Holiday Ever After

Also by Hannah Grace

Daydream

Wildfire

Icebreaker

Holiday Ever After

A Novel

HANNAH GRACE

ATRIA PAPERBACK
NEW YORK   AMSTERDAM/ANTWERP   LONDON
TORONTO   SYDNEY/MELBOURNE   NEW DELHI

An Imprint of Simon & Schuster, LLC
1230 Avenue of the Americas
New York, NY 10020

For more than 100 years, Simon & Schuster has championed authors and the stories they create. By respecting the copyright of an author's intellectual property, you enable Simon & Schuster and the author to continue publishing exceptional books for years to come. We thank you for supporting the author's copyright by purchasing an authorized edition of this book.

No amount of this book may be reproduced or stored in any format, nor may it be uploaded to any website, database, language-learning model, or other repository, retrieval, or artificial intelligence system without express permission. All rights reserved. Inquiries may be directed to Simon & Schuster, 1230 Avenue of the Americas, New York, NY 10020 or permissions@simonandschuster.com.

This book is a work of fiction. Any references to historical events, real people, or real places are used fictitiously. Other names, characters, places, and events are products of the author's imagination, and any resemblance to actual events or places or persons, living or dead, is entirely coincidental.

Copyright © 2025 by Hannah Grace

All rights reserved, including the right to reproduce this book or portions thereof in any form whatsoever. For information, address Atria Books Subsidiary Rights Department, 1230 Avenue of the Americas, New York, NY 10020.

First Atria Paperback edition September 2025

ATRIA PAPERBACK and colophon are trademarks of Simon & Schuster, LLC

Simon & Schuster strongly believes in freedom of expression and stands against censorship in all its forms. For more information, visit BooksBelong.com.

For information about special discounts for bulk purchases, please contact Simon & Schuster Special Sales at 1-866-506-1949 or business@simonandschuster.com.

The Simon & Schuster Speakers Bureau can bring authors to your live event. For more information or to book an event, contact the Simon & Schuster Speakers Bureau at 1-866-248-3049 or visit our website at www.simonspeakers.com.

Manufactured in the United States of America

1 3 5 7 9 10 8 6 4 2

Library of Congress Control Number: 2025942288

ISBN 978-1-6682-1373-5
ISBN 978-1-6682-1374-2 (ebook)

For Becs,
my Christmas girl

Holiday Ever After

Chapter 1

CLARA

I can't deny that technology has done miraculous things for human beings in every aspect of our lives.

Living in the twenty-first century has given me an unimaginable advantage over my ancestors (with the small exception of getting on the property ladder without the assistance of my parents) and I accept that I live a life that my relatives, with their humble beginnings, would hardly believe.

But even as I start my day in my beautiful West Village apartment, I can't escape the bone-deep jealousy of those family members who never had to wake up to twelve different people texting them "Have you seen this?!" and four missed calls from their father.

It's a shock to the system that not even a cold plunge could achieve, and the twisted sense of terror that coiled in my gut when I saw three different social media platform links in my inbox lingers as I head into the boardroom at Davenport Innovation Creative headquarters.

Monday is my least favorite day for a work crisis, but a Monday crisis on only my second week back in my role? The stuff of nightmares.

I drop myself into a chair in the back corner of the room facing the window and place one of two coffee cups on the table in front of me and the second to my left. The overhead lights glare off the glass stretching from one side of the room to the other. My reflection sits to the right of the Empire State Building, the rest of the city lit up around it beneath the gloomy November sky.

At 7:58, all my colleagues who undoubtedly also had their morning schedule ruined by this impromptu meeting pile into the room, taking their seats and muttering among themselves.

The floor shakes as an overstuffed Birkin lands in the empty space beside my pumps. I smile at Sahara as she sits in the chair next to me and practically lunges at the coffee I bought her on my way into the office. She takes a sip and sighs contently. "I love you, Clara Davenport."

"You love coffee," I respond, dodging her hand as she tries to playfully ruffle my hair. My dad finally enters with Roger, the VP of publicity, and takes his usual spot at the head of the table, which, thankfully, keeps me out of his eyeline.

After the world's fastest debrief, Roger clears his throat and draws attention to the buffering screen behind him. "Good morning, everyone," he says, his deep voice bellowing around the room with ease.

The face of an older woman appears behind him with a large play button covering her nose and lips, a face I've seen a dozen times this morning. Her blond hair is so icy it's practically silver; a wide, voluminous lock frames her face and sits behind her ear, the rest looks like it's tied up in a French twist.

I can't assign an age to her, not accurately, at least. Sixties, maybe? Her skin is white but lightly tanned, with a glow that speaks to a foreign vacation somewhere a hell of a lot hotter than here. Her eyes are bright behind thick brown cat-eye glasses; the telltale lines of time gather at the edges, in contrast to her suspiciously smooth and wrinkle-free forehead.

The play button hides the rest of her beauty, but I know from the amount of times I've seen her this morning that she is both radiant and mildly intimidating. She's a total natural in front of the camera.

Ultimately, I want to be her when I'm older.

"Most of you are already aware of this video that went viral over the weekend, but for the sake of everyone being on the same page, I'm going to play it now. We know that this has impacted the social teams already, and we anticipate that will continue."

Sahara's borderline-screaming voice note this morning said where they'd usually expect to see a problem hit its peak and then start to calm down, this was still climbing.

She's the director of social media, and her department has just survived an outpour of anger after an AI-generated video of a Davenport toy exploding went viral. Everyone is still recovering from the extra work and really doesn't need this, hence the borderline screaming.

The boardroom lights are turned off and the video begins to play.

> *Hello. My name is Florence Girard, and I'm asking you to support my small town this holiday season after Davenport Innovation Creative stole from us.*

It's an incredible hook, I have to give her that. Her American accent is diluted with something European better suited to an Old Hollywood movie than my For You page.

> *Three weeks ago, Davenport announced they were releasing the Evie doll in time for the holidays. Their doll is a direct copy of a product made here in Fraser Falls, the Holly doll. Last year, our doll gained popularity after a famous visitor to our prestigious Small Business Saturday event posted about her, and we were inundated with orders and visitors. Including Davenport themselves.*

Holly is a community project and supports multiple independent businesses in our town. Every part of her is made right here in the United States from recyclable, nontoxic materials. Everyone involved is paid a living wage and every doll comes with her own unique certificate of authenticity.

I love Holly and everything she's done for our town. I love our community that comes together to make her a possibility. Most important, I love our customers, who choose us over the dozens of other options on the market.

The softness of her expression morphs into something harder. More jaded and tired. The smile lines at the corners of her mouth disappear as her lips straighten.

Davenport doesn't love you.

Several people in the room wince at the harshness of her tone.

And they don't love Holly, like they claimed to when they showed up here in January trying to get us to sign up for a predatory scheme purporting to help small businesses expand. They told us that they'd help us protect our design, and when we didn't sign up, they copied us.

Their copy, the Evie doll, is the antithesis of everything we're trying to achieve here in Fraser Falls. Holly comes with six adventure stories, brought to life by the Green Light bookstore and the Fraser Falls Art School. Evie's stories are credited to AI. Holly has wooden toys, each one made by hand at the longstanding town staple Harry's. The amount of work meant

> that during the summer apprentices could be employed, with money going into the pockets of the young people in our community. Evie's toys are plastic, made by a machine.

Florence Girard continues listing all the ways in which the Holly doll is far superior to Davenport's Evie doll. I listen, quietly seething that this is happening at all. She's reaching the end of her dragging, and the worst part of the whole video.

> Since Davenport's announcement, including their doll being half the price of ours, half our orders have been canceled, and we have seen a significant reduction in new orders over the past three weeks.

> Companies like Davenport think they can do anything. Think they can get away with everything. I'm asking you to help me show them that they can't. Fraser Falls has so much to give, and we would love to welcome you this holiday season, whether you buy a Holly doll or not. This time of year is when our community is at its absolute best and we'd really love to show you. We have a number of holiday events planned, which will be listed at the end of the video.

> So support local, hardworking businesses this year. Even if it isn't our town, there's a town near you being bullied by a large corporation, too, and they need your support.

The word *bullied* hangs in the air like an unwelcome smell. It's still heavy in the room when the lights come back on.

"'Cancel Davenport' is trending on every platform," Roger announces. "While Ms. Girard didn't call for a boycott in so many words, online . . . activists, we'll call them, are running with it, trying to generate engagement where they can. They're unfortunately doing a great job. Sahara, can you expand?"

Sahara nods and puts her coffee cup back on the table. "It's generally the same handles we see over and over. Internally, we call them the drama vultures. They'll feast on anything so long as it's negative.

"They're offended by everything, which is amplified by bot activity. But they do move on as soon as complaints lose momentum, which allows incidents to peak and decline quickly. Unfortunately, this has spread outside of the normal online echo chamber and is reaching consumers who typically wouldn't engage with this type of content."

"Why do you think that is?" Dad asks, leaning forward to look down the table toward us.

"If we compare the situation to our last major social incident, which was the AI video, a large number of viewers were able to quickly identify that the video wasn't real without us saying anything," Sahara explains calmly. "We mobilized online messaging rapidly, which not only highlighted that the video wasn't real but gave advice on how to fact-check in the future. Our customers engaged with shares to point out it was fake, which reduced our workload and helped the message spread quicker."

"So why can't we do that here?" Dad asks. Sahara doesn't answer immediately, most likely doing mental gymnastics trying to work out how to say the truth.

I lean forward so he can see me. "Because we can deny a video is real when it's AI generated. We can't say we didn't copy their design or impact their town when we did."

There's surprisingly little benefit to being the boss's daughter, but it does make it a little easier to say what needs to be said in these kinds of situations.

"The small business program is your initiative, Clara. How do you propose we resolve this?" Dad asks.

I'm waiting for someone to point out that I've been covering a long-term sick leave in an entirely different division of the company for the past year, and this mess has nothing to do with me, but it doesn't come.

I didn't try to onboard Fraser Falls. I didn't even know about it until my six accounts were handed back to me two weeks ago when I returned to my job in PR. Someone mentioned it when I talked about how hideous the Evie doll is, and that's the extent of my knowledge on the situation.

The small business program was born in a corporate social responsibility working group. I was told in my annual review that if I wanted to climb the ladder, I needed to implement something with a positive impact on the business.

My intention was to make our image as a monopoly more palatable by helping select independent companies that have a lot of potential to upscale. Creating a more competitive market and improving our reputation were the obvious wins, but given Davenport started as a small independent business fifty years ago, I pitched that it spoke to our core values and history.

It was signed off on immediately and I helped onboard six different businesses across the US—who have been *thriving*, might I add—before I unexpectedly moved to cover a more senior position in Distribution, another choice designed to give me the experience to get a promotion.

I don't know how they messed up with Fraser Falls so badly. My dad is still staring at me like I'm somehow going to magic up the perfect answer. How about *go back in time and don't rip off a small town relying on the income from their star product*?

I drag a hand through my hair; auburn waves tangle around my fingers. "We need to make a meaningful apology to the town. Through investment or publicity, or both. We need to take the image of us robbing someone's grandma and replace it with something easier to swallow. A sorry company looks better than one that steals money from the pockets of hardworking Americans."

"Apologizing makes it look like we did something wrong." The voice is like nails on a chalkboard. It takes everything in me not to flinch. Mindful of the room full of people, I do my best not to scowl at Daryl Littler. He looks every inch the smug asshole he was twelve months ago when I last had the displeasure of seeing him. "I disagree that it's the right call."

Being on a different floor works miracles when it comes to avoiding people you hate. I remind myself that in eight short weeks, Daryl will be retiring, and center myself. At first I don't know why he's in here in a marketing and publicity crisis meeting, but I quickly realize that his team worked on the Evie doll.

Daryl is the director of innovation and his department is supposed to focus on introducing innovative technologies to our brand. When your core audience moves on quickly and generally has a short attention span, it's vital to always be one step ahead.

So far, all he's done is replace real human creativity with artificial intelligence and cut corners. My dad thinks he's brilliant because he runs the most cost-effective department, but in reality, he's the opposite of everything the company is supposed to be about.

Aside from the fact that he's morally bankrupt in every way a person can be, I've never heard him give his team credit for anything. The ideas that he doesn't steal from small towns are taken from his own staff, and I think it'd be impossible for me to hate him more than I do.

Knowing he was going to be retiring in the near future, I've focused all my effort on doing enough to take over when he's gone. Everyone knows I'm gunning for his job and my passion is in the creative side of the business, not bouncing from problem to problem like I do now, but I still haven't managed to convince my dad to let me replace Daryl.

I'm kind of certain he's going to give it to my brother, but that feels like a worry for another day. I shoot Daryl a tight smile. "I appreciate your input but pretending we've done nothing wrong isn't an effective recovery strategy. Someone needs to reach out to Ms. Girard to talk to her about her grievance directly and what we can do to make it disappear. In the meantime, we need to provide the brick-and-mortar teams an approved statement in case they're confronted in stores."

Roger is nodding as I talk, which gives me a tiny amount of relief. He's my boss's boss, and she's currently on vacation in Cancún, making me the most senior member of my team until she's back Friday.

"I agree," Roger says. "Clara, you reach out to Ms. Girard to establish her mindset now that she's getting the attention she wanted. There will be something we can give her or do for her that fixes this problem. Sahara, you . . ."

I zone out while Roger dishes out tasks to people in the room. Potential press release options, social media responses, in-store answers. A whole day's work for a room full of people because Daryl was too lazy to green-light an original idea.

I really cannot wait for him to go.

Chapter 2

CLARA

"The thing nobody tells you about nepotism is anybody can be a victim when you're not the favorite child."

"I—" Honor says before the line goes quiet. My eyes dart from the sparsely leaved trees lining the highway to my phone screen to check the call is still connected. I hold the phone to the window like *somehow* that'll fix the problem.

"Hon? Did I lose reception?" After several seconds of silence, I finally hear a sigh that sounds like it came from the depths of Honor's soul.

"Is everyone in the Davenport family allergic to critical thinking or do you catch it from your dad when you see him at work?" A surprised laugh chokes its way out of me so brutally that my driver, who hasn't said one word since he picked me up, checks on me through the rearview mirror. "Don't answer that, I know the answer."

Having a grounded and straight-talking best friend is great until you want to have your ungrounded thoughts and feelings justified. "You can't just humor me a teensy-weensy bit?"

"No," she says. "I won't be responsible for making you worse. You're capable of doing that all on your own."

"You're mean today. I'm not saying I don't deserve it, but I definitely don't like it."

I hear her fail to hold back a yawn. She's getting ready for another night shift in the emergency room. "Yeah, well, someone vomited on my feet last night, and there's a very high chance that will also happen tonight."

"So what I'm hearing is we both hate our jobs . . . and we should quit?" It's an idea one of us has floated at least once a month since we were old enough to have jobs. Playfully, *most* of the time. Being a nurse like her mom has always been Honor's dream.

"You don't hate your job, Clara. You hate that your dad is probably going to give your brother the position you've been busting your ass to get. You need to quit your job and work for someone who appreciates you."

I wrinkle my nose. "Ouch."

It didn't occur to me to be worried about Max, my younger brother by one year, getting Daryl's job over me until four months ago. After finishing business school, he took an eighteen-month contract at a company out of Boston. A year passed by quickly, and it was at a Fourth of July barbecue that Dad first casually dropped a comment about Max joining the family business at the end of his contract—which is now next month, perfectly in sync with Daryl's retirement date.

Max's contract expiration has been hanging over my head like a metaphorical rain cloud since summer, but I can't work out a way to bring it up. We've been competing against each other our whole lives, for attention (where Max usually won), in challenges Grandpa created to keep us busy (where I usually won), and academically (where Max *always* kicked my ass).

It was a relief when we hit our teens and I didn't have to compete with him at work. When I was spending my weekends at Davenport Toy Emporium, our flagship toy store in the city, hauling boxes and dealing with sticky children, Max was at the movies watching *Star Wars* marathons with his friends.

I spent my college summer breaks at Davenport headquarters, fetching coffee and learning as much as I could about how each department functions. Max spent his in places like Japan, playing real-life *Mario Kart* through the streets of Tokyo, or in California, learning to surf.

I graduated, started as close to the bottom as being the CEO's daughter would allow, and have spent the last decade working my way up. He graduated, immediately started working for Silicon Valley tech bros until he decided he wanted to get his MBA, and has shown zero interest in Davenport.

It's not that I think Max shouldn't work with us; it's our family business after all. I just don't want him to get the job I want. The one I've worked for.

I lean my forehead against the window, the quick stream of traffic blurring into the darkening sky. Honor's daughter shouts something unintelligible in the background of the call. "Is he late picking her up?" I ask.

"Of course he is. He's a lot of things that I can't say out loud right now." I hear the strain in Honor's voice. It happens when she talks about her daughter's dad. "I'm changing the subject. How far away are you?"

I tilt my head toward the center of the car. The console screen is lit up with a map. "Twenty minutes."

"You nervous?"

"Not really. I'm annoyed that I couldn't get this woman to take my call and now I have to show up in person." Twenty-four hours of attempting to reach Florence Girard amounted to nothing but her mailbox being full of my annoying customer service voice asking her to return my call. "But the town looks cute and a change of scenery for the night is fun, I guess."

Honor sighs. "All this over two dolls."

I mean, it's a little more than that. Corporate greed, creative theft, reputational downturn, et cetera, but essentially, yeah. All this over two dolls.

Dolls have existed in different forms for thousands of years. Something about this specific doll from Fraser Falls has caught the attention of parents and kids across America. Like most people, I can't put my finger on why *her* versus all the other products available on the market.

Problems seem to multiply when something holds a special kind of magic that people can't explain. People want to re-create the magic for themselves, even when they can't work out what the magic is.

It's the beauty and misery of virality in the digital age. Everything is so amplified it becomes inescapable, and in certain circumstances, it can bring unfathomable, life-changing levels of success. But how is anybody supposed to re-create it when nobody knows how it happened in the first place?

How are you as the person benefiting from the attention supposed to cling to it when everyone is trying to replace you at the top? When companies like Davenport have more money and more resources and, likely, less shame?

But there's no manual on how to re-create it, as much as people hawking online courses would love for you to believe them when they say that there is. Most of the time it's lots of different things aligning at once, plus a dash of something that can't actually be bottled.

We all know this. We talk about it at work all the time, and yet they decided to try anyway and thought undercutting a small business wouldn't backfire on them. My grandpa would be *seething* if he were still here.

"Dad's worried it's going to drag on and hurt sales or overshadow the Clara party," I say. "He's determined to break the donation record, hence the goodwill tour."

I can just picture Honor's face. She's never liked my dad. "If he's so concerned he should go himself. And that's another cursed doll, add her to the list."

My hand covers my mouth to smother my laugh. Twenty years ago, Davenport debuted the Clara doll. She's eighteen inches tall, with soft auburn curls that brush her shoulders and a neat center part tucked back with two velvet ribbon barrettes.

Her eyes are hazel, more green than brown in the right light, and framed by the perfect amount of dark lashes. She wears a thoughtful expression, and a sensible oatmeal-colored cardigan layered over a crisp Peter Pan–collared blouse and a wool pleated tartan skirt. On her feet are brown leather Mary Janes.

Each doll comes with a miniature canvas satchel embroidered with the letter C; tucked inside are tiny paper books, a pencil stub, and a coin purse. Unlike all the other dolls that were popular at the time, Clara wasn't bright or flashy. She didn't have glittery outfits or fancy accessories. She was a good friend, a role model, and our most popular toy for a long, long time. Her success put Davenport on the map and funded our growth.

It's as fun sharing a name with a toy now as it was when I was fourteen. When the bitchy teens at my school would tease me about it, Honor was the first person to tell me not to worry. The doll was named after me, obviously. Not because my dad thought it would be a sweet nod to his only daughter, but in recognition of the fact I came up with her during one of my grandpa's challenges when I was ten.

Dad wanted to call her something else; it was Grandpa who insisted she have my name.

This year, our annual charity Christmas party is also a celebration of two decades of Clara. In fact, the reason Daryl's department was able to get the Evie doll green-lit is they pitched her as Clara's modern sister for her anniversary year.

"I have to go, Hon. It's my job."

Would I prefer not to be visiting the businesses signed up to our program? Of course.

I'm still finding my feet after being away for a year. The last thing I want to do is spend my week being the human equivalent of the Energizer Bunny running from company to company. Since Florence Girard mentioned the small business program in her video, I need to fly out to check in on every company signed up.

They all admitted they'd looked over their contracts after hearing about the video but didn't find anything suspicious. Two put me off until January because they're busy, but the other four happily accepted a free business outing.

Thankfully, the two that turned me down are on the West Coast. One's in Maine, another in Pennsylvania; the other two sit within a few hours' drive of each other in Illinois. So assuming everything goes according to plan, I'll be back in the city by Friday late afternoon.

"Speaking of jobs, he just pulled up so I'm gonna head to mine." How Honor keeps this calm when her ex almost makes her late every single time it's his turn for custody amazes me. "Stay safe and let me know how it goes. You're gonna win them over, I just know it."

"Love you."

"Love you too. Paloma, come say love you to Auntie Cla—she's gone. Never mind, she does love you. Bye."

The map says five minutes when I put my phone back into my purse and slip my headphones back into their case. I'm booked into a charming bed-and-breakfast less than five minutes' walk from the bakery and café that Ms. Girard runs.

My research tells me that the dolls are handled by Harry's, a handmade furniture store opposite Ms. Girard's businesses. Tomorrow, I'm going to Bliss Café and finding a table to observe at. Then I'll approach her after the morning rush has cleared. After I've gauged how she's feeling, I'll head across the street to introduce myself to Harry.

Hopefully, smoothing this over will be quick and easy and I can get to Maine early for the second stop on my tour. And if it isn't quick and easy, at least I'll be eating lobster for dinner.

My plan tonight is to grab something to eat from a nearby bar that has great reviews and make it an early night. The roads have been getting narrower for the last five minutes and now we're moving steadily down a quiet lane bordered by fields. I stare out of the passenger-side window; the orange hues of sunset that were cascading a warmth between the trees have now melted into the deepening blue of the night sky.

A "Welcome to Fraser Falls" sign is erected in the grass, the thick white letters illuminated by two lights shining from the bottom of the frame, making each word stand out against the forest-green-stained wood.

"Nearly there," my driver calls from the front of the car. "This is Main Street."

Everywhere is bathed in a golden glow from the tiny lights decorating the town as far as I can see. There are dozens of fairy light strings draped above the sidewalk between the buildings and the trees and lampposts lining the pavement. Small, glowing snowflakes dangle from the string, giving a floating effect that feels magical. Each trunk and post is wrapped in an evenly spaced spiral of tiny bulbs leading up to a thick red ribbon.

It feels like something from a holiday card.

I'm so distracted by the lights I forget to look out for the café, but from what I can see, most of the stores are closed or closing.

The car slows as it approaches a stop sign, and directly in front of us is a beautiful white gazebo at the start of a U-shaped grassy field. Lights drop from the center of the roof and drape outward; they're softer and more delicate than the other lights on Main Street. The wide entrance at its front is split into stairs and a ramp; the same muted lights weave between the spindles of the handrail up to a seating area.

I want to sit and look at everything in this picture-perfect town.

Fraser Falls feels like an amalgamation of every cheesy holiday movie I watched growing up in the best way. It makes me understand why the Hallmark single city girl chose the small town. Its clean streets and easy roads are worlds away from Manhattan, from most places I know actually.

The one strange thing that I can't quite shake as I climb out of the car in front of Maggie's B & B is I haven't seen anyone. Ms. Girard asked people in her video to visit to support her town this holiday season and now I understand why.

Chapter 3

JACK

"I'm glad our band never took off. I wouldn't have been able to cope with the fame."

I watch Tommy, patiently waiting for him to expand and give me some kind of idea what the hell he's talking about. Not an unusual or infrequent reaction to my best friend. The explanation doesn't come. He continues wiping down the beer taps with a cloth.

I rest my elbow on the bar, drop my chin into my hand. "What the fuck are you talking about? When were we in a band?"

"That summer Luke got the drum kit for his birthday. When we said we'd lie and say you were our brother so we could be the next Hanson."

My brows pinch together. "Hanson?"

He throws the towel over his shoulder and leans against the bar, dragging his hand through his perfectly coiffed chestnut hair. "Okay, it might have been the rock 'n' roll version of the Jonas Brothers, I can't remember. We were going to practice every day in the barn. But then . . . well, never mind, but my point is"—he looks down and fiddles with something behind the bar out of my view—"I'm glad we didn't see it through. I wouldn't be good at being famous. Avoiding that news crew is giving me hives."

I have very vague memories of Tommy's younger brother, Luke, getting a drum kit. I must have been thirteen, maybe? There are blurry images of me holding a guitar somewhere in the dark depths of my memory from twenty years ago.

I realize he's avoiding looking at me, because he worked out before I did that he fucked up by bringing up *that* summer.

"I don't think I'd be a good famous person either," I say, moving past the awkwardness. Even though we're the same height at six foot four, there's something that seems small about him when he puts his foot in it. He lifts his head to look at me again, an unspoken apology in his dark blue eyes. "I'd be one of those rock stars who punches a pap."

"I can see that happening," he says.

The doors to the tavern open and we both quickly turn to look, breathing out a synchronized sigh of relief when it's Melissa and Winnie and not the camera crew that's been roaming Fraser Falls trying to talk to someone about the mess Flo caused over the weekend.

Melissa and Winnie run the florist, Wilde & Winslet, opposite my store. Winnie grew up here in Fraser Falls. She's younger than me and Tommy by a handful of years, but her father is the town pastor, which makes her the second most popular thing talked about every Sunday. She met Mel at school and convinced her to move here and open a flower shop.

"Don't think I've ever seen you two so happy to see us," Winnie says as she heads to the armchairs by the fire at the back of the room. A sweet floral smell follows her as she passes me and I notice a red rose tucked into the band securing her black box braids at the back of her head. "Your sign is very direct. I don't think you need to worry," she calls over her shoulder.

The sign is the result of ten seconds, a piece of paper, and a Sharpie: "NO CAMERAS ALLOWED. REPORTERS WILL BE ASKED TO LEAVE IMMEDIATELY." Despite being told not to,

Flo posted a follow-up video this morning thanking people for their support and inviting them to visit us again. It caught the attention of someone who, Winnie told me, was on *Dancing with the Stars* and their share made the original video take off again.

I love Flo like she's my own grandmother, but she didn't know what she was doing when she decided to air town business on the internet. She thought the public support would result in visitors and orders, but in reality the only visitors we've had so far are unwelcome.

The problem is, the Holly doll was originally my project. Which means the website is now struggling with traffic, the customer service email is blowing up, and the new orders have all been dropped on me. Flo didn't even tell us she was posting a video, let alone multiple videos, which means I now have a ton of orders I don't have inventory for because my naïve and forgetful ass didn't set the order cap when half of our existing orders got canceled a few weeks ago.

To put it lightly, Flo has caused a massive fucking headache, mostly for me.

But we love her, and she loves this place more than anyone I know, so we're going to support her anyway, and grumble about it in private like adults.

Mel stands at the bar to my right and orders drinks from Tommy. "Still getting hounded?" I ask.

She rolls her eyes, drags her short brown curls away from her face with her hand. "Yes, all mostly time wasters. Three different influencers have messaged to ask if we want to do their wedding for free for the 'exposure.'" She emphasizes the word with finger quotation marks. "I'm tired."

Tommy puts the two glasses of wine on the bar in front of Mel. "On me."

"Thanks, Tommy," she says sweetly, heading over to Winnie.

I watch him watch her walk away, a wistful look on his face that feels totally out of place. I finish my beer. "You've never given me a free drink. Why is that?"

"Because you're an asshole. Next question."

Before I can ask how long he plans to pine after Melissa before asking her out or what he thinks his odds of being shot down are, he's saved by a customer at the bar ordering food. He disappears to tell the kitchen, putting an end to what could have been a fun night for me.

I slide off my stool and walk around the bar to the other side, immediately spotting a bag of chips that Tommy told me he was out of under the counter. Serving myself isn't something I'd usually do, but he gets into a long conversation about God knows what every time he goes to the kitchen, so who knows how long I'm going to be waiting for him to come back.

I grab a ginger ale from the fridge and a clean glass. With my back turned to the rest of the room, I freeze when I hear the heavy wooden door open again. *Please don't be a reporter.* I turn reluctantly, and my eyes land on a woman standing near the entrance, taking off her gloves as her eyes drift across the room.

When they land on me, she smiles a full, beautiful smile. I almost look behind me. She walks toward the bar, unbuttoning the blue buttons of her coat as she does. With her free hand, she pulls her auburn hair from beneath the collar and shakes it until shiny waves cascade down her back.

She's three steps away from a stool before I realize I'm standing in the middle of the bar area staring at her like I've never seen another human being before. The quick fire of embarrassment is enough to unstick my feet. I put my drink down in front of my seat as she reaches the edge of the bar.

"Hi," she says, her voice soft. "Are you still serving food?"

I grab a menu from under the counter and hand it to her. "Yeah."

What's weirder—telling her I don't work here or just walking back to my seat and saying nothing?

"Thanks," she says, placing the menu down on the bar and climbing onto the stool next to mine.

"What can I get you to drink?" I ask. I don't know why I ask. Tommy is going to kill me for asking.

Her eyes flit up from the menu, pale green and bright. "Can I get a—"

"What the hell are you doing? You know you're not allowed back here!" Tommy yells, nudging my shoulder to send me away. He's still shaking his head at me when I climb sheepishly back onto my stool feeling like a bad kid who got caught—a feeling I've grown to hate in the last fifteen years. He turns his attention to the woman beside me. "Sorry about that. Are you a reporter?"

"Uh, no?"

"Definitely not undercover?" I frown at my best friend.

"Definitely," she says slowly.

Tommy glares at me when I open the can of ginger ale and it cracks loudly. He turns his attention back to her. "Good. Sorry about that, can never be too careful. What can I get you?"

She orders a cheeseburger and fries with a lemon-lime soda. Tommy makes her a drink and hands it to her before heading back to the kitchen. She takes a sip and places it down gently on the coaster, twisting the glass so the bear emblem, the mascot of the local high school, is straight. She turns slightly on the bar stool to look at me.

"So what's the deal? Does everyone get to play bartender when the real one disappears?" she asks, taking her coat off and letting it hang over the back of her seat. She's wearing a thick cream turtleneck sweater, dark blue jeans, and heeled boots. When she moves her hair over her right shoulder, I get a glimpse of an expensive-looking watch and a cluster of diamond earrings.

I shrug. "Only if you have an unyielding passion for craft beer and don't mind Mitch the Moose watching your every move." She follows my eyes to the giant plastic moose head hung above the bar and pretends to consider the criteria.

"I guess I'm out. I'm not a beer fan, arts and crafts or otherwise." A sharp laugh bursts out of me. I study her more closely now, watching as she pulls a napkin from the holder and dabs her mouth gently where the ice from her drink has wet her top lip. Each delicate movement has every ounce of my attention. "But I've been stared at in bars by weirder things than a plastic moose."

Another laugh. Damn, what's with me tonight? Something about pillowy pink lips and high cheekbones on a beautiful woman makes me act up. My cell phone buzzes on the bar. I reluctantly take my eyes off her and spot a text from Arthur reminding me I promised I'd help him fix his drainpipe tomorrow after his grandson smashed a hole in it with a hockey puck. I lock my screen and focus back on her. "You just passing through?"

She lowers the napkin and starts folding it neatly. There's no ring on her left hand. "Something like that. I'm on my way to Maine technically."

"What's in Maine?"

She tilts her head, a soft smile on her lips. "Lobster. Rain. People who mind their own business."

I raise my hands in surrender. "Fair. You won't find people who mind their business around here."

It's her turn to laugh. Tommy is going to be back any minute and will take over this conversation with something interesting and fun. He has that barman charm that makes him able to talk to anyone about anything that I've never managed to replicate.

I'm the practical one. The one you call when your internet isn't working or, if you're Flo, when you need hundreds of lights hanging a month early to impress a travel blogger. Sure, I rope Tommy into helping, but he's the one you'd go to for a good time.

The tavern is quieter tonight, everyone staying home to prevent being accosted in the street by the rogue news crew I'd guess. Aside from the crackle of the fire, the only sounds in the tavern now are Winnie and Mel whispering in the corner and the gentle thud of people playing darts in the back.

"I'm Clara, by the way," the woman beside me says, snapping me out of my daze.

"Jack." She rotates her body so she's fully facing me and rests her elbow on the bar. Her heels are hooked on the foot rail, her long, slim legs angled between my open ones. "Has your visit to Fraser Falls been enjoyable so far, Clara?"

"Let's see, I've encountered someone impersonating a bartender, been accused of being an undercover journalist by the real bartender, and on my way here someone offered me her condolences for an unknown reason."

"That tracks," I say, gesturing to her outfit. "Usually anyone arriving in town dressed in anything above casual is here for a funeral."

Her eyes widen like it suddenly makes sense. "You're local then?"

"Born and raised. Never left. Although, I did go to sleepaway camp in Rhode Island one summer when I was ten. If that counts."

She nods assuredly. "That definitely counts. It's practically Euro summer."

I bite the inside of my cheek. "What brings you to Fraser Falls? On your route to Maine where people mind their business?"

"Heard good things about it. Rumor is there are really nice people here." I nod knowingly. "I can't say I disagree so far, and it's just as pretty as it looks online. Prettier, in fact. I love the lights. You should keep them up all year."

"You're lucky. They're not usually up this early, but don't give Flo any ideas. They're nice to look at but the wind tangles the stars and I'm the one who gets the call to fix it."

Clara's eyebrow creeps up. "Flo?"

How to describe her. "She runs a café and bakery over on Main.

Technically owns the building. Spiritually owns the town. Think of her as the unofficial mayor, the town crier, and the neighborhood watch all rolled into one."

"Oh my God," Clara says, clapping her hands. "Florence! She's the one who posted the doll videos, isn't she? With the very serious background music and the finger pointing?"

I smother a groan. "Unfortunately, yes."

She laughs. "No offense, but from the Fraser Falls social pages, this whole town seems . . . aggressively quaint for all the drama. Internet fame and reporters? That's a lot."

"That's putting it mildly." I don't add anything more. The last thing I want to talk about is Dollgate and Flo's recent internet fame. "There's so many other things we could be talked about for. Better things."

I think Clara senses my reluctance because she changes the subject. "Is the school mascot really a bear wearing overalls?"

Not one of the better things I was thinking of, but sure. "Yup. Fraser Falls Bears. Our one and only victory was the '98 regional football championship. The town still celebrates it every year. It was our moon landing, but we can't call it that openly. There's a guy who thinks the moon landing was faked and it sets him off."

"Ohhh." Her eyes widen. "One of those people who think it was all filmed on a soundstage?"

Also not one of the better things I was thinking of. "Kinda. He thinks the moon is a hologram."

Clara twirls the ends of her hair around her finger as she nods slowly, absorbing. "I saw someone trying to catch a drone with a net earlier today. Like an actual net. Like he was a butterfly catcher. Same guy, by any chance?"

"Yeah! That's him, Donald. *Huge* conspiracy theorist but excellent landscaper if you ever need your garden fixed up. The drone's lucky it got away. He's wicked fast with that net. Caught Tommy in it once." I nod toward my best friend over by the fire. "Accused Flo of being a CIA operative, too, and only narrowly escaped with his life."

Clara chokes on her soda laughing. "This place is wild. Aggressively quaint, but also wild."

Her food appears as I take the last sip of my drink. "You don't know the half of it."

Chapter 4

JACK

I GO HOME TO GET Elf and bring him back to the tavern while Clara eats her dinner.

The gasp she lets out when she sees him is one I'm used to, and one he loves. "Bully mix?" she asks, hand scratching the white patch in the center of his otherwise silver body.

"Or something. He was a stray, so they weren't one hundred percent sure."

After stealing her attention away from me for five minutes, he follows Tommy and settles in the bed kept behind the bar especially for him.

With her focus back on me, Clara lets me talk about the colorful lore of Fraser Falls. I introduce her to Tommy and let him recount his traumatic experience of being trapped in Donald's net. When he's done answering her questions, he makes himself scarce, which I appreciate.

I tell her how some people in town staged a protest outside the art school when Wilhelmina wanted to use a nude model for a painting class—their three placards said, "No class needs ass"—and she almost chokes on her drink.

When she's finished with her meal, Clara tells me about her mom's obsession with horoscopes and how her brother has been in love with her best friend since they were kids. She skips over her dad and I'm happy to do the same. I beam when she gasps as I recall the infamous Fraser Falls love triangle of '09 that rocked the foundation of the town.

The conversation is flowing so easily that I want to ask if this happens to her. The instant rapport, the sparks crackling between us, the desire to learn everything. Because it doesn't happen to me. I don't ask; instead she laughs through a story about getting stuck in an elevator with Jennifer Aniston on Halloween while dressed as Chucky and I tell her about the time I accidentally set the summer play set on fire.

Clara laughs with her whole body, leans forward when she talks like every word is a secret she only wants me to hear. It's impossible not to like her. She's polite to Tommy when he refills our drinks and pats my forearm gently with an understanding smile while I apologize profusely that my phone ringing has interrupted her for the third time.

"Is this the part where I find out you're the town drug dealer?" she asks when I end the call.

I place my phone back on the bar and put it on silent. "My life isn't that dangerous or exciting. I'm the guy that gets the call when someone has a problem."

"Like an *I need help blackmailing someone* kind of problem?" she asks playfully.

My eye flicks to my screen as I see a text come through. "More like *There's a raccoon that keeps getting into my garden and ruining my vegetable patch*, or *Can you fix the hole in my fence?* Or something glamorous like *My toilet is backing up and flooding my house, what do I do?*"

"Wow, that is glamorous. Surely the correct solution is domesticate the raccoon and launch a social media career?"

I nudge my phone toward her. "You're good at this, you can take the next call."

"I hope it's something juicy. Do you want to play pool while we wait for my time to shine?" She's already shining pretty bright from where I'm sitting. I don't even like pool but I find myself nodding. "I should warn you, I'm not very good."

"That's what all the pool hustlers say before they reveal they're some kind of prodigy."

Clara slides from her stool and I follow her to the table. "Just for fun," she says, chalking the end of her cue while I rack the balls. "No bets."

I pull a coin out of my pocket. "Heads or tails?"

She presses her lips together, thinking. "Tails."

The quarter spins in the air before landing on my palm. I press it onto the back of my hand and reveal it. "Heads. I break."

Clara grips the top of her cue with both hands and leans against it. "Don't be nervous. There's nothing at stake but your pride."

"Oh great, that makes it less stressful." I pull the cue back and surge it forward, connecting perfectly and sending the cue ball careering toward the triangle. The crack is loud as they break and roll in opposite directions across the green felt, bouncing off the rails. I silently thank whatever cosmic force made me not miss.

Two solids and a stripe roll into the pockets. "Now who's hustling?" Clara says, leaning her hip against the table. I focus on the orange stripe away from her and breathe a sigh of relief when I sink it.

"Looks like I'm stripes." My growing confidence immediately stops when my next shot bounces off the corner of the pocket. "You're up, solids."

I take a step back from the table and watch her survey it from all angles. Her legs look even longer in her heeled boots, ass tight and round as it moves side to side. "I hit it with the thin end, right?" she says, flipping her hair behind her shoulder when she stands up straight. "I'm kidding! I'm totally kidding. I know it's the thick end."

I rub my hand over my jaw, watch her try not to laugh at her own jokes. There's something irresistible about how she doesn't take herself too seriously. "Take your shot, Clara."

Her movement is smooth but the red ball bounces off the pocket and rolls diagonally to the center of the table. "I think this table is wonky," she says, side-eyeing it.

"It must be. Couldn't be your aim." I line up my next shot, face six inches from the table when her elbows land in the spot next to me, her head level with mine. "You're not going to distract me."

She leans in, the sweet smell of her perfume engulfing me. She lowers her voice. "You haven't seen how good I am at it."

Clara winks and I go too far to the right on the cue ball and miss my target entirely.

"See? And I'm not even trying yet."

She sinks her orange. Then her purple. Just touches her blue.

"Do you need some help?" she asks when I spend ten seconds evaluating the table.

I hit the ball and sink my maroon. I lean toward her, our faces only inches apart. Fuck, she's so gorgeous. "I think I'm okay."

I miss my next shot, but it doesn't matter. I do exactly what she just did to me. Lean in as she's lining up and whisper, "Do you need some help?"

"I do, actually." She straightens up and watches me patiently while the words *oh* and *fuck* run through my head on a mental conveyor belt.

"Bend over." I swallow the lump in my throat. Yeah, I can see myself saying that to her in an entirely different set of circumstances. I don't make a habit of lusting after strangers, but it's not every night a gorgeous woman walks in here and I have instant chemistry with her. "And line up your shot like you would normally."

She does as I say and looks up at me from the table expectantly. "And now?"

I adjust her left hand with mine and reposition her right hand, reach across her back, and grip the bottom of the cue. She inches closer to me. "Hold it closer to your body like this. Don't grip it too tight, you want a smooth stroke," I say quietly.

"Good technique." I'm very aware that we're being watched right now, but Clara either doesn't care or hasn't noticed.

I guide the cue back with her and hit the cue ball into the blue. She wiggles in excitement when it rolls into the pocket, the soft curves of her body brushing against mine. "We're a good team."

I let go of her and take a safety step backward. I rub my neck where my skin feels red-hot. Losing it over a game of pool. I need to get a grip.

Clara continues to distract me every chance she gets and I continue to let her, enjoying her constant fight for my attention over the game.

"What does the winner get?" Clara asks, chalking her cue again. She brushes the blue dust off her hands, wedging the cue between her forearm and biceps.

"I think it was just pride, wasn't it?" I clip the side of my yellow but it goes nowhere. "Are you telling me there's been a prize this whole time?"

"I didn't want the pressure to crush you." She tilts her head to the side and pouts. "I had your best interests at heart."

"How about . . . the loser buys the next round of drinks?"

Clara's eyes widen like I just said something magnificent. "That's a totally new and unique take and I love it. Let's do that."

Clara takes a deep breath and lines up to pot her red. I make a slight noise and she shushes me. I already know she isn't going to sink it, her angle is all wrong and her cue is too high. She's more likely to chip the cue ball off the side of the table. "Hey, permission to work as a team?"

She looks across the table to me, her pert ass in the air. "Planning to sabotage me?"

I push my hands into my pockets and shake my head. "Nope."

She looks me up and down, eyes taking longer over my chest and face. "Okay, but only because I like your raspy whispering in my ear, not because I think I need your help."

I drag my hand over the crown of my head, temporarily at a loss for words. "Understood."

"Move this way a little." I guide her closer to the center of the table with my hand on her hip. I settle over her again like earlier; my hands are steady when I tweak her form. My body is a little closer than before. When I reposition her left hand everything falls into place, almost like she was being bad on purpose. "You're doing so good, you didn't need my help."

"I know, but there's that whispering again." She draws her arm back, eyes fixed on the shot, then strikes the cue ball clean. It smacks the red exactly where it needs to, sending it speeding into the pocket. "You want to help me beat you or watch from the bar while you buy us drinks?"

"I'll help. Feeling like I was involved will probably boost my ego."

Clara cheers when she sinks the eight ball into the closest pocket. I let go of the cue and give her space. Well, give me space. She holds out her hand and I shake it carefully. "Good game," she says. "I'll have a mojito, please."

"Coming right up."

"Biggest town scandal?"

Clara grips the straw of her third mojito and swirls it around her glass. After Mel and Winnie left, we took over the love seat by the fire and Clara's been questioning me on Fraser Falls ever since. I expected her to sit in the empty chair on the opposite side but she slid herself into the tight space beside me.

We're twisted slightly to face each other, so close it eliminates any reason for her to lean in. Her body is relaxed against mine. I try to return the questions that she's firing at me, but she's more interested in asking them.

"Biggest town scandal . . ." I scratch at my jaw while I think it over. "Teen pregnancy. Resulted in Sailor, my goddaughter, who belongs to Tommy's brother, Luke."

"Teen pregnancies happen everywhere. What's so scandalous about it?"

"Luke got down on one knee to propose to Dove and she told him to get up. They weren't even dating, they just grew up next door to each other and made a pact. They still live next door to each other. Healthiest parent relationship I've ever seen."

Clara takes a sip of her drink. "I was sorta hoping for a cult or, like, a murder you all made a promise to cover up forever or something."

"Closest thing we have to a cult is book club. Sorry to disappoint."

"What's *your* biggest scandal?" she asks.

I have too many from my teen years that I wouldn't ever want to admit to. They're not fun, laughable moments for me. I search for one she might like. "Butt-dialed one of my neighbors while I was working out and they started a rumor I called them while I was having sex." Clara's hand shoots out and grabs my arm; with wide eyes, she pinches her lips together to keep in her reaction. "It got brought up at a town meeting and it made me die inside. I was only twenty-three."

It's enough to tip her over the edge and she howls laughing with her forehead pressed to my shoulder. When she eventually recovers, she apologizes, the multiple mojitos she's had giving her a giddiness that's endearing.

"I'm trying to figure out what your workouts sound like for someone to think that's what you were doing," she says, her brow furrowed.

"I haven't had enough drinks to give you an example."

"We have time."

The hours blur in the warm flicker of the fireplace.

I like her. More than I should ever like someone I just met. I do finally manage to sneak in some questions. I learn she loves food, specifically breakfast food and Italian. That she lives alone in Manhattan. That her favorite movie is *Pretty Woman*.

But then she's back on me.

There's something about the way she watches me talk. Like she genuinely cares about what I have to say. It's been a long time since anyone has wanted to hear me talk about anything other than the doll. That's my favorite thing about her: she hasn't once brought up work.

Eventually, the tavern is empty. Tommy starts wiping down the bar, giving me the look he always gives me when I linger too long without offering to help.

I glance at Clara, who's finishing her drink.

"Come on," I say. "The B & B is on my way home. Let me walk you back."

Tommy waves his goodbyes to her, says he'll borrow Elf for the night, and winks as I follow Clara out the door. Outside, the cold air slices through us. Clara shivers and wraps her coat tighter; I do the same. Our breath clouds the air in front of us. Fraser Falls is nearly silent, just the sound of our footsteps and the distant barking of a dog.

"I'm surprised more people don't know about how dreamy this place is," she says, pushing her hands into her pockets.

"We had more visitors last year than in the past. Hoping they come back this year, but who knows. Flo has this dream of us hosting a big Christmas market like they do in Europe, but we need consistent visitors to make that happen."

She looks up at me, her breath visible between us. "I can see why. I'd come."

We reach the front steps of the B & B. The porch light flickers above us, casting her face in soft gold. She turns toward me, still wrapped up in her coat. "I'll send you the first invite when it happens."

She looks at her feet, then back at me, still smiling. "Thanks for the drinks. And the walk. And the invite back."

"You definitely need to go to Maine tomorrow? I could find a lobster for you. Can't promise rain, but could probably find a sprinkler system or something." I smile, trying not to let my sadness at the night ending show.

"I definitely need to go to Maine tomorrow," she says, sounding disappointed. "I wish I could stay."

"I wish you could stay too." There's a pause that stretches out too long, where something could happen, should happen. I want to kiss her. I should kiss her and I don't know what's stopping me. Rejection ruining a perfect night, maybe? I don't know.

"I should get inside, it's cold. Good night, Jack. Thanks for giving me such a warm welcome."

The moment passes and I've missed my chance.

I nod. "Good night, Clara. I mean it, come back anytime."

She studies me, then smiles. It's a little pensive, like she knows the moment is gone too. She squeezes my arm affectionately before disappearing through the main door, and I stand there for a beat longer, hands buried in my pockets, cold settling into my bones.

I take back what I said earlier. Not every new visitor is unwelcome.

Chapter 5
CLARA

My alarm blares and I open my eyes in a bed that's too soft, on a street that's too quiet, with a headache that's too loud.

Truly, I have nobody to blame but myself. And also Jack. Mostly Jack. I laughed until my stomach hurt and won at pool for the first time in *years*. He had the audacity to be charming and gorgeous and a very encouraging drinking partner.

As a tall girl at five foot nine, I'm a sucker for a man who makes me feel small when he's next to me. Jack certainly ticks that box. Jack ticks a lot of my boxes actually. Broad shoulders that relaxed more and more every time he laughed. Dark brown hair fighting between messy and curly that he'd drag his hand through every so often so I had no choice but to stare at his huge biceps. We didn't talk about work, intentional on my part and another tick for him, but he doesn't look like he works in an office. His build is solid, earned. I'd guess he works in construction or something.

But there's a softness to him, as contradictory as that sounds. The way he'd apologize every time his cell phone interrupted us. A dimple that appeared beneath the dusting of stubble along his jaw when he smiled. How he went home to get his dog because he didn't want him to get lonely.

I can't remember the last time I felt so drawn to someone. I can't remember the last time I felt disappointed that someone didn't kiss me at the end of the night.

Pushing all thoughts of Jack aside, I peel myself out of bed, forgo my ten-step skin-care routine, and scrape my hair into a sleek ponytail that I hope says *serious businesswoman* rather than *woman in crisis*. I throw on a black knitted dress, my most weather-appropriate heeled boots, and my wool coat. It's as casual as I can be while in work clothes, and I hope my outfit says *I'm definitely not here to crush your charming local community spirit for corporate gain.*

Maggie, the B & B's owner, is a sweet woman in her sixties hellbent on making sure I have the best possible stay. She tries to fill me full of oatmeal and fruit as I'm heading out the door to stealthily observe Flo.

The bells above the door jingle as I step into Bliss Café. It's barely 8 a.m., but I'm eager to get the day started and head up to Maine. I have an unusual amount of confidence that today is going to be a success. I think it's because I have a better idea of the town dynamic after spending last night with Jack.

Bliss Café is as dreamy as everywhere else in this severely overlooked town. The paneled walls are painted a dusky blue. Late fall sunlight spills in through the frosty windows. The air smells like espresso and powdered sugar. French instrumental music floats from a speaker somewhere in the back. A young waiter is delivering a plate of croissants to a nearby table with the delicacy of a museum curator.

Bliss, as I read in exactly nine gushing reviews, is Fraser Falls' answer to a Parisian bistro, with Flo's Fancies next door serving as a patisserie. Instead of on the Champs-Élysées, Bliss and Flo's are wedged between an ice cream parlor and a hardware store. The café's handwritten chalkboard specials menu is aggressively themed, featuring classics like pain au chocolat, croque monsieur, and a questionably authentic crème brûlée iced latte. It's impossibly charming.

If this were Williamsburg the line would be around the block.

I try not to squint under the soft lights and make my way to the counter, weaving between small tables of locals sipping coffee and reading copies of the town gazette. The glass cabinet is full of golden, flaky pastries, each with a delicate paper label written in loopy cursive. Behind the counter is a woman wearing a floral apron, her hair in an immaculate French twist. I recognize her instantly from the videos, only she's scarier in real life. Like Julia Child if she had been raised by Tony Soprano.

"Good morning. You must be Ms. Girard," I say, mustering my best and brightest PR smile.

She eyes me over her glasses like she can smell the city on me. "Oui, Florence Girard," she says in an exaggerated French accent. Fake French accent, to be clear. "Your driver ran a stop sign last night on his way out of town."

My smile falters. "I'm so sorry, I'm sure he never meant to—"

"Coffee?" She cuts me off, turning her back on me to make it.

"Oh yes, please. Black."

She works the machine like it's second nature, then hands it to me in a porcelain cup that probably predates me. "Two dollars."

"I was hoping to speak to you, actually," I say, handing over a five. This isn't part of the plan. The plan was to sit my ass in the corner and observe until people headed to work, *then* talk to her. The confidence I felt earlier is slowly dwindling away as she watches me, saying nothing.

She feels like the kind of woman who would appreciate a direct approach, but she's *still* staring at me. Should've stuck to the damn plan. "I'm heading over to Harry's later this morning, but I wanted to have a conversation with you first—"

"He isn't available for interviews." She cuts me off again.

"It's not an interview," I say quickly. "It's . . . it's something else.

I'm here for business reasons. I need to speak to him about the doll, but I wanted to talk to you about the viral videos."

"This isn't one of those triangle schemes, is it?" Flo eyes me suspiciously. "I've seen posts about them online. I know they're no good. Besides, Jack doesn't need a business meeting. He needs to find a reliable website host and get a good night's sleep."

Jack?

Before I can ask what Jack has to do with anything, the bells jingle again. I turn, cup halfway to my lips.

Jack is standing in the doorway. As in, flannel-shirted, smirky, ruggedly handsome Jack. He yawns as he walks to the counter, rubbing the back of his neck, unaware that I'm about to disrupt his quiet morning.

He hasn't seen me yet. Flo, of course, has. She tilts her chin toward me and mutters to him, "Your timing is impeccable as always."

Jack blinks. Turns his head and his face moves from sleepy to surprised. "Clara?"

I raise my cup in a weak toast. "Morning, Jack."

"What are you doing here? I thought you were heading to Maine."

"Just getting some coffee before I try to score a meeting," I say, attempting to sound casual. "With Harry. From the store across the street."

There's a beat of silence. Then Jack presses his lips together. He looks like he's trying to swallow a laugh.

"You good?" I ask, eyes narrowing.

He exhales and pinches the bridge of his nose. "There is no Harry. Well, there was, but he's not here anymore."

I blink. "I'm sorry?"

"Harry's is the name of the store, but I'm the owner."

I short-circuit. My brain actually pixilates. "You're Harry."

"No. I'm Jack," he repeats slowly. Flo snorts so loudly it echoes. "I'm the one you . . . came to score a meeting with?"

Well, this is just perfect.

I let my guard down and flirt with a handsome man in a bar for the first time in forever and this is how the universe repays me for putting myself out there. For the second time today, I mentally assign blame for my circumstances to Jack. Although I can admit this is probably my fault.

I'm not here to flirt. I'm here to put an end to this nightmare. Namely, the PR nightmare that is *The People (of Fraser Falls) vs. Davenport Toys*. Which has its own subreddit, trending hashtag, and now commentary videos from at least twenty-three prominent mommy bloggers.

"She's here to talk about Holly." Flo cuts through the silence, sounding decidedly less French. "Says it's not one of those schemes Maggie got scammed by, you remember? But make sure she doesn't try to talk you into buying anything, Jack. Lord knows this town doesn't need any more Tupperware parties. I can't even open my cabinets without an avalanche of lids."

"Thank you, Ms. Flo, I'm sure Clara hasn't come here to recruit me to her down line." Flo pours him a cup of coffee and he swaps two dollar bills for it.

I decide that this couldn't possibly get worse so I should go bold. "Can I buy you breakfast? And talk? Please?"

He gestures toward a table at the back of the room and I lead the way.

"This is the most beautiful place. I feel like I'm in Paris," I say to break the silence as we take our seats.

"I did my job right then," Jack says, nursing his coffee. "Flo lived in Paris for years. When it came to making the tables and chairs, she didn't give me or Dad a moment of peace for weeks. After we finally did the wall paneling to her tastes, Dad took himself fishing for four days just to recover alone in silence."

"You did this?" I ask.

He shrugs. "Chairs. Tables. Dolls. Whatever keeps the lights on."

We study the menu in silence; it's a high-quality card bound in leather, with an impressive breakfast selection. Just as I'm trying to find the courage to start talking to Jack about the doll, Flo appears at the table, shooing the approaching waitress off and snatching the notebook and pen out of her hands.

"What can I get you two?" she asks brightly. I smile up at her sweetly, the surprise written all over Jack's face confirming for me that her waiting tables is not a regular occurrence, and she is blatantly attempting to snoop on our conversation.

We both order French toast and more coffee, but Flo doesn't move; instead she pulls a chair from a neighboring table and sits herself in the middle of the conversation, which feels less like a meeting and more like the world's most awkward continuation of last night.

"So," she says, folding her hands neatly on the table, "what exactly is it that brings you to our humble little Fraser Falls, Clara . . ."

"Davenport." I fill in the obvious blank Flo left.

Flo's eyes sharpen. "Of Davenport toys?"

"Yes. I'm here about the doll. I'm not a journalist. I—"

Flo claps her hands together. "I wondered how long it would take for a spin doctor to turn up here."

I clear my throat and can feel my cheeks flushing. "As I mentioned, I was hoping to speak to you first. Then I was planning to head over to talk to you, Jack, not Harry, because I saw on the doll website that you manage distribution." They're both just staring at me, blank faced. "But of course that plan is a little mixed up now. And I just want you both to know I want to help the community. I'm here to find a way forward and work out how we achieve that."

Jack reaches for his coffee cup, taking a long sip. "You want us to take the videos down."

"Well, yes, but more important I want to make things right," I say. Jack looks more guarded than the carefree man I met last night.

"Davenport is sorry that it took the video to get our attention. I'm still learning about the history of your relationship with us, I've been working in a different division for the past year so I wasn't involved in the Evie project. I firmly believe that there's a pathway to fixing our professional relationship and regaining your trust in our business."

"I firmly believe that you came here to fix your company's image," Jack says, his voice even. "We don't need Davenport's guilty offerings."

Flo's smile widens. She looks proud of him. "You know, that's my handwriting on the box. I took a calligraphy course in the nineties and the talent has never left me."

"Oh," I say weakly.

"I sewed the dresses for the first hundred dolls or so, too, but then Jack here went and got himself a viral infection and—"

"It went viral," Jack interjects quickly. "The doll went viral online. I don't have a viral infection."

Flo tsks at him and continues, "My hands couldn't take it. Now I oversee the younger ones and their sewing machines. We have a little club at the art school."

"That's . . . incredible," I say, and wonder if it would be rude to ask Flo for her notebook to write this down. I decide it definitely is.

"It's a collaborative project," Flo continues, launching into the same doll history she covered in her videos. This time explaining about how it was all started by Jack of Harry's. Feels a little different when the man in question is sitting in front of you.

"Ms. Girard, there's nobody more in awe of what you've created here than me. Davenport was once a small business, too, and it's with those values in mind that I started the small business program. I'm sad that I didn't come here a year ago, before I left for my new role. I'd love to know everything there is to know about your project."

"Haven't you already copied enough?" Jack says.

The words catch in my throat. I was naïve to think this wouldn't be difficult. This community is hurt and it's Davenport's fault. Of course they weren't going to welcome me with open arms.

"I can see that you're hurt, and I understand why. I'd love to talk about things we can do to make this right. I have a very generous investment budget available to me and lots of ideas about how we could elevate what you've achieved."

"Ms. Flo," Jack says firmly, like the mention of money triggered some kind of guard-dog mode, "I wasn't expecting to be so delayed and I haven't opened the store yet."

She gives him a look that could curdle milk and walks away to put in our order, muttering something in French that I can almost guarantee is about Jack and doesn't sound complimentary.

When she's out of earshot he turns back to me. "It's cruel to get an old woman's hopes up."

"Are you kidding?" I say. "I've met CEOs with less fire in their belly. She might be old in age but she isn't in mind, *clearly*." He raises an eyebrow. "I meant what I said, Jack. I'm here to fix things. You should be proud of what you've achieved so far. I'm sorry that this . . . incident . . . has impacted you as well as your neighbors."

He gives me a small, begrudging smile. "You need to get to your point, Clara."

"I know you probably don't want to have anything to do with our company after the incident that inspired the videos."

"You mean the theft," Jack says dryly.

I wince. "I know you've got a great thing here. But what if you had someone with experience, with expertise, to help you capitalize on this, to grow it and manage it? To make this bigger and better."

"You've missed a chapter, Clara. I've already had the spiel from one of your colleagues. It was a scam."

"I'm not scamming you. I have six other businesses signed up to the program that I'm back overseeing. I can arrange for you to meet them." Onboarding Jack was *not* the purpose of my visit but there's something about this quiet little town and the community it's fostered that makes me excited.

Maybe I'm looking at things under the hazy glow of the stories Jack told me that made me laugh. But maybe signing him up *would* fix things. I can't think of one person who wouldn't be impressed by a community assembly line of what's already a bestselling product. With Davenport's small business program, it could be huge.

Jack finally speaks after letting me sit in silence for a minute, desperately anticipating his answer. "Why would I trust anything from Davenport?"

"Because it's not Davenport, it's me. I'm here. And I don't want to take anything from you—I want to help you, help the town. Help you deal with the viral success of the doll."

There's a long pause. Then he says, "You talk a really good talk."

I blink. "I can't tell if that's a compliment or not."

"It's not," he says. Then he adds, "The people in this town are good, decent, hardworking people, and they've been hurt before. Their confidence in your company is nonexistent, and I can't let their confidence in me shake too. As charming as you are, Clara Davenport, you can't charm me into being screwed over twice."

I don't know what to say. As much as I want to shake him and beg him to let me fix this, I can't say I blame him for not wanting anything to do with us. With me.

We sit in silence for a moment as the teenager from earlier drops off our French toast. He retreats faster than Flo did. Jack picks up his fork and plays with his food. "You really want to help this town, Clara?"

"I do."

He stares at me for a long beat. "Then go back to New York and tell your fancy executives to take their doll off the market and leave us alone. We don't want you here, we don't want your money, and we don't want your help."

I nod, trying not to show how rattled I am. "Jack, I—"

He puts his hand up to silence me. "I need to open my store, Clara. Have fun in Maine." He stands, throwing a few bills onto the table and lifting his plate and cutlery.

He doesn't say another word to me and holds up his stolen tableware to Flo on the way past, saying, "I'll bring these back later."

She tuts at him, then turns her head to me and tuts again.

Flo's eyes bore into me from behind the counter as she reties her apron like she's preparing to go to war. And she's got a town behind her.

Chapter 6

JACK

It is a universal truth that being a man in a close-knit community means that if you sass the town matriarch, and later forget to return the plate and cutlery you took during your dramatic exit, she will immediately begin making phone calls and tattle on you to the entire town.

By the time I'm walking into the Hungry Fox after closing the store, I've had two texts from Maggie, one from Winnie, and a voice note from my high school basketball coach telling me he's worried about the choices I'm making.

Tommy, naturally, is busying himself behind the bar and pretending he didn't send me a text that read "DID YOU STEAL FROM FLO" in capital letters and with twelve alternating question and exclamation marks.

"You're really robbing local businesses now? In this climate?" he says as I settle myself on a bar stool. "What's next, knocking over the post office? Stealing from the collection plate at church?"

Pastor Akinola, who usually does an excellent job of pretending not to be listening in on our conversations, chokes on his club soda and turns to me. "I did hear you've taken up petty theft, Jack. I do hope you plan to return Ms. Girard's tableware. I'd hate to have to prepare a new sermon on coveting thy neighbor's crockery."

I groan. "It was a misunderstanding, Pastor. I meant to return it this afternoon. I just got busy."

His eyes narrow skeptically. "With what? Planning how you'll go back for the rest of the dinner set?"

Tommy snorts.

I stumble over my words. For someone who gave zero fucks about authority as a teenager, as an adult I'm a bumbling mess. "With orders I—"

"I'm joking, son," Pastor Akinola says kindly, patting me on the shoulder. "But I do want you to know that Ms. Girard is spreading the word around town at an impressively rapid speed. If only she'd be as enthusiastic spreading the word of our Lord."

She's unbelievable.

"I *texted* her about it," I groan. "She'll have it back first thing in the morning."

The pastor nods solemnly. Then without breaking eye contact he swivels to Tommy. "And I trust you're behaving yourself this week?"

Tommy, who has been smugly smiling through this entire interaction, suddenly looks sheepish. "I—of course, Pastor Akinola, sir."

"Good. Now, I need the name of that witch you hired on Etsy."

Tommy blinks. "Uh . . ."

"Don't try and tell me *Etsy witch* is the name of a band again, Thomas. I've visited the internet and I've spoken to my daughter. I know what you have been up to." Tommy looks more panicked than he did when we were fifteen and he set a field of sheep free by accident. "Now, I need the name of the woman you instructed so that I may send her the outline of my sermon on the occult hiding in plain sight."

Tommy tries to recover. "I'm sorry, Pastor, I was kidding. I—" He fumbles in the tip jar and pulls out a crumpled twenty-dollar bill. "I'd like to give you this as an apology, for the church roof fund. And"—he gestures to the pastor's drink—"your club soda is on the house."

Pastor Akinola eyes him warily before nodding. "Common sense is not a flower that grows in every garden, Thomas Brookdale, but your community thanks you for the two roof shingles your donation will cover." And with that, he glides out of the bar, his wool coat trailing behind him.

"He terrifies me," Tommy whispers, his eyes wide.

"Do you want to tell me what that was about?" I ask, putting my head in my hands, knowing already that I probably won't like the answer.

He sighs as he slides a can of ginger ale across the bar to me. "I paid a witch online to find you a date. Expedited results. Seven-to-ten-day guarantee. And the pastor may or may not have heard me talking about it to Luke and called my mother to tell her his concerns."

"You what?"

"And then Clara showed up and you sent her packing." He throws up his hands like this is somehow my fault. "So now you have no date, I'm down fifty bucks, and my mom's mad at me."

I can't stop staring at him in disbelief. "You're telling me Clara Davenport was delivered to me . . . by a spell?"

"Yes! I didn't expect it to work! But then she showed up here in her nice coat with her shiny hair and big smile and—"

I groan for what feels like the millionth time today. I rest my forehead against the bar. "She works for Davenport, Tommy. She *is* a Davenport. You summoned the devil. Maybe Akinola does need to come back in here."

Tommy shrugs. "You liked her until you found out her last name. Now you're acting like she arrived with a can of gasoline and a box of matches."

"I'm not acting like anything. The thing she arrived with was an agenda. We can't know that it wasn't all an act."

Tommy eyes me and pours himself a soda. "I know that you liked her from the moment you met her."

"I don't even know her," I say indignantly.

"You liked her," he repeats, ignoring me.

I focus on opening my soda and pouring it into my glass and not my best friend's judgmental glare. I don't know what else he expects me to say. "It doesn't matter."

Tommy leans on the bar, suddenly serious. "Flo said Clara wanted to make things right. Big investment budget or something."

"She said she did—wait, when did you speak to Flo?"

"When she called me to tell me you burgled her, but never mind that. Heard you had your big dramatic moment. Told Clara to leave and never return, and then you left and so far haven't returned Flo's possessions. Why?"

I scrub a hand through my hair. "I panicked."

"Because she's from Davenport?"

"Yes. No. Sort of. Mainly because she made it sound so easy. Like she could wave her magic marketing wand and fix everything, give us everything. I don't want her to strut in and fix it. We can do it ourselves."

Tommy stands quietly for a moment. "Do you know how many wreaths I've zip-tied this week?"

"Too many?"

"Far too many. Winnie has early-onset Christmas vision. She thinks this year will be the year they really hit the big time. Like now that you've gone viral with the doll, and Flo went viral with her rampage, it's her and Mel's turn next. I've been going to the flower shop before I open up here to help them."

I huff a laugh. "That's because you want to spend time with Melissa."

"It's because I believe that they deserve to hit the big time. To not panic every month. Flo made us put up triple the lights, and we did it. Why? Because I believe in her vision." Tommy pinches the bridge of his nose. "And she's talking about ordering fake-snow machines. Something about global warming. Snow machines. Here."

I shake my head. "I heard."

"And when they arrive, we'll be the ones who get made to drag them around. But we'll do it anyway because she wants our town to be known for something."

"Yeah, we'll be known as the laughingstock that has their snow machines running in the middle of a snowstorm."

"You're the guy who made the doll that made everyone's dreams feel possible," Tommy says, quieter now.

I stare down at my glass.

"So yeah," he finishes, "I get it. You don't need anyone else, especially not the people who stole from us, to swoop in and get the credit for what we have."

"It's not about credit," I say, shaking my head.

"It's about control."

I don't say anything.

Tommy points a finger at me. "You're trying to do everything yourself. You can't let anyone else help because you need everything to be perfect, otherwise you feel like you've let everyone down. Which isn't true, by the way. So you're working yourself into the ground trying to be in a million places at once to get the town ready for the holidays, and meanwhile, that blogger isn't even coming."

"Bad vibes and need for professional distance from an ongoing crisis is such a shitty excuse." It was the last thing we needed. "*Crisis* is an exaggeration."

"Yeah, I know, but Flo's still crushed."

His words sting. For all Flo's eccentricities, she means so much to me, and the thought of her being sad or let down cuts me deep.

"Clara wasn't the problem, Jack," Tommy says gently.

"She's a Davenport. She's a representative of the biggest problem this town has right now."

"She's also someone who spent less than twenty-four hours in this town and during that time charmed you, was treated with nothing but suspicion by everyone, and still faced Flo head-on with a promise of redemption."

"Like I said, she also came with an agenda." I press my fingers to my temples, trying to massage the stress of the day away.

Tommy shrugs. "Maybe. But she also came with a promise to help."

I lean my elbows on the bar and rest my head in my hands. "What if I made a mistake? Walking out on the conversation before finding out exactly what she had in mind?"

"You did," Tommy says cheerfully. I glare at him. "But lucky for you, everyone will still love you. You make sleighs for kids and fix people's front steps and get handwritten thank-you notes from third graders. You can still fix this."

"How?"

He shrugs. "Start by returning the plate. And the knife. And the fork."

I groan.

"And maybe, just maybe," he continues, "if you see her again, don't go all sheriff-in-a-western on her and tell her to get out of your town."

I cringe as I replay the conversation with Clara in my head. "I hate you."

"I can't understand why." He grins. "I'm the guy trying to get you a date."

"I can't date a Davenport, Tommy. You should've given your witch more guidelines."

He scoffs. "You could. Flo said she didn't even work on the copycat doll. She's just a fixer here to throw money at us to get the videos down. You've dated worse. That one woman who cut holes in all your clothes? She wasn't great. And that one who hit Arthur with her car! Definitely worse than someone just doing their job."

I'm beginning to see why my best friend thought he needed the intervention of magic to get me a date. I rest my chin on my fist and watch the Christmas lights blink around the edges of the top shelf. "Thanks for the walk down memory lane."

"You weren't your dad when you worked for him. What's to say she's even anything like hers?"

It's his landing blow before Tommy walks off to serve someone else. Fraser Falls is still my favorite place, but it feels like we're holding it together with string lights, cinnamon sugar, and a whole lot of hope. Flo's banking on this being the year that turns everything around, for tourism, the florist, the café—hell, even the tavern. I still feel like the guy who started it all, gave my neighbors hope and couldn't see it through.

Tommy returns and I seize the opportunity to move the conversation off Clara and my disastrous dating history.

"I don't know if I can cope hearing Flo talk about that town in Illinois again this year," I say, glancing at the "Upcoming Holiday Events" flyer Flo made and distributed all over town. "They've got a carousel this year. And the twenty-foot-tall advent calendar that they open every day is back. All we've got are Flo's temper and a church bell with a two-second delay."

Tommy snorts. "Don't forget that we may soon also have fake snow. Besides, that town cheated last year. They had a drone show choreographed to Michael Bublé. They emotionally manipulated everyone by pulling on their festive heartstrings."

"Well, we don't have emotional manipulation money," I say, shaking my head. I sent the emotional manipulation wallet holder to Maine.

"And you can't afford to suffer any more emotional damage. So stop moping around, get out of my bar, and go home and kiss your dog. Tomorrow is a brand-new day," Tommy says, opening a bag of potato chips.

I start laughing slowly, and it rolls into something uncontrollable until I'm wiping tears from my eyes with the backs of my hands. "Sorry, sorry. I got a vision of Donald trying to stop a drone show with his net and Mariah Carey playing in the background."

Saying it out loud sets me off again and soon Tommy is laughing with me. "I needed that laugh. Okay, I'm going home. It'll be fine."

"It will be fine, buddy. It always is."

"Thanks, man," I say, pulling my wallet out of my pocket.

He smacks it out of my hand. "Absolutely not."

"You're only saying that so you can tell everyone I stole from you as well," I argue.

"I just think it could be fun for you to rebrand as the Fraser Falls kleptomaniac."

"Good luck getting anyone to believe you after I start a rumor you're into witchcraft."

I try not to think about today's events on my walk home, but I can't help it. I don't know if I made the right call sending Clara away. She caught me off guard after we spent last night together. As soon as she identified herself as a Davenport, I couldn't see her as anything other than someone untrustworthy.

If I hadn't laughed and flirted with her last night, would I have been more open to hearing her out today? Did I just screw over my town for my ego?

The worst part is I *did* like her. I liked talking to her. Liked looking at her.

But liking isn't the same as trusting and right now, I don't trust her.

Chapter 7

CLARA

WHEN I FIRST STARTED WORKING at headquarters, taking the elevator up to my dad's office made me giddy.

Now it makes me nauseous. Dad wants me to act like any employee, but he wants to talk to me like I'm his daughter. It's hard to navigate and even harder to tolerate after working here for ten years.

The metal doors open onto a bright white hallway. Despite the bitter chill outside, the sky is a cloudless blue. The sun streams onto the white marble floor, making it shine. Dad's assistant isn't at her desk so I take myself to the door, knocking lightly, pressing the cold metal handle down and nudging the door with my hip to push it open when he instructs me to enter.

"Clara," he says, his voice impassive. "How was your trip?"

I take a seat on the other side of his desk and smooth down my dress. Looking at Dad has always been like looking into a mirror. My red hair comes from his mother and skipped a generation with him, but we share the same face. Narrow nose, high cheekbones, green eyes, and a snatched jawline I've always been thankful for.

Dad's more suntanned than my pale, borderline-allergic-to-the-sun skin, and his previously dark hair is more salt and pepper these days. There are lines etched into his forehead from frowning and a faint line across his top lip from the cigarettes he thinks nobody knows about.

My brother looks like my mother's side, with brown hair and blue eyes. Max has a square face to my heart shaped, but we were both hit with the same tall and lean Davenport gene shared by my father and grandfather. Mom frequently complains about being five foot four and surrounded by "giants."

We're a small family with both my parents being only children, and I can't help but think that it's a good thing there aren't more versions of my father roaming the streets.

"Successful. Three businesses couldn't make time to see me until after New Year's. I was scheduled to see one, but they rearranged last-minute. The three I saw are very happy with how our partnership is going."

"A half-successful trip then."

I try to match his smile but it makes my face feel tight. "I took some feedback about comms, which I'll distribute to the team, but overall no issues," I add. "The family business in Rockford is doing some interesting stuff, I'd love to tell you more about it. There's definitely an opportunity for a good news story there. They're—"

"I don't want to know about Rockford, I want to know about Fraser Falls. I assume you have no successes to share given the video is still live."

I swallow. There's a tiny alarm in my head telling me to run. "Fraser Falls didn't go as we hoped it would. I wasn't able to secure an agreement on how to settle the matter. They don't trust us, Dad. Their doll was bringing much-needed attention to their town and with one move we wiped it away."

He looks uninterested. The irritation bubbles in my chest, threatening to grow into something more explosive. "I don't think I need to remind you that Daryl is retiring next month, Clara."

It's like being zapped with lightning. Every nerve feels frazzled. "I know that," I say carefully.

"Your name has been mentioned more than once when talking about his replacement. It's no secret your goal is to move into the design sector." My lungs might have actually stopped working. "I'm just not sure how anyone can advocate for you to step up into that role if you can't resolve something as simple as a small business dispute."

"Your other candidates are welcome to try." My shoulders sag as my chest deflates. Max's skinny ass would never make it past Jack in guard-dog mode. "My objective for the trip was to establish Ms. Girard's mindset, which I did. It was also to establish if she feels there's something we can do to fix it; she doesn't. I don't believe this is the kind of thing that is going to be resolved in one conversation."

"Then why did you give up after one conversation and come home?" My mouth opens and closes like a goldfish's. "If you can resolve this mess in Fraser Falls, the promotion is yours, Clara. I thought that was obvious."

There is nothing about my dad that is or has ever been obvious.

"I expect you to have a plan by Monday."

I know it's my cue to leave but I have so many questions I know won't get answered. Suddenly, the morale-raising karaoke invite sitting unread in my inbox feels a hell of a lot more appealing.

THERE'S SOMETHING INCREDIBLY HUMBLING ABOUT spending a Friday night drinking with colleagues who have a median age of twenty-four.

I in no way believe that women peak at a certain age—and if we do, it's certainly not south of ninety—but there does come a point where I *do* just want to be in bed. Or at least in a pair of comfortable shoes.

When I've overheard people in the staff kitchen talking about a new club opening or some bar, I've always thought, *I'm young . . . that should be me . . .* but now that it is me, I'm happy to admit I was wrong and want to go home.

Sahara texted while I was in Maine asking what she could do to reinvigorate the spirit of her tired and demotivated team. I suggested an exorcism. You can't expense that though, so singing Whitney Houston loudly and off-key was the next best thing.

A bottle of wine and minimal food mixed with several nights of bad sleep is going down as one of my more ridiculous choices this year. We haven't even made it to the karaoke bar yet and I'm ready to be in bed. I wrap my coat tightly around my waist, shielding myself from the wind while honking taxis serenade the city.

"Please, don't go!" Sahara begs, but all I hear is *Please don't leave me with them*. My brain is fumbling to come up with something motivational, but the wine is making it difficult to do anything other than wrap her in a bear hug.

"You can do this," I mumble. Her out-of-work friends are meeting her at the karaoke bar, so I don't feel bad about leaving her. Whitney will have to wait.

My car pulls up to the curb and I've never been so happy for a blasting heater. We crawl into slow-moving traffic and I fight to stay awake.

My fingers travel across my cell phone screen to my work inbox. Email after email scheduling meetings and looking for approval. Wine-brain me looks up "Harry's store Fraser Falls" and navigates to the contact page. He doesn't even have social media pages for his business.

There's an email address though.

It isn't a good idea to contact him out of the blue, but I click the link anyway and choose my personal email account over my work one.

> **From: Davenport, Clara (claradavenport@gmail.com)**
> **To: inquiries@harrysfraserfalls.com**
> ***Subject: whun?***
>
> Are yup going to let my help yet???

My stomach immediately sinks as I hear the whooshing noise of my email sending. Why the hell did I do that? My clumsy fingers search for the option to recall but I can't find it.

I might be sick.

A mail banner appears on my screen.

> **From: Kelly, Jack (jack@harrysfraserfalls.com)**
> **To: Davenport, Clara (claradavenport@gmail.com)**
> ***RE: whun?***
>
> Did you let AI write this the same way you let it write your kids' books?

I switch to speech-to-text and concentrate hard to change the subject bar without accidentally pressing send.

> **From: Davenport, Clara (claradavenport@gmail.com)**
> **To: Kelly, Jack (jack@harrysfraserfalls.com)**
> ***RE: WHEN?***
>
> Are YOU going to let me help yet?
> Smart ass

> **From: Kelly, Jack (jack@harrysfraserfalls.com)**
> **To: Davenport, Clara (claradavenport@gmail.com)**
> *RE: WHEN, smart ass?*

Are you drunk emailing me, Clara?

Shit.

> **From: Davenport, Clara (claradavenport@gmail.com)**
> **To: Kelly, Jack (jack@harrysfraserfalls.com)**
> *RE: WHEN, smart ass?*

Obviously not. I just want to know it's the house on the left with the red door thank you why you're being a broody bodyguard and not accepting my where are my keys help. It isn't very nice of you send email

> **From: Kelly, Jack (jack@harrysfraserfalls.com)**
> **To: Davenport, Clara (claradavenport@gmail.com)**
> *RE: WHEN, broody bodyguard?*

Has anyone ever told you you're a great communicator? Helping people by taking over and throwing money at us isn't the desirable thing you think it is. You don't actually want to help us. You want this to go away.

> **From: Davenport, Clara (claradavenport@gmail.com)**
> **To: Kelly, Jack (jack@harrysfraserfalls.com)**
> *RE: WHEN, broody bodyguard?*

I do want to help fraser falls!! And I don't need to throw money to do that
And I know I can if you stop acting like a guard dog

From: Kelly, Jack (jack@harrysfraserfalls.com)
To: Davenport, Clara (claradavenport@gmail.com)
RE: WHEN, guard dog?

Prove it then.

From: Davenport, Clara (claradavenport@gmail.com)
To: Kelly, Jack (jack@harrysfraserfalls.com)
RE: WHEN, guard dog?

Fine. I will
I have a lot of ideas and experience and connections

From: Kelly, Jack (jack@harrysfraserfalls.com)
To: Davenport, Clara (claradavenport@gmail.com)
RE: WHEN, guard dog?

Good night, Clara.

From: Davenport, Clara (claradavenport@gmail.com)
To: Kelly, Jack (jack@harrysfraserfalls.com)
RE: WHEN, guard dog?

See you tomorrow, neighbor

Chapter 8

JACK

I KNOW HUNGOVER PEOPLE AREN'T famously renowned for their reliability and accurate recall of details, but I swear I've just seen a ghost.

Not the sheet-over-the-head kind, or the type that'll drag chains down the hallway of the B & B. No, this ghost has auburn hair that flickers like fire. And it moves with the kind of urgency not seen from a ghost since Ebenezer Scrooge got his shit together.

She's just a blur of movement on the other side of the gazebo, a swish of navy, a flash of red, head down, marching toward Maggie's with the same graceful stride my body recognizes.

I blink, shake my head, blink again.

She's gone.

I tell myself that she was never there to begin with. I imagine ghostly apparitions are probably quite common after extensive beer tastings and three shots of a liquor Tommy claimed was flavored but tasted more like lighter fluid and bad decisions.

I feel like a truck has run over my head and I have nobody to blame but myself.

And Tommy. I can always blame Tommy.

It's around this time every year the Hungry Fox, his bar, receives its selection of holiday ales from the brewery a couple of towns over. It's tradition every year for us to sample them.

It's also tradition for us to dodge any town leaders and their clipboards while I still have remnants of "BrewDolf the ReinBeer," "Ho Ho Hops," and "Hoppy Holidays" seeping out of my skin.

Which is why dodging Bliss Café and Flo's Fancies is also required on days like today whether she's working or not. Flo has her little minions well trained and they'll snitch if they see me red eyed and clammy skinned, smelling like beer.

I should be in the store making a start on all the orders I now have thanks to Flo, but instead I'm leaving it to Joe, my Saturday kid, and Deena, my old Saturday kid who left me for Flo but helps out occasionally when she wants extra money and I have weekend plans.

There's something about a hangover at thirty-two that chips away at my soul in a way it didn't at twenty-one.

I concentrate on my feet hitting the sidewalk. A mistake when I get slapped upside my head by a snowflake light hanging too low. When I get past the Frozen Spoon Ice Cream Parlor and nobody has called my name out the door of the café, I breathe a little easier. Two stores later, when I'm passing Wilde & Winslet, I feel like I see another flash of auburn hair in the bakery.

My mind strays somewhere I won't let it go, and I brush it off. I'm already hungover, I don't need to also torment myself with her.

Especially after I dreamed about her last night.

Still.

That hair. That walk. The specter of Clara Davenport has been haunting me all damn day. She has taken up residence behind my eyes, curled up in the pit of my stomach, and clenched in the line of my jaw every time I think about her.

Flo always says nothing good ever comes from anger, and given

I appear to have accidentally summoned Clara in some spite-fueled séance, she might be onto something.

"When the reviews on Google complained that we don't have enough places to sit, we put Jack on the case and the new benches will be installed before Small Business Saturday."

I look up at the sound of my name. I zoned out up until now with the various issues that crop up at these long-ass town meetings. Some new and related to the incoming tourism, some old that people repackage under the guise of tourist needs.

Unfortunately for Tommy, who wants permission to extend his back patio to offer "opportunities for more patrons to take a seat and grab a drink," Flo can smell a phony request a mile away.

His first mistake was not bringing it up at the town meeting six months ago when it was hot as hell and people actually wanted to drink outside and watch baseball. The second mistake he made was fighting for outdoor drinking space in November.

Elf's nose nudges at my knee, swiftly followed by his paw stepping on my foot. "What?" I mouth at him. His tail wags, hitting the leg of my chair with such force that it projects the sound around the room. "You love me again now?"

As much as I hate town meetings, I don't miss them because if I'm not here I always end up signed up for some project I don't want to do. One time Elf was sick and I didn't want to leave him home alone so I brought him along with me.

He spent the whole meeting going knee to knee, hand to hand, and mouth to mouth, getting pets and kisses from everyone here. Now if I don't bring him, I get complaints from my neighbors and Elf ignores me when I get home.

I can't be sure, but I think that even he isn't that impressed with spending his Saturday night here, but today was the only day people could agree on after Wednesday's meeting was canceled because of the news crew that showed up. The proposed Monday date clashed with a Patriots-Jets game so that was swiftly rejected.

The fact that Elf is only halfway around the room and has returned to me doesn't tell me that he wants my attention more, it tells me he needs to pee.

There's a flash of red in my peripheral vision as I stand and turn toward the door. I blink hard, rub my eyes with the back of my hands, like that'll somehow remove her from my line of sight.

I blame everything from stress to being hungover as I unstick my feet and take slow steps toward the back of the meeting. My eyes cover every inch of her in a desperate attempt to convince myself that like all the other times today, she isn't really there.

Her foot bobs up and down as she scribbles furiously onto a notepad on her lap, her hair twisted messily and secured out of her face with a hair clip shaped like a watermelon. She's wearing an oversized chunky knit cardigan over a black T-shirt scooped low to show her cleavage and a delicate diamond necklace sitting between her collarbones.

Clara Davenport isn't a ghost and she's sitting in the back of a town meeting looking like she's supposed to be here. Which couldn't be further from the truth.

And Elf, being the traitor that he is, leaves my side to go and stick his head right on top of all her notes while wagging his tail. She smiles at him like she smiled at me the first time she saw me. The thing that stopped me in my tracks before I even realized how beautiful she is, or funny, or any of the other things I learned about her that night.

I stop in the space beside her and crouch down so I'm closer to her eye level. I focus on her face while I ignore the sweet smell of her perfume. The way her cheeks flush and how hard she's focusing on Elf. "What're you doing here, Clara?"

"I'm busy," she says softly, not bothering to look at me.

"Get unbusy real quick. We need to talk. Outside."

Tucking her notepad and pen into the bag, she grabs her coat as she stands, leaving me looking like I'm kneeling at her feet. It's an image I had that first night after I went home alone but this doesn't live up to it.

There's a twisted satisfaction to her smirk becoming a swallow when I stand and tower over her. Her chest is only inches from mine, her face tilted up defiantly. "Fine."

I move out of her way so she can walk ahead of me out the door in jeans that cling to the curve of her ass, Elf trailing close behind her with his tail still wagging. The second she pushes open the town hall door and we're hit with the bitter-cold air, Elf changes his mind about going outside and runs back into the meeting.

I push my hands into my coat pockets. She puts her coat on and does the same. "What are you doing here, Clara?"

"You invited me," she says innocently.

"I did not invite you," I reply, my voice flat, but my mind begins to race.

"I said I wanted to help the town and I'd prove it. So here I am, to prove to you that I'm ready to help."

She looks so confident, and I feel anything but. Cloudy memories of a dream I had last night with Clara come back to me, but trying to fully remember things that happened feels like smoke slipping through my fingers. "That didn't happen."

"Don't try to gaslight me, Jack. I went to an all-girls school so I can confidently tell you that you're not even good at it. I have the emails."

As soon as she says the word *email*, the two packs of instant ramen I wolfed down pre-meeting and post–hungover late-afternoon nap threaten to come back up. "I . . . I would never say that."

The uncertainty in my voice is so fucking obvious it's embarrassing. I don't remember talking to Clara last night. I was more drunk than I've been in a really long time, which I blamed on tiredness and stress, but too drunk to remember something I did? I haven't gotten myself into that kind of mess since I was a teenager.

"It looks like you need to have a little recap with your inbox so I'm going to head back inside because it's cold and I have notes to take."

She tries to move past me to reach the door but I block her. Her arm presses against mine. She stands a little straighter, chin tipped up defiantly like earlier. "You can't just show up to a town meeting, y'know. You don't live here. And you can't just take notes of people's private business."

"Private business . . . at a town meeting? I can't help people if I don't know what their issues are." Clara doesn't back down. "And actually, I do live here. I moved in this afternoon."

That explains why I *thought* I saw her near the B & B—I did. It's unbelievable that she woke up this morning and was here by late afternoon. How much has she even packed? How long is she planning to stay?

I have two Claras in my head. The one I met first, who made me laugh while she pretended she couldn't play pool. Stunning and witty and easy to talk to. Then there's Davenport's Clara, who comes here with an agenda. The one who's just as beautiful and charismatic as the first one but will leave as soon as she gets what she wants.

I don't believe her when she says she only wants to help and now I have to watch her float around town trying to be everyone's fairy godmother. Part of me is a little jealous I can't offer to do that for my neighbors myself. I don't begrudge all kinds of help, I just don't like the kind tied up in strings that lead back to Davenport.

"What's your grand plan then?" I ask.

She purses her lips, looks down at her feet. "I don't know yet, because you dragged me out of the meeting to cry over my being here."

"I haven't cried." I raise an eyebrow skeptically. "So you don't have a plan? You want everyone to believe that you want to help but you don't know how you're going to?"

"The plan comes after I work out what the problems are, Jack. I bet you've never turned up at someone's house to fix something they didn't tell you was broken, right? But you expect me to. I need time."

The problem is Clara needed practically zero time to win me over the first time; I can't say how long it'll take for her to do it again. I don't want to let people down by being fooled by Davenport again.

"How about I say I forgive you, and you leave town in the morning? I'll even give you a ride to the station."

She scoffs. "How about you let me do my thing and learn to play nicely with others?"

I scratch at the stubble on my jaw. The thought of playing with her is the last thing my mind needs right now. "I don't trust your thing. That's the problem. I know who you represent."

There's a flicker of hurt that lasts less than a second. I think back to what Tommy said about how I wasn't my dad when I worked for him, and how she's not necessarily hers.

"Then think of it as I'm representing myself. Think about how much you care for Ms. Girard, and the dreams she wants to achieve, and the fact I want to help her do that if that's what will make her happy." Bringing Flo into this is a low blow. Her hands land on her hips and she cocks her head. "Or think about the fact you told me to come here. I don't care."

"I was inebriated. I didn't know what I was saying." It's a shitty excuse but it's the only one I've got.

She smiles. "And you think I send emails full of typos to men late at night while sober?"

I shrug. "I don't think about you, Clara. I don't know what you do in your free time. I don't care either."

"Good," she says cheerfully. "If you don't care then you have no right to tell me what to do. I want to make Fraser Falls better, so just stay out of my way."

"You clearly haven't lived in a place like this before," I say, trying not to laugh. "There is no staying out of someone's way."

"You better get used to looking at me then."

I'm positive under normal circumstances, looking at Clara Davenport wouldn't ever be a struggle. "I don't want you to hurt my neighbors. I've already let them down by opening the door to Davenport once, and I don't want to do it again."

"I'm only here to help and I'll prove that to you. Just like you asked me to."

And with that, she pushes past me and through the door back into the meeting, leaving me standing in the cold, vowing to never drink again.

Chapter 9

CLARA

I'M SLOWLY GETTING USED TO a giant gull being the first thing I see when I open my eyes in the morning.

Maggie's B & B is decorated in a way that the interior designer who furnished my apartment would describe as kitschy, and she wouldn't mean it in a loving or appreciative sense.

When I stayed here earlier in the week, I was in a guest room in the main part of the house that was musical theater themed. When I politely asked Maggie why she picked *The Phantom of the Opera* as a design choice, she said it was the first show she ever saw. Each room is decorated with something that represents her or a point in her life so that guests get to experience her as well as her home.

I'm in what's essentially a self-contained condo at the back of the main building. It's an extension that they built for Maggie's mother when she wasn't able to live on her own. I have my own entrance at the back, but there's an adjoining door to the main building for going to breakfast or accessing the reception desk.

My bedroom is sea themed, with anchors and lighthouse ornaments adorning multiple surfaces in equally measured spacing.

There's of course the aforementioned ceiling gull, and I'd bet the air freshener is called Sea Breeze or something similar.

The aqua-blue walls were a shock to me when I first arrived, but it's nice to be surrounded by color and *things* instead of the minimalist beige approach I took in my home. I like it a lot.

Maggie told me the whole space was previously booked out for a blogger who wanted to review the town, but he canceled, saying the energy wasn't right anymore after Flo's video went viral. Given there's only one other couple here right now, I imagine it was a big disappointment for Maggie to have him cancel.

My Sundays are usually spent booking Pilates and brunch and then skipping the Pilates part. Today I'm sitting in front of my closet surrounded by sticky notes and the most delicious macarons I've ever had.

As much as I hate to give credit to a man, Jack made me realize something very important last night: for people to trust me enough to let me help them, they need to like me.

I don't know if Maggie would like me if she came in here to clean and found my plan stuck up on the wall. So, in the interest of being discreet and *not* strange, it's on the inside of the closet, where it can be hidden behind my clothes.

Ten out of ten for not being weird, Davenport.

I'm a visual person and I need to see my actions laid out in front of me. I know I'll continue to be met with a six-foot-four wall of resistance if I bulldoze through the town trying to change things without support from people. It's funny that Jack, the man who received no fewer than three calls the night we met from people asking for things, is so against having another pair of hands around here.

Before I can truly do my best work, I have the very simple task of making everyone love me. Okay, I'll settle for liking me. I write *Gain Town's Trust* on a pink sticky note and add *be proactive*, *be helpful*, and *be visible* in parentheses underneath. Something I kicked off this morning when I bought coffee from Bliss Café and macarons from Flo's Fancies, then signed up to volunteer at the nativity tomorrow night.

I drank my coffee on a slow walk back to Maggie's, smiling and saying good morning to all the people looking who were definitely questioning who I am.

A lot of my job—the real one I have, not whatever the hell this is—involves finding achievable objectives within the noise. Listening to people talk at the town meeting last night, before Jack rudely made me stand in the cold, proved what I already knew. This community just wants to grow and make enough to live comfortably and peacefully, and they want to share the love they have for their town with other people.

Flo has a very clear dream—that she loved recapping last night at the meeting, and, to be honest, I loved hearing—of the town hosting winter markets similar to what she's experienced in Europe. Having been to Cologne in December on a business trip, I know exactly what she means. I can imagine the grass in front of the town hall lined with red-roofed stalls filled with independent businesses. People would flood here to experience the magic, but before they can bring in outsiders, the businesses already here need to be okay.

To grow and be successful, people need to know Fraser Falls exists. When people know it exists, they need to come here. While they're here or while they're looking up town businesses, they need to spend money.

I write *Raise Profile*, *Increase Visitors*, and *Spend Money* on three individual blue sticky notes and put them side by side on the wall beneath my pink sticky note.

I have contacts I can use to get media attention to raise the town's profile, but it needs to be the right kind of attention. If I call them right now, all they're going to latch on to is the fact I'm here and the video. I need to find the perfect story to hand to them that isn't "toy company scandal at busiest time of year."

Getting people here is trickier unless I start running bus tours from the surrounding cities. I can imagine how confused finance would be when they got my expense report after I started my own Greyhound operation. Raising the town's profile goes hand in hand with increased visitors. I can also look at special events to get people here.

The sticky note with *Spend Money* has a question mark under it.

I pull the blue paper from the wall and write *small business saturday?* underneath as a reminder to really think about how I can link them together. It came up a couple of times last night at the meeting and I'm sure (kind of) that there's something I could suggest here.

Flo mentioned in the meeting that during last year's increased visitor flow following Holly's virality, they collected a lot of email addresses and have been doing blasts to remind people of upcoming events.

I reach for the orange sticky notes and separate them from the rest of the pile, trying to think about what would make this trip a success I can be happy about.

Flo deleting the video and going home to a promotion, obviously. Looking up at the clothes hanging in front of my plan wall, I get the feeling it'd take longer to pack up my desk to move into Daryl's office than it'll take to pack up here. Apart from all the loungewear and sweatshirts, I brought one dress that would be perfect if Fraser Falls opens a nightclub inspired by Ibiza. Not my finest work but I was packing with a deadline.

My point is, I do want to feel like I'm leaving the town better than I found it when I head back to my real life. I feel like the people involved in the doll need more from Davenport. More from me.

I write each of their names on the orange sticky notes and line them up beneath my other notes: Winnie and Melissa from Wilde & Winslet, Miss Celia from the Green Light bookstore, Wilhelmina from the art school, Dove from the animal sanctuary, and Jack.

Under *Miss Celia* I put *Matilda Brown?* to remind me to talk to my friend about a potential book event with one of her authors, but the rest are currently question marks. There's definitely a way to tie all these things together, but I just can't see it right now.

Maybe I should've bought string.

I pat the floor around me until I hit the hard case of my phone beneath a purple sweatshirt I've yet to put on a hanger. Scrolling to Honor's name, I navigate to FaceTime and smile when she fills my screen.

"How can I make people like me?" I ask, leaning against the side of my bed.

Her eyebrows pinch together, dipping beneath the thick rim of her glasses. She only wears them when her eyes are too tired for contacts because Billy Poston told her she looked like Velma Dinkley from *Scooby-Doo* in eighth grade. No amount of showing her Hot Velma from the second movie has ever changed her mind.

When Paloma was a baby, I turned up on Halloween dressed as Daphne with Velma and Scooby-Doo costumes for them. I thought it'd help her move past something that happened a decade earlier, but Honor shut the door in my face.

She has zero to feel self-conscious about. In addition to being smart and hilarious with excellent taste in friends (but not men), she's ridiculously hot. It feels like an unwritten rule that every tall girl has a short best friend, and we're no exception. She's half a foot shorter than I am and becoming a mom added to her curves (that I'd die for, honestly) in every way.

Her brunette hair is a few shades off being black, and even with it tied up like it is right now with her overgrown bangs hanging out, she looks effortlessly gorgeous.

Honor takes a bite out of a bagel with cream cheese and nudges her door closed with her shoulder. "Show them your titties."

There's a flash of Jack's shocked face in my head but I push it away. I scowl at her. "I'm not trying to leave town with a criminal record, Hon. I need to work out what my best qualities are so I can play to them, and I'm not sure I have any."

"Stop looking like you have a stick up your ass. I'm thinking." Honor sits down and I spot her shampoo and duck-egg-blue bath tiles in the background.

My nose scrunches. "Are you eating your lunch in the bathroom? That's disgusting."

She takes another unbothered bite and wipes cream cheese from her top lip with the back of her hand. "Girl, shut up. I'm hiding from my child, otherwise I'll have to share my lunch and this conversation. You're the first adult I've talked to face-to-face this weekend. Why do you want to know how to make people like you?"

"It's the core of all my plans to fix the Fraser Falls mess and get my promotion."

"Why can't you just have normal problems? Seriously. Like, one Sunday I'd love you to call me with a pregnancy scare or a flat tire or something."

"I called you three weeks ago and said I was dying of a cold and you told me to grow up! Also, I don't have a car and if I was having a pregnancy scare, my first call would be to the church to report a miracle, not you."

"Told you to grow up but made you lunch. Don't make me a villain, drama queen. Anyway, there's tons of things to like about you. You always say yes to everything. You rarely freak out even when it's a huge thing, like when *I* called *you* with a pregnancy scare."

"It wasn't a scare. You were pregnant."

"Moving on . . . being levelheaded and practical is great to have in a friend. Let's maybe exclude some of the things you do from that one, but most of the time you're levelheaded."

My jaw hangs open. "Excuse you, what are we excluding exactly?"

Honor frowns. "Your weird competitiveness with your brother."

I should feel outraged and a little embarrassed. She's totally right though. "Okay, fair. Continue."

"You're kind. You're generous with your time and your money. You encourage people wholeheartedly. You're funny . . . most of the time. There are dozens of things that might make those people like you, so you should probably just be yourself."

There's a soft throbbing in my chest. "This is so weird."

Honor sighs and leans against her knees. "*So* weird. I hate being nice to you."

"I think I hate you being nice to me too." It feels like the truest sign of friendship. One forged over more than twenty years after we met at summer camp as kids. Honor is one year younger than me, the same age as Max. When it was time to go home we forced our parents to swap information so we could meet up in the city. If anyone knows my good and bad traits, it's her.

The corners of my sticky notes are starting to curl off the wall. I sigh. "This would be so much easier if I could just bribe everyone."

"There's that Davenport charm you should definitely suppress. You got this. Just think what your dad would do, then do the opposite."

"You should be a motivational speaker."

Honor finally leaves the bathroom after taking the last bite of her bagel and licking her fingers. I can hear Paloma's annoying YouTubers blasting from a TV in the background. As someone in the toy industry, I'm pretty hot on what kids like, but I'll *never* understand how so many people got rich from slime.

"Just be yourself, Clara. They'll fall in love with you."

Honor sits at her breakfast bar and balances her phone on the top tier of her fruit stand. I feel like I'm there with her and not miles away from home surrounded by people who don't want me there.

When she's done updating me on every aspect of her life, I reluctantly end the call.

I wrap my arms around my shins and rest my chin on my knees. My plan looks like the work of an overenthusiastic child, but I think it's going to work.

I guess I'll have to try being myself.

Chapter 10

CLARA

ONE PLACE I NEVER EXPECTED to find myself is in an accidental standoff with a reindeer on a Christmas tree farm.

Maggie looked exhausted and uncomfortable at breakfast, a fibromyalgia flare-up she said, so I told her to let me know if she had anything I could help her with. She explained her daughter is usually around to help out but she had a baby a few months ago and Maggie doesn't like to bother her.

I was very clear that I am here to be bothered with anything that makes her life easier and more comfortable. I left the breakfast table with a grocery list and petty cash.

When I went back to my room I opened up the closet and pushed my clothes to the side to reveal my curling, barely-holding-on plan and added the name *Maggie* beside everyone else. Sure, she isn't directly involved in the Holly doll project, but she did lose business because of it when the blogger canceled their reservation. I added *make her life easier* underneath her name. Everyone else's question marks got a little bit bigger in my mind.

The grocery store trip gave me a false sense of achievement. Which means when Maggie mentioned she'd been planning to pick out the B & B's *multiple* Christmas trees, I confidently volunteered myself for the task, despite the fact that I've never been to a tree farm or even decorated my own tree. My mother has hired decorators my whole life.

I thought getting my own apartment sophomore year of college would be the start of my reenacting every Christmas movie ever. Soft festive music playing in the background while I battled golden lights, the smell of cinnamon and sugar cookies, hot chocolate and mismatched ornaments.

In reality, when I got home from a seminar, my mom had let herself and the decorators in and my tree was good enough to go into a store window. I think I was the only college kid in the whole of New York to have a model train playing "Santa Claus Is Comin' to Town" circling her living room.

How intimidating could a Christmas tree farm be? Now that I'm avoiding eye contact with a giant beast who looks as unimpressed with me being here as everyone else, I can confirm the answer is *pretty intimidating.*

"Mikayla! You don't live here, girl!"

My head turns alarmingly fast at the sound of a name that isn't my own. I'm just grateful to have another human around. A five-foot woman with hot-pink hair, pale skin, and very thick eyeliner is storming toward me and the reindeer, who apparently goes by Mikayla.

"Sorry, she's a bit of a diva," the woman says as she ushers the hooved trespasser toward an open gate into the next field. "She's supposed to be rescued from being forced to interact with humans, and here she is, staring you down."

A lightbulb illuminates above my head. "You're Dove, right? From the animal sanctuary?"

I'm trying not to be excited that being helpful to Maggie and being visible has led me right to someone on my list. After a long day of staring into my closet and hoping that the most perfect and easy-to-execute idea would hit me in the face, I decided to look up people in town for inspiration.

Dove & Friends saves animals in need, from either being used in entertainment or going to slaughter. I made an anonymous donation to the rescue and veterinary fund on the website after crying over a cow called Custard who only has half a tail.

"And you're Clara. From the doll-stealing company." Oh, man. My heart falls out of my ass. "I'm just messing with you. You're the one who has Jack's panties in a bunch. I'm not supposed to talk to you but I make it a point not to listen to the desires of men, so, here I am. You're not as evil looking as I thought you'd be. No horns or anything. Kinda disappointed."

The fact Jack is telling people not to talk to me is annoying and amusing at the same time. "Thanks . . . I think. I didn't mean to get anyone's panties in a bunch. Seriously, I found out what was happening here at the same time as everyone else. Just know I'm trying to un-bunch quickly, I promise."

She stuffs her hands in her coat. A lemon-yellow puffer with hearts on the pockets. "I mean, I'm no expert but you could get the greedy corporation you share your name with to stop selling the Holly rip-off. If they're feeling proactive they could also stop selling millions of dollars' worth of plastic that nobody really needs and ruining our planet, but like, maybe start with the small thing first."

Dove gives me a glowing smile that almost softens her request a little, but an uncomfortable feeling blooms in the center of my chest.

"I'm working on it," I say with a meek smile. "And I meant it when I said I'm going to be around for a while, so if you have anything you need help with, reindeer maintenance aside, I'm your woman."

Dove's eyes widen. "Do you want to help with the toy drive?"

"Yes! What's the toy drive?"

"Every year basically since the dinosaurs, the town collects toys and donations over the holidays. We use the donations to buy extra gifts, usually for the older kids who get left out, and we donate everything to hospitals, family shelters, charities that distribute to low-income families, et cetera," Dove explains. "My mom was in charge of it but she up and died so now I have to do it. I have a huge pile of flyers to put up and a list of businesses to email who've helped out in the past."

I slow-blink. "I'm sorry for your loss. If it helps, I can arrange a huge donation of toys from the warehouse at work. Plus, I know *tons* of rich people and businesses who are super easy to guilt into being generous. I can email everyone!"

Dove claps her hands together excitedly. "I'd normally be against accepting anything from Davenport *but* I'll put my personal beliefs and morals aside for the good of the children. And I hate emailing so yes, I'll accept your help."

I'm scared to be arrogant, but not scared enough to not admit that this is starting to feel a little too easy. A small town that rallies annually to give gifts to sick kids and low-income families during the holidays? It's a feel-good news story gold mine. I just need the right time to pitch it and get maximum attention on the town. One step closer to people knowing Fraser Falls exists.

"I'm here to pick out Christmas trees for Maggie so I'll grab the flyers and list from you before I head back to the B & B."

She nods toward the huge red barn a hundred yards away. "Luke will know which ones she's getting already, go talk to him. He promises her first pick but he knows the cold gets her down so he's usually prepared."

I guess my tree-choosing virginity lives to see another day. "I'll talk to him, thanks."

She starts to head toward the gate Mikayla was sent through but stops, turning on the heel of her glittery rain boots. "When you walk through the gate be careful of Simon. He's a sweetheart but he doesn't know that he's a donkey. He's body-checked Luke more than once."

There's probably as much chance of the same thing happening on the subway. It's also the reason I rarely use the subway anymore. "Thanks for the heads-up."

The crisp earthy smell of the tree farm is far better than any candle or car air freshener could work up. As much as I love the city, it feels good to spend my Monday weaving around branches instead of people. That's until I curve around a huge tree with wide branches and smash into something solid that knocks me on my ass.

My first thought is obviously Simon the donkey. But mid-falling I reached out for something to hold on to and pulled the "something solid" down with me. Something that can curse my name into my hair.

"Fuck, Clara." Jack's arms box both sides of my head and his chest lifts from mine, but I can still feel the rapid inhale-exhale moving through him. His nose is an inch away and I notice the flecks of amber in his brown eyes for the first time. I wriggle my leg out from underneath him, ignoring his sharp intake of breath when his hips sink between my legs. "Are you okay?"

That's when I realize his hand is cupping the back of my head, protecting it from the hard ground. I nod silently, my hair brushing against his fingers. "There are easier ways to get between my legs, Jack. You don't have to knock me down in public. Dinner and some flowers would work."

There's something special about watching him try not to laugh close-up. "Don't you watch where you're going?" he says, sounding as breathless as I feel.

"I thought you were a donkey." I try to push him off sideways but I'm not strong enough. "What're they feeding you up here? Why are you so hard?"

"You really have a way with words." He frees himself from the back of my hair and pushes himself up by his hands. I can immediately breathe easier but there's an empty aching feeling in my core now that the weight of him is gone. He gets onto his feet and holds out a hand for me. I eye it suspiciously. "I'm only going to offer once."

I take it reluctantly. His palm is rough but warm. "Thank you. Even though it was your fault I was down in the first place."

Jack fists his hair at the top of his head. Gives me the same exasperated look as last week. "You bulldozed into me and then pulled me down with you."

I wave a hand flippantly. "Details. Besides, there's no way I could pull you down if you didn't want to be pulled. If you wanted to cuddle you could've just asked."

He pinches the bridge of his nose between his thumb and forefinger. I don't know where getting on Jack's nerves fits into my plan; I might need a new sticky note for that. "What're you even doing here?"

"It's a Christmas tree farm. I'm picking out Christmas trees . . ."

"But you're not here for Christmas." There's almost a question in his statement. It sits somewhere between him reassuring himself and mild panic. Maybe a touch of curiosity if I'm kind to myself.

It's tempting to play into his obvious fear, but I remember the question mark under his name and that I've already had my fun with him today, so I decide against it. "I'm helping Maggie. She isn't feeling great today."

His expression immediately changes to real concern. "Why didn't she call me? What does she need?"

The night we met, Jack was constantly being asked to help with things. Even though he sighed every time the phone lit up, he didn't once screen anybody's call. The town meeting was full of updates on things Jack had fixed. His role in this community is very clearly problem solver.

"I'm sure she'll call you if there's something I can't do for her," I say, deflecting. "I'll tell her you're around if she needs you."

Jack's mouth opens like he's going to say something but closes just as quick. I feel like the words *thank you* were on the tip of his tongue, but I might be being optimistic. "Okay."

I want to tell him I have a plan, that even when I'm joking with him, fixing things is on my mind, but I don't. Jack's going to see what I can do.

Chapter 11

CLARA

"Miss Celia?"

An older woman stacking the classics section turns around at me calling her name. She puts down a leather-bound copy of *War and Peace* and looks at me. "I wondered when I'd be seeing you, Clara."

It's a slightly creepy introduction, I can't lie. It's honestly the last thing I expected her to say. Top of my list was *Get out* or something equally unwelcoming.

The only way I can describe Miss Celia is she looks like a feminine version of Gandalf the Grey, which isn't an observation I'll be voicing out loud. Her ashy silver hair is long with a slight wave as it flows on either side of her face down her chest. She's tall with a lean silhouette. The deep lines on her alabaster skin show the passage of time, but like how I felt with Flo when I first saw her, I can't put an age to her.

Someone needs to look at what's in the water in this town, I swear.

"That's nice," I say. What else can I say? "Do you have five minutes for me to tell you about an idea I've had?"

I ask to be polite but the Green Light bookstore is empty other than the two of us. "Of course. I was told you're on a mission to save the town from despair. I've been looking forward to your visit."

It feels less like sarcasm and more like playful banter. Maybe I'm giving her the benefit of the doubt because she looks like she'd be a really nice grandma—or wizard—and Arthur, one of the town leaders, said almost the same thing to me yesterday. I assume it's messaging that originated with Flo, but who knows.

All my words are stuck in my throat, something that hasn't happened to me during a pitch in *years*. She looks at me over the frameless glasses perched on the end of her nose. "I don't think the town is in despair. I'm trying to find ways to get positive attention on Fraser Falls to increase visitors and spending. Are you familiar with Matilda Brown? The author?"

Miss Celia taps on her hearing aid. I hope she isn't turning me off. "Yes. She's very popular with our book club."

"I also love her books. I'm friends with her publicist, we went to college together. Matilda has a new book coming out—I'm sure you already know that. She starts her US tour on release day but she has a three-day break after she's in New York. I asked her publicist if she'd be open to considering a last-minute addition to her schedule to support an indie bookstore."

Miss Celia's expression doesn't change, but she leans against the bookshelf. "What did she say?"

"Well, last-minute changes to book tours are the kind of thing that gives publicists hives, but Matilda gave a provisional yes. I was totally honest that I was inquiring without talking to you first, so if you say no there's no hard feelings, but they need an answer by tomorrow."

Miss Celia pushes her glasses up her nose and dusts her hands off against her dress. "You're quite the meddler, Miss Davenport."

I've been called worse. "The Northeast dates sold out immediately and they were looking at doing another one in Philadelphia or Boston, but I convinced them to do it here, knowing people will travel anywhere for Matilda. Also, people love supporting indies and since I know you ship, this is a great way for people to find out about you."

She looks at her feet instead of my face. Fiddles with a button before looking up again. "I assumed you'd buy out my stock or something financially frivolous. However, I can see you've put quite a lot of thought into this one."

My heart pounds. I stare at the dozens of stocked shelves lining every wall of this place. "I can absolutely buy out your stock, Miss Celia. I'll give you my address and credit card right now, but I thought giving your store some exposure would benefit you long-term. But to be clear, I'm happy to do both."

Miss Celia smiles and waves me off, shaking her head. "I'd be happy for your publicist friend to contact me to discuss the finer details. No purchase necessary."

I FEEL LIKE I'M WALKING on air as I head over to the Hungry Fox Tavern to get something to eat and use their Wi-Fi.

This town is turning me into a cliché but I'm struggling to be mad about it.

I tug the zipper of my coat up a little higher and use my headphones as earmuffs to combat the cold wind. After thirty seconds, I get a strange feeling in the pit of my stomach, like I'm not alone. I lift one ear of my headphones and hear a soft jingling. When I turn around, pulling the headphones down to my neck, there's a furry face at my knees.

"Hi, buddy." I crouch to stroke Elf. I look up at his owner. "You know, if you don't want to walk your dog alone, you can just ask me to walk with you. You don't have to walk ten paces behind me like a serial killer."

Jack rubs the back of his head with the hand not holding the leash to stop me from being charged by a seal-looking dog. "I'm walking to the tavern. I'm not following you."

"That's where I'm going." I watch him realize that he needs to either walk with me or continue walking behind me after I just compared him to a serial killer.

He looks like he's weighing up his options. Polite conversation for a few minutes or me telling Tommy that he followed me the second I walk through the door. Jack lets out a defeated sigh and I get my answer. "Cool."

It's amazing what a difference a week can make. Last Tuesday, Jack walked me to the B & B with a smile on his face. I even thought he might kiss me. Now I'm the lesser of two evils. Life really comes at you fast. "Can I hold Elf's leash?"

Jack looks between me and the dog. "He's strong and he'll pull you over if he sees a squirrel. Or an interesting leaf. Or another person."

"Like his owner then." He doesn't match my smile. "I'll be careful with him, promise."

Jack takes my hand in his. The rough calluses scrape against my knuckles as he removes the hoop from his wrist and slides it over mine. He taps his finger over where the fabric is stitched together. "Hold this bit tight. He'll walk next to you until he spots something."

I take a testing couple of steps away from Jack, and Elf follows next to me like the good boy he is. Jack also follows like a good boy.

"I begged for a dog when I was a kid," I explain. "It was the only thing I asked for that I was never allowed to have. That and a belly button piercing when I was thirteen."

Jack pushes his hands into the pockets of his pants. "Why couldn't you have one?"

"My mom didn't want dog hair in the house. Then I lived in buildings that didn't allow pets. Now I own my apartment and . . ." I pause, waiting for the reason to come to me. Jack looks at me, waiting for an answer. "I don't know why. I guess dogs have always felt like a family thing to me, and I live alone."

"I understand what you mean. I didn't plan to adopt Elf, which sort of goes against everything they say about being prepared and really thinking about getting a dog." We slow so Elf can intensely sniff a patch of grass that looks like all the other grass out here. "I was helping Luke out with a tree delivery to a shelter. When I got there, I saw a sign that said Elf was their longest resident and I couldn't leave him."

"That's so sad. He's such a sweetheart." I look down at Elf; his gray ears are blowing in the wind.

"Yeah, he was super shy when I took him home. He'd never lived with someone so it took a bit of getting used to, but now he's the biggest diva. I have to remind him he used to live outside when he won't go for a walk in the rain."

I smile and tuck my face into the top of my coat. "He has standards."

"Apparently," he says. "Clara, watch—"

Jack's hand wraps around my middle as the other shoots across my front, gripping the leash beneath where my hand is just as Elf pulls away urgently. My body freezes as Jack holds him back. The top of my head sits right below his jaw but I don't look up, scared of the judgment. "I'm sorry. I don't even know what he saw."

I unloop the leash from my wrist, letting Jack take it back. He slowly lets go of my waist, clearing his throat. He points to the tree on our right. "Don't worry about it. There's a cat on the branch."

He hardly strains against Elf pulling in the direction of the tree. "Is it stuck?"

"No. He likes to sit up there and survey the local area–slash–aggravate passing dogs." The sign outside the Hungry Fox flickers to life as we approach. I look both ways before crossing the street, a couple of steps ahead of Jack. "His name is Prudence."

My head snaps back to look at him over my shoulder. "*His* name is Prudence?"

"Donald started feeding it one day when it kept showing up in his yard. Didn't bother to check before naming it."

A laugh bursts out of me. "Donald the butterfly-net guy?"

Jack pushes the door to the tavern open, letting me walk in first. "I can't believe you remembered his name."

I turn around when I'm through the door, nodding enthusiastically as he and Elf follow me in. "He made a huge impression on me! I've never seen one that big!"

It feels like the whole room went quiet the exact moment I opened my mouth. Jack closes his eyes briefly; I turn to face the rest of the room. I turn back to Jack to make a joke but he walks past me, heading for the bar with Elf following him, leaving me standing alone.

Five minutes a day is obviously his maximum tolerance for me. I brush off the sting and head to my favorite seat in the corner of the room. It's close enough to the fire to be warm but far enough away that I don't end up itchy from the heat.

I've started coming here to work on my laptop because the internet connection in the B & B is the worst I've ever experienced. Tommy is quiet and sweet. He makes polite conversation when I arrive until he takes my order, then leaves me with my work.

I begrudgingly set up my computer at the table and grab a menu. I don't pay attention to Jack laughing at the bar with Tommy.

"The burger is good, if you need a recommendation." I look over to the armchair beside the fire where Melissa Wilde is sitting. Winslet Akinola is in the chair next to her. I have to pretend I don't know that they run the town flower shop and go by Mel and Winnie, all of which I read on their "about" page.

"Thanks! I was thinking about getting the lasagna."

"Great choice," Mel confirms, Winnie nodding beside her.

Jack and Tommy walk toward us and I go back to studying the menu. Jack fills the empty seat in front of the fire next to Mel and Elf lies at his feet. Tommy stops at my table and leans against the back of the chair opposite me. He nods at my laptop. "Do you ever stop working? What's gonna fuel you tonight?"

"Lasagna and a still water, please. I'm harassing every contact I have for toy drive donations. I know a lot of people." I'm not kidding. It took me fifteen minutes to email all the people in Dove's list and twenty minutes to make a list of my own. Nobody is safe and I won't be taking no for an answer.

"Can't you just raid your attic at home? Bet you have more toys up there than anyone." I just laugh, because how can I explain that my mom threw that stuff out the second we outgrew playing with it? Max played with his stuff on a rotation so nothing caught her attention.

"I think my mom and dad still have my Clara doll in their garage," Melissa says, laughing. "I was literally the coolest kid in school when I got one for my birthday."

"I wanted one *so bad*," Winnie says, pouting. I don't think that's what I should write on my sticky note under her name. "My dad used to tell me they were always sold out, but I'm now realizing he was probably lying. Did your sister have one?"

Jack sips his drink quickly so I almost miss that he nods.

"It's so cool that you have a doll named after you. Was it a surprise or did you know? You must have been a little girl, right?" Mel asks. She seems to be genuinely interested but it feels borderline illegal not only to be talking about Davenport in Fraser Falls, but to be doing it in front of Jack.

"She's called Clara because I designed her. My grandpa looked after me and my brother a lot when we were kids and my dad was trying to scale up the business he'd inherited. Grandpa made me and Max design toys and pitch them. I came up with Clara and Dad liked her, so they made her. It was the first popular toy we did."

Jack instantly sits up a little straighter in his chair. "How is it possible that I didn't know this?"

I lift an eyebrow. "Do you have a specific interest in dolls from twenty years ago?"

He rolls his eyes. "I researched every popular doll from the past fifty years when I was working on the prototype for Holly. I read *everything* about that doll and nowhere does it say she was designed by Clara Davenport."

I feel defensiveness prodding me in the center of my chest. "I was ten, Jack."

"You aren't credited anywhere."

"I was ten," I repeat. "I hardly even remember it. I probably drew it in crayon."

Not quite the truth, but Jack's sudden and urgent interest is throwing me off. I remember working on my design pack for the whole week. I used the special pencils I'd received for my birthday to make sure everything was as tidy as possible.

My mom thought my grandpa's childcare techniques were giving me an unattractive competitive streak but Grandpa loved it. He said it would give me all the life skills I needed. Not sure which of them is supposed to be useful right now though.

Jack's still staring at me, his brown eyes lost somewhere not quite here. He blinks slowly. "You're their first victim."

My heart slams into my chest. "Excuse me?"

"They stole your design and didn't credit you, Clara. You're their victim just as much as we are. Of course they knew they'd get away with doing it to us. They've been doing it for twenty years."

All the blood in my body rushes to my cheeks. My face feels like it's on fire. The skin on my chest begins to itch. Mel, Winnie, and Tommy are frozen in place. "You're so far off."

"Dude," Tommy says, standing up straight. He's shooting his best friend a look of disbelief. "Come on."

"It's the truth," Jack says.

"Jack," Winnie says quietly, staring at her feet.

I suddenly feel very far from home. "I think I'll put that lasagna order on hold." My computer snaps as it shuts from the accidental heaviness of my hand. "Lunch tomorrow, maybe," I mutter as I push my things back into my purse.

"Tomorrow," Tommy says, his voice gentle. "See you, Clara."

There are gentle murmurs of *bye* behind me as I head toward the door. I hear Tommy snap, "Sit down," behind me, but I don't turn around to investigate.

Chapter 12

JACK

"To the left. More to the left. I said left, gentlemen! Unless the United States issued some kind of direction revision memo that I wasn't privy to, then I am correct when I say you are all going to the right!"

Tommy and Luke groan as they drop their side of the bench, bending over to breathe. To Flo, who has no issue with continuing to bark orders at them in their fragile state, they're just unfit. Like me, they're so hungover their livers feel like they've been used as punching bags.

Being hungover twice in one week isn't the norm for me and I don't plan to make a habit of it. I needed to blow off some steam. I'm so fucking behind at work and it feels like Clara Davenport is constantly in my line of vision with that smile and that attitude and that determination. Plus, last night I managed to piss off absolutely everyone, which contributed to the decision to move from soda to soda whiskeys.

Tommy and Luke—being the great friends they are—wouldn't let me drink alone. Flo doesn't care that we're feeling delicate.

So here I am, doing manual labor to resolve a seating issue in time for the visitors who may or may not come, when I should be watching my guilty-pleasure show, *The Traitors*, with Elf on the couch and enjoying the patisserie I bought from Flo's Fancies this morning.

It was venturing into Flo's this morning that landed me, and by extension Tommy and Luke, with the task. My own fault admittedly, because I clearly looked too free and too eager to be bossed around today. I wouldn't be so pissed if I hadn't had the benches ready to go for three weeks and it was Flo who couldn't find the time to supervise.

The whole town has bought into Flo's European Christmas dream, which means saying no isn't an option. We're expecting the town to start to get busier right after Thanksgiving on Small Business Saturday. Everyone has put in effort to improve the town; I even heard Arthur say they're going to start caroling this year.

"Is there a reason we have paused, gentlemen?" Flo yells from fifteen feet away.

"Because I'm gonna throw up," Luke mutters.

"What was that?" Flo says, continuing to yell. The yelling has really helped the whole hangover situation.

Just as I get my focus back, a blacked-out SUV turns in front of the gazebo and stops in front of Maggie's. The engine shuts off but nobody gets out.

"Who's that?" Tommy wonders, nodding toward the parked car.

"How the hell am I supposed to know?" I say, but deep down I know. I blame Tommy's witch for the connection I seem to have with this woman.

Flo claps her hands at us impatiently. "For goodness' sake, it's probably Clara Davenport. Now can the three of you stop moving in slow motion and get back to work?"

"Whose car is that?" I ask, unable to get a better look.

"I suspect it's the young gentleman who picked her up this afternoon. I thought she might be giving up and leaving, but Maggie said she'd be back and here she is."

Did I upset her so much last night I sent her to another guy for comfort?

Why does the idea of that bother me so much? Maybe it's because I genuinely didn't mean to upset her last night and I know I did. Not only because of how she reacted but because every one of my friends told me so right after she left. Repeatedly.

God, I have too much on my plate to spend this much time thinking about one woman. It's irritating to let one single person pull so much focus in my day.

"I wish she'd give up and leave," I mutter. "I'm sick of seeing her everywhere."

Flo tuts at me loudly. "If I was young and that beautiful, I would be in Monte Carlo or Marrakesh, not here. Yet she is here, and she does seem hell-bent on tethering herself to our little community. She's been very helpful, in fact. More helpful than some people," she says, eyeing Luke and Tommy, both now sitting on the bench.

"We have our own businesses, Ms. Flo," Tommy says. It sounds more like a cry for mercy than a statement of fact.

Flo waves her hands flippantly. I readjust my gloves and sneak a look back toward the SUV now exiting the road and heading up Main Street before looking at Flo again. I'll admit I'm curious to see what kind of guy Clara goes for when she isn't limited to the boundary of Fraser Falls.

"Why don't you care about her being here? You said Davenport was corrupt. You're the one who made the video about them."

"Oh, Jack. I support your vendetta against that company, but I cannot support your vendetta against that woman. If you listened to anything beyond your own internal monologue, you'd know Clara didn't have anything to do with the doll situation. She was gaining experience in a different department." Flo folds her arms across her chest and tilts her head. "You are more likely to find corporate greed wearing a suit and tie than designer pumps. You would do well to remember that when you're upsetting people who are here to help."

"I don't have a vendetta against her." She raises an eyebrow at me. "And are you suggesting that she can't be corrupt because she's a woman? That doesn't make her trustworthy."

Tommy and Luke are notably quiet. Flo tuts at me again, probably for the millionth time in my life.

"You're a ridiculously stubborn man, have I told you that? Women are capable of all things. Should a woman put her mind to it, she can excel beyond men in anything she sets her heart on, corruption included." I interlock my fingers on the top of my head, regretting saying a word. "Now, I don't think young Miss Davenport has set her heart on being a supervillain, do you? I've never seen the Joker organizing toy drives and painting nativity sets, have you?"

I want to roll my eyes at her so badly. I would never, but the urge is throbbing behind my eyelids. "I don't think we know young Miss Davenport enough to speak on what her genuine intentions might be."

"Do you really think she would repeatedly bring herself here to be grunted at by you if she was the corporate menace you seem to think she is? Davenport may be suffering in the court of public opinion, but they're unlikely to be suffering at the bank. Which is what they care about. It's highly unlikely that woman needs to be here, and I believe she is in fact choosing to be here to try to make amends with the town."

"What lie did she offer you to buy your forgiveness?"

I see Flo's expression change into something nobody would want to see. "Do you think so little of my intelligence that you believe I could be led up the garden path by a pretty face and very nice hair, Jack Kelly? Does the fact I have conversed with many experienced businesspeople and lived all over the world mean so little to you, that you think I'm a prime target to be the victim of an elaborate manipulation?"

Flo was a flight attendant out of Boston in her younger years and ended up meeting and marrying a French opera singer. She left Fraser Falls for years to live in Paris, then England, and has probably seen more of the world than everyone in this town combined. She came back here every December, her accent and colloquialisms different from the year before, and shared her European life with anyone who would listen.

I know I won't win this argument. Not because she's right when she says she's met experienced businesspeople or lived all over the world, but because this woman is the most stubborn person I know. Despite being divorced from the aforementioned opera singer for fifteen years, she refuses to change her name from Girard as she enjoys that it upsets her ex-husband's new wife.

When she was a teenager in the seventies, she wore a Santa beard every day for two months to protest the town's exclusion of women in the annual Santa run that kicks off December. When she introduced an accompanying Santa hat, the town council finally gave in and allowed women to run alongside the men. There's a plaque about it in Bliss suggesting that the Boston Marathon may have been inspired by her actions.

Basically, I'm not going to change her mind, and I don't have surviving a Flo lecture in me today. "Of course I don't think that about you, Ms. Flo."

Her hands are on her hips now. "Then tell me, why is she receiving the brunt of your anger? What's she done to you that's so terrible?"

"Should we maybe get back to . . . ," Luke says carefully, but Flo holds up a hand to stop him.

"Don't you try to get him out of this, Luke Brookdale, or I'll be calling your mother to let her know you turned up to official town business smelling like a brewery."

His mouth opens and closes like a goldfish's. Luke is twenty-six years old, a father, and a successful business owner, but that shuts him right up.

Her attention is back on me, and I don't have an answer for her that I'm willing to share out loud. The truth is, that Davenport offer last year got my hopes up that we could turn our small project into something bigger and better for our town. That I could be the one to contribute something great to my community. That I could finally put the guilt of being a shitty teenager and always apologizing for my dad's flaky behavior behind me.

Then the legal papers arrived, and we realized Davenport was trying to screw us and it gutted me. I can't move past the feeling that they're trying to screw us again and using Clara to do it. Given what we learned last night, they have no problem using her. "I just don't trust her. I'm allowed to not trust her after everything that's happened. After what Davenport did to us."

"But look at everything Clara is doing for us now. She's secured funding for the toy drive. Celia is hosting a book event next month that's going to bring dozens of people here." Flo's expression softens. Something close to pity. "You're allowed to be wary of her and it doesn't surprise me that you would cling to distrust because you inherited your skepticism from your grandfather. You would be a fool to fully trust someone you don't know. But perhaps you should get to know her and decide whether she's worth trusting then. What do you have to lose?"

"My sanity." An apology for my rudeness sits in my throat but I ignore it.

Flo sighs and closes the distance to rub my arm affectionately. "You're a smart man, Jack. You'll figure it out."

"You're really not upset about her being here?" I ask, even though I know the answer.

"Until the business is hers, she's going to answer to the decisions of her father plus likely many other people. Just like you did with yours. I'm still upset with Davenport but look at everything she wants to do for us. What do I have to lose by giving her a chance?"

I stare at Flo. "Your sanity."

She bops me on the arm and smiles. "That's long gone."

Chapter 13

JACK

THERE ARE THREE WOMEN MAKING my life exponentially more difficult than it needs to be and their names are Florence, Holly, and Clara.

I don't think why Flo is making my life difficult needs a lengthy explanation, but the other two have me exhausted.

Ever since the Davenport videos went viral I've had a surge of orders and I'm so behind it makes me feel sick. Everyone else is keeping up their side of the work. The outfits are ready, the boxes are here waiting to be filled, the books are printed, and I have almost all of the toys prepared thanks to the weeks of prep work we did in the summer.

But because I'm so behind with shipping, I've had to temporarily pause taking orders, which means I'm limiting the income for my neighbors. Which means I'm a massive dick.

I should be focusing on that. I'm here on a Sunday morning looking at the stacked boxes in the corner of my workshop while I drink my coffee trying to hype myself up to make some progress.

Instead, I'm drawn to laughter on the other side of the door to the shop floor. Which leads me to the final lady making things hard for me: Clara.

Despite disappearing out of town and not turning up to the tavern to work like she usually does, yesterday morning Clara Davenport was up a ladder outside of my store helping fix the wind-tangled lights decorating Main Street. Which meant for some reason, I put on my coat and found Arthur with his clipboard and ended up on my own ladder helping fix lights too.

Joe and Elf watched me through the store window, probably questioning what the fuck I was doing, just like I was.

When I got back, cold and confused about why the hell I'd done it, Joe asked me if he could tell people he's the store manager now since I keep leaving him in charge to do town business. It was a hard no.

It feels like I'm spending all my time watching the Clara show and I hate it. I preferred it when I thought she was a figment of my imagination. I don't have time to be so distracted by her pretty laugh and shiny hair charming the people I've known my entire life.

I know I still owe her an apology for the victim thing, but she hasn't stood still long enough for me to be able to talk to her. She's everywhere and nowhere all at once and I feel like I'm losing my mind.

I want to get her on her own. Hell, I'd accept her crashing into me at this point. If she wanted to pull me on top of her again, I think I'd cope with that too. Sometimes I think that's exactly what would solve this weird energy between us. Flo thinks I should give Clara a chance. Flo clearly hasn't considered that she doesn't stop moving.

I follow the sound of a light melody to the shop floor and find her. I don't hear exactly what she says to Joe but I swear she says the word *nutcracker*. I watch his face drop from a wide smile to panic as he mutters something back to her. My feet move a little quicker.

She spots me crossing the room and holds up her hands in surrender. "Don't yell. I'll get out of your hair before it starts receding from the stress of being in the same room as me."

"I wasn't going to," I say as she turns on her heel and walks herself out of the store. My hand goes to my hairline. Joe clears his throat into his fist, trying to hide a laugh. Little shit. "What did she want?"

"She was asking about the woods, boss," Joe says sheepishly.

"The woods?" I repeat.

"Yep."

"What about the woods?"

"She asked where would be best to go for a walk."

I know he's lying to me but I can't work out what about. "Okay. I'm going back to work."

Joe nods and there's something very suspicious about the whole interaction. I brush it off, putting Clara somewhere at the back of my mind, and focus on my current main headache and all her accompanying stories and accessories.

Sunday afternoons are quiet so I let Joe close up the store early so he can get home to do his homework.

I stay out back putting the finishing touches to a set of chairs that need to be shipped to Vermont tomorrow. Each design carved with care and love and every ounce of my concentration. It means no two things are identical; everything has its own unique difference, practically impossible to identify to an untrained eye.

It's not a skill I even wanted to learn, but over years of being forced to hang out in this room because Dad thought if he could see me I couldn't get myself into trouble, I needed to do something to pass the time.

Now I voluntarily spend hours in here, although you couldn't tell that from how long my order list still is. I know I need to spend more time working instead of running all over town trying to be one step ahead of Clara, but I forget that in the moment.

There's a snowstorm landing tomorrow according to the town newsletter I received twice earlier. Twice because nobody who sends the newsletters knows how to work the newsletter website properly. It's the perfect opportunity to catch up while I'm here alone.

Starting tomorrow, since as soon as the email landed three people called to ask me to help them do various things to prepare. The first was Tommy, who has a broken window frame I've been promising to fix for three weeks. In my defense, the duct tape I secured it with has been holding up just fine as long as you don't touch it or look at it too hard.

Tommy promised to feed me for doing free labor, so I'm heading there first, then I'll tick off everyone else. Nobody wants anything difficult; it's time consuming more than anything.

As I take a left toward the tavern, Clara walks out of Maggie's front door and slowly descends the steps until we both reach the pavement outside the B & B at the exact same time. She's wearing the same sweatpants she was wearing when I last saw her. Navy blue and oversize. Her normal sleek coat is replaced with a sky-blue one with hearts on the pocket. It looks like Dove's. She pouts. "Where's Elf?"

"Busy sleeping next to a radiator."

"He should live with me," she says. "I'd never leave him."

"You've already stolen my doll. You can't have my dog as well."

It freezes the air between us more than the weather could ever. "Always a pleasure talking to you," she says, walking away.

If Flo saw my version of giving Clara a chance the tutting would be heard across state lines. Remember when it was easy to talk to her? I need to embody how I acted that night. I'm supposed to be getting to know her. Working out if she's worth trusting.

"Clara, wait," I say in panic. "Dove has that jacket," is the only thing I can think to say. She stops and turns to face me. "In yellow."

She looks down at the puffer, then back at me like I've lost it. "I know. We had some time after going through the toy drive inventory, so she took me to the store she bought it from."

"Oh." Why am I suddenly so fucking bad at talking? She's walking away again. "Where are you heading in the dark? You know a storm is coming, right?"

She doesn't stop walking this time, just calls to me over her shoulder, "Yeah, I got the newsletter twice. Arthur added me to the distribution list."

Fraser Falls is as safe as safe can get but that doesn't account for people who are likely to get lost out in the dark. Clara doesn't add anything, she just keeps going, and now I'm following her. She's going to call me a serial killer again, I just know it. "Does Maggie know where you're heading?"

"Maggie's busy baking something for book club," she calls back, still not stopping as she crosses the road.

Here she goes again with not standing still for two minutes. Falling on top of her is the closest I've gotten to keeping her in one place probably since she got here. She looks so determined but I can't help but worry about what that actually means. She's definitely the type of woman who would do something dangerous to prove a point.

"Clara, wait! Are you heading into the woods for some reason? Is that what you were talking to Joe about earlier?"

She turns to face me. Her auburn hair is tucked beneath a wool hat. She pokes at the few hanging strands near the rim, pushing them under. "Why do you care if I go in the woods?"

"Because I don't want you to get hurt." It's an honest answer so why does it make me feel so vulnerable to say it? I rub at my jaw awkwardly. "Plus it'd be bad for the town's publicity before the holidays and I have too much shit to do at work to be roped into joining a search party when you go missing."

She smiles. "You wouldn't be in the search party. You'd be their number one suspect."

I can't help but laugh. It feels kind of good to be laughing with her again. The frustration I've been feeling eases. Her eyes widen, in surprise, maybe? Something stirs in my chest.

I close the distance between us slowly until we're toe-to-toe. "You shouldn't go into the woods on your own. It isn't safe. Especially in this weather. Especially in the dark," I explain gently. "What do you even want to do in there? Bury a body?"

There's something captivating about her smile. I noticed it the first time I met her. She'd lean in like everything was a secret she *only* wanted to share with me. I get the same feeling when she smiles at me, like I'm the only thing she's concentrating on. She hasn't smiled at me much recently. "Maybe. Depends how mean you are for the next sixty seconds."

"I'm never mean to you," I say, not sure if I believe it as the words come out of my mouth. "Not intentionally."

"No, I guess you aren't outright mean," she agrees. She holds up her hand and counts off each of my indiscretions with her fingers. "Just unwelcoming, unforgiving, unhelpful, and grumpy."

I capture her wrist gently in my hand and fold her four fingers down slowly. Her hand is small in mine but she's warm and soft. She doesn't pull away and I don't let go. "Last time before I walk into the B & B, interrupt baking, and snitch to Maggie. What're you up to?"

She huffs in defeat and frees her hand from mine. "I want to find the missing nutcracker. Wilhelmina asked me to find it when I volunteered at the nativity. Dove said the high school kids probably stole it and hid it in the woods. Joe told me—and someone needs to teach that kid to lie better—that it might be where the seniors hang out and drink. But that he doesn't know anything about it because he only does his homework and his job."

The damn nutcracker again. "You don't need to look for it. They return it on December first because after the month is over they win.

It's a prank that happens every year. Wilhelmina has no idea, she just thinks it turns up."

"A prank I hear *you* started," she says smugly. "I don't care. I told her I'd find it and I want to stick to my promise."

Her determination is what's so attractive about her but fuck, it can be borderline infuriating. "Helping Wilhelmina really means that much to you?"

She nods, her green eyes shining beneath the streetlamp, and I honestly believe her. "I'm here to help, Jack. This is me helping like I promised I would."

"It's twenty minutes on foot to the edge of the woods, and you have no idea where the kids hang out. This is a you-frozen-in-the-leaves situation waiting to happen."

"And then I'd be here in your town forever . . . haunting you." She laughs at her own joke, but I want to tell her she already fucking haunts me daily. She pushes back her hat from her ears so I can see the white earbuds. "I have a backlog of podcasts and nothing but time. Joe said he *thinks* it's only slightly off the path. Honestly, go do whatever you were on your way to do, I'm fine."

There are multiple arguments happening in my head as Clara turns and walks away. One being she's an adult and not my responsibility. Another being if she's so determined to get herself lost over something I've told her doesn't matter, then I should let her. Finally, and the one that's the loudest, is that I'd never forgive myself if something did happen to her.

"Clara, wait," I say, more defeated than the first times. She turns slowly, beginning to look as frustrated as I feel. "The path Joe is talking about is from the parking lot. It's too far to walk to and the ground is too uneven in the dark. I'll drive you; just let me grab my truck keys."

She's quiet. Too quiet. Finally, she walks toward me, closing the short distance we've been talking across. "Can I pick the radio station?"

I raise an eyebrow. "No *Thank you for helping me, Jack*?"

"Hey, you invited yourself. But if we're saying thank you for invitations, thank you for inviting me to town, Jack."

"I didn—"

"I really like it here," she says, interrupting. She sounds like she really means it.

"Come on," I say, nodding back the way I came. "You can pet Elf while I grab my keys. But if he knocks you over with excitement, I'm not helping you up. I don't like that he seems to like you more than he likes me."

She beams and my heart slams against my ribs. "There's that not-being-mean-to-me thing you were talking about."

Chapter 14

CLARA

"Remind me again why we are doing this?" I call out, breathless from trying to keep up with Jack's superior stamina.

My words fog in the air between us. Jack is several steps ahead, with the assured strides of a man who has done this a hundred times. Meanwhile, I'm shuffling in the leaves, trying to avoid tripping over half-exposed roots, and trying not to snap an ankle on the uneven trail.

He glances back, his cheeks flushed from the cold. "I did attempt to warn you that this wasn't a good idea, but in what is becoming a recurring theme, you didn't listen."

I step over a gnarled root and immediately stumble. I manage to catch myself on a tree trunk just in time to stop me from face-planting into a patch of mud. "Helpfulness waits for no one," I mutter, brushing moss from my hands.

"I'm not sure how helpful you'll be to anyone if you get seriously injured out here," Jack replies, shining his flashlight at the ground in front of my feet. "And stop shining your light at my head. I'd like to be able to see when I check that you haven't fallen over."

"It's a safety measure so you can't land on top of me if I fall down," I tease.

"You wish," he grumbles in response.

Something hot sparks below my belly button. "Wouldn't you like to know."

The woods swallow the quiet groan he lets out. The trees create a canopy over us, which would be beautiful if it weren't so damn dark and creepy. The woods are perfectly peaceful, apart from the sound of my boots skidding every few steps. It reminds me to concentrate on staying upright and not wonder what it might be like to be horizontal.

"Tell me again why you're so sure the nutcracker is in *this* part of the woods?" I ask, wiping sweat from my forehead. It shouldn't be possible to sweat in this kind of weather.

"Not many places to be a rebellious teenager in a town like this, which means there aren't many places to hide things. Stealing the nutcracker is a beloved Fraser Falls High tradition. One you're fucking up, I should point out."

"Sorry for ruining your legacy, but I'm more concerned about my own. I want to make Wilhelmina happy by finding it."

"I don't want a stolen prop to be my legacy, Clara. I was young and acting out and it became a thing accidentally. I'm just saying, don't be surprised if you get pelted with snowballs walking through town by pissed-off teenagers."

"I'll just deny it. I'll tell them it was you." I'd be feeling pretty smug if I didn't immediately trip over a tree root. Jack catches my elbow and keeps me upright, hardly even breaking his stride. There's something sexy about being outdoors with someone who actively wants to keep you safe, I realize. I mutter a quiet thank-you and focus on my feet and not him.

"They've gotten lazy. We didn't always hide him in the woods. One year we tied him to the water tower and nobody noticed. Flo wasn't here that winter, otherwise we wouldn't have gotten away with it."

"I think I'd have liked to see that."

Jack digs his hands deep in his pockets. "It was awesome when I was fourteen. Probably crap my pants if I tried to climb that tower now. Danger feels like fun when you're young, I guess."

I'm successfully keeping up with him but too scared to point it out in case the woods decide to humble me. "Can I ask you a question?" I say.

"I suspect you're going to anyway."

"Have you ever thought about leaving Fraser Falls? I'm just curious if you've ever thought about starting somewhere new. There's so much to love about this place and I'm trying to work out if I'm looking at it through rose-tinted glasses as an outsider."

He doesn't answer right away, and for a moment I think maybe he won't. Maybe I'm prying. Then he exhales, slow and deliberate. "Maybe once or twice when I was a teenager. Sometimes anything else feels better than home and I'm sure I had visions of myself in Chicago or somewhere cool. Knew I'd never make it there deep down."

"Not New York?" My flashlight is pointing at the correct angle to catch the way he grimaces. "Oof, *not* New York."

We reach a fallen tree on the path and Jack holds out his left hand as he easily steps one foot over it. I take it and his other settles at the bottom of my back, keeping me steady while I put one foot on the trunk and step over it. Jack's still holding me when he brings his other leg over, only letting go when we're ready to walk again. "I like knowing who my neighbors are. What they like. What they stand for."

"Hey!" I protest. "I know who my neighbors are. Mr. Eighties Perm lives on my right. He likes to play Phil Collins late at night and he gets more takeout deliveries than I do. I thought Mrs. Upstairs was dead at one point, because she's old as hell and I hadn't seen her in weeks, but it turns out she just got *really* into Netflix. And Ms. Won the Apartment in the Divorce lives on my left. She never acknowledges me but I think she runs a pyramid scheme so that's probably for the best. I'm impressionable."

Jack snorts. "Sure you are. They sound like great neighbors."

"I haven't even told you about Dave! I don't know if that's his name but it's what Honor and I call him. So, Dave lives opposite me and doesn't wear clothes or close his blinds."

"If I want naked neighbors I can get that right here in town," he says. "Wouldn't even need to move that far."

I almost fall down. "*Who?!*"

"I can't tell you that. Classified town secrets." I want to call him a liar but the way he's trying not to smile, I *think* he might be telling the truth.

"It's Arthur, isn't it?" It's hard to tell navigating the dark with limited light but I swear he nods. "As a naked-neighbor expert, Arthur gives me a vibe."

"You'll never know. Unless you move into a house with a view of his windows, I guess. He lives next door to Donald. You three could be quite the trio."

"Is this the part where you tell me Donald caught a naked Arthur in his net?" I'm so glad there's nobody around to listen to this conversation. At least, I hope there's nobody around. That's the true-crime podcast listener in me.

"I'm not telling you anything. Like I said, classified town secrets."

"Oh no," I groan. He stops immediately, grips my arm, and shines his flashlight over me. "Hey, what're you doing?"

"You said 'Oh no,' are you hurt?"

I lower his hand from where he's pointing light directly into my eyes. "Because I got a mental image of Donald catching a naked Arthur in his net! Not because I hurt myself."

"Oh."

"You care a lot about people, don't you?" I ask, squeezing the hand still gripping my arm with mine. He lets go but doesn't step back.

"Are you being sarcastic?"

"No." I hold my arms out as if to show the woods. "You're giving me an X-ray with a flashlight because I said two words. Look where we are, look what you're doing tonight because you were worried I was going to get myself into trouble."

"Which you would've," he mutters.

"And the first night we met you were fielding calls from people just wanting your input or your help or reassurance. People don't call people who don't care late at night. It was an observation, Jack. I'm observing that you take care of people. It's a very generous thing for a person to do."

He's contemplative, letting the quiet roll on as he starts walking again. I sneak a glance at his face and he's chewing the inside of his cheek until he catches me looking. "I guess," he eventually concludes. "I don't think of it like that."

"Have you always been so selfless?"

Jack laughs so loud it makes me jump and something rattles the branches. "I'm not selfless, Clara. Far from it. A lot of people in this town helped raise me, forgave me when I didn't deserve forgiveness, and kept me from screwing up when I was determined to. I owe them answering their questions and helping them feel better when sometimes it can take hours to get actual repair guys here. I wouldn't want them wasting their money when I can deal with it anyway. It's just not how we live around here."

"And who takes care of you?"

"Who says I need taking care of?"

"Everyone needs taking care of, Jack," I say.

He sighs, something he does a lot of around me. "You ask a lot of questions."

I smile at him but he isn't looking at me. "Wouldn't want you to get bored."

"We wouldn't want that," he mumbles, pulling me out of the way of a puddle by my waist before I plunge myself into it. His hands hover there, my skin, which wants to feel his touch, shielded by the padding of my coat. He realizes and pushes his hands into his pockets.

"Is Holly the first toy you've designed?" I ask, thinking maybe talking about work is better suited to his personality.

"If I say no, will you steal the others?"

Okay, *naïvely* thinking talking about work is better suited to his personality.

"Depends if you can get them to go viral." I'm trying to make a joke, but it lands as flat as I'm probably going to on my face during this late-night excursion. Especially because I just upset the guy keeping me upright. "That was a poorly worded joke, I'm sorry. I'm just interested in what took you from furniture to kids' toys."

Another sigh. I should start a tally. "It was a present for Sailor, my goddaughter. Dove isn't into plastic toys and it got me thinking. It was a passion project that spiraled into something more."

"That's the best kind of project."

"When I had my finished doll, I was talking about it to Sailor's dad, Luke, and people started chipping in on how to make her better. Next thing I know it's a group project. Then neighbors started asking to buy them for their kids and grandkids. So I bought a tiny shipment of stock and thought anything left over could go in my store. Then it went viral."

"'Then it went viral' is such a funny end to an amazing journey," I say, trying not to sound like too much of a kiss-ass to a man who wants my lips nowhere near him. "Do you think you'll release more?"

He shrugs. "It's already a lot. Especially after Flo's videos put the spotlight on us. Sometimes it feels like it's shining in my eyes. But she's got these big dreams about town fame and success and an espresso machine that works consistently. So who knows, I might need to keep going to keep up. Especially with such ruthless competition."

"I'm sorry." I mean it when I say it but I don't think that matters.

"Don't apologize. I blame myself as much as I blame Davenport," he admits. It's an unexpected show of vulnerability from Jack, and it catches me totally off guard.

"What?" I squeak, my voice high and grating against the quiet. "Why do you blame yourself?"

"I should've done more to protect us. Trademarked, copyrighted, patented. I don't fucking know which is the right one or if it's even possible but I would if I'd even looked into it. I just got so busy and ended up letting everyone down."

"It's a community effort, Jack. *Anyone* could've looked into those things. That's not on you." I want to stop and shake him. This isn't his fault. This is Daryl and countless people at Davenport who pushed the Evie doll through.

"I'm the one who got everyone's hopes up when Davenport approached us. The guy said they'd help us with legal stuff, 'lighten the load' were the words he used, and I foolishly believed him. Showed him every step of our process. Showed him all my prototypes. Sent him home with a free doll." He laughs but it's humorless. "Must've thought he'd hit the jackpot."

I want to argue for the program I created, that it isn't what we stand for, but I'm trying to pick my battles and I don't think me fighting to defend my own project is what Jack needs to hear right now. I grab his arm impulsively, pulling him to a stop. "Listen to me. It isn't on you. You've done an amazing thing. You're going to do more amazing things. If you don't believe anything else I ever say, please believe that, because I really mean it."

His lips part and I watch in real time as his face flits between different emotions. It's like a roulette wheel of which one he's going to stop on; I hold my breath in anticipation. I want him to know that I see him and the responsibility he carries on his shoulders. In the end, his mouth closes and he sucks his bottom lip into his mouth. He nods slowly. "Thank you for saying that."

We walk in silence for a few more paces, and I let the quiet stretch, giving him space. Something snaps in the trees behind us. Loud and abrupt. Sharp. I freeze, my pulse hammering, and without thinking, grab Jack's hand. .

He glances at me, calm and faintly amused, and squeezes, rubbing his thumb across the back of my knuckles. "Hey, you're okay. It isn't a bear. Probably a squirrel."

I hold him a little tighter, clinging to the feeling of safety it gives me more than the man. That's what I tell myself, anyway. "Do squirrels sound like murderers?"

His thumb draws spirals on my skin, calm and reassuring. "Only the very ambitious ones."

"Sorry." I realize I'm still holding his hand, warm and steady in mine. I let go, suddenly self-conscious. "I'm disappointed. I thought this was my big chance to see one of Fraser Falls' famous denim-overalls-wearing bears."

Another laugh achieved. It's embarrassing how much breaking through Jack's frosty exterior feels like winning. We don't talk for a while until eventually, Jack veers off the trail and points to a clearing. "This is where we usually stash it, but I'm guessing now that apparently the entire town knows where the nutcracker takes his vacation, they've had to start hiding him slightly farther off the trail. Stay where you are, I'll go look."

"Wait," I say, squinting at something between two trees. "Is that—"

It is. Tipped slightly sideways, wedged between two tree trunks, half-buried in leaves, stands a life-sized, slightly chipped wooden nutcracker. His mouth is less of a smile and more like a grimace. His eyes are wide with mild alarm. He is old and faded and looks homemade. He's perfect.

"I did it," I whisper.

Jack scoffs and brushes past me, reaching for the nutcracker's arm to pull him free. "You didn't do anything. In fact, you slowed me down because I was so afraid you'd fall and twist your ankle."

I'm too excited to care about his grumbling. "I actually found it!" Without thinking I launch myself forward and throw my arms around Jack's neck. He catches me easily, holding me above the ground until my nose brushes the side of his neck accidentally and the realization sets in for both of us.

He lowers me slowly, his hands tight against my hips, where the coat doesn't disguise his firm grip. We stand there for a second, in the cold silence of the forest breathing with our bodies pressed against each other and my hands gripping the back of his neck.

Jack's eyes travel down to my lips but he doesn't make the move. I'm scared to, knowing that it could ruin the friendly footing we finally feel like we're reaching together.

His hips inch backward, I see a flicker of embarrassment, and that's when I realize what's happening. I'm suddenly very aware of my limbs and take a step back. "Oh God. Sorry. Sorry."

He drags his hand down his face. "You're going to keep surprising me, aren't you?"

Maybe I should go and hide myself between those two trees and hope Flo hears of me embarrassing myself, takes pity, and deletes the videos to make me leave. As flushed as my cheeks are, there's still something powerful about having an effect on him. "Trust me, I'm surprising both of us."

I let Jack have some alone time while he retrieves our wooden third wheel.

Jack shakes his head. "I can't believe they still do this."

"Tradition," I say. "You said it yourself. Maybe someday the kids who stole him this year will reminisce about it fondly with their newest friend while attempting to locate it in the middle of the night."

He gives me a long, unreadable look, then smiles. "Who says we're friends?"

THE TREK BACK TO JACK'S truck is even slower than our initial walk into the woods.

Finding the nutcracker, I quickly realize, was the simple part of tonight's activities. Dragging him back to the car is proving more challenging, since he insists on getting caught on every stray branch and tree root.

We haul him back between us like a third, deeply uncooperative band member. Even Jack, who is definitely fitter than me, is slightly out of breath as we reach the parking lot.

"Hey, Jack?" I say softly as we load the nutcracker into the bed of his truck.

"Yeah?"

"Thanks for taking me to find this."

He nods. "Thanks for not breaking any bones."

We ride back to town in silence, the nutcracker bumping off the sides of the truck rhythmically. Jack drives at a crawl along Main Street, so our festive companion stays in his assigned seat and doesn't accidentally get launched through the Wilde & Winslet window.

I rest my head on the passenger window and watch the town go by. Fraser Falls isn't shiny or sleek. It doesn't try to impress with scale or spectacle. But it's special, layered. Its roots run deep, and for not the first time since I arrived here, I find myself wondering why anyone would want to leave this place.

Beside me Jack drums his fingers lightly on the steering wheel. He hasn't said anything in a while, but his gaze flicks toward me as he makes the left onto the street that leads to the back of Maggie's.

"I meant what I said," I murmur as he pulls up. I climb out of the truck and hover at the passenger-side door. "You're going to do more amazing things. Don't let this one thing deter you from creating more."

Jack smiles, my final win of the evening. "Good night, Clara."

Chapter 15

CLARA

"I'm tired of being single. It's unfair to be this hot and have my longest healthy romantic relationship be with my vibrator."

My turkey sub suddenly feels very phallic as I two-hand it into my mouth. I frown at my screen, where Honor is leaning against her kitchen counter in her work scrubs. "Tired of being single? Since when?"

"Since you ran off and I'm *bored*!" she says, leaning her chin against her crossed forearms.

"My brother is still madly in love with you if you feel like dating the less fun Davenport. I had dinner with him last week. Talked about *Jurassic Park* the entire time. He's a total dork but he won't cheat on you."

Honor snorts. "*Jurassic Park*?"

"Specifically about whether Dad would open Jurassic Park if he could, even after watching all the movies." It wasn't a conversation about work so I just let it roll. I was feeling lousy after Jack called me a victim in front of people I hardly know. I wanted to ask Max what he thought but I was worried it would progress to talking about my promotion. Or lack of promotion, as it could turn out.

"Your dad *totally* would if he could make money from it. No doubt about it. But I can't date your brother, Clara. What if it all went wrong? I don't want to make our friendship weird."

I scoff. "Grow up, I wouldn't care if you potentially dated Max. I'd feel sorry for you. Imagine dating someone that annoying *and* having my parents as your in-laws—you'd deserve my sympathy."

"I don't even think I want to date anyone. I think it'd be too weird for Paloma meeting someone new, plus Kyle would be a huge dick about it. I just wanna be taken out for dinner, then bent over afterward when she's at her dad's place. Is that too much to ask?"

"Definitely not. I refuse to talk about you hypothetically doing *that* with my brother, but I should point out that Paloma knows Max. Have you considered putting up a flyer? I'm sure you'd find someone real quick," I tease.

Honor flips me off. "You're less helpful now that you're helping everyone else. Stop being selfish and come home to give me attention so I don't end up having sex with someone I will later start to hate. Or worse, marry into your family."

"I can't stop it. It's a canon event. Does it help to know I got worked up last night over minimal friendly touching? That's how long it's been since I had sex." I already told Honor about Jack falling on top of me at the Christmas tree farm, which made her laugh for like five minutes.

I haven't worked up the courage to explain finding an old, faded nutcracker made me launch myself at him. I can see the funny side of it when I push past the embarrassment. I didn't start overthinking it until I was back in my room alone. I was still buzzing with excitement and pride at achieving another goal, but as soon as I was greeted with the silence it fizzled away. It reminded me of every time I walk into my empty place with nobody to tell about my day. Nobody to share my achievements with.

It can be lonely. Lonelier than I'd like to admit. That's why it felt so good to have someone with me last night, someone to share the moment with, even if he was only there to save me from my own lack of coordination.

"You should take a ride on the carpenter. I—" Honor's face and voice distort as my laptop freezes.

"Hon?"

The banner at the top of my screen tells me my internet connection is weak, and then the screen disappears completely. I want to scream. The internet company sent someone here just this morning after I complained to them on Maggie's behalf. They replaced the router and things were so much better for the past few hours. I send Honor a text letting her know my internet is down, possibly because of the storm, possibly because it's the worst internet provider, and promise to call her back as soon as I can.

I'm supposed to be having my check-in call with work this afternoon. They'll definitely think I'm lying if I say a storm knocked out the internet. I'm sure half the office believes I'm on paid vacation already.

I finish my sub watching the Wi-Fi icon closely, waiting for the little white curves to appear telling me I'm back online. Nothing happens and then my lights go out. I open all the blinds to let in as much natural light as possible, which in this climate isn't a lot.

"Great," I mutter.

The storm hasn't even fully landed yet and it's already being a pain in my ass. I opt to climb into bed for warmth instead of making a nuisance of myself by asking Maggie what's happening, so I'm secretly relieved when there's a knock on the internal door to the rest of the house.

Maggie's worried face is on the other side of it. "I'm so sorry, Clara, but we've lost power. A tree has probably come down on the power line; that's very common around these parts. The backup generator kicked in, but it's tripped and I can't get it going. This has never happened before."

I *hate* seeing Maggie upset. "That's totally okay! Is there anything I can do to help? Do you want me to call someone? My cell is fully charged and if I stand very still near the shower I get three bars of service."

"You're very sweet, but I've talked to the engineer already. He can't get to us for two days. Unfortunately, it means you can't stay here, but we have a contingency plan and my very generous neighbors have agreed to take in guests."

Thanksgiving is only a few days away so I could theoretically go home early, but I don't feel even close to ready to leave town yet and the roads might be too dangerous. I feel like I'm *really getting somewhere*. I'm so visible that people aren't surprised to see me anymore, and I've been so proactively helpful that I'm getting trusted with more and more tasks.

People return my emails for the toy drive daily, Miss Celia is planning her event with Matilda's team, I found the nutcracker for Wilhelmina, and I painted a nativity stable. Leaving early for Thanksgiving feels like I'm giving people the chance to forget about me.

"It'd be very kind if someone could take me in," I tell her.

"I will be back with a bed for you as quick as I can. Thanks for being understanding, Clara. I'm not expecting anyone else to be as nice," she says nervously. Three couples checked in two nights ago. It's the busiest I've seen the B & B. I strongly suspect they're swingers, which wouldn't bother me in the slightest if I weren't totally bitter about everyone but me—and Honor, apparently—having a sex life. Maggie gives me a hug, which prompts zero reaction from my body or brain. Just Jack then. "This has never happened before. I'm so careful with preparations in the colder months."

"I believe you, Maggie. Hey, why don't you let me handle them? I'm really good at being yelled at and I can smooth things over while you organize who needs to go where. We could offer them free breakfast at Bliss and a voucher for a coffee and a pastry, maybe? As an apology."

She looks like she's about to turn me down, but then to my surprise she nods. "Breakfast and vouchers is a great idea. If you don't mind talking to them for me it would be a huge help! Here are the room numbers." She hands me a sticky note. "I don't know what I'd do without you at the moment, Clara. Thank you."

A glowing feeling settles in the center of my chest. Fifteen minutes later, when I reach reception, Maggie is pacing around the small space with a cell phone decorated in monster stickers to her ear. I hold up one finger to her and she covers the microphone of the phone with her hand, tilting it away from her ear. "Just me to be rehomed. The three couples are going to find somewhere new out of town."

Maggie mouths *thank you* and removes her hand from the mic. "Flo has family visiting this week . . . Mm-hmm, I could ask Dove if she'll take her . . . Yes, her . . . Yes . . . No, Arthur had to take in Donald because there's a tree down outside his house . . . I know, but he thinks the government controls the weather . . . Okay, she'll be over later."

It's funny how even only hearing one side of the conversation you can guess the other side of it. It's also funny to ask a question I'm almost certain I know the answer to. With a tight smile, I watch Maggie hang up. "Who am I staying with?"

"Jack said you can stay with him."

There's a huge part of me that thinks I can survive here without any power. If I don't share the same space with him for multiple days, then I can't throw myself at him. Staying here and turning into an icicle feels like the only way I can 100 percent guarantee I don't do that. I can feel the stress radiating from Maggie so I keep smiling. "Great. I'll pack a bag and head over there later."

THE HUNGRY FOX TAVERN HAS become my daily safe haven with its always-roaring fire, good food, and excellent Wi-Fi.

Tommy mostly sits and reads his Kindle when it's quiet. It's the perfect place to unabashedly email everyone I know while also delaying heading over to Jack's place.

I lazily break off a piece of almond-topped peppermint chocolate bark and pop it in my mouth. Tommy placed the plate to the right of my computer ten minutes ago. The kitchen is trying different treat options for Christmas and I've been assigned the role of taster. Mostly because I'm here more than anyone else, but I'm not complaining.

"Thoughts?" Tommy asks, approaching my table.

"The almond isn't working. It needs crushed candy canes, the way Jesus would've wanted for his birthday month." He sighs. Tommy ordered ten times his usual almond order by accident and now he's trying to use them up. "Mix some sugar and cinnamon and do candied almonds. You can put them in little jars."

"Good idea." He looks past me to the window; the snow is really starting to come down. "The weather's getting pretty bad out there. I'm going to close up early since no one will be coming in. You ready to face the music?"

I pin him with a look, then roll my eyes. Tommy bent over laughing when I told him who's taking me in in my hour of need. After he stopped laughing he did say if I end up with the urge to strangle Jack in his sleep, I can snooze in the chair in front of the fire here. I wouldn't be the first person to fall asleep there, apparently. "I'm ready."

"I'll give you a ride. The temptation to run away might be too strong and Flo will call Jack to find you. Then he'll call me to help the search party, and I have book club tonight."

"It isn't canceled?"

"I can't think of anything that would convince Miss Celia to rearrange. Zombie apocalypse, maybe, but I'm not certain that'd be enough."

I close my computer and cross my arms on top of it. "Well, I can't interfere with book club. I promise not to run away."

"Appreciate it." He puts the strap of my bag over his shoulder and spins his keys around his index finger. "I don't want Miss Celia putting a mark against my name for not being there."

The second we step outside I'm assaulted by my own hair whipping into my face over and over until I throw myself into the passenger seat. Tommy cranks the heater all the way up and turns the radio low.

I ask him about the book he's reading and he confesses he hasn't finished yet. Another thing that could earn him a mark from Miss Celia. The drive only takes a couple of minutes. The snow hitting the windshield is oddly hypnotic but I'm glad I'm not walking in it.

Tommy pulls up behind Harry's. There's a red front door beside a larger delivery shutter. He kills the engine and climbs out, grabbing my bag from the backseat. "I'll show you up," he says when I try to take my bag from him. He's making sure I don't get him in trouble with Miss Celia by running away.

I follow Tommy up a set of stairs, noting another door on the right that I presume goes to Jack's workshop. Tommy walks straight in when he reaches the top of the stairs, not bothering to knock, and I feel awkward following him. Which leaves me clumsily lurking on the top step. He looks back at me, eyebrows pinched together in confusion.

Am I really behaving like this because of one mostly friendly trip to the woods? Yes, apparently. It's almost like you shouldn't press your body against someone who is only just learning to tolerate you.

As soon as I brave walking across the threshold I'm tackled by the wiggling body of Elf. "Hi, buddy," I coo, crouching to cuddle him. It results in a chin to my brow bone but it's worth it. "Have you had a good day? Did you have lots of naps? Did you watch the snow?"

Each question is met with a wet tongue against my ear, or forehead, or hand. I don't care. I love him.

"He isn't going to answer you, y'know." Looking over to the kitchen, Jack, whom I temporarily forgot about, is tossing a salad. It's strange and domesticated, and, if anything, it makes me feel a little suspicious. "He did have a good day though. He did have lots of naps, and he did watch the snow."

"Good to know."

Jack looks to Tommy, who's watching us interact like we're on *National Geographic*. He puts my bag behind the couch. "You staying for dinner?"

"Can't. Need to finish my book."

"He doesn't want a mark from Miss Celia," I add, freeing myself from being climbed on by Elf.

I take a slow look around the room. Plush brown couch in an L shape with an older-looking black leather couch that I would bet is for Elf. Lighter scatter cushions propped up against the ends of the brown couch with a cream blanket neatly draped over the back. Whereas the leather couch is covered in older, darker blankets.

In the center is a coffee table with sleek, clean lines that looks like it belongs in *Architectural Digest*. Design books are piled in the middle, a huge three-wick candle beside them. Jazz music is playing from a speaker below the television. And he's cooking. From scratch, judging by the kitchen surfaces being covered in vegetable peels.

My face isn't on a dartboard anywhere so I can only assume he removed it before I came over. Tommy says his goodbye and I debate asking him to stay for moral support.

This might be the first time I've seen Jack out of work clothes. He's opted for gray sweatpants and a black Henley. His gray baseball cap is on backward, flattening down his hair. He looks relaxed and comfortable. I feel very out of place.

"If you keep staring at me, I'm gonna start to feel self-conscious," he says, looking up from cheese he's hand-grating.

I walk over and lean against the empty side of the kitchen counter. "Sorry, seeing you in your natural habitat is weird to me."

He smiles, not taking his eyes off the cheese. "Seeing you in my natural habitat is weird to me. I made spaghetti Bolognese for us. I hope that's okay."

"I love spaghetti Bolognese, thank you."

"I know you do." There's a vague flash of a memory. Talking about food the first time we met, me declaring it my favorite meal. Him telling me it's the most boring Italian dish. "It'll be ready in a few minutes."

My eyes narrow. "Why are you being so nice? Is it because I'm a damsel in distress with nowhere to stay?"

"Damsel, my ass. We both gotta eat."

There's a slight blush on the apples of his cheeks that tells me he's lying. "Did you poison it?"

He rolls his eyes and throws a pinch of cheese into his mouth. "No."

"Glass?"

"Do you want the damn spaghetti or not?" He grips the edge of the counter with both hands; his biceps flex as his hands tighten. It's a simple question that requires a one-word answer. But my eyes move up his arms and across his hard chest. Eventually they reach his face and the smug amusement is enough to snap me out of my temporary lapse in restraint.

"Yes, please. Where can I wash up?" He nods toward a door on the other side of the room. "I'll be quick."

I hear him sigh as I rush to hang my coat up by the door and scuttle to the bathroom to wash my hands. There's something incredibly personal about being in someone's bathroom, especially when that person is Jack.

I feel like an intruder in his space, in his life, more than ever.

Drying my hands on a towel, I take one last look in the mirror and promise that no matter how much I get the urge to, I won't start a food fight.

Chapter 16

CLARA

"This is really, really good, Jack."

He mutters a coy thank-you and continues to twirl spaghetti around his fork. I've always prided myself on being able to get conversation out of the shyest people. I don't think Jack is shy, I think he's just not used to having a conversation partner during dinner.

"Have you ever been to Italy?" I ask, ignoring the awkward gut feeling that's telling me to stop embarrassing myself. "Wait, don't answer that. I know you haven't."

"Good memory," he says. "I'd like to go one day, maybe."

"It's beautiful and the food is amazing. I like New York pizza, but Naples is another level." He nods politely, concentrating on his food. He isn't even being rude, but I feel like I'm *dragging* conversation out of him. Sure, I could just shut up and eat, but who wants that. "I think the Yankees are better than the Red Sox."

There's a harsh clang as his fork falls from his hand and hits his plate. Fiery lasers practically burst from his eyes as he looks at me in disgust. His jaw is so tight it might shatter. I can almost hear the words he's biting back. I know they're dancing on the tip of his tongue.

Truth is, the only Yankees game I've ever seen is the one Carrie goes to in *Sex and the City*. I don't know anything about baseball, but I'll become the team's biggest supporter if it gets this out-of-practice man to make small talk with me.

Instead of releasing a barrage of statistics and abuse in my direction, he picks up his beer and takes a long drink. I watch his Adam's apple bob. My fingers clench around my own cutlery in anticipation. I get nothing. I sigh loudly. "Really thought I was going to get you with that one."

"I'll get kicked off the emergency list if I curse at a guest." Jack puts his beer back on its coaster. "I'm being boring, aren't I?"

Yes. "No. It's just going to be a really miserable time if we live in silence."

"You were under the impression this was going to be enjoyable?" he asks playfully. "I'm kidding . . . And I'm sorry. I guess I'm out of practice. I've lived alone since I was eighteen and I can probably count the number of times someone's been over for dinner on two hands."

"You should host more often. You're a really good cook," I tell him honestly.

"What do you want to talk about, Clara?" He leans back in his chair and takes off his hat, smoothing down his hair before putting it back on again. For possibly the first time in my life, I don't know what to say next. He lifts an eyebrow. "Silence. You're telling me you don't have a long list of questions in that head of yours?"

The window creaks from the increasingly aggressive snowstorm outside. It only amplifies the fact that I'm not saying anything. "I'm overwhelmed by choice." I chew on the inside of my cheek. Think about what I really want to know. "Isn't eighteen a little young to live alone?"

He immediately looks like he regrets upgrading his grunt to real words. "Did you not move out for college?"

"Yeah, but that was college, it's different. The freedom was only pretend." I look around the living space again. "This is a real grown-up place. What made you rush to move out?"

I grab my near-empty glass and cradle it in between my hands. It'll stop me from nervously tapping against the table.

"Living with my parents was frustrating. Well, living with my dad was frustrating is more accurate. I got tired of his constant overcommitting and underperforming. Tired of him bringing it home. We get along better when we're not always around each other, so I moved out."

"Do your parents live locally?"

He shakes his head. "They moved to Florida."

It feels so strange to imagine them down there when Jack is so committed to this place. "Did you always want to take over the family business?"

"Well, my sister wasn't going to do it."

"Does your sister live in town?" I ask. "I don't think I've met her yet."

"Nope, Oklahoma. Moved to Boston because she hated living in such a small community and fell in love with a farmer in town for a friend's wedding," he says, scoffing.

"So you're the last Kelly standing. Do you like your job?"

His eyebrow quirks. "I feel like I'm at a job interview."

My cheeks flame. "Sorry, you're just interesting. I like learning about you."

"Yeah, I like my job." I don't ask anything else, letting the silence hang between us. I think he realizes what I'm doing because he sighs in defeat. "I've never considered what else I could do because I've been training for this my entire life. I like being my own boss. I enjoy creating stuff, working with my hands. It's generally minimal drama . . . unless your designs get stolen."

We were doing *so* well. "At least you're the second victim. I have to be stuck with the title of the first."

I watch as the fun slowly drains from Jack's face. Way to usher in the elephant, Clara. We haven't talked about what he said, and the hint of regret in his eyes is enough to make me glad I brought it up. At the time it felt like a dagger, so if he feels uncomfortable, good.

"Clara," he says slowly, my name rolling off his tongue like he's said it a million times.

My heart feels like it's being squeezed in his hand. "What, Jack?"

"I'm sorry I upset you that night in the tavern. I stand by what I said because you deserve better. You deserve to be credited for your work. Fuck the excuse that you were just a kid." He flattens his hands on the table, spreads his fingers wide, and takes a breath like he's trying to regulate himself. "But I shouldn't have said it in front of people. I shouldn't have said it in a way that made you feel attacked. I really am sorry. I didn't do it to intentionally hurt you, I was angry *for* you. I'm sorry I was angry *at* you."

Deep down, I never expected to hear an apology from Jack. He's made it so clear that he only sees me as the corporate version of myself, and that corporate version is tied tightly to a company he hates. This feels like he's finally beginning to see me for me, and an apology feels like a huge leap.

"You're forgiven." I finally put down my emotional support glass. Roll my shoulders back to ease the tension built up in them. "For now."

"Appreciate it. Now I'd ask you about your job and family but I hope you can understand that I don't really want to hear about the company." It's the most tactful I've heard him be since I got here. "And last time we talked about it, I upset you, so maybe let's set a boundary so that doesn't happen again."

I reach down and stroke Elf's head. He's been patiently waiting to see if I'll drop anything on the floor since I sat down at the table. "That's okay, there isn't much to say. My dad will probably hand everything over to my brother anyway and that's far too depressing a thought to discuss over spaghetti. I prefer asking you questions."

There's a ghost of a smirk on his face. "Because I'm so good at answering them?"

"You *are* good when you try. What was Harry like? I walk past your store with his name on it every day to get coffee and I can't help but wonder. In my head I imagine him looking like an older version of you."

Jack digs in his sweatpants pocket and pulls out his cell phone. He taps and swipes until he hands it over to me. It's a picture of a picture. Young Jack holding a saw proudly, over half his face covered by safety glasses. Beside him a man who looks exactly like an older version of the man sitting in front of me, just like I suspected. "He was a great man. Kind, patient, he'd do anything for anyone. Nothing was too much hassle for him, he was always there when he promised he'd be. Could fix anything you could imagine, no problem. It amazed me when I was a kid."

"Sounds like someone I know," I tell him, offering a soft smile.

"I wish. It was easy to him, as simple as breathing. Never let anything overwhelm him. But he died when I was thirteen. It was summer and Arthur's air-conditioning unit was broken. Granddad had a heart attack on the way back with the new part. He was sick all summer, back and forth to the hospital. He passed right before school started." Almost twenty years later and it doesn't look like it's any easier for Jack to talk about. "I didn't take it well."

"My grandpa died when I was thirteen too. I'm sorry, Jack. Everyone who says time is a great healer is a big fat liar. It doesn't get easier."

"It doesn't, you're right. But I handle it much better than I did as a teenager." Jack walks over to the refrigerator and picks up the water jug. He tops up our glasses and puts it on the table.

I take a sip. "I cut my hair into a pixie cut with kitchen scissors and got my nose pierced, what did you do?"

"Crashed my car into the gazebo," he says flatly.

I nearly splash my water everywhere. "At *thirteen*?"

"No, my anger just got worse over time. Acting out lasted *years*. I didn't hit the gazebo on purpose though; I lost control on ice, it was my first winter with a driver's license. Nobody believed me when I said it was an accident. Flo threatened to send me to military school if I didn't get my shit together."

I shouldn't laugh but I can hear it in my head. I shake the thought away and push off the smile threatening to happen. "Can someone who isn't your parent or guardian send you to military school?"

Thankfully, Jack starts laughing. "I didn't trust the military to say no to her. We made it safe and as not ugly as possible while the ground was frozen, then as soon as spring landed she had me repair all the damage I caused and put in a ramp for wheelchairs and strollers."

"What an exciting spring break."

"Seriously," he says, chuckling. "Donald and Pastor Akinola helped me. They both had some experience renovating. The pastor from repairs he ended up doing himself because of limited church funds. Donald from soundproofing his house so the government can't listen to him."

I press my lips together, bouncing the question around in my head. "Your dad didn't help you?"

"He said he would but he got sidetracked doing something for my sister. Flo tore him to shreds when she saw him the following Monday. After that she was my shadow. Couldn't get away with anything no matter how hard I tried. So I stopped trying. Spent more time in the workshop and less time hiding beloved Christmas treasures in the woods. Became a grown-up."

"I feel like you missed a stage. No wild party-boy early-twenties Jack stories to tell?"

His teeth dig into his bottom lip, his head tilted to the side as he shrugs. "Nope. Fraser Falls isn't a wild party-boy kinda place. And my parents decided to retire to Florida pretty suddenly so I didn't have much time to try it out elsewhere. What about you? Any stories to tell?"

"*Tons*. But none I'll be sharing with you. I don't want to ruin your perception of me by muddying the angelic impression I've already made."

"Angelic," he repeats like the word is in a language foreign to him. "Sure, Clara. That's what I think you are."

It takes us thirty minutes to load the dishwasher and clean up the dinner leftovers in the kitchen.

We're slow and careful, dancing around each other in the small kitchen space. I bump into him once. He brushes his arm against mine twice. I wipe down the counters while he takes the trash out. It's worlds away from me collecting takeout from my front doorstep and battling to fit the excessive amount of packaging in my overcomplicated recycling system.

I'm putting the seasonings back in the cupboard when Jack returns, brushing snow off his shoulders. His hands are a deep red shade; he rubs them together as he nudges the door closed with his hip.

"Come here," I say gently, holding my hands out to his. Surprisingly, he does. I take Jack's cold hands between my warm ones. I quickly realize it's doing basically nothing to help him, but he stands in front of me anyway, letting me try. "I should've put the oven mitts on you instead."

His eyes travel across my face and down to our hands. "I prefer this."

I clasp his hands, bringing them up to my neck slowly. I press them beneath my ears into my hairline. The contrast of his cold skin on my warm neck stings at first, sending a chill down my spine. I press my hands over his and watch as his eyes flicker down to my lips briefly.

I feel like we're back in the woods, both not being the person to make the move, worried to rock the boat. "That helping?"

"Yeah." His fingers flex against my neck so I lift my hands off. He removes his hands slowly, then pushes them into the pockets of his sweatpants. "It's getting late. I think I'm going to head to bed. You can stay up and watch TV or whatever. I'll show you where everything is."

I nod and follow him, saying nothing. If I thought hugging was bad, Jack's hands on my neck is much worse.

Chapter 17

JACK

IT'S BEEN A LONG TIME since I've had to jerk off in the shower and pray nobody hears me moan.

I'm too old to be embarrassed about masturbation but just old enough to be embarrassed that I couldn't get the fucker to go down this morning. Thoughts of Clara's creamy skin under my hands had tormented me all night. Her pulse punching into my palm. Blush-pink lips and green eyes looking up at me.

I almost caved. I almost said fuck it and did what I've wanted to do since the night I met her. I had my opportunity in the woods, but I spent too long questioning it. My body knew what I wanted and when I pulled my hips away, attempting to hide how hard she makes me, it snapped her out of whatever could've happened.

Apparently, kissing her when I have the chance to is too easy. Instead, I've resorted to groaning her name into my bicep, one hand pushed up hard against the shower wall while the other grips me. Imagining my hands in her hair when I slide between those pink lips. I feel like they're all I can focus on recently.

My thighs strain tight when the orgasm crashes into me. My stomach flexes, my heart pounds, and the confusion about what I'm doing follows right after. Maybe it's been too long since I had sex and I'm not thinking clearly. Maybe it's just been that damn long since I've spent time with someone up here that I'm having delusions about what it might mean. Maybe I'm just a man and she's just a beautiful woman.

I hear her as soon as I leave my bathroom. She's singing something I can't work out. She isn't loud but living alone has given me scary-good hearing. I tighten the towel on my hips and venture just far enough out of my bedroom door to see her in the kitchen.

Clara's singing Whitney Houston, I quickly realize, and making pancakes. I should call out and let her know I'm here but I want to watch her be so carefree a little longer. Her body is moving completely off beat with the rhythm of the song and she's trying to flip pancakes at the same time. Her red silk pajama shorts sit high on her hips; the matching camisole hangs low on her back.

She scoops a pancake with a spatula and I realize how fucking creepy I'm being. My door creaks as I push it open; she looks over and lets out a short scream. She recovers quickly but the pancake falls off the spatula onto the floor. Elf pounces on it but she doesn't seem to notice, she's busy staring at me with her mouth slightly open.

"Sorry!" I yell as I retreat into the safety of my room.

I pull on my sweats quickly and drag a towel over my wet hair, cursing myself under my breath. I'm going to get kicked off the emergency accommodation list. When I leave my bedroom again, Clara's only humming to the music.

"Mornin.'"

"Good morning," she says, not taking her eyes off the stove as I approach the kitchen.

I rub the back of my neck. "Sorry about earlier, I was trying to work out what you were singing."

The apples of her cheeks are rosy pink. "That's okay. I'd just forgotten what a naked man looks like, so you made me jump."

"I wasn't naked," I protest. "I had a towel."

"A *tiny* towel. A low, tiny towel clinging to your thighs." She pops a blueberry in her mouth. "It was borderline nakedness. I almost had to call Donald for his net."

"I'm sorry I broke your streak of only seeing fully clothed men." I don't mean it. There's a weird obnoxiousness brewing that I'm going to blame on testosterone and forced proximity that likes hearing Clara say she hasn't been seeing guys naked recently. "That guy who took you out last week never walks around after a shower?"

Asshole. Why did I just say that? I don't want to know the fucking answer.

Clara's eyebrows pinch together. "Guy? What are you . . . Ew, Jack. That was my little brother."

Massive, massive asshole. "Oh. Flo suggested he was someone else." I'm lying and simultaneously praying that Clara never brings it up with her.

Clara looks thrilled by the information. "Were you jealous?"

Ah, fuck. "No."

She pouts playfully, then turns back to the stove. "That's a shame. That could've been fun."

It would be fun, but I can't think about that right now while she's living in my apartment. I look across the kitchen worktop at all her efforts. My eyes squint at the pancake sitting in the now-cooling pan. "Is that—is that supposed to be me?"

It's a series of interconnected blobs with a skirtlike bottom and two chocolate chips for eyes. She picks up another blueberry. "Maybe."

"Wow." I pick up the spatula and tuck it under what I think is supposed to be one of my batter legs.

"Hey," Clara protests, slapping my hand away lightly. "He's mine." She points to the pile of pancakes on the counter. "I made you the snowmen."

Frankly, there isn't much difference between the blobs of the snowmen and the blobs of my limbs. "Have you ever seen a snowman before?"

"I'm rusty, okay?" she says sheepishly. "I normally eat breakfast on my way into the office. Never feels like there's any point just making them for me."

"It looks great. I can't remember the last time someone made me breakfast." Or saw me almost naked before 8 a.m. "Thank you. Sit down, I'll grab the syrup, it's on the top shelf."

"Are you working today?" Clara asks when I take a seat with a couple of options.

"Yeah. I can't afford not to. I'm really behind with Holly orders and my regular stuff. Flo didn't tell us she was posting the video and I didn't have the maximum order cap set on the website. Got flooded with new orders before I realized and set it to out of stock."

Clara pours coffee from the pot into a reindeer mug I know she's dug out from the back of the cupboard and pushes it in front of me, then does the same to her own matching mug. "Do you have the stock?"

"Mostly. Around half my orders were canceled when the Davenport doll and its price was announced." She pokes at her pancake version of me with her fork. "I have some more stock coming in December. What's your plan today?"

"Sit at the window and watch the snow. Maybe strike off a few things from my Christmas movie list. If your Wi-Fi doesn't suck maybe I'll do some scheming for the greater good."

"Christmas movies in November is illegal, Clara. December first is the earliest acceptable time to start," I say seriously.

"You need to find some handcuffs then, because I watched *The Muppet Christmas Carol* three days ago. Zero regrets." I don't need the image of Clara handcuffed distracting me from working today. "If I'm being super honest, I watched *Love Actually* in September."

"I can't listen to this," I tease. "I'll be downstairs if you need anything. November-appropriate movie recommendations included."

My email inbox is full of order update requests that vary in levels of hostility depending on if it's related to Harry's or Holly.

Dad would say that this isn't a way to run a business, but Dad sent me a picture of sunny Florida this morning while I'm stuck here in snow, so he doesn't get to dictate how I run my business right now. Badly, is how I'm running it, and that's my choice.

My workshop is cold as fuck even with the heater blasting and I'm struggling to get motivated, but I make myself look busy when I hear paws and feet on the stairs.

There's a light tap on the door before it opens. "Jesus, it's cold in here."

"No kidding."

Clara turns to close the door behind her. Her gym leggings cling to her long legs, the black fabric scrunching above the curve of her ass. This isn't helping my ability to concentrate, and I can't decide if it's better or worse than what she wore at breakfast.

I'm telling myself that the reason I can't get her off my mind is because she's in my space, not that I'm pathetic and horny and haven't stopped thinking about this woman in one way or another since I met her.

"I made us lunch. I was going to bring it down but then I thought maybe you don't allow food in here. Also, I'm now worried if you turn into an icicle down here people will think I locked you out or something. Don't you have a heater?"

It's amazing that a simple offer of lunch is enough to make me slow-blink. I'm starting to like this coexisting-in-one-space thing; I can't remember the last time it felt like someone was looking after me instead of the other way around. "The heater is on. It's just a piece of shit. You didn't need to make me lunch."

"I wanted to. Keep your expectations low—it's only tomato soup and grilled cheese." I follow her out the door and keep my eyes on the stairs instead of her ass as I let her and Elf go ahead of me. "Am I allowed to ask how work's going?"

The word *no* is on the tip of my tongue. "Only if you want to hear me complain."

We take our seats at the table. Clara sits to my immediate right instead of opposite me like last night and this morning. I warm my hands on the side of the steaming bowl of soup. "That bad?" she asks.

"No. I hate the admin side of work and my inbox has become unmanageable. I can't face tackling it so it's getting worse every day."

Her face is practically angelic as she smiles innocently.

"Why do you look like you're plotting something?"

"No plotting, just ideas. Hear me out before you immediately turn me down, okay?"

My suspicion is at an all-time high. "I'll try."

"Let me clear your inbox for you. Wait, wait, wait!" She holds up her hands to stop my oncoming interrupting. "I've dealt with customer service problems since I was in high school. We can agree on a script because most things will be the same couple of questions. I'll work downstairs and run any answers by you that fall outside of it. I'll be *so* quick, Jack. Then you don't have to worry about it."

"Don't you have your own job to do?"

Clara shrugs. "Resolving problems in Fraser Falls is my job right now. This is a problem, and I can easily help you. Then you can keep the answers for whenever you need them. Please let me help you."

Having an empty inbox would be a weight off my shoulders, but there's something tugging at my gut that doesn't want to hand over my work laptop to Clara.

"You can't be in my workshop while I'm running the machines because of health and safety. Can we do it together later?"

Her whole face brightens up. "Of course we can."

"Because I've been the recipient of your emails, and I have a few concerns about the professionalism you're going to give to my customers."

I dodge the paper towel that's thrown in my direction. "I should've left you freezing your ass off downstairs. Soupless."

"Too late now."

The afternoon passes surprisingly quick knowing my email problem is going to be taken care of soon. I find myself smiling when I can hear her and Elf moving around above me while I'm working. When I eventually clean up and take myself back upstairs, Clara is making a salad to go with the pizzas she put in the oven ten minutes ago.

"I think my mom was onto something with this housewife business, y'know? I don't know why I try to prove myself to my dad when I could just get a husband and hang out with dogs all day."

"You'd be bored without someone's problems to interfere with."

"I know," she admits. "But it's nice to pretend for a little while."

I agree, it is nice to pretend.

Dinner is another meal that consists of Clara making me talk about myself. When she's satisfied she's heard enough about my elementary school crushes, we move on to a more controversial topic.

"It happens on Christmas *Eve*!" I say, almost knocking my soda can over with my arm. "At a Christmas party, for God's sake! He says 'Ho, ho, ho' at one point. What's more Christmassy than that?"

"But the main theme of the movie is violence and terrorism, not holiday spirit! I'm sorry, Jack, but *Die Hard* isn't a Christmas movie. Bruce himself said it isn't."

I immediately reach for my cell and swipe away the messages from Tommy asking if Clara and I have murdered each other yet.

She's wearing the smuggest grin I've ever seen as I furiously type on my phone to find out if Bruce Willis did say that. I quickly find a YouTube video from a roast. "It's AI," I declare, locking my phone and putting it face down.

"The video from a million years ago is AI? That's what you're going with?"

"Listen, how about I find us a tub of Ben & Jerry's buried in the back of the freezer and we agree to just never talk about this again." Clara holds out her hand to shake. Her hands are always so soft and warm compared to mine. "Great to do business with you."

I stick to my promise and find an unopened tub behind a bag of turkey dinosaurs. Clara's already wrapped in a blanket with Elf loyally tucked into her side when I join them on the couch. She looks alarmingly excited. "Are you ready to enter the professional realm of bullshit bingo?"

The laptop is balanced on Clara's crossed legs. Her foot is pushed up against my thigh, forearm flush with mine. She encases me in the blanket, too, and leans across to tuck it under my leg. Clara said earlier that seeing snow makes her feel cold even though the house is warm. She's had a blanket on her in some capacity all day.

It's a surprisingly comfortable setup and the casual touches since we tackled the woods together have felt more and more normal. It feels like the first night we met, a memory that felt distant and unobtainable until recently. Somewhere along the way the two versions I separated Clara into in my head have merged.

"Bullshit *what*?"

"It's a very serious game we started at work to make dealing with complaints more fun." Clara brings up a new screen: a four-by-four board with different statements in each square. "Look, this first email is complaining that their order hasn't arrived yet, but if you look at the estimated delivery date on the confirmation email they've forwarded, it isn't due for another two weeks."

She clicks the pen tool on her bingo board and puts an X through the box that says *no delivery but it isn't even due yet.*

"This feels like the opposite of good customer service." I watch her long fingers type rapidly against the keyboard. She's apologetic and sincere, promising that it'll be there by the delivery date outlined in the confirmation email, signing off as Holly's Customer Service Team.

Clara highlights and copies what she's typed, quickly pasting it into a blank Word document. "It's kinder than not responding to it until it's past due. It's not illegal to have fun while working, grumpy. You happy with this?" When I nod, she fires off the email. "Okay! Next one."

Every time the little "unread" number on the inbox goes down, I breathe a little easier. So many of them are for things that aren't overdue yet, which makes me feel lighter. I make a note of the order numbers to prioritize as Clara uses the small list of answers she's collected to create the right response.

"You're good at this," I tell her honestly. The reason I've put it off is because of how long I have to fight the urge to just respond with *It'll be ready when it's ready.*

"I worked in our flagship store when I was in high school. After you get yelled at in person on Christmas Eve for three years in a row, responding to emails is easy. An email has never made me cry in a stockroom."

"Can't relate. I've had a work email make me cry before."

Clara's head whips around quickly. Her hair fans out behind her; the smell of her shampoo fills the space between us. Coconut and something sweet. "Oh my God. What happened?"

She closes the laptop and twists to give me her full attention; her knee meets my hip, the length of her shin presses against my thigh. Her eyes are big and green, concerned and fully focused on me.

I rub the back of my neck. Give her a tight smile. "I was just minding my business with my friends, having some drinks, trying to unwind from the week. I saw I had a work email and normally I wouldn't check but I'd been super-aware of them, being behind and all. So I checked it and honestly, I couldn't believe it. I tried to make sense of what she was unhappy about but then she resorted to name-calling."

Clara's jaw drops; her pink lips form the perfect O shape. "That's wild. What did she say?"

I drag my hand down my face, cover my mouth, squeeze my eyes tight. When I open them Clara is still staring at me with her doe eyes. I can't laugh. "She called me a smart ass and broody bodyguard. What does *broody bodyguard* even mean? I—"

Clara's fingers poke right in my ribs, winding me. She huffs and she twists back to her original position, her feet on the floor this time, the length of her thigh pressed against the length of mine again. Her shoulder sitting a little lower than mine. "I hate you. You're writing the next email."

Chapter 18

JACK

"Hey! Repeat offender!"

I don't know where the enthusiasm comes from as I point my finger at the email on the screen. Clara's laugh shakes her, vibrating her body against mine in all the warm spots where we're touching.

"Good eye, Kelly. I'll hit them with a *Please accept this email as a confirmation of receipt. Please see our response to your original email for answers to your query.* Okay?"

"Sure." I obviously made my anxiety about letting Clara help out clear, because she's been checking I'm happy before sending anything. She sends the email and crosses off *repeat offender* from the board.

"Just need one email sent from an email address clearly picked in middle school to get a full house. Only ten emails left, you think we can do it?"

"I've never been more sure of anything in my life." There's something about gamifying a task I hate that's working for me. It might also be doing it with Clara that's helping.

"Oh my God," Clara squeals. "This lady is asking you out. She said she met you when she came into the store and wants to know if you're single. She's forty-two, soon to be divorced, and a mom to two eight-year-old twin girls. Why isn't *score a date* on the bingo board?"

"Very funny."

Clara holds the laptop up in front of my face, where I see she's not joking.

"I'm not trying to be anyone's stepdad right now."

"God, you don't have to adopt the kids to date their mom." She grimaces at herself. "I've spent too much time in the tavern recently listening to drunken men talk. My point is, you could date her if you wanted to."

I pinch the bridge of my nose. "I don't want to so you can delete it. Next."

Clara clicks the trash can icon without saying another word and moves on. It's a disappointingly normal email address and she boos at the screen. Another two emails get responded to without giving us the chance to cross off our final bingo box.

"When did everyone suddenly get so professional? Where are all the 'hotchick one-two-threes'?" Clara says, clicking into the next email. Another dud. "There's no individuality anymore."

Clara responds to the second-to-last email while I dig my cell phone out from under my leg. I make sure she can't see my screen and bring up my inbox. The whooshing sound happens a split second before the dinging noise my laptop makes.

She eyes me. When she clicks my name and opens the email her hand flies to her mouth. "'Jack is the coolest zero-five-one-zero at Hotmail dot com' wants to know if I want a fresh drink. I should email back and say no thank you."

I rub my temple, pushing through the minor embarrassment. "I think you can probably just ignore it. Sounds spammy. Can I cross the square?"

Clara hands me the laptop. "You've earned it. Incredible, incredible email address creativity from baby Jack."

I strike a line through our final bingo square and hand her back the laptop. "Full house."

"And last actual email. Come on, Jacqueline Stewart, don't be an asshole . . . oh my God."

"What?" My eyes dart to the screen as Clara bursts out laughing.

"'Cutie-pie Jacky zero-seven' wants to know if it's possible to change the design she picked on the table she ordered from you two weeks ago."

"So you're telling me if I'd just waited one more email I could have kept 'Jack is the coolest' all to myself?"

"But don't you feel so much freer now that he's out?"

Clara rubs between my shoulder blades in a bid to comfort me. Her hand stops and rests on the shoulder closest to her for a beat, then returns to the laptop. Every touch ends quicker than I want it to. "Don't respond to that one. I'll call her tomorrow to talk about it. Are we done?"

"We're done. Wasn't that bad, right?" She hands me the laptop and shuffles off the couch.

"You made it not that bad. It would've been bad if you weren't here to help," I tell her honestly. "I probably would've given up from frustration."

Clara stretches her arms and legs. She groans as she brings each knee up to her stomach and rolls her shoulders. "Do you have any other tasks for me?"

"Do you know how to make an oak table?"

I watch as she continues to move around, like she's got too much energy all of a sudden. Elf jumps off the couch to sit near her feet, equally unsure what's happening. "I'm one of those annoying people who were born believing that they can actually do anything. So while the answer is technically no, let me watch a few YouTube tutorials first."

"You're ridiculous," I tell her, smiling when she dips her head to hide her smile. "Are you okay? You look like you're warming up to go for a run."

She looks over to the window, where snow has compacted on the external windowsill. "I'm fine. I just sat in one spot for too long and I suddenly have energy because I'm happy I was able to help you. I'm morally against running."

"So I won't get to race you at the Santa run?"

She sits back down beside me, cross-legged, facing me this time. I make sure she has enough of the blanket covering her. Elf can't find a route to sitting next to her so he opts to lie in his bed next to the radiator.

She rests her chin on her hand, propped up by her knee. "I'm undecided. Why do you even have a Santa run?"

I tuck a strand of hair that falls into her eyes behind her ear. "It's to raise money for the toy drive."

Clara bolts up straight like she's been hit with a stun gun. "That's it. That's it! That's it! Oh, I need my laptop!"

"What just happened?" I murmur to myself as Clara sprints across my living room into her bedroom. "What happened to being morally against running?" I yell.

"It's for a good cause!" she yells back.

She reappears, laptop in hand and the biggest smile on her face. "Are you going to fill me in on what I'm missing here?"

The couch creaks as she launches herself at the cushion's end. "I have press connections because of my job, right? And I've been trying to get a news station to do a segment or story about the toy drive. Everyone only wants to talk about Flo's video but a friend of a friend of a friend said if I could find a better hook then they could maybe do something."

"And you've found a better hook?" I ask, feeling clueless.

"The Santa run to raise money is the perfect introduction to everything you're achieving with the toy drive. People all dressed up ready to run in the cold to make sure kids have something to open at Christmas? It's perfect." Clara is practically humming with excitement.

"You've really thought this through, huh?"

It feels like an obvious thing to say when, if I'm honest with myself, she's been a whirlwind since she got here. The frustration I felt about constantly seeing her has subsided, leaving behind the truth that she's been trying hard for all of us since she arrived.

"If I can get you on the news, then people will know about Fraser Falls. If people know how great it is here, then people will visit. When people visit, they'll spend money here, and money makes the world go round." She doesn't look up at me while she explains her thought process. Her teeth are digging into her bottom lip while she concentrates on typing. "Almost done."

"Take your time," I say gently.

When she eventually closes her laptop she beams at me. "Who knew running could make me this happy?"

"You really care, don't you?"

"About running? No."

I roll my eyes. "About Fraser Falls, Clara."

"Of course I do." She wraps her arms around her legs, rests her chin on her knees. "I haven't lied to you once, Jack."

I hesitate. "So when you said you had nothing to do with the doll or the contract, you meant it?"

"I meant it. I started the small business program because I needed to pad out my résumé to climb the ladder. My grandpa would've loved it. He started as a small, independent business and remembering our roots was important to him. It's literally written on the wall of our reception area.

"Then the opportunity came up to cover someone on long-term sick leave in a higher position than mine in a different division, so I took it to get the experience. I didn't know about the Evie doll until

I got back a couple of weeks before Flo's video. I haven't even seen the contract, Jack."

"Do you want to?" I ask.

The conflicted look on her face makes me want to wrap my arms around her. "Yeah."

She nibbles on the corner of her thumb while I find the emails from the start of the year that include the contract. "Holly went viral when a reality TV lady shared her with a link to the store. Everything blew up from there and the town was busier than we'd ever seen it. Flo was thrilled, obviously."

"Obviously," Clara adds.

"Few weeks into the New Year, a guy from Davenport shows up asking if I'd be interested in scaling up my operation with the help of an experienced backer. He explained about the small business program and gave me the names of some other companies who participated. Encouraged me to look them up."

"They're the ones I onboarded before I left."

"It sounded great. The others were excited, so I said I'd be interested, then they sent over the paperwork." I pass the laptop to Clara. She balances it on her knees and tilts the screen back. Her eyes bounce from left to right rapidly but her breathing slows.

When I was a kid, my parents tasked me with teaching my sister how to ride a bike. I'd picked it up much quicker than she had and they thought she liked their attention too much to try. One Sunday I spent hours showing her what to do, and right after she started to get the hang of it, Mom and Dad came out to watch.

She got so distracted by their cheering that she stopped looking where she was going and was heading straight for a tree. Their cheers of pride turned into screaming at her to brake. I knew she was going to hurt herself and I couldn't do anything to stop it. My gut twisted in the worst way, voice stuck in my throat when I should have been telling her to stop.

It's how I feel right now watching Clara read the contract that's the antithesis of everything she says she stands for.

When she reaches the last page, she takes a shaky breath that feels like it sucks all the oxygen from the room. The kind you get between sobs. A noise that is so revealing that it doesn't need her to explain how she's feeling.

I feel it in the center of my chest, that ache of knowing someone is hurting and you can't do anything about it. I hate seeing her deflate, not when she's so loyal to what she thinks Davenport should be about. It makes me hate them even more.

"I failed you," she says, voice hardly above a whisper. "I'm so sorry."

When Clara turned up to resolve things full of fire and determination, she said she hadn't read the contract. If I'd shown her then and there, and she'd reacted like this, I don't think I would have been suspicious of her intentions.

You can't fake this kind of devastation.

"Hey," I say gently, getting her attention. Her bottom lip quivers. I pull her to my chest, cradling the back of her head while she fights away the urge to cry. She wraps her arms around my torso as I rest my chin on her hair, her body melting into mine as she takes big, unsteady breaths. "You're okay. You didn't fail me. They failed both of us."

"This isn't what it's supposed to be like. We're not supposed to be this kind of business. I promise you, the program is about a partnership. I didn't want this. I don't even know what this is." She lifts her body from mine and points a finger to the contract still on the screen. "This isn't what we do. They let me believe you were lying and being dramatic for attention."

I don't know how it happened, but I find myself wanting to apologize to her. A few weeks ago, I'd have taken great pleasure in proving I'm right, but there's no joy to be taken from shaking the foundation of the only thing someone's ever known.

"This isn't what Davenport is supposed to be about," she says quietly, possibly to herself.

There's a large tear rolling down the side of her face. I catch it with my thumb; her face turns into my palm and I cup her cheek for a short moment. "I'm sorry this is hurting you. I know how important your family business is to you."

It's a punch to the gut—no, worse—to see Clara cry. She looks so vulnerable when she's upset, a stark contrast to every version I've seen of her. I'm stuck between regretting showing her and being relieved she finally knows. She deserves better and I want her to believe that for herself.

Clara lets me hold her while soft sobs wet my shirt. I stay quiet, alternating between rubbing her back and stroking her hair until she untangles herself from me and wipes both eyes with the back of her hand. "This is just . . . a lot to process. I think I'm going to go to bed. Is that okay?"

"Of course. G'night, Clara."

"Night, Jack."

Chapter 79

CLARA

JACK'S WATCHING *DIE HARD* ON the TV in the living room and I'm smiling into the dark like a weirdo knowing I can call him a hypocrite for watching what he believes to be a Christmas film in November.

Maybe we can take turns handcuffing each other.

The room is like a freezer that no amount of blankets can save me from but the idea heats me up, just a little. I spent the first twenty minutes of "going to bed" crying in the bathroom on FaceTime to Honor. If Jack could hear me, he was polite enough to pretend he couldn't. When I eventually emerged, he was downstairs letting Elf use the bathroom.

I planned to sleep off the miserable feeling that comes with realizing that the people you trust are liars and it's a very real possibility that the company you've dedicated your life to is actually bad.

Unfortunately for me, my brain doesn't want to shut off when my nose is going numb from the cold. It doesn't help that all I have with me is silk pajamas that do nothing to keep me warm. I finally admit defeat and fumble toward the door in the dark. Jack and Elf are on the couch illuminated by the glow of the TV. Jack's feet are resting on the coffee table. Elf is sprawled on his weathered couch.

"Hey," Jack says warily. "How you doing in there?"

"Can I hang out with you guys? I don't want to report you to the police for watching what you think is a Christmas movie in November, so I may as well be an accomplice to the crime." Jack's mouth opens immediately but I hold up a hand stopping him. "If you keep going you'll have to either admit it's not a Christmas movie or admit it's not illegal to watch Christmas movies in November."

"Take a seat." He pats the empty space next to him. His eyebrows pinch together the closer I get to him. "Are you okay? Your nose is bright red."

"I think the heating in my room is broken." I hold out my hands for him to feel how cold my fingers are.

He gently squeezes them and looks horrified. Jack's on his feet before I can tell him it isn't a big deal. Next thing I know I'm being pushed down onto the couch and there's a huge knitted blanket being wrapped around me and another fluffier one being thrown across my lap. "Thank you," I say, but he's already charging toward my room.

I pause the movie to listen to him call the radiator useless and other derogatory names. Elf is snoring loudly. Jack eventually emerges, shutting the door behind him. "You should've told me you were cold."

"I didn't want to bother you," I admit.

"You love bothering me," he says playfully. He crouches in front of where I'm sitting on the couch, his hands clasped together, paired with a worried look on his face. I want to run my hand over his jaw and tell him it'll be okay, but I think it's me being upset that's upsetting him. Plus, I think I might have used my personal-contact pass already tonight when I turned into a blubbering mess on his chest.

I try to force a smile. "That's true. I like it when you get frustrated and pout."

The corner of his mouth creeps up. "I know you're lying; I don't even know how to pout. Do you want me to make hot cocoa?"

I nod. "That'd be nice."

"Whipped cream?" I nod again. "You got it."

I scoot to the end of the couch and rest my forearms on the arm. The storm has started to calm, the frantic blizzard slowing into a soft curtain of white. It's soothing to watch something so peaceful. "I feel like I'm in a snow globe," I say to Jack when he approaches me with a mug piled high with whipped cream.

"Stand up," he says, putting the drinks on the windowsill.

I move out of his way as he drags the coffee table and maneuvers the couch in front of the window looking out onto Main Street. I'm fighting to keep all the blankets on me in some capacity but lose one when Elf lies down on top of it. "There you go."

Jack switches his movie to the Christmas Jazz playlist. A jazz instrumental of "Have Yourself a Merry Little Christmas" fills the room. It feels cozy and peaceful. "Hey, I don't think I've heard your cell phone ring tonight. Did the snow magically solve all the problems in Fraser Falls?"

He shakes his head as he lifts the drinks from the windowsill and sits. "I've had a few texts but nothing urgent. People wouldn't drag me out in this weather if it wasn't urgent. Any other weather is fair game."

"Or the cell tower fell down," I offer.

"Or that."

I carefully lower myself next to him, tucking my feet under the back of my thigh and accepting my drink. He lets me take one sip before he's covering me in blankets again. "Does my skin offend you or something? Why are you trying to smother me under additional layers?"

Jack lets out a precarious laugh. "Your skin doesn't offend me, no. But you almost froze earlier out of politeness and you're hardly wearing anything so I'm stepping in."

"I'm not *hardly wearing anything*! These pajamas are from a boutique in Paris."

"I don't care about your Texas pajamas, Clara. I want you warm and not getting sick. Should I turn the temperature up?"

I raise an eyebrow, for multiple reasons. "Only if you're trying to cook me. Everything is good, Jack. Here, share so I don't feel like a human blanket basket."

I spread the fluffy one across both of our legs and attempt to put the heavier knit one across his shoulders too. All without tipping my drink onto him. "You happy now?" he asks, a hint of amusement in his tone.

"Yep."

"Are you actually? I didn't mean to upset you earlier, Clara. I really didn't."

"Oh, that? No, that still totally sucks. But I'm happy in this pretend snow globe with you."

Jack gives me a sympathetic look, one that makes me want to cry again. "You need another hug?"

I pinch my thumb and forefinger together. "Little bit."

We're sitting so close that he could argue we're already cuddling and I wouldn't have much defense. But he raises his arm anyway and lets me curl under it. His fingers stroke my arm lazily, occasionally trailing up to my shoulder and making my heart hitch before journeying back down. His chin rests on top of my head and I try my hardest to listen to his every heartbeat. "Better?" he murmurs gently.

"Yeah, you're pretty good at fixing problems. Don't know if anyone's ever mentioned it . . . except bedroom radiators, obviously," I mumble, squirming when his fingers tickle my waist.

"I admit, I gotta step up my heating game, but it's complicated. It could be worse. You could be at Tommy's place; he keeps his A/C on all year round. The man is like the Human Torch."

"You're not exactly Iceman yourself."

"Hey, you'd be grateful if we ever went camping in shitty weather."

I snort. "Okay, Jacob Black. You know, I've actually never been camping before."

"You're joking." Jack twists to get a better look at my face. Maybe to judge if I'm trying to play an elaborate prank on him . . . about camping. "You're not joking?"

"Why would I joke about something as apparently sacred to you as camping? Do I look like an outdoorsy girl to you?" It's funnier that Jack's sudden movement has disrupted our blankets so he's reminded that I picked out silk shorts and a cami to wear in this weather. His eyes skim over my thighs where my shorts sit high lazily; I watch him swallow and rub at the back of his neck. "I wouldn't survive the night."

"I think you're capable of anything you put your mind to, Clara. Indoor, outdoor, upside down. Even in your Kentucky pajamas." I try to hit him lightly, but he catches my hand and tugs me back under his arm. I fit too easily and settle too quickly. "And you tried to tell me violence isn't a theme of Christmas. Let's watch your snow globe and stop fighting."

I don't want to laugh at him but I can't help it. "I'm impressed with your Paris, USA, knowledge."

He buries his face into my hair as he laughs too. "Thank you."

The soft soothing jazz continues to play from the TV while we watch the snow fall and drink our hot cocoas. I'm not sure at what point I stopped needing comfort and started wanting to sit here intertwined with Jack.

"You can take my bed tonight," he says quietly. "I'll sleep on the couch."

"I can cope with sleeping in a cold room for one night, Jack. You have an unusual number of blankets for a man. You can just layer them on top of me."

"Let me just check the radiator again." He's gentle as he frees himself from the cocoon we've turned ourselves into. I immediately miss his warmth. "Maybe there's something I can do."

I follow him to my room and stand in the doorway, head and

shoulder leaning against the white wooden frame. There's a stark contrast between this room and every other room. "Stick my duvet in the bathtub. I'll sleep in there."

"The fuck you will. Grab your pillows," he says, pulling the duvet off the bed and bundling it up in his arms.

"Hey! Where are you going with that?" I protest as he tries to nudge past me. I take a step closer instead, pushing him back into the room.

"You're sleeping in my room where there's heat. I'll sleep on the couch . . . where there's also heat. You can't sleep in there."

"But it's fine. You don't have to sl—"

"Out, Clara," he says firmly. "Now."

"Or what? You're gonna throw me over your shoulder and carry me out?" I ask.

He grins. "Sure. That's definitely easier than arguing with you."

He takes one purposeful step toward me and my hands shoot up defensively. There's a playfulness in his eyes that I'm not used to that I fear I'll miss as soon as it's gone. "Okay, I concede, caveman."

"Even easier."

"But *I'm* sleeping on the couch. I can't take your bed off you and—Jack!" I cling to his neck as he scoops me up on top of the duvet already draped over his arms. It's the most comfortable I've ever been while being carried against my will. "You're a cheat."

I poke my finger into his cheek to try to kill the smile there. He looks too pleased with himself. He's careful as he maneuvers me through the doorway, feet first.

I wonder if I'm more or less easy to move than a table.

Jack drops me onto the mattress; the duvet underneath cushions the fall as the mattress springs creak. He seizes my moment of distractedness to grab his pillows and take them out to the living room. He's already moved the couch away from the window and back to its regular spot by the time I get out there.

He looks at me, eyebrows pinched together. "What's your problem? Get in there and go to sleep."

I fold my arms across my chest. "There's only one situation where I'll listen to a man tell me to get in his bed, Jack. To sleep alone isn't one of them. I'm taking the couch."

He crosses the room toward me, stopping only inches away. There's something hot stirring in me at the idea of Jack finding out what that one situation is. His glare pierces me; my eyes flick to his lips. There suddenly isn't enough oxygen in the room as I drop my hands to let them hang.

Jack's fingers brush my jawline gently until he reaches my ear, tucking my hair away. Goose bumps spread across my skin and I watch his throat bob as he swallows. "You're a pain in my ass. You know that?"

I nod slowly. "You're one to talk."

His fingers travel down my neck and along my shoulder until he finds the skin his fingers spent the night traveling. "I'm taking the couch, Clara."

I don't say anything as he passes me to head back into his bedroom. I stare up at the ceiling, trying to find the exact moment I found myself losing it over Jack Kelly. He walks past me with his duvet and throws it on the couch with his pillows.

"Night," he yells as I gracefully walk (read: stomp) toward his bedroom. I get the pillows and duvet he's sweetly straightened on the bed and bundle them into my arms.

Jack's in the kitchen by the sink when I walk out of his room. I quickly lie down on Elf's couch and tuck a pillow under my head. He stops at the foot of the couch and sighs.

It's the feeling of victory that I might be getting slightly addicted to. But it's short-lived when he gets under his duvet on the other couch.

I prop myself up on my elbow. "What're you doing?"

"I told you, I'm sleeping on the couch."

"But your room is empty," I say, gesturing to the open door and bed.

"I'm aware of that," he says calmly.

"Are we having a sleepover?"

"No."

"Can we build a fort?"

"No."

He sits up to look across to me when I go quiet. I'm doing an exaggerated pout. "Can I tell people we built a fort?"

He shakes his head. "No. Go to sleep."

"I don't think you know how sleepovers work, Jack."

He lies down and I roll onto my back. "There's only one situation where I'll let a woman keep me awake all night, Clara. To build forts isn't one of them. Good night."

I sigh through the butterflies. "Night."

Chapter 20
CLARA

Jack talks in his sleep and I'm trying to decide if it's funny or weird to mention it.

I know it was weird to record it, which I *won't* be telling him about, but otherwise what's the reasonable thing to do? In my defense, he was saying either *Clara* or *karma*, neither of which is necessarily good for me.

I'm as quiet as possible as I tiptoe around the kitchen to make coffee. I don't want to wake Jack. The strong lines of his face soften in his sleep; his sharp jaw fades beneath a dusting of facial hair that I quite like.

I'm ignoring the fact Maggie texted me to say the repairman is coming today and I'll be able to go back to the B & B. A car service is supposed to be picking me up tonight to travel home for Thanksgiving tomorrow but I'm itching to tell them not to bother.

The idea of leaving Fraser Falls to be locked in the house with my parents for forty-eight hours makes my skin feel too tight for my body. I don't know how I can be expected to sit opposite my dad after reading the contract Jack showed me last night.

The one that would have cut him out of the decision-making

and let Davenport develop the line without him. The one that would have let them produce his work without giving him credit, just like they did to me. I wouldn't say I'm an especially irrational person, but it makes me want to cause a scene. Something my mother has specifically asked me not to do my entire life.

I'm not anxious to talk about what I've learned with my dad, I'm anxious because I know that he knows and doesn't care. He let me come here to work toward a better relationship with these people, knowing we're everything they believe us to be.

Part of me wonders whether he even wants me to succeed. Watching me fail would give him a plausible reason to not promote me.

The other part of me questions if a trip home to reconnect and update my dad will soothe my concerns. *Concerns* is a nice way of saying "paranoia about Max," I guess.

Will a trip with familiar home comforts be good for me? Do I miss Uber Eats? Yes. I also miss important things like Honor and Paloma. Gossiping with Sahara. The bodega near my house. Masturbating without the fear that Maggie is going to burst into my room with a vacuum cleaner at any moment. The full spectrum of important things.

Either the coffee smell filling the room or the loud screeching of Jack's ancient coffee machine wakes him up, distracting me from my Davenport-related rumination. He squints at me from the couch. His hand rubs his hair, then his eyes. He looks confused to see me at first, then smiles.

Call it the result of forced proximity, call it maturing, I don't care, but I like where we've landed. I would've settled for not being treated with suspicion, but being comforted and encouraged is more than I ever expected after he found out who I was.

Sure, my skin feels hot every time he touches me and every time I catch him looking at my mouth I want to close the distance, but I think that's a normal reaction when it comes to a man like Jack.

Acting on those things would be a conflict of interest, which is funny since I learned I work for a company with zero moral integrity. But he was the one who was here to soothe me, even though they hurt him too. I think, all things considered, that speaks to a pretty exceptional kind of person. One that I'm going to miss sharing space with when I go back to the B & B.

"The screeching was the machine, not me," I say, in case it needed clarifying.

"Good to know." His voice is gravelly and deep. "Good morning."

"You should ask Santa for a new coffee machine." It finally finishes filling and makes a noise that sounds a lot like it giving up. "This one just wants to be put out of its misery."

"I'll put it on my list." I fill two mugs and walk over to him, perching on the edge of the couch when he rolls onto his side to make room for me. "Why do you look so pensive this early in the morning?"

I shrug and he watches, patiently waiting for an answer. "Thinking about how I don't want to go home later."

He sips from his mug, then puts it on the coffee table. "Home to Maggie's or home home?"

Both. "Home home. I don't think spending time with my family is what I need right now. I might call my mom and see how she reacts to the idea of me staying here. What are you doing for Thanksgiving?"

"I think you should do what makes you happy. Not that you asked for my opinion." He gives a tight smile. "I'll be doing this, mostly. Watching football and eating a cherry pie by myself. Nothing fancy."

"You're not seeing your family?" He shakes his head, pushes himself up into a seated position. I shuffle farther away from the edge. "Why not?"

"My sister is at her in-laws' and my parents changed their mind about flying up. Heard about the storm and decided to stay in Florida."

"So they're leaving you alone? What about Tommy? Or Flo?

Maggie?" Despite the fact I was *just* thinking about staying in Fraser Falls alone, I hate the idea of Jack not having anyone. "You can't be alone."

He laughs awkwardly, scratches at his growing stubble. "I can. It's only one day. Tommy and Luke take Sailor over to their grandparents' house up in Portland. I've been before but they're old now and I don't like to intrude. Flo and Maggie both have their own families. I'm okay here hanging out with Elf."

"Maggie texted me to say I can go back there." I watch his face closely for a reaction. A tiny part of me hopes to see the disappointment I felt when I read the message.

"That's good news," he says, giving *nothing* away.

"It is." I'm not even convinced by me, wow. "I'm going to jump in the shower and start packing up my things."

Still nothing. "I'll make us breakfast."

IT'S AMAZING HOW A LARGE bath towel can start to feel like a napkin when Jack takes one indiscreet look at me from head to toe. I'm pretty sure my whole body blushes as I shuffle into my room and close the door behind me.

The room is still freezing but I was too busy spiraling over what to do tonight to remember to take my clothes into the bathroom with me. I'm paying for it with rock-hard nipples and a risk of frostbite in places frost should not be reaching.

I settle for something comfortable and oversized.

I follow the smell of cinnamon and vanilla to the kitchen and lean my forearms against the counter. "Are you making French toast?"

Jack flips a thick slice of bread in the frying pan. "I am."

"I *love* French toast."

He dunks another piece in the mixing bowl on his right. Ordering breakfast to my house will never feel good enough after this. "I know you do."

My eyebrows pull together. "You keep claiming to know things. How?"

"You told me the night we met," he says simply, confirming that he does remember. "Were you worried I'd learned to read your mind?"

I steal a chopped strawberry from a bowl on the counter. "Learning my food preferences would be the least of my worries if you could read my mind."

Jack finally looks way from the pan, eyes wide. "And what would I learn?"

"All kinds of wickedness and debauchery. I'm not sure you could handle it." Realistically, I'm not sure I could handle it.

"I think you should try me," he says coolly.

I move onto my tiptoes and lean against his shoulder, pulling him down until his ear is level with my mouth. I lower my voice to a whisper. "I think I should sit at the table for breakfast, and you should just use your imagination."

I muster every bit of confidence I can as I drop onto my heels and walk to the table. Jack's still shaking his head when I take a seat.

There's a quiet that occurs directly after that resets the balance, and the temperature, of the room. Jack puts a plate stacked high with French toast and strawberries in front of me. "Bon appétit, as they say in the home of your pajamas."

"Arkansas?" I ask. Jack bursts out laughing as he loads his plate. "Are you going to the nativity rehearsal later? I was personally invited by Wilhelmina after I found her nutcracker."

"*You* found her nutcracker? Did *we* not find her nutcracker? And yes, I'm going later. I'm Joseph."

"Not in the version of the story I tell." I think about what else he said, and I almost knock my cutlery off the table. "I'm sorry, did you just say you're Joseph in the nativity?"

"You think I'm growing this beard for fun?" he asks, rubbing his hand along his jawline. I've been actively avoiding thinking about the blossoming beard. I just assumed he was going for the rugged lumberjack look.

"I didn't realize you had a passion for acting."

He pins me with an unimpressed glare. "It's a lottery because nobody ever wants to do it. My name got pulled out of a hat. It's been Tommy for the last three years and I think he added my name a dozen times, but I can't prove it. So, I'm Joseph."

"I'm in awe. I have so many questions. Have you always felt a calling to a story about a carpenter?"

"Eat your toast, Clara." Jack shuffles on his feet, nudging at something on the floor that isn't there. He clears his throat. "Will you be around to watch it? It's on the seventeenth."

The big question. "I don't know."

I watch for a reaction. Still nothing.

A PICTURE OF MY MOM and me at last year's Davenport charity gala is the background of my call while I wait for my mom to accept my FaceTime request.

She finally answers and I can see the inside of her ear. "Mom, it's FaceTime."

"Sorry, sorry." She brings the camera to beneath her chin. It looks like she's moving at speed through the house but it could also be Saks. "I'm having a disaster day, Clara. Are you okay, darling?"

"I'm fine. What's going on?" A disaster for my mother is a broad spectrum of possibilities. "Is there anything I can help with?"

She sighs heavily. "I doubt it. Unless you know a floral designer who isn't completely booked all of December. The Rose Garden double-booked us with the DAR for the Christmas Eve fundraiser.

It's a ridiculous hassle. I'm about to go shopping to calm myself down."

"A floral designer is just a fancy name for a florist, isn't it?" She repositions her camera so I can see that she's frowning at me. "If the answer is yes then I might know a business who can help, but if you like them you have to tell all your friends."

"No, Clara, that's how I ended up in this mess in the first place! Betsy Hannigan saw the Rose Garden invoice and I've been at war ever since. I won't go through it again."

"It's a small business in a tiny town, Mom. Their work is beautiful, I'll send you some pictures and if you like it, you can contact them. Spreading the word about them would help them massively. I'm sure they'd prioritize you as an early client."

I'm just saying what I think will convince her at this point. Hosting events is my mom's pride and joy and she's very good at it. She knows people all over the Northeast who would keep Mel and Winnie busy all year.

I need to update my closet plan as soon as I'm off the call.

"Send them over, darling. I'll take a look at their work. Now, why are you calling?" I chew the inside of my cheek, working out how to word what I want to say. "Oh, here's your dad and brother. Say hello to Clara!"

Mom flips her camera to show Dad and Max walking through the front door laughing with each other. They each have a tennis racket; Dad's arm is draped over Max's shoulder. Both of them wave at the camera and I unenthusiastically wave back. Mom flips the camera back to her. "Why isn't Dad at work?" I've *never* known Dad to take the day off.

"Your brother had a voucher."

A voucher. "Seriously?"

She nods. "One of those stamp book incentives where you get your seventh game free. Max is quite enamored with it. Strange since he hated every sport we tried to make him do when he was a child."

"Very strange." The image of my dad and brother arm in arm isn't one I thought I'd need to get used to. I might not want to go home, but it feels like I have to. I feel like I'm trying to keep up with them when I wasn't invited in the first place. Most important, it feels like my promotion is slipping through my fingers. "I was just checking in. Nothing urgent. Enjoy shopping, Mom."

"See you tomorrow, darling. Love you."

Chapter 21
CLARA

I HAVE A HUGE PAPER cut because Elf is onstage dressed like a donkey and I don't know how to be normal about it.

It's totally my own fault, but when Jack walked him out, his little chunky body wiggling beneath the grayish sweater—Elf's, not Jack's—I completely lost my mind and managed to drag the lethal edge of the pamphlet right down my index finger.

It immediately resulted in Dove squealing loudly about not getting blood on the paper, rightfully so, and I was sent to the table in the corner away from anything of value to wait for a first aid kit.

I take a seat at the center of the table and watch everyone working around each other while simultaneously working with each other. It's a fascinating system of people who have clearly done this together many times.

"Causing trouble, Davenport?" Jack's deep voice is laced with humor as he approaches holding a Band-Aid.

"They're making you help me? When your wife is about to give birth?"

He smiles as he takes my wrist, holding my hand up to inspect my finger. "I have time. Only been turned away by one innkeeper so far. Mel keeps messing up her lines so I'm free while Flo drills them into her."

Mel looks like she's about to run away as Flo works with her on the edge of the stage. Nobody can tell me why she's wearing a fake pregnancy stomach when this isn't a dress rehearsal. I've asked at least three people.

"I got so excited at your donkey that I gave myself a paper cut."

"Understandable." Jack moves closer until his thighs are pressed up to my knees. He leans over my straightened finger and pulls out a disinfectant wipe sachet from his back pocket. "This might sting."

I mumble a series of curse words into my uninjured hand's fist as he wipes the blood away. "How can a paper cut feel like a stab wound?"

"I'm sorry. Nearly done," he says gently.

The Band-Aid has dinosaurs on it and frankly, it's the only good thing to come out of the situation. "Thank you. You're going to be great putting those skills to use during childbirth."

"Can you be trusted to return to the playbill station or should I get Flo to assign you the role of placeholder sheep?"

"I'm a really bad actress. We did *Annie* when I was in middle school and I couldn't even handle the pressure of Unnamed Orphan. I'm much more of a judgmental audience member than an artist. You'll see when you receive my review of your performance."

Jack steps back and holds out his hands to me, taking mine to help me slide off the table. "Can't wait to hear your in-depth thoughts."

"No man has ever said that to me about anything, ever," I say teasingly. "I'll be giving Elf a rave review, just so you know."

"Obviously."

"Did he miss me today? It was weird having no one around to lick my feet."

"I think there are apps that can help you solve that problem, Clara." He dodges the poke to the ribs. "Yes, he missed you today. It feels super quiet and empty now. As soon as Luke fixed the radiator in your room, Elf went and slept on your bed."

I swear I hear my heart crack open. "I'm going to cry. You can't let me go back to the program table, I'm going to flood it with tears."

Jack wraps an arm around my shoulders, guiding me slowly toward where I'm supposed to be working. "Think happy thoughts."

He smells like aftershave and soap, something woody and spicy. It's completely distracting in every single way possible. "I can't think happy thoughts. I'm being picked up soon to be taken to my parents' house."

"Patched her up for you," Jack says to Dove, pulling out my chair for me to sit back down.

"Well, aren't you a hero," Dove says playfully. "You technically patched her up for Flo, because I'm not cruel enough to subject anyone to such a boring task."

"Guys, speaking of Flo," I say warily, "I've had an idea that I want to run by her, but I'm scared to. I'm both in awe and terrified of her."

They both nod like they know the exact type of fear I'm describing. Flo is so sure of every single thing she says that it begins to wobble the confidence I have in myself. I feel like as soon as she has a question I'm not ready for I crumble under the pressure of wanting her approval so badly. In the beginning it was because she's the deciding factor in my promotion. Now it's because everyone in this place respects her so much and I want her to like *me*.

"Hit us," Dove says enthusiastically. Sailor doesn't look up from her book on the other side of the table.

"I've been thinking about how to encourage people to spend as much money as possible at Small Business Saturday. What about a passport? Each store is represented and when someone buys from that store it gets stamped or crossed off, or something. If you buy from every store you get a prize."

Jack and Dove are listening carefully. "What would be the prize?" Jack asks.

Great question. "Uh, I don't know. Something simple and inexpensive. People love earning something free. My brother's recent interest in tennis made me think of it."

"She's going to tell you that it's too late," Dove says. "If it isn't weeks in advance, she isn't interested."

I considered this while I was trying to figure out how to pitch this idea to her. "It'd take me thirty minutes to whip up something to print. I can buy thick high-quality paper on Friday and complete everything. I bet I could find stamps on Friday before I come back from the city."

"I can make stamps," Jack says. "Sails, want to make some stamps with me?"

Sailor doesn't look up. "No, thank you."

"Great, but that wasn't the right answer," he murmurs. "I like it, Clara. I think it's a good idea. I'll get Flo."

I want to tell him to wait as he heads toward the stage, where Flo is still guiding Mel. I feel like I need more time to come up with a well-thought-out pitch, but in reality, my car will be here soon. Flo is the most intimidating woman I've ever met, and yes, I'm slightly obsessed with everything about her.

"I believe you have a proposal for me, Clara," Flo says as she approaches our table.

I relay my idea to her in a slightly more enthusiastic and professional version of how I told Dove and Jack. As expected, she says there isn't enough time.

"I think it's a really good idea, Ms. Flo," Jack says.

"I do too," Dove adds. "I'll come up with a prize."

Flo looks as shocked as I do that Jack is taking my side. "Okay, I'll tell Arthur. Give me an update on Friday, Jack?"

"You got it."

I don't even have time to celebrate because my cell phone starts vibrating on the table, letting me know my car has arrived. "I have to go," I say, the words struggling to come out. "But I'll be back."

"Have you finally replaced me in town as the fixer?" he says, cocking his head. "I know I always say you're capable of anything, but I'm not sure you could unclog a drain."

I smile, look down at my phone clutched between my hands. "Your role is safe for now. It's my car service calling to let me know he's outside."

Jack nods, pushing his hands into his pockets. "Have a safe trip home."

I debate if it'd be appropriate to hug him goodbye and settle on no, not here.

Time seems to move slower as I grab my bags from the back of the room and head out to the car. There's a longing I don't recognize as the car gets farther and farther away from Fraser Falls. My phone lights up with an incoming text from Jack. When I open it it's a picture of Elf in his donkey outfit.

I'm not even ten miles away and I'm already pining to go back. Knowing I'm trading in the simplicity and community of the place I've been calling home to overanalyze every mention of work my dad makes to my brother is the worst. Jack is going to spend the day alone and I'm going to spend the day miserable. I don't know why I'm doing it.

"Excuse me, I'm sorry, but could you please turn around?"

Chapter 22

CLARA

The last place I ever expected to be at 11 a.m. on Thanksgiving is Jack Kelly's doorstep clinging to a cheap bottle of wine.

I pressed his doorbell a minute ago, an old-fashioned thing I'm half convinced didn't work until I start to hear a bolt sliding on the other side of the door. My words are lodged in my throat as he stares at me, mouth slack.

He's wearing basketball shorts and nothing else. Heat creeps up my neck and the speech I mentally prepared on my walk over here is gone. All I can focus on is the hard lines of his body, the faint remains of a summer tan, dark hair dusting his chest and beneath his belly button.

Seeing him from across the room didn't do him justice.

I do my best to act like a normal human being as I hold out the wine. "I couldn't find pie, so I brought wine."

He accepts my offering, but he's looking at me like he's questioning if I'm real or not. Eyebrows pinched, lips pressed tight. It isn't exactly the smile I was hoping for. "You're supposed to be in New York."

I know I am. It's exactly what the last four text messages from my mother say. But the second the car turned around last night, the ache in my chest began to ease. "I was wondering if you maybe wanted to be alone on Thanksgiving together?" I tuck the wild pieces of hair blowing in the wind behind my ears and pray that he doesn't turn me away. "I could probably make a pie if it's an entry criterion."

I feel like I can pinpoint the moment the confusion passes. He blinks a few times, steps out of the way, and holds the door open. "I'll share my pie with you, Clara." I walk past and take the first step of the stairs as he closes the door. "I can't believe you're here."

"Neither can I," I mumble.

Elf is so happy to see me that he knocks over a chair. I turn to Jack to jokingly tell him that it's his turn but he's busy pulling on a hoodie, giving me one less thing to be thankful for today.

I hang my coat on the hook beside the front door and kick off my boots. Jack puts the bottle of wine in the refrigerator. I feel out of practice being here even though it's only been twenty-four hours. I lean my elbows against the kitchen counter, but I'm awkward and out of place. I go around to the other side and lean my back against it, switching from one foot to the other.

Jack doesn't seem to notice. At least he doesn't say anything when he turns back to face me. "So what made you stay?"

"A few reasons. I didn't like the thought of you spending the day alone." There's something about the person who does everything for everyone else being alone on a day for giving thanks that doesn't sit right with me. "Even though I know you said it was fine. It didn't feel fine to me." Vulnerability isn't something that comes naturally to me, but I push the discomfort to the side to be honest with him.

His eyebrows lift half an inch, eyes that little bit wider. "That, uh, that means a lot to me."

"Mm-hmm." I look at my cream socks against the gray tile flooring. He takes a few steps and stops in front of me. Jack pushes my hair behind my shoulders and nudges my chin up gently until his deep brown eyes are locked with mine.

"I mean it, Clara." He follows the curve of my jaw with his fingers, lets his hand settle on the side of my neck. I swallow as his thumb strokes over my pulse. He's watching me so carefully that it makes me want to look away. I feel like he's under my skin. "I'm really happy I get to spend today with you."

Jack's hand slips into the hair at the nape of my neck. "Show me how happy you are that I'm here," I whisper.

His head dips slowly; I angle my mouth toward him as he nudges my nose with his. He's teasing me, taking his time and testing how patient I can be. My hands cling to the front of his hoodie in desperate fists, pulling his body closer. "I've wanted to do this since I met you," he whispers.

There's no patience left in him as he melts me with a searing kiss. I creep onto my tiptoes to try to get closer; he lifts me at my hips and sits me on the counter, pushing himself in between my parted knees.

I lock my feet around his lower back, groan into his mouth when he squeezes my hips and drags me to the edge. The pressure of him in between my legs. His mouth on mine. His hands back in my hair. It's too much and not enough.

"I want to feel you on top of me again," I murmur when his mouth leaves mine to kiss down my throat. Jack wastes no time hoisting me up and striding toward the couch. His hands grip my ass; his mouth moves back to mine. He lowers me down slowly, moving a cushion behind my head as he settles between my open legs.

It's more intense like this. The kissing feels hotter. The pressure better. I slip my hand under Jack's clothes and run my finger down his spine. His hips grind into mine, his erection thick and heavy.

"Should we talk about what's happening right now?" he asks gently, pressing his forehead against mine.

I use my hand to tilt his face to find his mouth again; the

roughness of his stubble scratches against my chin. I shake my head between quick kisses. "No."

He ignores me, pushing himself up and sitting on the heels of his feet between my legs. My thighs are over his, feet flat on the couch behind him. I push myself up onto my forearms and shake out my hair.

If I knew I'd be seducing a man today I'd have worn something other than sweatpants. I have Halloween-themed bat panties on. Jack probably wishes he had on something other than the basketball shorts that are failing to hide how hard he is. He follows my eyes and pulls his hoodie down at the front.

"This isn't smart," he says. The uncertainty in his voice is almost funny. "Is it?" He rubs at his temple, eyes slowly trailing over me. I really wish I were wearing something sexy. He tilts his head back, looking at the ceiling like it'll somehow give him answers.

"Does something have to be smart to be good?"

"You're going to leave." It sounds like he's reminding himself more than me. "At some point. Some point soon."

"Yeah, I will."

"But there's this"—he points his finger to each of us repeatedly—"this thing. Right? Between us? An energy. I'm not imagining it."

I nod my head slowly. "You're not imagining it."

This poor man looks tortured when he was supposed to be enjoying having a pie to himself today. "Maybe now that we've kissed once it'll, I don't know, lessen the energy. We can go back to being normal after."

I give him a soft smile, run my foot up his thigh. "I don't know any time where that exact logic hasn't worked."

"I'm a man in crisis and you're making jokes." Jack laughs, rubs his eyes with his thumb and forefinger. He moves my foot from his leg and leans over me, placing it on the bottom of his back. I lift my other leg and interlink my feet again. The weight of his body reignites the ache that was starting to dull. He presses his forehead against mine again. "I can't fuck you, Clara. I know I won't be the same after."

Jack's hips grind into mine and I whimper. Now who's being tortured? "Just kiss me then. Nothing bad has ever happened from making out."

His teeth nip at my ear. My thighs tighten around his waist. A desperate fire is burning in my lower belly. "I deserve a medal for the levels of restraint I'm showing," he mumbles, sounding furious at himself.

"Yeah," I tell him, helping pull the hoodie from his body and over his head. "Won't be getting a medal from me. I'm team no restraint."

His skin is hot and smooth under my fingertips; every inch of him is covered in thick, solid muscle. I trail my fingers across his shoulders while he kisses me gently, letting me explore him.

It's slower and sweeter than earlier. He takes his time, almost like he's savoring it because he knows it can't happen again. He maneuvers us so I'm on top of him and spends time running his hands over every inch of me.

When I finally push us apart, my hands flush to Jack's chest with his erection hidden in his shorts at the apex of my thighs, he clears his throat gently. "Do you want some pie?"

THERE'S SOMETHING ABOUT EATING AFTER finally getting what I've been waiting for that is making this cherry pie taste incredible.

My family won't even be sitting down to eat their appetizers yet, so I feel very spoiled being allowed to skip straight to dessert. The pregame commentators are going over statistics but Jack is too busy spinning a strand of my hair between his fingers to pay attention.

"You're really going to let me sit here and eat this alone?" I hold up a forkful of cherry filling to him but he shakes his head.

"I'm enjoying watching you try not to get it all over your face." I roll my eyes and he kisses my temple.

In a surprising turn of events, "once" didn't make the energy between us any more manageable. I decide not to think too hard about it and just enjoy today for what it is.

He shows me pictures his family sent and reads the *Fraser Falls Thanksgiving Newsletter* out loud. There's a natural gap where it would be normal to talk about my family, but it's a boundary Jack set and I want to respect it.

I think he senses it too. "What are Honor and Paloma doing today?" he asks.

I smile and lean in, kissing him lightly on the cheek just above where his beard ends. When today is over, so is the affection. It's a one-time thing. A one-day thing at most. "Paloma is at her dad's house. He's named Kyle. We don't like him."

Jack nods very seriously. "Good to know, thank you."

"He only fought for custody to reduce his child support payments and he constantly messes with Honor. He cheated on her and is just generally an ass. Honor is at work. She's a nurse at a hospital in Brooklyn."

I launch into how we met, the stories that represent the best of our friendship, and how much I love being part of Paloma's life. Jack listens carefully, adding thoughtful questions, while we spend the rest of the day hanging out on the couch. When we get hungry, Jack throws a couple of frozen pizzas in the oven and opens my cheap wine that smells a little like vinegar. And when it's time to go to bed, there's no argument over the couch. He drags an old Red Sox shirt over my head and pulls me to his chest beside him.

I fall asleep wondering how long I can make one day last.

Chapter 23

JACK

It's really distracting to be intensely stared at while I have a knife in my hand.

"Can I help you?" Tommy, Luke, and Dove all stare back at me over their coffee mugs like they don't know what I'm talking about. "The staring has to stop."

"What did you do?" Tommy asks, his eyebrows pinched together.

"He definitely did something," Luke adds, propping himself up at the counter.

This is the worst part about spending time with Sailor like a good uncle; she usually comes along with these three assholes, who are determined to annoy me all day. "Where's Clara today?" Dove says in a singsong voice.

"That's a blush! He's blushing," Tommy yells, pointing dramatically at me across the table. Sailor shushes him and he apologizes to her immediately. "I'm trying to concentrate here," she says seriously. We're attempting to carve the stamps for Small Business Saturday, but we've been constantly distracted by her unhelpful parents and uncle since we sat down. Sailor is the only one acting like a grown-up.

"She's at a print shop an hour away picking up her rush order for the stamp books. That's what Flo told me anyway."

I'm lying. I haven't seen Flo today. I did see Clara though. This morning when I first opened my eyes. Her auburn hair was splayed over my pillow like fire. My T-shirt bunched around her waist. Her creamy soft skin pressed into mine while she slept peacefully.

She's devastatingly beautiful and I regret not telling her that yesterday.

"I thought Flo was visiting her sister this morning," Dove says, bringing her coffee cup to her lips.

Ah, shit. "Caught her on her way out the door." Another lie.

Tommy narrows his eyes at me like he's about to ask if I also stole a pie from a windowsill.

"You didn't rob Flo again, did you?" he asks, eyeing me.

"I need everybody to move on from that one error in judgment," I mutter.

Sailor holds up her stamp proudly. "Look! This one's a candy cane. It's for Sweet Caroline's."

I lean over to inspect it. "That's perfect, kiddo."

She beams, teeth and dimples and all. It hits me all over again—how much this town means to me. How much these people do. Even if they're annoying.

"I better get back to work," Luke says, ruffling Sailor's hair as he passes.

She brushes off his hand and holds up her next rubber block. "I'm making one for Miss Celia's store too. It's a book!"

"She's a baby," Dove says, nudging Luke with her elbow. "And already more productive than Tommy."

"I resent that," Tommy mutters, stealing one of Dove's muffins anyway.

"I resent being called a baby," Sailor says in her most grown-up tone.

"I'm sorry, sweet girl," Dove says gently, a tone that's exclusively reserved for Sailor. "Hey, let me help you. Pass me that one."

"That's for Flo's Fancies," I say.

She smiles, pushing her pink hair back into a ponytail. "Oh, I know."

Small Business Saturday has always been more successful on paper than in practice in Fraser Falls, but this year it might actually work. Because Clara came in and made it make sense. She designed stamp cards with little illustrations and shop maps. She scheduled social media posts. And when I said I was worried we didn't have the budget for the number of flyers Flo was requesting, she made them herself in the seat next to me while we hung out on my couch.

We haven't talked about what happened yesterday. About *what I did*. I don't know how to talk about it. Not without giving something away I'm not ready to lose.

Because she's going to leave. Eventually, she'll go back to New York, and Davenport, and whatever sleek glass office she came from. I'll stay here, answering my neighbors' calls, sketching new toy ideas I'll never bring to fruition, and trying not to think about the fact that I'm always only one tiny step from everything going wrong.

The front door creaks and then slams.

"Jack?" Flo's voice calls down the hallway of Dove's house. "You have a delivery. Apparently postal worker is something I can add to my résumé."

I stand and wipe my hands on a dish towel. "Watch the carving," I tell Sailor, who salutes me seriously before squatting down so she's eye to eye with the stamp.

"Clara dropped this off. I said I'd bring it since I need to speak to Luke about the Christmas tree," Flo says, handing me a flat cardboard box.

I nod. "Thanks."

Flo narrows her eyes at me. "You look like you didn't sleep."

"I slept a little," I lie.

"Well, make sure you sleep tonight. I won't accept sleep deprivation as an excuse for being rude to your customers tomorrow. I'll be checking the reviews," she says, patting me on the shoulder and floating out the way she came.

I carry the box back into the dining room and open it. Inside are the printed stamp cards. Each one is perfectly aligned, with thick paper and the Fraser Falls logo Clara embossed in gold on the cover. The inside features a map of Main Street, a space for each business, and a checklist of festive challenges like "compliment a barista" and "post a picture and hashtag Fraser Falls."

She thought of everything. Flo is going to be talking about this for years. I'm so screwed.

Back at the table, Tommy's whispering something into Dove's ear that I already know I won't want to hear.

"Don't," I say, pointing at him.

"What?" Tommy grins. "I was only saying I think I believe in love now. Or maybe witchcraft. Hard to tell."

"You're a total d—" My eyes move across the table to Sailor, who's working hard. "Doofus."

Dove tilts her head. "Do you think Clara knows what she's doing to you?"

I drag my hand down my face and drop myself back into my chair. "She's not *doing* anything to me."

They say "Hmm" at the same time and I want to scream.

I ignore my friends and focus my attention on the task at hand. "Do you think a heart with S-B-S in the center is okay for the welcome table?"

"Yeah," Sailor says. The only helpful person at a table full of adults is the child. "But make sure you don't write *Clara* in the heart, Uncle Jack."

I take that back.

• • •

Sailor presses the final rubber stamp block into the ink and tests it on her piece of paper.

I pull thirty dollars out of my pocket and put it on the table in front of her. I don't know what the going rate is for children in the workforce but I'm just happy I could talk her down from the fifty that she asked for.

We'd settled at twenty but she stood up to shake my hand (to seal our deal, like a real negotiator) and I told her she looked like the Fraser Falls bear mascot in her overalls. She stormed off and I got a lecture from Dove about self-esteem in young girls. Took an extra ten dollars to coax her out of her bedroom to start carving.

"Well done, kid. You've done me proud today." She really has.

"What do people win if they get all the stamps?" she asks, tucking her money into her overalls.

"A crown," Dove says. "And a free drink at Uncle Tommy's bar."

"No cash?" she says, looking disappointed.

Dove raises an eyebrow. "Go check on the goats before you start getting up to mischief, please."

She skips out of the room humming to herself.

"She's a good kid," I tell Dove.

"She is, and you're so good with her. You should definitely settle down with a nice woman and have one of your own."

"Don't you ever get tired of your own voice?" I ask her, throwing a piece of carved rubber at her when she shakes her head.

"I like Clara. There. I said it," Dove says, like I somehow forced the information out of her. "I know I'm not supposed to because her family business is an endless list of all the things I'm against, but I can't help it. She's kind and she's sweet and she's trying *really* hard. I've never tried this hard at anything."

"I know she is." I pull the rubber scraps into tiny pieces. "Not going to keep her here though."

Dove picks up the piece I threw at her and throws it onto the pile in front of me. "No, but it's nice to pretend."

Tommy comes back and the topic changes to work and family and town gossip that Dove acquires at an unfathomable rate. I listen and laugh and contribute, but deep down, I'm questioning how much longer I'm going to have to pretend with Clara.

Chapter 24

CLARA

Small Business Saturday is the kind of event that I should've trained for the way people train for marathons.

There's little evidence of this week's storm as I walk up Main Street. Every twinkling light is exactly where it should be, the sidewalks are clear of snow, and there's zero proof that any branches even snapped from the trees. There's a bitter wind whipping through but the energy is high, with every store open and ready.

Fraser Falls looks perfect for the visitors it's expecting to travel here today.

Arthur was in good spirits when I stopped by his welcome stand to pick up my stamp book. When I bought a Fraser Falls SBS T-shirt he gave me my first stamp. A little red heart with SBS in the center. He told me the town hall parking lot was already full of visitors.

My first stop is Flo's Fancies to place a delivery order for my mom. I told her about Flo's macarons the first week I was here, and I've been patiently waiting for Flo's one delivery day of the year to be able to ship two dozen. Flo doesn't mention that the booklets look amazing after I went to a special print shop to have them done professionally. Which obviously makes me all the more desperate for some kind of praise.

She takes the book from my outstretched hand and stamps it, handing it back. I squint at the drying brown ink. Why does the Flo's Fancies stamp look like a sausage?

Flo sighs. "Jack tells me it's a chocolate éclair."

"Of course, it looks exactly like one."

Neither her eyebrows nor forehead moves but I can still tell she's scowling at me. "Lying isn't an attractive trait, Clara. It looks like a sausage. Now, on you go, you're holding up my line."

She's right, I am, and it feels damn good. Normally in the morning when I go to Bliss to grab a coffee, or if she's in the bakery, I'll find a reason to lock her into an overly polite conversation with me for at least a few minutes. Today there's a line of people behind me, stamp books in hand, waiting. "Have a great day, Ms. Flo," I say before heading next door to Bliss.

Small Business Saturday is always the day after Black Friday. It was started with the intention to encourage people to shop locally when they're being bombarded with offers and discounts from big retailers. I'll never forget the one year a marketing blast was scheduled on the wrong day and Davenport got dragged to hell online for trying to steal focus.

I intend to do all of my Christmas shopping in town today because if I get all my stamps, I'll get a free drink of my choosing at the Hungry Fox and a crown.

Two things I've just learned are very important to me. The fact that I'm competitive is something I knew, but I didn't realize it applied to stamp books.

Maybe I should take up tennis.

It's nice, albeit a little strange, seeing so many people on the pavement when I leave Bliss, coffee tray in hand. I have to look both ways before crossing the street, something usually not required due to the distinct lack of cars.

Harry's is full of people and I can picture Jack being both happy and pissed about it. He wants Fraser Falls to thrive as much as anyone, but he also strongly dislikes the customer service side of being a business owner.

Joe, Jack's weekend guy and nutcracker stealer, is behind the register as I walk through the door. He gets a little whiter. I always thought I'd be one of those cool grown-ups but apparently not. I'm a narc. Nancy, Jack's weekday worker, is talking to a customer over by the candleholders.

"I bought you and Nancy a coffee," I say as cool adult-y as possible, lifting two cups from the tray and putting them on the counter in front of him.

He looks between me and the drink. "Uh, thanks. But my mom doesn't let me drink coffee. She says it makes me hyperactive and a pain in her ass."

"Got it, sorry. Is Jack around?" He gestures toward the workshop door with his head. "He hiding from customers?"

"Yeah. He always does when it's busy."

I reposition my hand on the tray to keep the drinks balanced and knock on the workshop door. I can't hear any machines running. I push it open and Jack's sitting with his feet crossed on a table, throwing a tennis ball into the air.

"Do you ever work?" I ask playfully, closing the door behind me.

I hand him his coffee and resist the urge to bend down and kiss him. "I'm resting because I've done so much work already. It's terrifying how productive I've been."

"I'm so proud of you. Suspicious, but proud."

"You here to get your stamp?" he asks, dropping his feet to the floor. I lean against the table in front of him, my feet filling the gap between his. He leans forward, hands angled outward like he's going to grip the back of my thighs. He doesn't; he stops suddenly, runs his hands through his hair, and leans back.

Nice to know it isn't just me.

"No, I'm saving you until last. Just wanted to bring you coffee." I dig my stamp book out of my pocket and point to my Flo's Fancies stamp. "Can you explain this sausage to me?"

Jack nearly chokes on his coffee. "Dove did it. I think she did it on purpose to wind Flo up."

It's enough explanation for me. I pluck my own coffee from the tray and put my book back in my pocket. "I'm going back to my quest. Stop avoiding your customers."

Busted. He hides his smirk behind his hand. "I'll stop avoiding them when you come back later."

Joe looks confused by the smile I'm fighting as I walk through the store toward the exit onto Main Street. When I'm outside I study the map for businesses I don't usually frequent in town. As the person who designed the stamp book, I really should've come prepared with a route.

Wilde & Winslet is my next target, and it's the first time I'm seeing Mel and Winnie in person after my mom called them on Wednesday. After I sent through the link to their portfolio she accidentally sent me back an emoji with sunglasses and then a thumbs-up.

Winnie is the first to spot me and squeezes me in the tightest hug. "Thank you, thank you, thank you."

Someone, who I assume, and hope, is Melissa, joins and hugs me from behind. "Don't thank me too much, you haven't worked with my mom yet. Her social status is her pride and joy. Losing their event florist weeks out pushed her to the closest thing to stressed I've seen in twenty years. I didn't even know her face could still be that expressive."

"Your mom is great!" Winnie says, letting me go. Melissa doesn't let go straightaway, which is good because the shock of what Winnie just said nearly makes me fall on the floor.

I love my mom, but I accept her for who she is and find humor in her quirks where some other people might find despair. She can be notoriously hard to please, especially when it comes to things through which she'll be perceived by others. It's always been a funny contrast to have a mother who offers her unconditional support and belief regardless of what it might relate to but is prepared to disown you over wearing an ugly skirt in front of her friends.

"She sent over the most detailed outline I've ever seen yesterday. We printed it out. It's basically a short story. She honestly couldn't have made it easier for us, especially on such limited notice," Winnie says.

"We were honest about struggling to get certain things from our suppliers with only a couple of weeks to go and she emailed straight back with suitable substitutes. Your mom rocks, Clara," Mel says, slowly detaching herself from me.

"I think I'm having an aneurysm. I once heard a caterer call her the Wicked Witch of the West Village. Anyway, I'm so happy it worked out for you guys! I'm going to celebrate your win by buying everyone I know a candle."

Winnie laughs. "Got your stamp book?"

The girls make all their own candles, and my temporary home at Maggie's already has a couple laying around. Thankfully, Honor *loves* candles, which makes her the easiest person to buy for. I choose a few from the brand-new Christmas line just out today, and a few of the bouquet collection. The stamp is a simple flower with W & W underneath and pink ink.

We, meaning Dove and I, made the executive decision to leave the hairdressers out of the stamp book, so I walked straight past their store, as well as the ice cream parlor, on my way to Wilde & Winslet. The Frozen Spoon is focusing on hot chocolate today and my plan is to hit them on the way back to Jack's.

The Green Light bookstore is next in my race to be the first person with a complete book. "Afternoon, Clara," Miss Celia says when I walk through the door.

"Hi, Miss Celia. How are you today?" There are visitors in earmuffs and matching black puffer jackets browsing the sci-fi section. She's perched on a step stool near them, but not too close.

"Can't complain. I've been busy preparing for our event." I love the way she calls it "our event" when all I did was connect her with the right people. It makes me feel part of something. Part of here, a desire that seems to increase every passing day. "Are you here to shop or chat?"

"I'm doing my Christmas shopping. Do you have any book recommendations for five-year-olds? And any books about dinosaurs."

Miss Celia stands up straight, throws her braid to her back, and storms off like a woman on a mission. I follow behind her like a puppy. "Is the dinosaur book also for the five-year-old?"

"He has the maturity of a five-year-old, but no, he's almost thirty."

It's incredible how Miss Celia is able to walk me through nearly every book on the shelves. She explained she only buys stock that she'd 100 percent recommend to her customers, and that makes it easy to recall.

After buying a stack of books for Paloma, two dinosaur books for Max, and a business mindset book for my dad, I get my next stamp. A green book.

Miss Celia fills me in on all things Matilda Brown until a dozen teenage girls come in looking for special editions.

I dodge strollers and dogs and cars until I safely end up at the part of Main Street that I never venture to. I end up buying more chocolate and fudge than any one woman needs, as well as jewelry for Honor, a stress ball for Sahara, a crocheted hat and scarf for Honor's dad, and a crocheted strawberry backpack for Paloma. And those are just the things I remember.

The amount of bags and stamps I now have tells me I bought so, so much more.

The air smells like fried food as I approach the gazebo on my way back to Maggie's to drop my collection of bags off. I thought I couldn't like this town any more; I was wrong. The taco stand on the other side of the gazebo is practically calling out my name.

"Clara!"

It takes a second to work out if I'm hallucinating being shouted at by food, but I quickly realize it's Flo. "Everything is looking great, Ms. Flo. It's so busy!"

A compliment feels like the right place to begin this conversation after she kicked me out of her line earlier. "Clara, look, do you think we have enough seating?"

I scan the area around the gazebo; multiple people are eating from the food trucks on benches and there are still some spare spaces. Large trash cans have been placed a foot behind the seating, close enough to be accessible but not too close to be off-putting. I've attended corporate barbecues without this much attention to detail.

"I think you have enough. Why?"

It's the first time I've seen Flo look truly stressed. "If we have a repeat complaint people will think we don't listen to feedback."

She makes a fair point. "How about you take the picnic tables from the tavern's deck? People probably won't want to drink outside in this weather, but they will sit and eat a taco or two. I do think it'll be okay. People don't mind eating street food standing up generally."

"Maybe in New York City, but we like to offer our visitors an element of comfort." That puts me in my place. "But the picnic tables were a nice idea. Thank you, Clara."

She's gone before I can say *You're welcome*. I study the map and aside from Harry's, I only have the antique store and the Frozen Spoon left on my list.

The B & B is full this weekend for the first time this year. Maggie is being hypervigilant that everyone is taken care of, so I walk the longer way to my personal entrance to avoid being accosted in the hallway.

The antique store is a little outside my normal safe zone around town; it's on the road past the tavern heading toward the Christmas tree farm. I lost track of who I bought what for around five stamps ago, but I'm committed and also financially irresponsible.

Leaving the bags at the B & B makes me feel lighter as I start my walk. I put my headphones in beneath the earmuffs I bought somewhere between books and tacos and keep my head down as I weave through the visitors flooding the streets.

The Christmas tree lighting will happen tonight around 8 p.m. I did kick myself for not thinking ahead when I arrived and offering to find a minor celebrity to do the honors, but I've been pretty busy being unescapably helpful.

It's starting to get dark as I reach the door of the antique shop a short time later. The second I walk in I spot a vintage butterfly brooch that my mom will love. This store is probably the busiest place in Fraser Falls right now and I have to fight my way to the cash register.

The room is thick with the smell of too many people and that musk that comes with old belongings. I'm relieved to be out of there. I squint at my stamp, then shine my phone on it to make it brighter. I have no idea what it's supposed to be. It doesn't look like anything other than a black blob. I make a mental note to take it up with Jack later.

After I wait in line for thirty minutes for a hot chocolate overflowing with marshmallows and cream, there's a yellow ice cream stamp in my book.

There was a little girl in front of me in line clutching a stamp book between her mittened hands when something terrible happened: I realized that it would be unfair for me to get a crown as the creator of the book.

I must have been high on stamp-based adrenaline not to see it before now. The fact I even know the prize is a crown is based on insider information. Which means I also know there's only a limited number due to everything being arranged on such short notice.

I feel like the Grinch at the end of the movie where he has his realization and his heart starts growing. I can't take a crown from an adorably tiny mittened child. God, I hate having a conscience sometimes.

I practically stomp across the street to Harry's, careful not to tip my decadent drink onto two women debating whether to buy a Holly doll near the doorway. "You should get it," I say as I pass them. "It's worth the money."

Jack is unsurprisingly still in his workshop, this time bent over a large dining table inspecting something instead of sitting with his feet on it.

I sigh loudly. I wish that were me.

"I'm annoyed," I announce when the workshop door closes behind me.

"I really need to start locking that thing," he says, standing straight. "What's got you all worked up?"

"I can't get the crown," I announce, possibly dramatically.

His bottom lip pouts out a little. See, I knew he could pout. I know he's teasing me. "Why not, princess?"

I hate how *not* mad I am about being called princess. "It isn't ethical. I was involved in the process. I shouldn't take it from someone else."

"But you bought all that stuff," he says, telling me exactly what I want to hear. "It shouldn't matter that you're involved."

I want to agree but there's something stopping me. Morals or something ridiculous. This definitely isn't a Davenport trait. I picked this up from school or summer camp or somewhere. "I can't do it. I'm sad."

"What can I do to make you not sad?" There are a lot of things. Many of them are the reason I'm still standing by the door, far away from Jack. "Do you want to go to the tree lighting? I'll buy you tacos. Will that make you not sad?"

I nod. "I'll meet you on the sidewalk in front of Maggie's at seven forty-five? I'm heading to the town hall to help Dove with toy drive donations people have been dropping off all day."

"Sure thing. I'll meet you outside Maggie's. Remember to get your stamp. You can't leave your book unfinished, even if you don't get the prize."

Chapter 25

CLARA

When Jack shows up, I'm going to whack him with the candleholders I bought from Harry's earlier.

It's 7:57 and he's late.

Given how close together everything in Fraser Falls is, I can see the Christmas tree from where I'm standing outside Maggie's. It's installed in front of the town hall and is a lot bigger than I was anticipating. I don't know how I've been walking past it oblivious. Don't get me wrong, it's not the Rockefeller tree, but what is?

Dove told me they were so worried about the storm at the start of the week that they didn't think they'd be able to get it ready in time. Arthur apparently suggested a hologram tree but wasn't sure where to source the equipment. *Apparently*, he said, "Ask Clara, she'll know," and I almost combusted with joy when Dove told me.

She then told me to "get a life." While she is totally right, it just showed that I'm starting to gain people's trust, per my closet plan. Even if every time I pull something out of there there's a sticky note attached to it.

I check my phone again for the time, then send Jack another five question marks to go along with my other messages asking where he is. The bubble appears on his side of the chat but disappears again. Then I spot him, weaving through the crowd at a light jog.

I fold my arms over my chest, unimpressed. I can hear the muffled garble of Arthur on a microphone near the town hall followed by the loud, synchronized counting down from ten from the sizable crowd gathered near the tree.

They all collectively chant *three* as Jack reaches me. "You're late, Kelly!"

"I know, I'm sorry. I had to get something." *Two.*

"What couldn't wait fifteen minutes?" *One.*

"This." The tree lights in reds and golds to the sound of applause as Jack lowers a small plastic crown onto my head.

"Congrats on completing your Small Business Saturday stamp book," he says proudly. His hands drop from the crown to my shoulders, squeezing. My hands cover his, my fingers interweaving momentarily before I readjust the crown, liking how it feels.

"But I can't get the prize. It's unethical."

"It isn't. I found it in the art school basement. You deserve to win something for all your hard work, Clara." My words stick in my throat. Knowing what a hellscape the art school basement is after venturing down there looking for a fresh paintbrush during nativity preparations, I know what it took for Jack to do this for me. There's a warm, comforting feeling blooming in the center of my chest when his hands run down my arms. "And I'm going to buy you that drink at the tavern."

Visitors and residents are everywhere, and we said that it wouldn't happen again, but the desire to grip the front of Jack's coat and pull his mouth to mine is fiercer than ever. "This isn't going to help your reputation as a kleptomaniac," I say slowly. Jack's laugh bellows against the noise of traffic and people. "Thank you. This is the sweetest thing anyone's ever done for me."

I wrap my arms around his waist and press my cheek into his

chest. One of his arms covers my shoulder, the other holding the back of my head. I look up as he looks down, our lips inches apart. It would be so easy . . . but we said we wouldn't. I take a step back, freeing myself from him. "I guess I can forgive you for being late."

Jack's eyes are brooding with something as he rubs his hand against his growing stubble. "I'm sorry I was late. It's a mess down there." Jack checks out the tree. "You want a closer look?"

"Mm-hmm."

"Come on," he says gently, throwing his arm across my shoulders.

Jack tells me about his productive day caused by avoiding customers. I give him a rundown of my food truck thoughts. It's an unremarkable conversation and yet I feel like I'm glowing from the inside out. When we're thirty yards away from the tree I hear my name called.

Flo is speed-walking toward us with a clipboard. Jack groans quietly but I'm immediately excited. I guess his is the normal reaction to potentially being assigned tasks on a Saturday night. I would *love* to be tasked with something by Flo.

"Hi, Ms. Flo," I say cheerfully as she reaches us.

Her eyes immediately go to Jack's arm on my shoulder. He drops it as I subtly shake it off. She clears her throat. "Clara." She says my name like she's holding the worst news of my life. It's more than a little alarming. "I just wanted to tell you." *That someone has died?* "That your stamp book idea was excellent. Everyone is reporting record-high sales. All in all, it's a roaring success. So, thank you."

It takes real effort to stop my jaw from literally dropping. My words are lodged behind a lump in my throat for the second time. "Yeah, I had a great day," Jack says, buying me some time.

"Hmm, don't think I don't know you haven't been seen all day, Jack Kelly," Flo snaps.

"Thank you, Ms. Flo," I eventually manage to choke out. "I'm glad it helped."

"Enjoy your evening."

I watch her walk away in a daze. I'm going to be chasing this high for the rest of my life. Jack takes one look at my lovestruck face and bursts out laughing again. It drags me from my mental fairy tale where I'm Flo's right-hand woman and we run this town together like a well-oiled machine.

"Let's get you to the tavern before you start chasing after her like a puppy," Jack says softly, nudging me out of my minor Flo-related trance.

JACK DOESN'T LET ME TAKE my crown off even though the tavern is full of people.

It's so busy that he ends up helping Tommy behind the bar, something he did when Tommy first opened and didn't have money to pay for another pair of hands. The irony that Jack spent the day avoiding his own customers to end up dealing with someone else's isn't lost on me. Or him, as he confirms when he finishes up for the night.

The streets are a lot quieter now that it's late. "It's going to snow," Jack says, angling his face toward the sky.

"Oh my God, are you one of those people who can *smell* when snow is coming? That's so cool." He holds out his phone; the weather app notification is right at the top. "You could've just lied to me. I would've believed you."

"I'll keep that in mind. So, do you like your crown? Was it worth maxing out your credit card for?"

I can't help but smile as I nod, careful not to tip it off my head. "I do. I haven't been given a crown since college."

"College?" he asks, confused. "What were you doing to get a crown in college?"

"I won a wet T-shirt contest in Miami during spring break."

"Great." He rubs at his temple, shaking his head. "Congratulations. Have you recovered yet?"

"From the wet T-shirt contest?"

"From Flo, Clara."

"Oh. No. She thanked me," I say. We're approaching my door, it's the end of the night, and I'm *still* in shock. "My idea helped. I actually did something to help."

"Why do you underestimate yourself? You've been helping since you got here."

We come to a slow stop just outside my front door. "I owe you a thank-you. For vocalizing your support to Flo, for working your ass off to finish the stamps, for believing in the idea. So thank you, Jack."

"I already told you, Clara. You're capable of anything you put your mind to. I'd back you every time."

That glowing feeling in my chest gets a little brighter. "I guess this is good night."

"I guess it is." The air between us is heavy. I flex my fingers, will myself to head to the door, but I can't move. Jack's eyes burn into mine so intensely that it's hard to breathe. It's like I can hear the threads of restraint holding us back from each other quietly pop as they snap.

Jack's mouth crashes into mine, his lips hot and bruising. My back hits the wall beside the door and his body presses into me. My hands pull at his hair, trying to get him closer somehow. He grips my hips, squeezing tight. This wasn't supposed to happen again, but I can't find it in me to care. Or stop.

His tongue slips into my mouth and the moan I can't hold back seems to snap him out of it. He stops, resting his forehead against mine as we try to catch our breaths.

"This isn't very one-time-thing of us," I murmur quietly, even though we're the only people around.

"I know. I should probably go back to my own house and my

own bed." His nose brushes mine gently. "It isn't the same without you in it."

"You definitely shouldn't come inside." I peck a kiss to his swollen lips. "That wouldn't be good."

"Definitely not."

"Unless," I say, my breath catching as he kisses my jaw.

"Unless," he repeats.

"Unless we just don't overthink it. One time doesn't need to be literal, right? It could be an umbrella term for a collection of times." Jack sucks beneath my ear and my legs shake. "One could be for my one visit to Fraser Falls. Casual. Super casual and string-free."

"Is that a smart idea?" he asks into my neck, giving no indication that he cares. His hand slips beneath my sweater, his cold hand up my spine spreading goose bumps across my body. My hands cling to his muscular shoulders as I try to stay upright.

His free hand squeezes my ass and travels down the back of my thigh. "Doesn't have to be smart to be good."

To my surprise, Jack frees himself and takes a cautious step backward. His eyes travel over every inch of me, but he says nothing. I wait to hear him be the voice of reason. Remind me I'm going to leave, that we said one time and we should mean it, that nothing good will come from being impulsive and reckless.

I watch his shoulder move as he takes a deep breath and I mentally prepare for the smile and nod I'll give him when I tell him he's right.

"Fuck it."

He's back on me instantly, his mouth more brutal and impatient than before. My fingers shake as they dig through my purse for my keys. Jack waits behind me, his body pressed to mine as he sweeps my hair to one side away from my neck and plants kisses there. I finally get the key in the door and we practically fall through it.

It's a battle of who can get the other person's clothes off quicker and my crown is a victim in the chaos. By the time we reach my bedroom he's down to jeans and I have my skirt and tights. "You're so beautiful, Clara," he whispers into the dim light of my bedroom, kneeling in front of me. "I can't stop thinking about you."

His fingers deftly work the zipper of my miniskirt and it falls to the floor. His hands move to grip the waistband of my tights, pulling them down quickly to reveal . . . another pair of tights.

He looks up at me, perplexed. "Well, this hasn't happened to me before. Shittiest magic trick ever."

I cover my face while I ugly-laugh at the mixture of confusion and horror on his face. He removes the second (and last) pair just as quick as the first. I could explain to him the need for thermal tights in this climate, but it'll kill the mood, I fear.

"You next," I say. He stands and reaches for the button and zipper of his jeans. He doesn't need to try to be sexy when they drop to the floor. Everything about him is sexy. He kicks them to the side with his socks and leaves himself just in his boxers in front of me.

He tilts my chin up so I'm looking at him; his thumb drags across my bottom lip. "All I ever do is stare at this mouth."

I kiss his palm. "It does more than just talk back at you. I can show you."

"Later," he says, his voice rough. "Right now, I need to taste you."

Heat spreads across my chest all the way up to my cheeks. I've had a lot of guys try to sell me crypto before we slept together, but Jack Kelly is the first man to say *that* to me.

I shuffle back on the bed until I reach the pillows. Jack crouches at the end of the bed; I hear clothes rustling and the crinkle of foil. He throws the condoms down on the bed beside my knees and takes his place in front of my open legs. "You're confident," I muse, pushing the packets out of my space.

"Maybe, or just a man aching to be inside of you."

Jack's fingers skimming my skin as he pulls my panties down is a sensation I never thought I'd get to experience. He doesn't take his time and is on me like a starved man. His fingers grip my hips to stop me from wiggling away from the pressure.

The way he laughs a "Shhh" into my inner thigh is enough to remind me that the adjoining wall to the rest of the B & B isn't that thick and he's making me loud. There's red-hot pleasure licking its way up my body, lighting across my skin like firecrackers. Jack's fingers slide into me and I'm gone. My hips try to lift off the bed and when he resists, my thighs press against his ears. The wet sound of his mouth working against me is too much as the pleasure rolls through me in waves.

Jack looks pleased with himself when I eventually manage to force my eyes open again. He reaches for a condom, ripping the corner with his teeth. I push myself up, my shaking legs screaming as I try to control them.

"You're the hottest man I've ever seen," I tell him honestly.

He looks down at me, his face twisted somewhere between a smile and a frown. "Thanks."

He doesn't believe me. What part of him wakes up and looks at his broad shoulders and thick biceps and solid stomach and doesn't see what I can see? "I'm not kidding. You're *the* hottest man I—" He cuts me off with a kiss. He tastes like him.

He also tastes like me.

My hand reaches for the band of his underwear; he straightens up, lifting onto his knees, making it easier for me to pull them down. I stumble over my breath as his hard cock springs free from behind the fabric.

My eyes flick up to where he's watching me intensely, dark eyes following my every move as I slowly grip the base of him and circle my tongue around the tip.

The guttural, raspy groan of my name makes my core clench. I'm trying to keep my eyes on him but his head rolls back when I suck lightly on the head. It's a powerful feeling, to disarm a man of his senses so easily.

Shortly after the thought, Jack recovers and pulls himself out of my grip. He rolls the condom on while I unhook my bra, and finally, we're ready.

"I'm out of practice," I admit when Jack positions his body over mine and a sudden flood of nervous energy bursts in my stomach. It's like a dance that I've done several times but can't quite remember the steps to.

His eyebrows lift in surprise. "You're nervous?"

"Maybe a little." He doesn't lower his body onto mine yet.

"We d—"

"I want to." I really, *really* want to. "Butterflies are a good thing."

Jack kisses the corner of my mouth as he lines himself up between my legs. I take slow, steady breaths. "I promise I'll help you practice until you're not nervous anymore."

And then he slides himself home.

Jack's forehead presses into mine, our stomachs fighting for space as we each take deep, labored breaths. Adjusting to him is, well, an adjustment, and he hasn't started moving yet.

"Are you okay?" he whispers, trailing kisses down my jaw. "You feel so good, Clara."

I nod, finding any part of him I can nuzzle my face into as his hips retract and snap forward for the first time. One of his hands reaches back to grip under my thigh while the other pushes my hair out of my face. "I'm good."

He smiles before kissing me hard. The nervousness from a few moments ago disappears into the rhythm we've fallen into. My nails press into his solid back muscles. His fingers dig into my thighs. The tension builds and builds.

Our heavy breathing mingles in the dim light of my bedroom. "I'm almost there," I pant over the sound of his skin slapping against mine. It's delicious and fracturing, and now that it's happening, I can't believe we weren't going to let this happen.

"That's it, baby," he coos. "Show me how pretty you are when you come. You're so good at it, Clara. I love watching you."

A few weeks and this man has already guessed the way to get me off is to give me praise. Am I really that transparent?

I don't have time to give my question any consideration because Jack leans down and puts one of my nipples in his mouth. I wrap my legs around his waist and the change of angle heightens everything. "Oh, *fuck*," he says, going even deeper. "*Baby . . .*"

His movements lose their rhythm so I know without him telling me that he's close. I slip my hand between our bodies down to where we're joined. It only takes rubbing my swollen clit in rapid circles for me to finally climax. The heels of my feet push into the base of Jack's back, trying to keep him as deep as possible as I squeeze and pulse around him. "*Jack . . .*"

"Attagirl," he says, groaning. He's getting sloppy now, crazed hard thrusts that have the feeling of ecstasy building again. He kisses me until he breaks away to moan loudly as he comes. Jack twitches and shakes with his forehead against mine and his eyes shut tight.

He rolls off, keeping a hand on my ribs and pulling me toward him as soon as his body hits the mattress.

"That was . . . ," I start to say, not knowing where I'm heading.

"I know," he says back.

He kisses my cheek and my temple and lies beside me breathing steadily until he's forced to head to the bathroom to clean up. I go next and when we're both back in bed, beneath the covers this time, I finally realize there's an important question I haven't asked yet.

I push up onto my elbow. "Where's Elf?"

Jack rolls onto his back and holds out his arm for me to lie against his chest.

"Joe has him. He borrows him overnight sometimes when his

parents are out of town and it's just him and his older brother. His mom's afraid of dogs so they'll never get one. Elf loves it."

He kisses my head when I slide myself into the space he's created for me. "So . . . you can stay tonight?"

He nods. "I'm not going anywhere. We need to get rid of your nerves."

"Always so ready to fix everyone's problems," I tease.

"It'll be a struggle but I'll do it for you," Jack says playfully, leaning over to kiss my shoulder. "Clara?"

"Yeah?" I answer, quickly deciding there's no bad way for Jack to say my name.

"Why is there a gull on the ceiling?"

Chapter 26

CLARA

The ability of sticky notes to not do the one thing they're supposed to do needs to be studied.

Arthur peeled *Maggie* off my leggings this morning when I passed him on my way to Bliss for my morning indulgence. Okay, *morning* is a stretch. More like afternoon, because every time I tried to get up, I was pinned to the bed.

There apparently wasn't anything discreet about how Jack left out of my private door. Maggie called my name as I passed reception and asked me to remind Jack about his nativity fitting.

I stumbled over my words while she looked at me, unbothered. I was still reeling when Jack and I just happened to bump into each other in front of the gazebo and share a friendly, neighborly conversation on our walk to the same place that was a total coincidence.

I don't know whether it's a good thing or a bad thing that Arthur noticed the neon yellow nuisance near my ass before Jack did. Thanks for not objectifying me, I guess? But also, Arthur, I'm keeping my eye on you.

It's amazing how it can cling to flexible material on a moving human woman but it can't cling to the wall I stuck it to.

Jack and I talk in hushed volumes while we eat our lunch. I lean in close and his foot wedges between mine under the table, and I'm certain that we're in no way acting out of character or attracting attention. People who live here are known for minding their own business, right? That's what they say about close communities?

I play with the escapee note in my pocket on my way back to Maggie's. I tell Jack I have a very busy day of scheming ahead of the Santa run and he says okay. Seriously, no questions. Which makes me think the idea of me scheming is not a surprise to him.

The first thing I do when I get back, after putting my bedding in the washing machine, is return *Maggie* to its rightful home.

Sure enough, three neon-pink squares flutter to the floor like fall leaves. I scoop them up, trying not to scream at their insistence on testing my patience, and squint at the familiar scrawl of my own handwriting.

RAISE PROFILE
INCREASE VISITORS
SPEND MONEY

Not to sing my own praises *too* loud, but I feel like I'm on track. If anything I should probably add some more things to the wall, or just directly to my clothes and cut out the middleman.

I restick everything to the wall and close the door before I see them all fall back down and start an online hate campaign against the entire adhesive note industry. Everything else in this place hits the right side of the algorithm; there's no reason I can't have my own viral moment for something *I'm* passionate about.

I catch my reflection in the mirror next to the closet and I instantly decide, based on the slightly terrifying look in my eyes that I don't think I've seen before, I need to let it go. I think I might be getting too much unpolluted air.

I grab my laptop from the floor and rest it on my thighs, opening up my email inbox. There's a handful of toy drive responses that I forward to Dove, emails I'm cc'd on related to the Matilda Brown book event, three "we miss you" emails from food places I haven't been to recently, and the email chain I have with a regional news station trying to convince them to cover the Santa run.

To say they're vague and noncommittal is an understatement. It took asking multiple friends of friends and a shameless deep dive on LinkedIn to get this far.

Several stations just gave me a flat-out no. Others said they're only interested in talking about Davenport. But this one made the mistake of showing a slight bit of interest and asking for a better hook and now I play the role of relentless nightmare in their inbox.

I look at their last reply. A simple "Thanks, Clara. We'll get back to you."

Liars. I click reply, again, and quickly draft a polite but firm reminder that tomorrow is the only opportunity to cover the run as well as the toy drive. I press send and close my laptop, placing it on the duvet beside me.

My eyes wander toward my closet. Note frustrations aside, I should really do a thorough recap of my plan.

I slide off the bed onto the floor, open the doors, and practice deep breathing.

My first real action-setting progress here was something I realized because of Jack: people needed to like me to trust me.

Thanks to careful networking and my point-blank refusal to say no to anything that's come my way, I'm now on a first-name basis with the following key town figures:

Flo. Terrifying in a way that's inspirational. Could not want her approval more if I tried, and I will be attempting to emulate her fierce energy in every meeting going forward.

Maggie. Saintly but also extremely nosy. Seems to be everyone's aunt. Impossible to hide things from.

Dove. Sensational source of gossip. Strong supporter of women's wrongs. Opposite of an almond mom.

Winnie. Lawful good.

Mel. Chaotic neutral.

Tommy. Chaotic good.

Jack. Chaotic evil. Source: seduced me on multiple occasions.

I'm confident that these people like me and I'm hopefully moving into the trust category.

If all goes well with my mom and the flowers, I think I can cross Mel and Winnie off my list. Wilhelmina's nutcracker is another cross. Miss Celia is in progress, as is Dove's toy drive. The stamp books felt like a step toward crossing Flo off, but I know I still have a long way to go. If the news coverage happens tomorrow, I'll be even closer. Jack is still a question mark because I don't think sex makes the cut.

Mind-blowing, toe-curling sex, yes, but not enough to get him off the wall. I'll come back to him.

I stare at it for a bit longer, regretting my decision not to buy string, and dig the pad out of my bedside table with a Sharpie. I write *Tommy*, *Luke*, and *Arthur* on three separate sticky notes and add them to the bottom left.

Arthur needs someone to teach him how to use the newsletter website. Luke is a question mark of where to start because his website is one page but I don't really know the ins and outs of Christmas tree farming to take on the task myself.

I've been thinking about Tommy and his patio aspirations since the first town meeting, making notes here and there when inspiration hit. I have time today to start a presentation that will hopefully elevate his pitch in the eyes of his neighbors.

I know the goal is to have the videos taken down and get my promotion, but when I sit here and stare at my chaos closet, it doesn't feel like the important thing anymore. The people here do, and the skills and time I can offer to help them feel worth it.

Dare I say I feel appreciated?

I can be determined about two things at once: helping the town and getting my promotion. The problem is, one by default keeps me here, and the other takes me home.

It's obvious based on the unread work emails stacking up in my inbox and my delayed rescheduling of the check-in I missed when the power went out where my attention is. Sure, I've skimmed certain briefings and responded to a colleague or two asking for advice, but it's a stopgap until I can return to what's exciting me.

It's a balancing act to prevent my desire for one from outweighing the other.

A balancing act I'm not very good at, because right now, helping the town is the only thing I can focus on.

Chapter 27

CLARA

"Running?"

"That's what I said."

"Do you even know how to run?"

"Yes, Honor, I know how to run."

She hums like she doesn't quite believe me, which is fair, because I don't think I've run anywhere since gym class over a decade ago. "It's nice you're trying new things. I think the new thing you try should be getting laid, but I guess running will give you a high too."

In a surprising turn of events, I haven't told Honor about Jack. Mostly because she'll want an explanation of how it happened and I have no idea. One minute we're doing an *out of our system* thing, next we're naked in my bed. It's a mystery I shouldn't be expected to unravel.

Deep down, beyond the woman who last week said she only wants to be bent over, Honor is a huge romantic. Deep down, we both know that any kind of situation with Jack isn't going to last. His life is here and as much as I've said I wish I lived in Fraser Falls, I don't. So even if my smitten, tender heart doesn't want to admit it, I don't think a love story with Jack Kelly is in the stars for me.

"What an inspiring pep talk. Thanks, Hon! I gotta go get ready. Give Paloma a big cuddle from me when she gets home, please. And enjoy your sleep."

The Santa run is an annual tradition going back to the fifties. It started as a forfeit for a poker game between Miss Celia's dad and Dove's granddad, but after the town turned out to watch Mr. Pierce run a two-mile loop around town dressed in the traditional red and white Santa outfit, it became a formal event the following year.

The year after that they started taking a collection to support the toy drive.

It happens on the first of December, and unfortunately at 7 a.m. It wouldn't be safe or practical during the day and people have jobs to get to when December first falls on a weekday. The only bonus of this early wakeup is it meant I could entertain Honor on her drive home from her night shift while I got ready.

The start point is at the gazebo; from there you head down Main Street and turn left, to take the long way around up to the Christmas tree farm, past it and Dove's animal sanctuary, then back down the road with the antique shop past the tavern to the gazebo once again. It's totally flat and many people walk it, but I want to go back to bed afterward so my plan is to do it as quickly as possible and worry about my lungs later.

Maggie tells me organized running is everything she stands against when I ask her if she'd like to walk over together, which, honestly, is a belief I can get behind. It's still dark out as I walk down the front path, but my two layers underneath my Santa jacket and pants—kindly donated to me by Maggie from when her daughter used to participate—are succeeding in keeping me warm as I walk over to the check-in desk.

Behind the gazebo, I spot a news crew setting up cameras and microphones. "They came," I whisper to myself. I know people usually have a surge of adrenaline before a run, but I think this particular surge can be attributed to relief. A news story about Fraser Falls is *huge*. "Morning!" I say cheerfully when I reach the front of the line. I feel like I'm somewhere between cloud nine and tired enough that I could lie on the floor and go to sleep. There's an empty pop-up medical tent fifty yards away with what looks more like a spa massage table than a medical bed. I can definitely make it work with one of those foil blankets you see people with at the end of marathons.

"Morning," the sleepy-looking teenager at the desk says. "Here's your number. You don't need to wear it, it doesn't actually mean anything. Arthur said it makes it look official."

"Got it," I say, accepting—*Oh great*—number 1313 and handing over my donation money. Thirteen twice. The Taylor Swift fan in me is screaming. The slightly superstitious part of me is not. "Uh, thank you." There are a hell of a lot of people here I don't recognize, so I stand at the back of the crowd out of the way.

"Y'know, if you stand on the right edge of the crowd there's a shortcut up to Dove's and you can just wait there to rejoin the crowd when they run past."

Jack's all-black outfit screams Halloween but he pulls a Santa hat over his morning hair. "That sounds like you're encouraging me to cheat."

He takes a step closer and my breath hitches. "I'm encouraging you not to get a cramp at seven a.m."

"Are you trying to tell me I don't look like a high-performance athlete?" I ask.

"No, but I should tell you that your Santa pants are on backward."

I pull at the elastic waist of the red velour pants, grateful for the fleece leggings I'm wearing underneath, and immediately spot the label that's supposed to be at the back. "Trying to get me out of my pants, Kelly?"

Jack stuffs his hands into the pocket along the front of his hoodie.

"Not out here I'm not. Too many people. Unless you're into that kind of thing."

Heat rushes to my cheeks at the idea of the people around us getting a front-row seat to what has been a very strenuous weekend. Jack doesn't have neighbors on either side of his place so he made it his mission to see how loud he could make me scream.

Now would be a really great time to get my head in the game, or race, but all I can think about is last night. Jack's hands in my hair and on my waist. Him lowering me onto my back, the feel of his muscles under my fingers. His careful touches. The way he smells clean but like a *man*.

I'm so lost in my head I don't realize we're starting until the horn scares the shit out of me and Santas begin to rush past. I urge my feet to move but there's at least a three-second delay before my body falls in line.

The first thirty seconds are easy and I'm moving much faster than I expected. Maybe it's the adrenaline or maybe it's that spin class I did two months ago. Jack stands out in the crowd as the only person not in red and white.

"You're in my way," I say quietly as I pass down his left side and find the pocket of space between runners in front of him. I don't know how long has gone by—could be another thirty seconds, could be ten—but the little confidence I had begins to waver as my lungs sting with each intake of breath.

I'm approaching the turn off Main Street when my foot lands wrong on the road and my ankle crunches. "Shit, shit, shit, shit, ow." Every extra step I take to slow down, trying to move myself to the outside of the stream of runners, makes a searing-hot pain shoot through my ankle.

"Hey, I got you, come on." Jack supports me at my waist, lifting me to take the weight off my foot as I hobble to the start of the Main Street sidewalk. The runners swerve around us. Of all the embarrassing things I've done in my life, this might be top of the list.

Jack leans me against a wall and crouches to check out my foot. He holds my calf gently, inspecting my ankle from all angles. "How can you sprain your ankle running on flat ground?"

"You're awfully close to my foot to be being mean to me. If you think I won't kick you in the face, you're wrong."

"Go for it. It'll hurt you more than it'll hurt me." He places my foot back on the ground with a gentleness that doesn't match his sarcastic tone. "Let's get you back. Can you walk at all?"

I practice, instantly wanting to be sick from the pain. "Sure."

Jack shakes his head, pulling off the Santa hat when he remembers it's there. "Yeah, you're a really bad liar. I'm carrying you."

Normally, I'd fight, but right now I can't think of anything worse than having to walk back. Jack scoops me up with ease. "And you used to think I was an expert liar. Look how far we've come."

"Shut up, Clara," he groans, shaking his head. I want to kiss him. His lips pull into a smile when he glances at my face.

"I think it's pretty selfish that you're not offering to carry me around the route so I can get my medal." Annoying Jack is the most fun when he can't get away from me, is what I'm now learning. "Where's your team spirit?"

His brow furrows. "What are you talking about? There isn't a medal."

"Okay, my certificate then."

"What certificate? You don't get anything for finishing," he says.

"What the heck? Why do people do it then?"

It's funny feeling the laugh start in his chest being this close to him. It bubbles out of him. "Charity?"

"Oh, yeah." Kind of lost my eyes-on-the-prize there. "I love doing charitable things."

"Baby, if you want a medal I'll make you a damn medal. But I'm not carrying you two miles for no reason."

Him calling me baby outside of the bedroom melts me in a way I didn't think was possible. "I'll remember this massive lack of sportsmanship from you, Kelly."

"Okay." He sighs deeply. "Arms around my neck, please."

"Why? You need a cuddle?"

"I'll let you fall, Clara." Jack comes to a stop outside his store and his grip on my back starts to loosen. My arms shoot around his neck quickly, gripping him so tightly I'm looking over his shoulder at the few Santas walking.

The asshole laughs while he gets his keys out to unlock the door. I loosen what's a borderline chokehold and lean back so I can see his face. "You're not taking me to the medical tent?"

"Do you want to sit on Arthur's massage table that he brought from home? That probably hasn't been heavily bleached?"

I shake my head. "No, thank you." He locks the store door behind us. "I could try walking now."

"I'd rather not have you fall down on my business premises, thanks." He walks us through the workshop to the door to the staircase to his home. "I need you to wrap your legs around me. It's narrow and I don't want to hit your foot off the wall by accident."

"I've heard worse pickup lines." Another sigh to disguise his laugh. "You're grumpier in the morning."

"And you're more annoying, so I guess we're both different." Jack supports my back again and lets go of my legs. I wrap them around his waist easily. It feels smooth and well practiced, which after this weekend you could argue it is. Then I hear the one noise that could fix any injury, and all my recent sexual frustration melts away. "Hi, buddy!"

Elf jumps at Jack's legs and I try to lean back to stroke him, one hand still holding Jack's neck. "Okay, we're not doing this. You can pet him after! Your ankle is going to double in size."

He makes a fair point.

Jack lowers me onto the kitchen counter. My legs are still tight around his waist, hands linked at the back of his neck, finger twirling a tuft of hair. He puts his hands on either side of my thighs and leans in, his face inches from mine. "Are you allergic to any medications?"

My eyes flick to his lips. "Nope."

He nudges my chin up with his knuckle and my eyes are on his again, then he puts his hand back on the counter. "Concentrate, Clara. Have you eaten anything yet today?"

Why is he so close to me if he expects me to concentrate? "Toast."

"Good. I'm going to get you some painkillers and anti-inflammatories from the bathroom. Don't move."

"I can't promise that." Jack pins me with a look that has my ass staying where it's been told to stay. I forgot how seriously this man takes taking care of people. "I can promise that, actually, as it happens."

He kisses me gently and untangles himself from my grip. "I'll be right back."

"You should stay here until you can walk properly again."

I push onto my forearms. He's concentrating hard on rubbing my foot that isn't hurt instead of looking at me. "Is that your medical opinion, Doctor?"

"That's my opinion as someone worried about you taking care of yourself."

"You're quite sweet when you're not being a huge asshole, y'know."

Jack finally gives me his attention, and with it a coy smile. "That's what they tell me. So?"

"I don't have any stuff here." It's also a sure recipe for disaster when it's even harder to leave. "And you have a job. Not one that involves taking care of an adult woman who can definitely crawl around her own place if needed."

"But you don't need to crawl. At least if I'm downstairs and you fall over I'll hear the thud."

Charming. "It's already starting to feel better. Jack, seriously, I know you're so busy at work and you don't need me as a burden."

"You're not a burden. I like not coming home to an empty place, Clara. Let me look after you. Please."

This definitely isn't going to end well, right? As long as everyone is on the same page. "Fine, but you're going to need to take me to Maggie's when you finish work because there's no way I'm letting you fumble your way around my underwear drawer."

"Scared of what I'll find in there?" he asks, eyebrow raised.

"*You* should be scared of what you'd find in there."

"Now I'm really excited."

Chapter 28

JACK

When I went to work I gave Clara one rule: text me if you need something—don't get up from the couch, because you need to keep your foot elevated.

So obviously, I'm immediately pissed when I head upstairs to check on her and she's in my kitchen making hot chocolate from scratch.

She looks guilty as hell when she looks up from the chocolate she's chopping into smaller pieces.

"I can explain," she says slowly.

"And I'd love to hear it." She puts the knife down beside the chopping board, wipes her hands on a towel. "Start from the beginning, right when I told you to keep your ass on the couch."

I walk around the kitchen worktop to her side; she presses her back into the counter, looking up at me with big green eyes when I stop in front of her. I move the cutting board out of the way and grip her hips, lifting her onto the counter. Her legs wrap around my waist, arms around my neck. I breathe a little easier. "It honestly doesn't hurt that bad."

I follow the curve of her jawline with the backs of my fingers. "That's because your painkillers are working."

"Have you considered I just heal faster than the average human?" Clara leans in, her nose nudging mine gently. She smells so sweet and I want her so fucking bad. I squeeze her thighs and she scoots to the edge of the counter so her body is as close to mine as it can be. She kisses the corner of my mouth. "I promise I'm not as hurt as you think I am."

Tired of the teasing, I take her face in my hands and kiss her hard. Her being injured scratches at something inside of me that won't soothe itself. I've always been slightly anxious around sick people, but there's something about this that makes me want her in my line of sight.

I *need* this, to feel her real and breathing, and I think she does too. Her hands grip my hair, her breasts press into my chest. "This is not what bed rest looks like," I murmur into her throat, kissing from her collarbone to her ear.

"Take me to bed then, Jack," she says, her voice wispy.

"You're a nightmare patient," I whisper into her ear. I regain my senses. I don't want to hurt her by accident. "You need to keep your foot elevated."

"Why don't we compromise? I'll elevate it on your headboard."

Senses are gone again. I swallow hard. "*Fuck.* You're not making it easy for me to be a good guy."

"You started it. I just wanted to make a delicious festive drink." I press my forehead against her shoulder. She kisses the tip of my ear. It feels like a tap-out. "Okay, I'll behave."

I kiss Clara slowly this time; she hums happily. "Thank you."

Even though she groans in protest, she doesn't fight me off when I lift her off the counter and walk her to the couch. Maybe it's because her ass is in my hands and she thinks I'm taking her to my bedroom. "You're taking this doctor thing far too seriously. I *can* walk."

"I like holding you," I admit.

There's a span of quiet that stretches between us.

One that's broken with Dove shouting, "Sailor, knock!"

Sailor bursts through the door. Dove is behind her, hand immediately covering Sailor's eyes when she spots us in the middle of my living room. We quickly untangle; Clara's cheeks flush pink. She's quick to get herself on the couch, her foot propped up by cushions. Maybe she *isn't* as injured as I thought.

"Sorry, sorry, sorry," Dove chants, moving her hand from Sailor's eyes. "Sailor made you a get-well-soon card, Clara."

Sailor hands the card to her mom and rushes to Elf's couch, where he's been sleeping all day. She climbs onto it with him, something she's been doing since I brought him home when she was just a toddler.

Dove is giving me eyes that tell me she's going to give me hell later as she crosses the room toward Clara. Deserved, I'll admit. She hands the card to Clara and then looks back at me. "Shouldn't you be working?"

"Shouldn't you call before showing up uninvited?"

Dove checks Sailor isn't paying attention, then flips me off. She folds her arms across her chest. "So you don't want to hear about Flo being on the news tonight then?"

"Oh, I do!" Clara yells from the couch. She asked me to go across to Flo's and get an update but I got distracted by a couple who came in wanting a quote to restore a grandfather clock they bought at a yard sale.

Dove dives into her story. Clara practically beams light as Dove tells her about the segment they recorded talking about the Santa run, the toy drive, and our recent very successful Small Business Saturday event. They're going to air it on the 7 p.m. news *and* post an article about us online because the producer was so charmed by Flo. "Flo is on cloud nine. She's been looking for you, Clara."

Clara looks like she's about to dart off the couch and sprint across the street to Bliss. "You gotta rest your foot, ba—" I catch myself. "Basically. You basically gotta rest your foot, Clara."

They both look at me like I'm losing it, which I might be. "You all right over there?" Dove asks, a blue-tinted eyebrow raised. "We have toy drive stuff to discuss if you want to make yourself scarce."

"Perfect. I have work to do. Shout if you guys need anything."

Clara shoots me an apologetic look, but I know she wants to talk about town things with Dove. As time rolls on and Clara does more for Fraser Falls, it leaves me wondering what else could be left in her plan.

DESPITE OBVIOUS—AND WELCOME—DISTRACTIONS, TODAY HAS been one of the most productive days I've had in what feels like forever.

There's a knock at my door. Dove pokes her head through with Sailor's underneath. "We're heading home. Have a *nice* night." Dove winks and I'm glad she's leaving so I don't have to throw her out.

"Bye, Uncle Jack," Sailor says in a far less loaded tone than her mom.

"Bye, sweetheart. Thanks for coming over."

I lock up and make sure everywhere is clean for tomorrow. Things aren't as busy during the week compared to the weekend, but it's still busier than weekdays the rest of the year. Sometimes people take a few days' vacation to stay here during the week to try to get a better rate. It's mostly parents with kids on the weekend.

I don't know what I expect to find when I head upstairs. Clara cooking a three-course meal, probably. Her doing DIY, maybe. Definitely not what I do find, which is her asleep on the couch with her foot still on the pile of cushions.

She looks so peaceful. Long dark eyelashes, relaxed mouth, soft breaths. I throw a blanket over her and clear up the glasses and cookies left out.

Sunday is Italian night at Mr. Worldwide restaurant, so I put in an order for pizza. Elf curls up on the couch behind Clara's knees while I schedule the TV to record all the different channels' news broadcasts since Dove didn't say which it was.

I feel like a kid waiting for their parents to wake up on Christmas. It feels like every other second my eyes flit to the woman sleeping across from me to check if her eyes are still closed.

I complete the boring jobs like laundry and clearing expiring food out of the refrigerator. I collect up the pile of drawings Sailor did and tuck them in the drawer of the coffee table beside my own toy sketches. Finally, this time when I look over her eyes are open.

"Hey, sleepy." Clara leans against her elbow, looking around the room confused. There are pink lines on her cheek from where she's fallen asleep against her hand, and her hair is frizzy on the side she slept on. "Want some pizza?"

"I slept so hard I forgot that I let you kidnap me." She yawns into her hand and rolls her neck and shoulders to loosen up. "You made pizza?"

"I bought pizza."

Her eyes narrow. "From where?"

"From a takeout place? Where else would I buy fresh pizza?"

Her eyes open wide like I just threw a bucket of cold water over her head. "I've been here for weeks and I'm *just* finding out there's a pizza place? Where is it?"

"It's less of a pizza place and more of a world culinary experience. It's called Mr. Worldwide and it's a converted barn about a mile past Dove's place heading out of town. They do a different cuisine every day—Sunday is Italian night."

"I saw that place on the map!" she says enthusiastically. "I didn't look at what it was. I can't believe I've been missing out all this time."

"How's your foot?" She lifts it in the air, wiggling it slightly as if to demonstrate her perfect health. "Wow, so much movement."

"Sarcasm is the lowest form of wit, Jack Kelly," she muses. "It's not that bad. A little stiff but I can walk on it. Which means I can totally get out of your hair and head back to Maggie's."

I don't know why the idea of her leaving sucks so bad. "There isn't pizza at Maggie's . . . or pets. You don't have a car to drive over to Mr. Worldwide to get your own pizza, so I think the most sensible thing for you to do is stay here."

"Are you bribing me with pizza and your dog?" she asks, her voice light.

"I dunno. Is it working?" I really want it to be working.

"Absolutely. I wouldn't be hard to kidnap with the right set of circumstances."

I laugh as I stand to grab the pizza boxes from the table. "I'll keep that in mind."

"It was nice of Dove and Sailor to visit, right?" she says, but it sounds more like a question.

"Yes. Dove clearly likes you a lot."

It's the most coy I've seen Clara, who usually oozes confidence. Her cheeks are flushed from her nap but I think there's a small part that can be attributed to making a friend.

"Where's this pizza you trapped me here with?"

THE TOWN NEWSLETTER ARRIVES AT six thirty, letting us know where to find Flo on TV tonight. Clara literally bounces up and down in her seat beside me.

Clara clearly hasn't considered, like I have, that Flo might have used her fifteen minutes to bash Davenport again. I'm surprised there hasn't been another video after the original ones had a great impact on visitor numbers over the weekend.

I'm not against Davenport bashing and I never will be. But I am against Clara being upset and that puts me in a pretty tricky position.

"Hey, why don't we save it and watch it with Flo tomorrow so she can see our live reactions? We could put a movie on."

Clara twists to look at me, her eyebrows pinched together. "Are you serious?"

Serious that I want Tommy to watch it first and tell me if there's anything that might upset Clara, yeah. "She'd love it. She loves theatrics, and if she gets to watch us gasp and cheer knowing we're watching for the first time, she'll be overjoyed."

She sucks her bottom lip into her mouth and bites it. She thinks on it so long I start to sweat a little. "You know her better than I do, if you think she'll like that, then sure, I guess. What movie do you want to watch?"

I rub at the back of my neck. "You choose."

"*The Polar Express*?"

"The creepiest Christmas movie. Perfect."

Five minutes into the movie and my alarm goes off, telling me to get Clara more painkillers. She argues she's not even in pain anymore. I argue that it's because the medication is working.

Ten minutes later, she's asleep against my shoulder and there's something in my gut telling me to enjoy it while I have it, because I won't have it for much longer.

Chapter 29

CLARA

I think I might get minor running injuries more often.

It turns out after a decade of singleness and self-sufficiency, I really like being taken care of. Especially when I'm not *truly* suffering.

Honor saw the picture I sent of my slightly swollen ankle and responded with a voice note telling me to grow up because I asked if I should head to the emergency room. Having a best friend who's a nurse is both a curse and a blessing.

Thankfully, Jack doesn't have Honor's bedside manner. His face is buried between my neck and hair; his left arm is tucked under my head and crosses my chest, his hand resting over my rib cage under my right breast. His right hand is gripping the front of my right thigh, his right leg pushed through mine.

Every attempt to free myself from the tangled mess we've gotten ourselves into is useless. His lips touch my neck; his fingers dance up my thigh with devastatingly light touches. My back curves from the sensation of his mouth on my sensitive skin; his hips push into my ass. His deep moan rumbles next to my ear.

"Good morning," he murmurs.

"Good morning," I repeat.

"I can shoot over to Maggie's to get your things," he says, kissing along the top of my shoulder. "Brave your dresser to get you something clean to wear. I don't open the store until ten on Tuesdays because I have deliveries and pickup at nine."

"I'm going with you. You can't be trusted."

I don't need to see him to tell that he looks guilty right now. "Correct. Want to go now and get breakfast on the way back?"

"We could watch the news broadcast with Flo at Bliss!"

After living alone for so long it feels strange to start my morning with someone else. Five minutes of saying we're getting out of bed and pulling the other person back in if they made attempts to get up later, we're heading to Maggie's.

I can get used to coexisting in the mornings with a man, but I will never get used to going commando. With yesterday's Santa outfit and panties stuffed into a tote bag provided by Jack, I'm trying to not be grossed out by the feeling of my bare ass on my fleece leggings. "Why is your face like that?"

"Bad genetics," I answer, trying to stop the leggings from riding up when I walk.

Jack rolls his eyes. "The grimace, Clara."

"I'm not wearing any panties and the fleece is causing a bit of a sensory nightmare. Can we go?" I steal the coffee mug out of his hand and take a sip, earning a tut. He removes it from my hand and puts it on the table, grabbing his keys and ushering me toward the door.

"I'm going to take you the back way."

I frown at him over my shoulder. "At least buy me dinner first."

"Unbelievable," he says, but I can tell he's trying not to smile. "I'm going to take you the back way to Maggie's, so you don't have to do this walk you're doing in front of the other guests."

I can't exactly see what kind of walk I'm doing, but I can feel it. "I'm blaming my ankle."

"Your ankle is clearly fine today," he admits as we climb into his truck. "It's the fur up your ass that's the problem."

"So you admit there's nothing wrong with me and you just want me at your place?"

He nods. "There are plenty of things wrong with you, fashion choices for starters, but I think your foot is all right."

THE TEXT I SENT TO Jack asking if he needs anything still shows as delivered, not read. Even though I'm probably going to be lectured, I go downstairs anyway, knocking on the door when I don't hear any machines.

Jack is sitting in front of his laptop with his head in his hands. "Hey," I say cautiously as I approach him. "What's wrong?"

Please don't let the answer be Davenport.

"Nothing. I just don't know how to run a business." I pull up a chair beside him. "And it's letting everybody down."

"What are you talking about?"

Jack chews the inside of his cheek; his lips part. "It's okay. It'll be fine. I'm just behind on my Holly orders and I got a load more last night, presumably because of Flo mentioning them on air."

We didn't end up watching the broadcast with Flo. When we suggested it at Bliss this morning, she said no because she was busy. So we watched it together at Jack's place, and both laughed when Flo managed to get the topic onto the Holly doll. She's quite the marketer. "Okay, well, you have time. You can—"

"I forgot to change the shipping timeline. People are expecting their dolls before December twenty-third."

That's not ideal but not impossible to fix. "Do you have the stock to complete the orders before the twenty-third?"

"Over half. Maybe three-quarters. My supplier can do a rush

order for me that'll come in two weeks, but I don't think I'll have the boxes. Melissa and Winnie handle it and I don't think they're expecting another delivery this month."

"Jack, I'm so serious when I say this doesn't mean you're letting people down. It's a little complication in your day. We *can* fix it and we will. Give me a minute to think through the options."

Part of me expects him to tell me to mind my business, but Jack watches me closely. "Option one: we work out exactly how many orders you can fulfill, and we email everyone after that number to say that there's been an error and you won't be able to get them their order before the agreed date.

"The positive is you know you have the stock, everything just has to be assembled and then shipped, which I can help you with. The negative is you might receive bad reviews from disgruntled customers. Something to consider is that not everyone will be celebrating a holiday and some customers could agree to a delayed shipment for either a discount or maybe an added gift."

"I don't even care about reviews anymore," he says, sounding defeated. "I just can't believe I'm causing myself this headache. Why couldn't it have happened to someone who actually knows what they're doing?"

It's a very sad reminder that Jack's partnership with Davenport could have helped reduce the stress in his life so much. A real partnership, not the one originally offered to him. "Is this why you haven't done any more toys?" He gives me a sad smile. "I saw the drawings when I was looking for a coaster in the coffee table drawer."

"I'm out of my depth, Clara. It started as a fun idea and it's developed into this stress I can't escape."

I ask the question I've been wanting to ask since the beginning. "Why don't the others help you? It's supposed to be this collaborative project but it feels like you do the brunt of the work. Designing a box once and ordering repeat deliveries is not equivalent to managing customers, managing stock, and handling all the assembling and shipping."

Jack doesn't look surprised or offended by what I'm saying. He looks like I'm not saying anything he hasn't already thought. "What are my other options?"

"Your other option is to hustle and get it done."

"I don't know if I can get the boxes," he says, reminding me of his earlier problem.

"I can deal with that. If Melissa and Winnie's supplier can't produce a rush order, I'll find someone who can."

"I don't want to use a Davenport factory," he says quickly.

I don't blame him at all; seeing all his potential weighed down by the pressure of doing it alone is reigniting the rage I feel at my own company for screwing him in the first place.

And me. They screwed me.

"I won't need to. Are we going for option one or two?"

Jack chews on the corner of his thumb and contemplates. "You keep saying 'we,' but I don't expect you to help me."

"You tell me to shut up, too, but you don't expect me to do that either. I want to help. Let me prove it to you."

"Okay." One little word and I feel like I won something spectacular. He stands and moves in front of me, stretching his arms up lazily. "Option two. I don't want to let people down if I can help it."

"I believe in you, Jack. I'll make us coffee and then you can show me how to put her together and I'll start, okay?" Jack leans forward and kisses me gently. It says everything I know he can't, and it's enough for me. "I'll be back."

I'M TRYING NOT TO FOCUS on how monumental it is that Jack is letting me work on the doll that started this whole mess.

That means he definitely trusts me, right?

Jack goes into a cupboard on the far wall. He starts lifting out cardboard boxes and putting them on the floor behind us. "Do you want to take notes?" he asks.

"I should be good just watching. Show me how it's done, boss."

Boss earns me an eye roll and a scoff. He points at the first box. "Dolls, then dresses with hair ribbon, over here is books and accessories, this one is box stickers." I follow him from box to box.

He grabs a doll and puts a dress on her. Then the wheel of pink hair ribbon, cutting five inches with scissors, and tying it in her hair. The box is next, opening it out and pulling out the card she stands against. Jack puts her in place, followed by her toys. The final stage is the twist ties that hold everything in place. I know it's the most frustrating part of unboxing something. I suspect it's probably the most tedious part of boxing too. When he's done minutes later, he pushes everything into the box and closes the clear window lid.

"The box isn't big enough for the books without damaging them, so I put them in a bubble mailer and they go in the delivery box."

"Okay, I got it," I say, but in reality I'm picking holes in this whole system. "Do you just do one at a time?"

He nods. "I'm usually on my own."

"Can I interfere?" I ask, giving him my most angelic look.

He rolls his eyes, puts his arm around my waist. "Could I stop you even if I wanted to?"

"No. We need to streamline this process. The ribbons can be cut in bulk—we also need to run a flame over the end to stop them from fraying. The accessories are all mixed up so you're losing time trying to find one of each. I'm going to split them into separate boxes." He's nodding along, which is a positive sign. "With the books I'm going to do the opposite. I'm going to collate them and put them in the bubble mailers so you can just grab and go."

"Why didn't I think of this?" he says.

"Let's get through today, but going forward, I think you should leave the dolls with Flo's dressmaking club. They can add the ribbons and dresses, *then* send them to you. It'll be less work for you and a little more work for those already making dresses."

"Maybe," he says, kissing my cheek.

It's better than no, I guess. "I'll dress her. Do you want to cut all the ribbons and burn the ends?"

He nods and we fall into a quiet but productive rhythm. The head hole in the dress is a touch too small to make putting it on easy, and every time I drag it over her perfect brown curls I cringe, thinking I'm going to ruin them. I wonder if Jack's mentioned this to Flo.

Jack adds the ribbons to her hair while I switch to separating the toy accessories into different boxes. She has flowers to represent the florist, a slice of cake to represent Flo, a book to represent Miss Celia, a microphone to represent Wilhelmina, a bunny to represent Dove, and a hammer to represent Jack. Each of the stories that come with her relates to an adventure involving one of them. "I forgot you're the one who wrote these adventures."

"Mm-hmm," he hums. "If I'd known so many people were going to buy them, I'd have spent longer making them better. They felt good enough for what was Sailor's gift, but maybe not for all the people who paid good money for it. They're short; I guess that redeems them a little."

I look up, shocked. "You're ridiculously hard on yourself, do you know that? Who else writes multiple children's stories for a toy they designed?"

He kisses my forehead, his mouth hovering near my face. My chin tilts up; I'm hoping he'll kiss me properly. "Not Davenport," he whispers. "They use AI."

The sky outside darkens as the day rolls on. Jack and I fall into a rhythm with our miniature assembly line. We take turns with the annoying job of twisting the packaging ties until we realize Jack is twice as quick as I am. My job becomes shipping paperwork and organizing, something my year in distribution prepared me for.

There's a surge of dopamine watching the completed doll boxes pile up next to us. The order paperwork stack gets smaller and smaller and I'm getting giddy with excitement.

I watch the tension dissipate from Jack's shoulders. We eventually run out of dolls and boxes, toys and mailers. It's a natural halt to the process, seconded by my stomach making the loudest noise I've ever heard.

Jack sits against the table. He holds out a hand for me to take and guides me in between his parted legs. There's so much he's not saying yet so much I understand from him wrapping his arms around my waist and resting his forehead on my shoulder.

"Your stomach is screaming at me," he says quietly. "What do you want to eat?"

"We should finish putting the shipping labels on them so you can send them tomorrow," I say, ignoring the embarrassingly loud gurgle coming from my abdomen.

"After I feed you."

"You're bossy." Jack looks up, his hands sliding from my waist down to my ass. He pulls me closer. "And grabby."

"And you're hungry." He lists off the contents of his cupboards and every takeout place he likes in a twenty-mile radius. "What do you want?"

"The grocery store hot counter does a barbecue pulled pork sandwich. How about that? I can head over while you finish up. I'll walk Elf." He looks like he's about to argue, but I suspect he realizes if he goes to get the food, then I'm going to do the work. "And yes, I'm *fine* to walk."

Jack rolls his eyes. "Take my wallet."

I may be a strong, independent woman with her own money, but I'll never turn down free food. "You're very trusting that I won't rob you."

"You're overly optimistic that I have anything worth robbing." He laughs.

He kisses my forehead and taps my ass, which I take as my signal to leave. I can't stop smiling at what we've achieved this afternoon. I can't stop smiling at what I've achieved so far.

Chapter 30

CLARA

Jack's phone has woken me up four times this morning and I'm ready to launch it at the wall.

How can one community have *so* many problems? I'm beginning to think they just like Jack visiting. I can't be frustrated about it to him because he sees it as a badge of honor to be needed and relied upon.

He hasn't even dragged himself out of bed yet and he already has a full schedule of problems to solve. Seriously, he's working harder than I am and problem solving is my actual job.

It felt like the calls calmed down a little, but now I think I've just been missing them.

When he finally ends his call with Wilhelmina, who thinks there's a bird stuck in the roof of the school, he puts it on silent. Couldn't have done that three calls ago? Men.

"Sorry," he murmurs sleepily.

I try to slip out from his grip to start my own day now that there's no possible chance I'm going to go back to sleep this time, but it's like those finger lock magic tricks, where the harder you pull, the worse it gets. The more I try to escape, the tighter Jack hugs me.

I try a different tactic: twisting in his arms so I'm facing him and attempting to roll him onto his back. I get a face full of chest hair when I roll with him, but the angle makes it slightly easier to slip out of his hold.

"No," he grumbles, arms reaching out toward me, his eyes closed again.

"I need to get up and flush your phone down the toilet," I respond, dodging his hand grabbing near my biceps. Talking was clearly an error, because he finds a forearm and a thigh, using them to tug me back toward him. "God, you're so clingy."

"No," he grumbles again, eyes fluttering open. He kisses my collarbone, pulling me on top of him. My thighs are sore from being in this exact position last night for *way* longer than I'd normally be. I don't have the knees or stamina to go on top, but I put on the performance of my *life* last night. "Don't get up yet."

"I'm hungry."

"I'll get you breakfast. There's hardly anything in the refrigerator, I need to go grocery shopping," he says, voice raspy. He rubs his eyes with the back of his hands. "What do you want to eat?"

"What do *you* want to eat?" I'm buying myself time, because the answer is I don't know. I was planning to let the kitchen inspire me.

"Your pu—" My hand slaps against his mouth.

"For breakfast!"

Jack pulls my hand away so he can talk. "I think you know the answer."

You'd think it wouldn't be possible to feel shy in front of a man you're literally naked with, but it definitely is. I push myself into a sitting position, duvet clutched to my chest. His deep groan makes my stomach flood with butterflies. "I want a pain au chocolat and a festive coffee of some description, please."

Jack squeezes the front of my thighs. "You got it. But you gotta stay right here, completely naked, until I get back. Deal?"

"I think I can manage that." I climb off, taking the duvet with me, and lie back down. He swings his legs over the edge of the bed, pulling up a pair of basketball shorts and heading into the bathroom.

It's easier if he goes, that way I don't need to explain to eagle-eyed Flo why I'm emerging from Jack's store with a glow that tells her I've been thoroughly fucked.

I've spent a lot of the past few days in here hanging out with Jack, which means I've mostly avoided the intrusive questions Dove warned me to prepare for. I didn't ask how people would know, but I assumed it's because she knows she can't be trusted to keep it to herself.

I do need to stop fooling around with Jack all the time and get back to my plan. The success of Small Business Saturday and the report on the Santa run have given me the false impression that I can slow down, but I can't.

Flo still has the videos up and my promotion is still being dangled in front of me like a carrot. I'm not even sure I like carrots anymore.

THE CELL PHONE VIBRATING ON the bedside table wakes me up from the micro-nap I was having and I'm filled with rage until I realize it's mine. Jack's name is in bold at the top of my screen. "Hey."

"Hey." His voice is low and quiet. "Do you know anything about reporting malicious reviews?"

I sit against the headboard, the duvet tucked under my arms. "Like getting them taken down?"

"Exactly that."

"Kind of. I know people that know about it though. Why? What's wrong?"

I can hear a commotion in the background, the faint sound of a crying woman. "I think I need your help, Clara. Can you get dressed and come over to the bakery?"

"I'll be two minutes."

I try not to flush with embarrassment as I pass Nancy behind the cash register of the store after I walk through the workshop. Tucking my coat tighter around me, I check before crossing the road to Flo's Fancies.

Flo is sitting at one of the tables, a small pile of tissues in front of her. Jack's elbows are against his knees as he whispers something to her. The small queue of customers look on, likely feeling as confused as I do.

I stop beside them; Flo takes one look at me and bursts into tears.

"Oh God, what did I do?" I ask, crouching beside the pair of them.

She blows her nose on a tissue. "It's not you, it's *her*."

There's a small moment where I consider that this is the moment where Jack's evil ex shows up, not that I know he has an evil ex, but the level of theatrics would make more sense. Then Jack mouths *the doll* and all delusions of fighting over Jack Kelly disappear.

It produces new questions about if I'd fight for him, but I push them to the back of my head to focus on the disaster at hand. "I'm sure I can help fix whatever has happened, but I need to know where to start."

I look between them helplessly. Jack stands and offers me his seat, pulling another from a nearby table and sitting between Flo and me. He unlocks his phone and gives it to me.

My eyes almost bulge out of my head as I read one of the most vicious reviews of Flo's Fancies I've ever seen. The review isn't even about the bakery, it's about the doll being out of stock. Jack takes back his phone and swipes to a different tab, one for Bliss Café, equally malicious and equally not about the café at all.

I've known since I arrived how important reviews are to Flo. It's something she takes great pride in. This is devastating for her.

"It's going to bring my average rating down," she says between heart-wrenching sobs. "People won't want to come here."

Jack doesn't say anything, he just looks at me with a kind of pleading I've never seen before. "They will, Ms. Flo. We can fix this. Excuse me, I'll make some calls."

Moving to the corner of the room, I watch Jack rub Flo's shoulder to comfort her while the phone rings in my ear.

"I've forgotten what you sound like. I heard a rumor you'd run away and joined a traveling circus," Sahara says, the sound of what I expect is a Poppi lid cracking in the background.

"Hello to you too."

"What can I do for you, my little clown?" she says affectionately.

"Do you have any friends at Google? Someone's left fake, malicious reviews on businesses in Fraser Falls that have nothing to do with the actual businesses. I'm going to flag them but I want someone to actually address them. I haven't checked everywhere, but it's definitely two places here."

"Malicious? About what?"

"The Holly doll being out of stock. But these are reviews for the bakery and café. I need to check the florist, bookstore, and art school."

I hear Sahara's nails tapping against her keyboard. "Yeah, the florist got it. Why would people do that?"

"Because Florence Girard talked about the doll as a community project on the news, and Jack doesn't have the stock."

"Sucks," she says, sounding uninterested. I guess she's been dealing with the backlash of Flo's posts for weeks, so it makes sense she doesn't feel sorry for anyone. She's a good person, though, so it won't stop her helping me. "I have a contact at Google. Just flag them the normal way and I'll get them taken down."

Thank God. "You're the best, thank you."

"I know. When are you coming back to me? The office is quiet without you stomping around it."

"I don't stomp. I don't know when I'm leaving for good, but I'll be back for the charity gala." My chest tightens. "Miss you."

"Miss you too, see ya."

I feel like I've achieved something walking—not stomping—back over to Jack and Flo. Sitting in my chair, I tuck my phone into my pocket. "My friend knows someone at Google; she's going to contact them and get any fake reviews taken down. I'm sorry this happened. They won't be on there for long. She's very efficient and determined; you'd like her a lot."

I've become used to Flo's long, elaborate tales whenever I talk to her in the mornings while grabbing a coffee and a treat. She's a woman of many, many words yet she only gives me three. "Thank you, Clara."

She collects up her tissues and stands, nodding at both Jack and me before heading behind the counter and into a private area. "Will she be okay?"

"You're great," he says, his voice calm and matter-of-fact.

"I didn't do anything. Sahara is the one with the contact."

"You helped, Clara. Like you said you would. I'm sorry I ever doubted you. I don't know what I'd have done today without you. I wouldn't have been able to help her." I sit in silence, unsure exactly how I'm supposed to respond. "I'll go up and order breakfast."

There's only one girl behind the counter today and Flo has disappeared, so I don't think we're getting table service. "You stay here and let your cortisol levels come back down, I'll go up for us."

Jack takes my hand and kisses the back of it as I pass him. I don't know what's hurting him more, the stress that the reviews are because of the doll or that there's a scenario where he wouldn't be able to help someone.

The internet has offered so much and yet there's so much to despise about it. I wait in the line patiently, lost in my head about how people love to be negative online. I get being frustrated about a sold-out product, but to intentionally seek out the community of people involved to leave malicious reviews is astounding to me.

I'd like to think it's one person on multiple accounts being shady, but in reality someone probably posted a screenshot of their review online and it got likes. So then someone else thought, *I want likes and attention from strangers*, so they did it too.

I'm next in line, admiring the garland decorating the front of the counter. There's a wreath decorated with berries and pine cones in the center and a string of fairy lights running along the top of the structure.

Holiday spirit is really starting to come to life here in Fraser Falls. If it's possible, the Main Street lights look even more festive with the addition of holly wreaths on the lampposts and a six-foot inflatable snowman outside of the Frozen Spoon.

Flo appears from the private employee area looking nothing like the woman who was sobbing not that long ago. I admire her ability to get her shit together quickly. It's something I can't relate to, sadly. "Feeling better?" I say hopefully as she emerges from behind the counter.

"I always feel wonderful, Clara," she says confidently.

"Well, that's great then," I respond.

Flo pauses and looks around. The café is quiet with the exception of two couples sitting by the window. The line was full of people wanting takeout. "Did you watch the news?"

I smile. "I did. You were a natural in front of the camera. You did a great job, Ms. Flo. Are you happy with how it went? Fraser Falls looked magical."

"I am happy with how it went. I know that they wouldn't have been there if it weren't for you, Clara. A lot of things have been happening around here that wouldn't be if it weren't for you. The town appreciates your effort."

I'm stunned speechless. Something that has possibly never

happened before. She doesn't wait for me to say anything in response. Flo rubs my shoulder as she passes and walks through the archway into Flo's Fancies.

It's a step closer to truly winning her over.

It's also a step closer to going home.

Chapter 31

JACK

Watching the courier drive away with a truck full of orders going to customers is like they've individually been lifted off my chest.

I don't think Clara will ever understand the pressure she relieved helping me yesterday or the hope she's given me with the advice she gave me to make things quicker.

She's right, I should talk to the others about not having to do everything myself. Whether I will or not is a different argument. I'm so used to everyone here depending on me that it feels alien to depend on them.

Tommy is watching me eat my lunch, his eyes following my every move. "What's your problem?" I ask, reaching into my bag of chips. He complained he hadn't seen me recently—a lie—but I felt bad and said I'd visit when I took my lunch break.

Clara took my truck to go shopping for a dress for a work gala she has coming up.

"I don't have a problem," Tommy says, leaning against the bar. "Did you have sex?"

"Jesus, Tommy," I say, spluttering on my lunch. "What's up with you?"

He draws a circle in the air around me with his finger. "You don't look like you've got a stick up your ass anymore. You smiled when you looked at your phone. So I put two and two together."

I smiled at my phone because Clara sent me a picture of how badly she parked my truck. "And got five."

"And I was told by Luke, who was told by Dove, who was told by Aunt Maggie, that Maggie caught you banging Clara." He looks so smug. Maggie didn't catch me "banging" Clara. She came in to clean while we were fooling around on the couch, fully clothed. "Which is weird because I thought there was no way my best friend would do something like that without telling me about it."

"Thanks for the recap," I mutter.

He looks at me expectantly, like I'm going to tell him my damn business. "So? Have you had sex?"

"You need to concentrate on your own sex life."

"I don't have one, that's why I'm interfering in yours," he says matter-of-factly. "Thought you hated her."

"I never hated her," I say, an uncomfortable guilt rushing through me. "I hate the company she works for and the people she works with, and probably her dad too."

He wags his finger at me. "Nah, I'm pretty sure you hated her."

He's just trying to get under my skin. Unfortunately, it's working. The idea of not trusting Clara feels weird now. The idea of hating her is even weirder.

"I was mad at her, and who she represented, but she's a good person. They treat her like shit too. We have a lot more in common than I realized."

It's the truth. Plus, after finding out that they stole her idea when she was just a little girl, it's kind of hard to hold a grudge. She's done what she said she was going to do when she got here; she's convinced me that she does actually care.

"So are you going to keep seeing her when she goes home?" he asks, and my stomach twists.

"No. It's a for-now thing, not a forever thing. We agreed it would be one time. Her one-time stay in Fraser Falls."

My phone lights up on the bar; three messages from Clara all come through at the same time. As soon as I see the first picture I pick it up rapidly before Tommy can see the screen. The text says "Off or on?" with two pictures.

One with Clara wearing a gorgeous floor-length emerald-green dress, her hair clipped up with two curled tendrils framing her face. The other with Clara no longer wearing the dress.

"Why are you turning red?" Tommy asks, leaning over to look at my phone screen.

I clutch it to my chest and lock the screen. "You're nosy today. Tell me what's going on with you instead of annoying me."

I quickly text back Clara telling her I can't decide and she'll need to show me both later, then put my phone down to concentrate on Tommy. Apparently in his tired, "overworked" state he thought it was a good idea to ask out Melissa Wilde. He found it wasn't a good idea, because she said no.

He has a new plan to try to get his outdoor terrace expansion approved. It won't be, but who am I to stand between a man and his vision? He also tells me he's thinking of getting a dog for company, something I can actually get on board with. Even though the tavern is always busy, especially this time of year, he says it makes him feel the quiet more when he is alone.

I get it. Elf is asleep on the floor next to my stool and I know that having him around is going to make the quiet when Clara leaves town more tolerable. I hate thinking about Clara leaving town—a statement I'd have laughed in your face about a month ago if you'd told me it was something I'd say.

Tommy pressures me into heading outside with him to look at the never-going-to-be-approved patio extension space and we talk about that instead of my sex life. It's cold as shit out here and Elf immediately tries to climb me like he's a Chihuahua, not a fifty-pound seal pretending to be a dog.

I reluctantly pick him up and sit him on my hip like I did with Sailor when she was younger. He licks the side of my face, which I take as gratitude.

My phone buzzes in my pocket, Clara's name on the screen. "Hey."

"Hi," she says breathlessly. "I need your help."

I pass Elf over to Tommy, who looks confused about why he's now carrying a dog, and move away from the sound of Tommy struggling under the weight. "What's happened? Are you okay?"

"Yes and no. I was being super careful driving like you told me to. *Super* careful, I promise. But . . ."

"What the fuck, Clara. Are you hurt? Where are you?" I ask frantically.

"Chill, I'm not hurt and neither is your truck."

"I don't care about the truck. Why do you sound so stressed?"

She takes a deep sigh. "I reversed into a snowman."

A confused laugh spills out of me. "Okay . . ."

"Some kid is going to finish school and come home and find their snowman obliterated because I'm a shitty driver. It isn't funny."

I press my lips together. "Tell me what I can do."

"Isn't it obvious?" she says.

"Not even a little bit, Clara. You tell me what you need and I'll do it."

"We need to rebuild it," she says like it's the most obvious statement in the world.

"We do?" I ask skeptically. I clear my throat. "Sure we do. Where are you?"

"If you walk to my door at the back of Maggie's, then keep going,

I don't know, maybe twenty houses, I'm there. My phone wouldn't stop ringing so I pulled over to answer, thinking it was an emergency, but I pulled too close to a post to drive off so I had to back up and that's when it happened."

"Was it an emergency?"

She sighs. "No, it was my dad wanting to talk about work. I'll spare you the details, but it wasn't worth killing a snowman for."

I'm trying not to laugh because she sounds genuinely devastated. "Heading over now. Don't run anyone else down."

THE WAY CLARA IS ACTING you'd think she's been involved in a hit-and-run.

When I find her at the scene of the crime, she's pacing back and forth with her hands on her hips. "Stop smiling at me," she says as I approach her.

"I can't help it. You look like the police are going to roll up at any minute and arrest you."

She glares at me in a way that makes my arm hairs stand up. "Does Fraser Falls even have police?"

I lift an eyebrow. "Yes, we do." I look at the crushed snowman at my feet. "You really did a number on him."

"I'm going to do a number on you if you don't stop looking so damn amused by my misfortune."

I want to tell her that it was going to melt anyway, but if she wants to build a snowman I'm not going to stop her. The snow has been heavy and frequent over the past couple of days. We're due to get a lot more over the weekend and it feels like it's getting earlier every year.

The original creator's first mistake was building it on the grass verge in front of the house instead of their front yard. This kid clearly doesn't know there are people like Clara on the road. There's a snapped carrot sitting in the middle of the carnage. "Have you made a snowman before?"

She looks at me like I have three heads. "Of course I have. I grew up in Manhattan, not Miami. I used to have a competition with my brother to see who could build the better one."

"Of course you did. Do you have any stories from your childhood where you weren't competing with your brother?"

Clara thinks about it, her lips pouting out, eyes looking to the sky. "No, I don't think so."

"Sounds super healthy," I muse. I crouch down to evaluate the mess we're dealing with. I pick out the carrot and what I think are stones but quickly realize are frozen Oreos and put them to the side. I free the tartan scarf and add it to the pile. "Do you know how big it was?"

"It was two tiers with a face and scarf. I *think* it had some branch hair, I can't remember. It all happened so fast."

When I stand and hold out my arms she clings to me tightly. I kiss the crown of her head, consider telling her this really is just a waste of energy and snowmen get ruined, by either the weather or other kids. But if she wants to spend her time in town building snowmen with me, then I'm not going to argue.

I text Nancy and let her know I'll be late back to the store. Then I send one to Tommy telling him I'll pick up Elf when I'm done. Clara is pulling on her gloves, a look of determination etched into her face. One that disappears when she kneels on the ground and immediately realizes her mistake now that she has wet knees. "Do you want to watch and I'll quickly build it?"

My question is met with a handful of snow to the face. "I'm helping."

I start by getting rid of the original snowman. Mostly because the snow is too compacted to be rebuilt, but also to hide the evidence of Clara's crime. She gasps as blocks of ice hit the road when I start throwing them out of our way. "We can't work with this, baby."

I leave her crouched in the spot and start at the other end of the grass beside the road. The snow is wet and rolls easily as I push and pack it all the way back to Clara. I'm glad she decided to massacre Olaf on a road that isn't busy so I don't have to explain what the fuck I'm doing in the middle of a workday.

"Is it weird that I found that sexy?" she asks, smoothing her hands over the sides to round the ball.

"Yes." I get another mouthful of snow. Her hand covers her face as she tries to hold in a laugh. "Next time I'm not going to let you get away with it, so make decisions ca—"

This time a small snowball hits the center of my chest and explodes into powder. Clara holds her hands up defensively. "Truce?" I ignore her, packing snow in my hands until I have a snowball ready to go. She backs up, her hands still in front of her. "Play nicely, Jack."

"Oh, so now it's play nicely?" She gives me the most mischievous and dazzling smile, then she bolts away.

She's quick for someone who hurt their ankle at the start of the week, but I'm quicker. One arm wraps around her waist, pulling her back into my chest. "Truce, truce, truce," she squeals as I press the snowball into her hair.

Clara turns around and pouts, her bottom lip protruding all the way out as the clumps of snow cling to the auburn strands framing her face. I brush it away and kiss her. She doesn't respond at first, but when I cup her face with both of my hands she wraps her arms around my neck. "Okay, truce," I say, right as her hand pulls at the neck of my sweater and I feel slush sliding down my spine.

She leans back, her eyes wide, lips pulled into a line. "Oops."

Clara runs away as I move the bottom of my sweater to get what's now water out. I'm glad there are no cars in the drives to witness me chasing after her, *again*. I'm within reaching distance of her when I notice her start to wobble. It's like slow motion, the way her left foot slides and her knees buckle.

"Shit," I say, reaching out to catch her. My foot finds the same iced-over patch of ground hers did, and suddenly I'm falling with her. We both hit the pavement with a thud. "I'm too old for this," I groan, pushing myself into a sitting position. Clara stays where she is and moves her right arm and leg up and down. "Are you trying to make a snow angel?"

"Half of one. You kinda ruined my chance of doing a full one by lying down next to me." My mouth opens to argue back but I catch the look on her face and realize it's what she wants.

"Get your ass up. We have a snowman to finish." I push myself off the ground and hold out a hand for her too. We're both wet and freezing, but there's no one I'd rather be those things with.

"Yes, boss."

I brush the dusting of snow from Clara's jacket. "Hey, do you have plans tonight?"

She pulls me closer with my pockets; tiny droplets of water are clinging to the strands of her hair. "I don't."

"I want to take you on a date."

"A date. That sounds very romantic and formal," she says.

I scratch at my jaw. "I can make it unromantic and informal if you'd like. Tacos and sex on the backseat."

I'm slowly realizing that these kinds of days are numbered and that I need to seize all the opportunities I have with her while I have her.

Clara's arms wrap around my waist. Her cheeks and nose are pink from the cold, and she's never looked more beautiful to me. "Wow, you just described my dream date. I'll be there."

Chapter 32

JACK

Despite Clara's blessing, I don't have tacos and backseat sex on the agenda tonight.

I pull up at the back of the B & B and grab the bouquet of flowers I bought her from the passenger seat. The volume of the music playing in her bedroom lowers when I close the front door.

"Are you here to rob me?" she shouts from somewhere in the room.

"Yeah!" I shout back, taking a seat on the couch. "Someone got here before me though, this place is trashed."

"Ha ha," she says sarcastically, putting on earrings as she walks out of her bedroom. "I know I'm going to get cold but that's a sacrifice I'm willing to make to wear this dress. I have no idea where we're going but you said dress nice, so here I am."

"You look unbelievable," I tell her as she stops in front of me. Her dress is tiny, lace, and black. All other descriptive thoughts leave my head as I cast my eyes over her long, creamy legs. "You're gorgeous, Clara."

"I know. You just didn't realize before now because all you've seen me in is thermals and ponytails." She drops a pair of stilettos by her feet and slips her right foot into one. "I'm actually very hot."

"I definitely realized before now." I kneel down near her feet, lifting the stilettoed foot onto my thigh and fastening the tiny buckle. Her hand cradles the side of my face, thumb rubbing affectionately over my temple. I kiss the inside of her knee and switch her feet. "You shouldn't be wearing these shoes after hurting your ankle."

"I know you won't let me hurt myself," she says softly. "And you're forgetting I *healed* my ankle. A medical miracle, some might say."

"I don't know anyone who would say that other than you." I put her foot on the floor carefully.

"Thank you. I'm ready as soon as I have my coat on."

Watching her walk along the icy ground makes me sweat but she acts like she isn't at serious risk of falling over, and to her credit, she doesn't.

She brushes the snowflakes out of her hair when she climbs into the truck. "Do I get to know where we're going yet?"

"No."

Clara keeps saying she misses New York Chinese food, so we're heading out of town to a fancy Chinese restaurant Tommy and I sometimes drive to.

I think a small part of me wanted to show her she can get everything here she can get in the city, which is pointless, because she's definitely leaving soon. First, we're heading over to the art school to watch the dress rehearsal of *The Nutcracker*.

A bigger part of me wishes she had a departure date so I could stop thinking about it.

"What's been your favorite thing about Fraser Falls?" I ask to distract myself from a miserable stream of thought. "Other than Elf."

"Is it too predictable and cheesy to say you?" she asks, playing with the hem of her dress in her hands.

"You're lying," I say. "You don't need to boost my ego."

"I'm not." I look across to her in the passenger seat and she shrugs. "There's something about making a man who hates you become obsessed with you that really does it for me."

"I didn't hate you," I say, instead hating myself for how I acted in the beginning.

"But you are obsessed with me." There's no point arguing when she winks. "I also liked watching you working at the store and helping your town even though your phone wakes me up. You're always there for everyone and yet you're so scared that you're letting everyone down. I wish you could see how much they all appreciate you."

The confession stuns me. I wasn't expecting her to say something like that; I didn't realize how much I wanted to hear it. I feel like I spend so much energy *not* wanting to let people down that I forget to look at all the times I *do* show up. It's like Clara knows that without my ever needing to tell her. "I appreciate you saying that."

"And most of all," she continues, "I really, really like it when you're naked."

"Good to know." I pull up in front of the school and Clara looks confused, then concerned. "Don't worry, nobody will see us."

"Good," she says firmly. "I can't let Flo see me in this dress. I think she's finally starting to like me."

I round the hood and open her door, kissing her as she slides out. Her warm body presses against mine. "You should go inside before I change my mind and take you home."

I can hear Clara laughing to herself as she carefully walks toward the entrance. The thought of her slipping in those shoes is enough to stop all the blood rushing south. I grab the bag of snacks from behind her seat and jog to catch up with her.

"Wow, such a gentleman," she says teasingly when I hold the door open for her.

"Have guys in New York set the bar that low?" I ask.

"The bar doesn't exist in New York. It's already in hell." Her fingers work each large blue button of her coat. "I can hear music!"

I unbutton my own jacket and hold open another door, this time the one into the theater. "Wilhelmina said we're not allowed to make any noise."

Clara's hand slowly rises to her mouth, pressing into her lips. She looks at me quickly, then back to the stage. "Oh my, they're so cute."

I guide Clara to our chairs at the back of the room. The corner bathed in darkness is the only thing I could get Wilhelmina to agree to. She doesn't want us making her young dancers nervous so they're not supposed to know we're here.

"I'm named after the girl in *The Nutcracker*," she whispers to me when we take our seat.

"Seriously?"

She nods, leans in, and hooks her arms around my arm. "My parents were on their way to watch the New York City Ballet's performance when my mom went into labor. Maybe if they'd watched the show, they'd know she's called Marie."

"You're kidding. When's your birthday?"

Clara shakes her head enthusiastically. "Shock of my life when I watched it at Lincoln Center for the first time. It's December twenty-seventh. Shhh, they're moving!"

A child in a too-long skirt darts across the stage, trailing a ribbon of gold tinsel that detaches halfway across the stage. Behind her, a cluster of Sugar Plum Fairies twirl and flutter, some more successfully than others. Their glittery tutus sparkle under the bright stage lights.

One fairy is wearing light-up sneakers that flash with pink and purple strobe lights every time her feet hit the stage. Another has a tiara made from pipe cleaners. Another's wings are bent at a suspicious angle and I suspect they may have been sat on.

Clara squeezes my arm tight. Her eyes are wide and her grin is stretched across her face.

In the wings, Wilhelmina mouths a silent count, tapping her finger on her clipboard like a metronome. The sequined snowflakes on her black cardigan sparkle as she conducts the mayhem onstage. The music falters on a tinny Bluetooth speaker; "Waltz of the Flowers" skips, then restarts as Wilhelmina calls, "From the top, please!"

A boy dressed as the nutcracker prince fumbles his sword (a spray-painted wooden spoon) and mutters a soft "Sorry" in Wilhelmina's direction, before scooping it up and stumbling back into place just in time to be chased offstage by a trio of candy cane dancers.

One of the younger girls, a tiny soldier with one sock up and one sock down, comes to an abrupt stop in the middle of the stage and salutes enthusiastically before collapsing in a dramatic faint, her eyes squeezed shut and arms crossed over her chest. It might've actually been convincing if she hadn't lifted her head, opened her eyes, and looked around to make sure someone was watching.

"My God," Clara whispers, grinning so hard it looks like it hurts. "This is the best thing I've ever seen."

When the snowflake dance begins, a dozen kids in paper crowns and white dresses flurry onto the stage. One forgets the choreography completely and starts twirling on the spot, faster and faster, arms out like airplane wings. She collides with a tree, which is made of green paper and tape, but it remains upright and she just keeps on spinning.

I pass Clara a gingerbread snowman without taking my eyes off the stage. "Your namesake would be proud," I murmur.

She leans her head on my shoulder. "She really would."

. . .

"Do you think I'm too old to take up ballet?"

I know a trap when I hear one. "I don't think you're too old for anything. I'd bet they do adult classes somewhere."

"Where are you taking me now?" Clara has had a dreamy look on her face the whole evening. When she spotted Sailor on the stage I thought she was going to start crying.

"For food. Although, are you even hungry after you ate all that gingerbread?"

There's still a lingering smell of ginger and cinnamon in the cab. "Yep. You impressed?"

"By you? All the time."

Clara tunes the radio to her preferred station and keeps it low until a song I don't recognize comes on and she turns it right up to sing along. She uses my hand on her thigh as a microphone until she tries to bend it at an angle it will not go to. "Sorry," she whispers into the dark, leaning over to kiss me on the cheek.

The roads are clear so it doesn't take long for us to reach Jade, the best Chinese restaurant I know. The dark building is the first red flag and the Closed sign on the door is the second. "Fuck, I'm so sorry. I didn't check, I just assumed it'd be open. Why wouldn't it be open during the week?"

"Oh well," Clara says cheerfully, squeezing my thigh. "Tacos and backseat sex it is."

"You're not mad I've ruined our date?" I'm mad at myself. I should've checked.

"Of course I'm not. We've passed like ten places that are open; let's just eat somewhere else. But like, if it could be somewhere that serves tacos, that'd be great, because I've made the joke a couple of times and now I'm craving them."

"You got it."

. . .

Turns out, the tacos with the other thing is kind of a package deal.

My truck's parked up on an unlit dirt track far enough away from the road that passing cars aren't getting a front-row show.

I have handfuls of Clara's dress bunched up by her hips while she grinds on top of me on the backseat. I move the thin straps of her dress off her shoulders and pull the dress down at the front. She throws her head back when I cup one of her breasts and suck her nipple.

"I need you now," she pants, fumbling beneath her for my zipper. "No teasing."

I work my belt quickly and undo the top button while she pulls the zipper down. This isn't the sweet, romantic end to our date that I imagined. It might be better.

"I'm so hard for you," I whisper beneath her ear. Her hand slips under the elastic band of my boxers and grips me tight. My eyes roll into the back of my head. "*Fuck*, Clara."

I lift my hips so I can pull my underwear down enough for her to comfortably pull my dick out. I slip my hand beneath her dress, feel the hot fabric of her panties when I pull them to the side. "Is this for me?" I run my finger across her, and feeling how wet she is makes my dick throb.

Clara's hands hold my face; her forehead presses into mine when I run the head over her clit, making her shudder. She kisses me hard, her lips and tongue moving perfectly with mine while I roll a condom on. "It's for you," she moans when I line myself up with her.

She sinks down torturously slow. Every single nerve in my body comes to life. My hands grip her ass, guiding her as she makes testing movements with her hips. I can hardly see her in the low light of the dash, but I can feel her soft skin and hear her wispy moans. "You're so good at riding me."

Clara likes praise, I've learned in these moments together. She whimpers, picks up her pace. I kiss and suck every inch of her I can get my mouth onto. It's quick and desperate and so fucking good.

I slip my hand between her legs, find her clit with my thumb, and rub in a fast, circular motion. Her thighs grip me tighter, hands find my knees as she leans back to give me more space. "I need . . . I need . . . ," she pants.

"What do you need, baby?"

"*More.*"

"Put your feet on the seat," I tell her. I help maneuver each foot onto the seat on either side of me. I slouch in the seat and plant my feet wide on the floor. Clara rests her arms on the back of the front seats and lets me guide her legs open.

I keep my thumb the same and thrust my hips up as she brings hers down. "Yes," she moans. I do it again, and again, and again until I'm so close I can taste it.

Clara falls out of rhythm; her breathing deepens and her thighs start to shake. I keep pushing, thrusting into her until she's tightening around me and crying my name.

Her arms reach out for me in the dark so I pull her close, supporting her weight while she bounces up and down, her arms wrapped tight around my neck.

One, two more and she's dragging me over, swallowing each moan with her mouth. After what feels like forever I finish coming. There's a thick sheen of sweat on the back of my neck and my limbs feel heavy. Clara rests her head on my collarbone, spent. I pull her dress up at the front and reinstate her straps, kiss her on her temple.

"I couldn't have done that after Chinese food," she says, so I mentally cross Jade off the list.

Chapter 33
CLARA

I'm a thirty-year-old woman with a hickey and I don't know how I feel about it.

Relieved that it's a perfectly acceptable time to wear a turtleneck sweater, sure. But otherwise, the jury is out. Jack acted like it was the funniest thing he'd ever seen, then apologized profusely when he realized I wasn't laughing with him.

"I got carried away," he said. "Won't happen again."

When I called him a leech he started laughing all over again. Thankfully, I was smart enough to bring a thick knitted turtleneck sweater that covers up the evidence that I was a reckless slut last night on an empty lane. God, it was worth it.

It started snowing on our drive home, and it hasn't stopped yet. Seeing everything coated in a thick blanket of white makes it feel even more enchanting.

I take a sneaky look in the North Pole mailbox, full of brightly colored envelopes, outside of Harry's on my way out the door. Jack told me he built the red mailbox from scratch with leftover lumber and had Wilhelmina paint the reindeer postage stamp on the side.

When I asked him what made him build it, he said it was something his granddad had done when he was a kid. So he brought it back and the local kids love it. He said he writes letters back to the kids from Santa and I swear I started ovulating on the spot.

The roads have already been plowed when I cross over to head to the Green Light. As Matilda's event approaches I've been regularly sticking my head through Miss Celia's door to check if there's anything I can help with. Sometimes the answer's no, sometimes the answer is yes, make one hundred goodie bags for the readers coming to the event.

The publisher sent over art prints and bookmarks they had left over from the preorder campaign, which Miss Celia added to a collection of things she'd bought for the occasion.

As I reach the pavement on the other side of the street I hear my name. Jack's head is sticking out of the Bliss café doorway. "Got something to show you."

He holds the door open for me and as soon as I step across the threshold I can hear Flo lecturing him about how rude it is to yell at people in the street.

"Morning, Ms. Flo," I say cheerfully. She's putting out a fresh batch of cinnamon rolls and they smell divine. The low hum of Christmas music—no, correction, French Christmas music—is playing from the speakers. "That cinnamon roll will fix all my problems, I can tell."

"Good morning, Clara," she says back with an unusually delighted tone. Her eyes flick to Jack. "Don't you have a business to run?"

"I want to see her face when you show her," he says, leaning against the counter, his thigh pressing into the garland. Flo swats his arm with a towel as I hit the other arm with my hand. "What?!"

"You'll ruin the garland!" we both say in sync.

"That's not a reason to abuse me," he says, playfully rubbing his biceps. "Just show her and then I'll get out of your hair." Flo looks at him like he just told her to breakdance. Jack's Adam's apple bobs as he swallows hard. "Please. Thank you."

Flo gets an iPad from beneath the counter and unlocks it. After tapping a couple of times she hands it over to me. "They published the story."

I'm confident my face is giving Jack all he wanted as I fight between jumping up and down and outright crying with happiness. On the home page of the online news outlet that was here for the Santa run is the accompanying article. It already has thousands of reads. My eyes skim over the text. "This is incredible."

"I know," Jack says, and when I look up at him he's wearing an expression I haven't seen before. Pride, maybe? I might be getting ideas above my station because of all the sex.

"They called Fraser Falls 'a hidden gem in a magical winter wonderland.' That's, wow, that's quite the endorsement." Flo is beaming in front of me. "I'm so happy for you, Ms. Flo."

"Maggie has already had ten calls this morning with people making reservations." My words catch in my throat, leaving me unable to respond. I've dealt with big wins and equally big losses throughout my whole career, but there's something about this that feels miles above the rest. "We're talking about arranging a winter market in a couple of weeks! Very humbly sized to start, but if it's a success it could lead to something bigger and better."

I pull myself together. "That's incredible news."

Flo looks to Jack. "You've seen her react. She's very emotional, as you anticipated. Now back to work, we have an immaculate town reputation to uphold. Can't have you lurking around in the middle of the day."

It's 10 a.m.

Jack doesn't dare roll his eyes but I can tell by the way they crinkle that he wants to. His expression softens when he looks at me. "Bye."

As soon as he's out the door, Flo turns back to me. "Clara, I've taken the videos down." My throat becomes a desert. I cling to the edge of the counter for steadiness. "You look upset."

I shake my head, all I can manage right now. *She's taken down the videos.* I wasn't mentally prepared for this. "Not upset. Shocked."

"This isn't about Davenport," she says firmly. "What they did is still unacceptable, but Fraser Falls is getting attention for all the right reasons now. I don't want our good image to be associated with drama and online discourse. I see now that my actions, while done with good intentions, invited the world to our doorstep. And frankly, not everyone is house-trained."

That's a good way to describe it. "I respect your decision, Ms. Flo. I'm happy Fraser Falls is getting the recognition it deserves. I've fallen in love with your hometown. I feel very lucky to have experienced living here."

"I suspect you'll be heading home now that the videos have been deleted." My stomach sinks, and sweat starts to form at the back of my neck. "Is there a big prize waiting for you back in the city now that you've achieved what you came here to do?"

"The promotion I've been working toward, supposedly, but I'm not sure I *have* achieved all that I came here for, if I'm being honest. The toy drive is still ongoing and the author event, and, gosh, I have so much more I wanted to do. I've hardly even spent *any* time with the Christmas tree farm." I can hear my voice getting louder and higher, but I can't stop it as the pressure builds in my chest. "I want to help Tommy. I still haven't met Donald. I can't leave without meeting Do—"

"Clara," Flo says softly. "I'm not serving you with an eviction notice. You don't need to panic."

I am panicking. I wonder if they've noticed at work yet. Am I going to pull my phone out of my pocket to thirty victory messages? Or, worse, missed calls from my dad? "I just don't want to leave anything half done," I explain. "I want to see everything through."

"While I was cynical at first, I can see that your presence here, no matter what brought you to us, has been a blessing. Being honest, I'll be sad to see you go. I know I'm not alone saying that." Water lines my vision but I hold it back. Flo opens a food box and scoops out a cream-frosting-covered cinnamon roll for me. She closes the lid and hands it over. "It *will* fix your problem. At least for this morning."

Flo has a way of kicking you out without actually walking you to the door. Maybe she just doesn't trust I'm not going to have some kind of emotional episode in front of her, which is a fair judgment.

I'm in a daze when I walk back out onto Main Street. I should cross the street and tell Jack everything that just happened, but I don't. I turn right and head to the Green Light.

I don't have any messages or calls, which eases the lingering tension a touch. I know it's only a matter of time before someone notices the videos have disappeared. I know I should be excited. Flo taking down the videos should feel like a relief, but it doesn't. I don't know why it doesn't.

That's a lie. The *why it doesn't* is six foot four and has messy brown hair and brown eyes with hints of amber. He looks after me when I'm injured, he lets me warm my cold hands on his extraordinarily warm body, and he tells me that I deserve the best.

I know we said just for now, but this feeling fucking sucks.

MISS CELIA DOESN'T NEED ME to do anything. Wilhelmina doesn't either. Dove isn't at the toy drive station at the town hall when I swing by. Mel and Winnie are too busy to chat. Maggie won't even let me shine cutlery to be helpful.

I lie in bed staring at the gull on my ceiling. I don't bother opening my closet because I don't want to learn that I've completed my plan. I contemplate calling my dad, getting ahead of the situation, but the idea of hearing him telling me to come home immediately is more than I can handle today. Instead, I clock-watch until I know the Hungry Fox is open and head over there.

I'm the first person in, to Tommy's surprise when he looks up from his Kindle. I place my laptop down on the bar and open it.

Tommy eyes me suspiciously. "You have a weird energy today."

"Me? That's weird. I'm doing great. Not that you asked, but I am. So, I've been working on a presentation and I didn't want to show you until it was done, but it's kind of hard to do on my own. I was wondering if maybe you have time to do it together today?" *Because I don't want my time here to run out before I finish*, is what I don't add on.

"Sure, I can help you. What's the presentation about?" Tommy asks.

I twist my laptop ninety degrees so we can both see the screen. "Your patio extension."

Tommy rubs his fingers over his lips. "You've been working on something for my extension?"

"I know it keeps getting rejected, and this might get rejected too, but I've taken a slightly different approach." My different approach is not standing up in the meeting and asking for it, hoping people will say yes. "It's a draft but I'll show you what I have so far. It starts with a sketch of what the tavern might look like with more outside room. That puts a visual in everyone's mind."

He doesn't need to know I took a picture of Jack's design without Jack knowing. He won't care—well, he might when he realizes I was going through his stuff. In my defense, the man is messy and I was looking for a pen.

"You've really thought this through," he says, leaning closer to the screen.

"This slide outlines the potential benefits. People like things in threes, so I've stuck to that format, focusing on profitability, public perception, and return visitors. This slide is the cons, and you can change them if they're not right, but underneath I gave a way you'll tackle or handle each of them so it doesn't impact your neighbors."

"This is brilliant, Clara."

"When I went shopping out of town, I saw a couple of bars with outdoor sitting areas serving food. I put the pictures in here." I click to the next slide. "Which brings me to my next point: I think you need to ask for more than just a decking extension. You're limiting yourself because you won't be able to use it in the winter. If you put a retractable roof and walls system, you can add heaters and make it profitable all year round. That's what those bars I saw were doing."

"I like how that looks too."

I nod, grateful he sees the vision. "Fraser Falls is *so* beautiful right now, why would anyone want to go inside and stop looking at it? This way they can eat, drink, and enjoy the view."

I go through my other slides that need his help. Mostly ones with figures, visitor numbers, et cetera. When I'm finally done I tuck my hands under my chin and wait for his feedback. I'm waiting a long time.

"I'm speechless, Clara." The subtle nagging feeling that started when people stopped wanting my help has started to seep away. "This is incredible, thank you so much."

We make a plan for me to email the presentation to Tommy so he can insert all the facts and figures we need, once he's looked them up. Then we will go over it before the next town meeting. The meeting is just the first stage; if they approve it, he needs to get official planning permission, but it feels closer than it did an hour ago.

Tommy swears he has no other problems to fix, other than being single. I tell him I could introduce him to Honor but my brother might disown me. Sahara has a very specific type, and that type is rich and works on Wall Street. I promise him if I ever make any new friends I'll tell him right away.

I take my time walking back the long way to the B & B, absorbing every square inch of Fraser Falls. The family of light-up snowmen that has been added to the Christmas tree display. The sleigh on the roof of the gazebo. The Christmas and Hanukkah books in the window of the Green Light. Holly wreaths for sale in Wilde & Winslet. Mistletoe above the door of the Frozen Spoon. Jack's North Pole mailbox sitting proudly outside his store.

I keep walking back to the B & B instead of going into Harry's. I'd love to see him, but I don't know if I could concentrate over the sound of the ticking clock I can hear.

Chapter 34

CLARA

THERE'S A SADNESS FOLLOWING ME around and I can't shake it.

It's like a black cloud that only I'm stuck under. Wilhelmina is hosting a pottery class to make Santa plates, but I can't find the energy to go and pretend to be happy.

Elf is lying across me like a fifty-pound anxiety blanket, whipping me with his tail every time I speak. Jack is still downstairs working. He's using our bullshit bingo card while replying to customer emails—ones he didn't want my help with—so I'm alone with my thoughts.

I tell myself that the black cloud is just because I don't feel Christmassy yet. But in reality, I'm blaming the lack of Christmas spirit because it's easier than facing the truth: I just don't want to leave. I pull out my phone and breathe a sigh of relief when I still don't find an influx of activity and car service confirmation email.

I google basic gingerbread recipes and click on the one by Martha Stewart. I scan the ingredients and shuffle Elf off me so I can check the kitchen cupboards. It's a workout but I manage it and find everything I need.

This will fix things, I decide. I had a momentary reprieve from the ticking clock of doom while eating my cinnamon roll earlier, so maybe the cure to my grief is sugar.

I send Jack a text that tells him not to be scared if the fire alarm goes off. Ten seconds later he's walking through the door. "Why are we burning things?" he asks, leaning on the end of the kitchen counter.

"Because it isn't festive in here," I tell him, reaching on my tiptoes for the flour. He walks behind me, his firm body pressed into mine as he reaches over my hand to grab the container for me.

"I see. And fire is festive?" He makes an overdramatic grunt when I elbow him gently in the ribs. "What else do you need to get festive in here?"

"Baking soda, baking powder, brown sugar." Jack stays behind me, getting things down off the shelf one by one. I turn around and wrap my arms around his waist, burying my head into his chest. "Ground ginger, ground cinnamon, ground cloves. Do you have molasses? I can't find it."

"In the refrigerator," he says. "You'll have to let go for me to find it."

"It isn't supposed to go in there," I tell him as I free him. He responds by kissing the top of my head. I already have the unsalted butter, salt, pepper, and eggs ready to go. I move the molasses jar he hands me from side to side and watch dark, sticky liquid move slowly. "I'll let you get away with it. It's still pourable."

Jack blows out a puff of air and wipes his hand across his forehead theatrically. "Thank God, you had me worried you wouldn't let me get away with it."

"Sarcasm is the lowest form of wit." I look for mixing bowls and find nothing. I don't want to ask him for help because he already looks like he's in a good mood and I have no patience for it. I don't know what it is about being around happy people when you feel bad that makes you feel even worse. I open another pointless cabinet and only find protein shakes.

"Baby, why don't you just ask me to tell you where to find what you're looking for?" he says softly.

"Because . . ." I don't have a reason. I'm just being a grumpy asshole who needs to get out of this funk. I should be happy I'm not needed anymore. The town is thriving. People are delighted. I'm getting my promotion—well, as soon as I call Dad I am. The thought makes me feel sick. "Because I don't know."

Jack's cell phone starts ringing, probably with someone asking him to do something or fix something or give advice on how to do or fix something.

He's a better person than me because there'd be a certain point where I'd just start asking people if they bothered to google it before deciding to call me. To my surprise, Jack sends the call to voicemail and puts his phone on the counter. I practically gasp. I've never seen him miss a call.

"They can wait," he says as a partial explanation. "We're doing your thing. Now, tell me what you're searching for, please."

"Mixing bowls," I answer sheepishly. He turns around and takes them out of the cabinet behind him. "Baking tray, rolling pin, and parchment paper."

Jack pulls out drawers and opens the correct cabinets easily, putting each thing on the counter in front of me. "What else?"

"That's it. I know where everything else is."

"Why do you look so sad?" Jack says gently.

I push the ingredients to the side and slide myself onto the counter. "I don't even want to make gingerbread."

Jack moves between my legs and runs his hands up and down my outer thighs. "You don't need to make gingerbread. I can put all this away and we can pretend it never happened. Do you want me to get my laptop and work up here?"

I shake my head. "No. I think I'm going to nap this funk away. I'll be nicer when you're done with work."

He kisses my temple. "You're always nice. I won't be much longer, okay? Then we can make this place festive."

I help him put everything back onto the shelves and ignore it when he puts the molasses back in the refrigerator. "I'm sorry for being a grump. I'll snap out of it."

"You're allowed to be whatever you want to be, Clara. You don't have to pretend for me. I'll be back up soon."

It's funny because I don't feel like I've needed to pretend the whole time I've been in Fraser Falls. Everyone has accepted me as I am.

I grab my phone from on top of the chopping board and immediately spot a missed call from Max. I suddenly wish I were distracting myself by making gingerbread.

My fingers hover over his name in my call log. I press his name and decide it's probably nothing. Max picks up on the fourth ring.

"Hey, sorry I missed your call."

"That's okay. I wasn't sure if you were busy tipping cows or whatever," he says, the sound of loud honking cars behind him.

"We don't do that on Thursdays. It's a rest day. So what's up?" There's a long, drawn-out beep in the background. "Where are you?"

"Walking through Midtown," he says, his voice becoming muffled. "Nothing's up. I wanted to see if we could have lunch on Monday."

"Sorry, back up. Why are you in Midtown?" I brace myself to be told it's for a work meeting. That this is how I find out I'm not getting the promotion.

"My project finished early so when I went back to Boston after Thanksgiving, we agreed to end my contract now instead of January. I've only been back a few days," he says. "So, lunch?"

"I'm not coming back until Wednesday, before the gala," I say, figuring out exactly how I can ask Max if he's going to be working at Davenport without sounding like a bitter bitch.

Max makes a noise somewhere right between a sigh and a groan. "I *really* wanted to talk to you before the gala."

My stomach drops. "Just say what you need to say now, Max."

"No, I want to see you and talk to you in person. Let's do Thursday morning then if you really can't make time."

I force a smile even though he can't see me. "I'll put you in my schedule. See you at the gala."

I stare at my phone after Max is gone. I could call my dad now and tell him about the videos. He could say the words *congratulations on your promotion* and it'll make me feel less paranoid and twitchy.

But then I'd be forced to leave.

It feels like an impossible choice between the discomfort of not knowing and the heartbreak of leaving. I still have so many ideas, so many things I want to achieve. So many things to learn about the people that make this town what it is.

The door opens again, and Jack appears in the doorway with his laptop. "You look more miserable than you did when I went downstairs. What's wrong with you today, Clara? Please, just talk to me."

Realistically, I could unload every single thought and feeling onto Jack right now and see if it makes me feel lighter. But all it's going to do is make him feel heavier, or worse, trigger an argument about my job. There's one thing I can tell him that is truthfully the root of all the bad things I'm feeling right now, and he deserves that honesty.

"I don't want to leave," I admit. "I haven't had enough time. I need more time."

Jack looks at my cell phone clutched between my hands warily. "I'll cause a PR crisis for you and you can stay forever. I'll make criticizing Davenport my life's work if it means you don't have to leave. I'll get social media accounts and one of those ring lights and I'll terrorize them."

I rub my eyes on the backs of my hands. I'm not crying yet but there's a heavy, weepy weight sitting on my chest and it might bring tears. "I can't believe you know what a ring light is."

"Is this why you're so sad today? Have you been told to go home?" There's a cautious undertone to his question. Jack *hates* talking about my job and, by extension, my family. It would matter if this thing between us didn't have an expiration date, but it does, so I don't push him.

"No, I just know it's coming soon. I have a weird relationship with my brother when it comes to work and you don't want to hear about it, Jack. I'll be okay."

He puts his laptop down on the back of the couch and holds his arms open for me. "I wish you'd talk to me properly about what's bothering you. I hate not being able to fix it."

Beneath the words, I know his intentions are good. Jack is *the* fix-it person. He takes on everyone else's burdens. It's programmed into him to try. But I can't pretend it doesn't rub me the wrong way that he's acting like I'm holding things back from him. I lean away and scowl.

"What do you expect me to say?" I snap. "My problems are all intertwined with the one thing you don't want to hear about. Don't act like I'm not an open book when you're the one who wants to rip some chapters out."

"I don't want . . . Clara, I—" He takes a deep breath. "I just wish you'd stand up for yourself when it comes to them. I hate hearing about them because it's always how you've been used and not appreciated. I hate how talking about Davenport ends up with you upset."

"Forget it," I say. "I'm sorry I snapped at you."

"I don't want to spend the time we have left together fighting. I'm sorry, you're right. It's my boundary and you're respecting it. We can turn this day around. It isn't festive in here at all. Will you come with me to pick a Christmas tree?"

I take a step back and fold my arms. "That depends, are you going to knock me to the ground this time?"

The corner of his mouth quirks. "Only if you're on the nice list."

"That's a no then." Jack grips the front of my sweater and pulls me toward him. His kiss is gentle at first, like he's not sure if I'm still ready to fight. He tastes like peppermint. I lean back, eyeing him suspiciously. "Have you been eating candy canes? Without me?"

His eyes widen. "I can explain. Nancy gave me one. Only *one*. I would never not share with you."

"I'm so mad at you right now." *What a day.* "I can't believe you'd do something so . . . *not* festive!"

"How about you stop being mad at me immediately, and I detour to Luke's via the grocery store and buy you a whole pack. Plus"—he holds out his hands like an overenthusiastic car salesman going in for the verbal kill—"you get to choose the tree."

"Is there hot chocolate available while we're choosing this tree?"

He nods. "Or mulled wine."

"And when we decorate the tree, do we have anything on in the background?"

Jack watches me carefully, considering all the options to what is quite clearly a question designed to trip him up. "Destiny's Child's Christmas album?"

He shies away from his answer like a nervous game show contestant. I wish I had a buzzer I could set off. "Okay, I guess I can stop being mad under those conditions."

"Thank fuck. Wrap up, it'll be cold up there and we're due a lot of snow tonight."

"You wear sensible shoes then, because I don't want you falling on top of me again," I say, totally lying. "Wait, I need to go to Maggie's and get my boots."

Jack digs in his pockets and tosses me his truck keys. "You go. I need to do something here first. I'll walk over in around twenty minutes? Then drive us over to Luke's farm."

My eyes narrow. "What're you up to?"

"It's a surprise. Drive safe."

Chapter 35

JACK

"You get a text to tell you to water it!"

I look between Clara and Dove, shaking my head for the third time. "No."

"You're a monster," Dove says. "Sailor painted those pots. You're saying no to Sailor."

I fold my arms across my chest, tucking my hands under my armpits. My breath is a cloud of white air in front of me. "Fine. Bring her over here and I'll say no to her face. I want a big, normal tree."

"Size isn't everything," Clara says, gesturing toward the potted tree from Dove's eco project.

I raise an eyebrow and Dove makes a vomiting noise. "In this case it is. I don't want your hippie recycling tree, Pierce. I want one that's going to die in a few weeks so I know the holidays are over. Like Santa intended."

Talking to Dove is like talking to a younger sister who never stopped acting like a teenager. Which is annoying, because I remember Dove as a teenager, so I've had to suffer for years. She rolls her eyes. "I bet your three brain cells found that one super funny."

Clara laughs, then holds up her hands defensively when I shoot her an offended look. "My three brain cells found it funny. The rest of them are frozen."

"I give up," Dove declares. "Follow the crowd. Be a sheep with your boring Christmas tree. I don't care."

"Will do!" I grab Clara's arm and practically pull her away toward the trees I actually want to look at. I'm a big fan of sustainable practices, but Tommy has one in his apartment and he's forgotten to water it three times in three days even though he received the text reminder.

I have enough trouble keeping me and Elf alive, I don't need a replantable tree to worry about. Especially when Dove is the person I'll have to tell if I fuck it up. And especially when I plan to be miserable when Clara leaves.

I *know* we basically said casual, no strings, but I think I'm strung up pretty tight.

"Do you want the first one we see or are you a size queen?" Clara asks, dodging a family and their tape measure.

"What the fuck is a size queen?" The way she's laughing to herself tells me I don't want to know. "You can't just pick the first one. You have to walk around for a bit."

She crunches the end of her candy cane. "It's so busy."

The tree farm always gets a steady dose of visitors through December, and Luke never turns down a delivery request, but this amount is something I haven't seen in a long time. "Yeah, Luke said people are saying they saw him online. Weird because he hasn't bought ads or anything."

"Yeah, weird," she says slowly. "Good for him."

I watch her out of the corner of my eye. The subdued smile on her lips. "Anything to do with you?"

"I haven't had time to meddle in Luke's life," she says dramatically. "You keep taking my clothes off when I try to do anything important."

"You're a bad liar, Clara." She looks up at me, brow furrowed. "Good person though."

"Jury is out on that one... Hey! What about this one?" She points at a seven-foot fir. "I like it."

She stands next to it and it sprawls far above her head. "Let's get it then. Guard it with your life."

Clara salutes me playfully. "Don't worry. I'm not above fighting a family."

I'm laughing as I walk away to find Luke or one of his staff, secretly hoping that Clara isn't above fighting *her* family.

ON REFLECTION, I SHOULD'VE COVERED Clara's eyes at the top of the stairs, not at the bottom.

She laughs all the way up to the top step, one hand covering my hand on her eyes, the other clinging to the railing. It feels good to hear her laughing after she was acting out of character since this morning. "I'm scared about what kind of surprise can be whipped up in twenty minutes and requires me to climb the stairs without the use of my eyes. You smell like a car air freshener, by the way."

"Yeah, my bad. You probably could've climbed the stairs." We reach the top step and I reposition my hands. "Are your eyes closed?"

"No, but your massive hands are causing a blackout, so does it really make a difference?" I push open the front door and brace to be charged by Elf, but he isn't waiting for us, weirdly. "Don't let me bump into anything, okay? I already have enough bruises on my thighs from you and your hip bones."

I help her dodge the couches, which aren't in their normal spot after I moved them out of the way. I can hear snoring from the tent I set up in front of the window, revealing the location of Elf.

"You ready?" I ask.

"Show me!"

There's a split second as I pull my hands away when I worry that I've built it up too much, but her hands fly to her mouth. "You remembered," she whispers, her voice unsteady.

She turns to face me, eyes wide and watering. I pull her hands away from her mouth to see her smile. It's just as stunning as the first time I ever saw it.

"I remembered," I respond. I fix problems all the time, but nothing quite compares to seeing this reaction after she was so down earlier. I feel like I know her and how to make her happy. It's a better feeling than anything I've ever done. She kicks off her shoes and coat, dropping them at her feet, to crawl into the tent beside Elf.

Clara being so upset about leaving made me think that there are so many things I haven't done with her. She loved sitting in front of the window when it snowed, so I thought I'd try to re-create it but with camping, something she's never done before.

"You happy?"

"I know I say this basically any time it snows and I'm in front of this window, but it really does feel like a snow globe. This is so fun, Jack. And I don't have to pee in the woods!"

I laugh at that being her concern and not how cold it is outside. "I'm going to bring the tree up while you get comfortable."

She pokes her head out of the doorway. "Do you need help?"

I shake my head. "No, thanks. I'll be right back."

Twenty minutes later, a steaming cup of marshmallow and cream is placed on the coffee table in front of me while I try to thread a piece of gold string through the deer Christmas ornament.

"Is there even any hot chocolate in that mug?" I ask. She dips her tongue into her own mug; it reemerges covered in cream. "Taking that as a no."

She shrugs. "There's some near the bottom."

I miss the hole of the ornament again, cursing under my breath.

Clara sits down on my knee, taking the deer and string from my hand gently. She wets the end of the thread between her lips and twists it. It threads through on the first try. "Thank you."

"You're welcome. Where should I put her?" She holds the deer up against the tree, moving it around from top to bottom. "I think top right."

She could tell me she wants to put it on Mars and I'd nod along. "Top right it is."

"Are you just agreeing with everything I say?" she says, twisting in my lap to look at me. I move backward on the couch until I hit the cushion. Her ass slips off my knee into the empty space beside me and she lifts her snowman-pajama-covered legs to rest them over my thighs.

"No. I just don't have strong tree-decorating opinions." And I also learned that Clara hasn't ever decorated her own tree. "And you make great choices."

"You're a kiss-ass, Kelly."

"When it's yours, for sure."

She runs her finger across the deer in her hand, head resting against my shoulder. "I think in another universe, if I lived here, I'd want an animal sanctuary like Dove when I retired."

"I think in another universe, if you lived here, that would be nice."

"This deer would be a perfect contender." She holds it up in the air. "Why does it only have three legs?"

I take it from her, turning it over in my hand. "I don't know. I've never noticed before. I could blame Elf but he never chewed anything when I brought him home. He was a good boy from day one. I think it's just my own negligence."

"Stay away from my animal sanctuary then."

"Some of these decorations are older than me. My parents dumped them on my doorstep when they moved to Florida, along with school report cards and kindergarten art projects. Too sentimental to throw away but not enough to go in a U-Haul truck."

"What do your report cards say?" she asks, crisscrossing my chest with her finger as she follows the plaid pattern of my flannel button-down.

"'Disruptive and unlikely to meet his potential.'"

"You're still pretty disruptive," she says. "All you do is talk, talk, talk. To everyone. Never quiet or brooding. Just yapping away to anyone who will listen."

"Sounds just like me," I say sarcastically. "You want to finish the tree? Or have you lost interest?"

"I don't lose interest in things that easily," she says, her hand cupping my face, thumb brushing along my cheekbone. "Except for this beard. I like the sexy overgrown stubble but this is too far."

I rub along my jawline. I know what she means. Part of me thought having a beard would somehow make me feel more masculine but I hate it. I wish I'd just opted for the fake beard like Tommy did every year.

A choice made out of necessity because Tommy can't grow a beard, but still.

"I'll send you a picture when I get to shave it off." *Because you won't be here.*

She looks sad but she smiles anyway. "I'd love that."

I take my time when I lean in and kiss her. I memorize the placement of the freckles on her nose, the exact green of her eyes, the curve of her lips. How it feels when her body relaxes and melts into mine.

"Let's finish the tree and go to bed," I say, breaking away from her reluctantly.

"Okay."

Clara puts on a new Christmas playlist while I drink my cup of cream, and between us we decorate the tree. Elf steals baubles and Clara complains there's no theme—something I argue against because the theme is Christmas—so it takes us another hour to reach a point where we're ready to put the star on top.

"The back is really ugly," Clara says, walking the perimeter of the tree.

"Shhhh." I grab her as she tries to walk around me to look from the other side. "Nobody cares about the back. That's why we put it next to a wall."

"I'm learning so much from you." She holds out the star to me. It's old and slightly crooked, but it's from my first wood shop project and my dad refused to ever throw it away. "I feel like there needs to be a countdown or something. Dolly Parton should be here."

I put the star on the top and crouch beside the wall socket, holding the plug for the lights in my hand. "I can wait if you want to sing '9 to 5.'"

"You say that as a man who has clearly never heard me sing. Okay, five . . . four . . . three . . . two . . . one!" I push the plug into the wall and the lights come to life, colors shining off the baubles. "It's beautiful. There's no color coordination *at all* but I love it."

"Good. Finish your cup of cream and we can go to bed."

Clara sits with her mug, Elf immediately taking the spot beside her, resting his head on her thigh. "I'm not that tired. Do you want to watch a movie in our tent?"

"That's what happens when you drink multiple cups of sugar." The truth is I am tired, but I don't want to pass up a couple more hours spending time with her. "Sure. You decide what we're watching."

I already know as soon as I hand over my iPad that she's going to find *How the Grinch Stole Christmas*. She's been talking about it ever since Tommy made a passing comment about *The Holiday* being the best Christmas movie.

The tent is a tight fit with the two of us and the dog, but we make it work. I roll up the side window so the lights of the tree shine through the netting and make sure we're in the right position to watch the snow cascading down.

Clara snuggles in, balancing the screen on my stomach, and I'm asleep before the opening credits have even finished.

Chapter 36

JACK

I CAN FEEL FLO'S EYES on me across the room but I'm trying to ignore it.

The café is packed today. The staff have been running around constantly to maintain Flo's required level of excellent service. Yet she still has time to stand behind the counter watching me eat my turkey sub.

Harry's has been full of people all day, meaning I've only had time to eat now after running back and forth with stock while Joe worked the register. I'm so relieved I took the extra time in the summer to make the Christmas decorations because they're unusually popular this year. Joe said at least twenty people have said "Shopping independent" to him like it's some kind of cult mantra and he didn't know what to do so he just saluted them.

I'm trying not to stare back at Flo so I opt to stare at the floor or table while I eat. Something I regret when two orthopedic-sneaker-covered feet stop in my line of sight. I look up expectantly, mouth full of turkey and bread. "No Clara?" she says, sitting herself in the chair on the other side of my table.

Christ. It's always been "No Elf?" and now it's "No Clara?" I want to tell her that I do come without an add-on and she can have me on my own, but I don't want to get smacked on the head while I'm eating.

I wash my late lunch down with my soda. "Nope."

"Has she gone home?" I don't know why Flo is acting like she doesn't know everything that goes on in this town. If Clara had checked out of the B & B she'd be the first person to know after Maggie.

"She's at the art school helping set up for the author signing later. Miss Celia sold a lot of tickets so she couldn't host it in the bookstore." I don't know why I'm telling her like she doesn't already know. Like I said, second to know *always*. "Do you need her?"

Flo crosses her legs and sits back in her chair. "I was talking to your mother earlier."

Here we go. "That's nice."

"It was good to catch up with her. She said she's going to your sister's house for Christmas and New Year's. Can't work out why anyone would pick Oklahoma over here, but she said your dad was excited." First I'm hearing about it. Cool.

"I'm sure they'll have a great time." My spidey senses are tingling. I know this is going *somewhere*, I just can't work out where. "I bet Oklahoma has its bonuses."

"She didn't know where you were spending your holidays," she says, reorganizing the seasonings and sugar on the table. "She didn't know anything about you and Clara. I was wondering if maybe you were heading to New York for Christmas."

This is what I get for not making my own food at home. "There isn't a me and Clara, Ms. Flo. I'll be in Fraser Falls for Christmas, like I am every year."

"Your grandfather was a very stubborn man. Now, I don't like to speak ill of the dead"—*So don't*, is what I want to say—"but he watched many opportunities pass him by because he was so stuck in what he knew. Didn't ever want to go off plan. Didn't always work out the best for him, Jack."

"I don't think I'm following what this has to do with me," I admit as politely as I can.

"I've seen you smile more recently than I think I have in the past ten years. Smiling is important. Keeps your heart healthy and helps you live longer. I'd like you to live a long time because at some point I'm going to need you to make my doors wider when I need a walker."

I let out an unattractive snort. "I'll add it to the list of jobs you have for me."

"I don't want you to let the reason you're smiling head back to the city with no thought of returning. She's a very nice woman, Jack. I know it was shaky ground in the beginning but she's done more than we could've expected of her under the circumstances."

Very nice woman feels like an understatement. "I know she has."

"The fact she's still here helping out when I told her I'd taken down the videos just shows that—"

My brow furrows. "You took the videos down? When? Why?"

"Yesterday. We're more than the bad things that happen to us, Jack. People should look us up and find all the positive things people have to say, not a feud with a corrupt corporation."

"And Clara knows?" Of course she does. It's why she was acting so strange yesterday totally out of the blue. "And she's still here? Helping at the book event?"

"Celia is delighted with her. The bookstore is full of people today and that publishing person mentioned doing a preorder campaign for Matilda's next book. Clara made that happen."

"You're not telling me anything I don't already know, Ms. Flo." Other than the fact the one thing keeping Clara here is now gone. "I know Clara is special, but I don't think what you want to happen is in the cards for us. There are too many things out of reach."

"The nativity has sold out for the first time in a decade, Jack.

Over one hundred people are here today shopping and eating before the event tonight. More are coming over the next few weeks. Everything feels in reach." She closes her hand over mine, her touch warm and maternal. "Maybe you can put that stubbornness to good use. You don't have to accept what you think is inevitable, Jack."

"Maybe," I say, unsure what else there is I could say in response.

Flo squeezes my hand and stands, leaving me with my half-eaten lunch and a hell of a lot to think about. Number one: Why the hell is Clara still here?

VISITORS ARE GREAT UNTIL I need to park.

Every single year we spend at least one town meeting going through all possible places to park; it used to be easy because of the limited tourists we anticipated. After last year's boom, Arthur bought double the signage for "busy periods." Which obviously meant I, plus Tommy and Luke, had to install it. It's how I know that where to park couldn't be clearer, because I froze my balls off earlier in the week making sure it couldn't be misinterpreted.

A waste of fucking time now that my truck is blocked in by a car with Massachusetts plates.

We have a tow-truck guy who lives fifteen minutes outside of town for emergencies, but I'll be publicly executed if I tow a visitor's car just because I'm pissed off that I have to walk when it's cold.

I get stuck behind a dozen women strolling after leaving Wilde & Winslet. They're each holding bags from the store in one hand and a bag from the Green Light in the other. I'm so happy for Miss Celia and even Wilhelmina, who's overjoyed for so many people to learn about her school, but there's also a swell of pride for Clara and the fact she was the catalyst. Back far before I even appreciated her.

I spot her as soon as I walk through the doors. Her auburn hair stands out against the sea of winter hats of the people arriving and finding their seats. She grins when she spots me and beelines across the room. Her arms circle my neck, and her lips press against my cheek gently. Her sweet smell envelops me. "Does it look okay?"

The seats are beginning to fill up already. On the outskirts of the room is a table manned by Miss Celia and her granddaughter; they're handing out books and totes to people who arrive. Behind me there are a hot chocolate stand and a business that must be from out of town selling licensed merchandise.

There are two comfortable seats for Matilda and the woman who's hosting the Q & A, on the stage. Information about the event is currently being projected onto a screen behind the seats, and a table is set up on the floor directly in front of the stage, ready for the signing element of the event.

"It looks amazing."

"I started reading the book while we were waiting and it made me cry. Then Matilda showed up and I had to meet her for the first time with black eyes," she says twice as quickly as she normally talks. Nerves? There's so much for me to learn and I don't have enough time. "How's your day been? I missed hanging out with you today."

It was fine until I found out there's no reason for you to be here. "I missed hanging out with you, too, but the store was a little chaotic so I wouldn't have had much time anyway. You have fun here? What's Matilda like?"

"I was kinda expecting her to be a diva but she's honestly so sweet. She spent an hour talking to Miss Celia about books while she signed all the stock she has at the store."

Behind Clara, Wilhelmina appears on the stage and starts testing the microphones. I watch as she takes a look around the room, smiling as she taps the mic. "I think we're almost ready to start. It's getting so full in here!"

I can't believe it myself. The nativity and the ballet usually draw a small crowd but nothing like this. I didn't even know this many seats could fit in here. "I'm proud of you. This wouldn't be happening without your persistence."

"Thank you," she says quietly, a mix of emotions on her face. "I can't believe how well the tickets sold. Apparently there were tons of people who didn't get tickets to her other events because she's so in demand, so they've all traveled in. I met a group who had rented a minivan to drive down here for a girls' weekend."

"I think I got stuck behind them leaving Wilde & Winslet."

Clara is visibly excited, clutching the front of my jacket. "That's them! They were early and we got to talking, so I told them how good the candles are in there and they said they'd go take a look!"

"Maybe we need to make you head of the tourism board or something," I say, only half joking. "You can be in charge of the Visit Fraser Falls page."

She gives me a dismissive look, hands on her hips, red hair swept over one shoulder. "You didn't even know about the Fraser Falls tourism page until I told you."

"Which proves my point. You're spreading the word."

Clara looks over her shoulder, kissing me quickly when she realizes nobody is paying attention to us. She tries to pull away but I hold her face, letting go when she starts to laugh. "I'm going to sit at the back out of the way, okay? I promised Tommy I'd save him a seat."

She looks over both shoulders. "Tommy is already here. He was one of the first people to arrive. I love that he's super into reading."

"He's super into gossip, which the book club provides a lot of. I also get scheduled to do a lot of tasks during book club time. I think Flo believes if she's busy, I should be too. Tommy always gets out of it because he's seated right next to her eating macarons or whatever it is she takes with her."

"He's smarter than you are."

I sigh heavily, rubbing my forehead with my hand. "I know. I need to pick up a book."

She gives me one last brief kiss and heads back toward the stage. I take a seat on the end of the back row; that way I'm not blocking anyone's view. I can see Tommy talking to a group of women our age on the other side of the room. One of them throws her head back laughing when he says something. I know for a fact that he's never said anything that warrants that reaction.

I wave at him to get his attention. He's got a shit-eating grin on his face when he sits down beside me. "This is where I'm going to find a wife."

Side-eyeing him isn't enough. "You sound like you're about to kidnap someone."

"That's weird," he says, pointing his fingers at me. "But I don't need to. I'm the only single man in the room."

"I'm single," I argue.

He looks at me skeptically. "Sure you are, man. Single men kiss the women they're sleeping with and never stop talking about in the corner when they think no one is watching all the time."

"I don't *never stop talking about* her," I argue, but he's already rolling his eyes.

"Clara doesn't like oranges. Clara has a scar on her wrist from falling over drunk in college. Clara's middle name is Rose. Clara's favorite vacation spot is Italy. Clara's—"

"I know all this. Why are you telling me?"

"I know you know it. Why do *I* know it?"

Despite what Tommy says, I think I talk about her a normal amount. It's not like she's all I talk about. Sometimes I talk about work too. Thankfully, Miss Celia appears on the stage and turns the mic on, giving me the perfect out for this conversation.

"Hello, everyone. I want to start by thanking you all for taking the time and effort to visit us out here in Fraser Falls. To see this room filled with people, especially on such short notice, makes my heart sing in a way I'm not sure *any* writer would be able to do justice with words.

"I've owned the Green Light bookstore for forty years and it's been a journey of highs and lows. This is certainly one of my highest highs. When you choose to support independent businesses, especially during the holiday season, you really are choosing to support someone's dreams.

"I'd like to thank Matilda for finding time in what I'm sure is a chaotically busy schedule to spend this evening with us, and her publisher for doing everything they could to make tonight as special as possible. A final thank-you goes to our very own Clara, who used her connections and persuasive spirit to make tonight happen for you all.

"With that said, I'd like to welcome Matilda Brown and her conversation partner and host, Dallas Ryan!"

The room bursts into applause as a young blond woman steps onto the stage waving. "Hi, everyone," Matilda says, her English accent standing out against Miss Celia's.

I'm too stuck on Miss Celia calling Clara *our very own* to listen to anything Matilda Brown or her conversation partner has to say. She has everyone in this room hanging on her every word and all I want to do is tell Clara how proud I am of her.

The problem is, it feels too much like goodbye.

Chapter 37

CLARA

EVERY TIME I OPEN MY eyes, it feels like there's a ticking clock of doom following me around.

And for once, it isn't caused by my mother reminding me about my biological clock. It's getting louder and more annoying and it is entirely in my subconscious.

There's this anxious feeling of needing to be doing *something*, which I sense Jack is feeling too. He was quiet last night when we finally finished at the book event. I thought he was tired because it took hours—Matilda wouldn't rush anyone away and spent time hugging and taking pictures with every single person—but he said he was okay, just had a lot on his mind. He blamed work before I could ask any other questions.

Matilda is a beautiful person inside and out, and I loved listening to her talk about putting her characters through the complexities of love and healing. So did Tommy, and he gave me a full rundown of his thoughts while we helped Wilhelmina clear up the theater.

Gossip lover, my ass. That man loves books.

Jack went home to get Elf and I walked over to the tavern with Tommy and Dove, talking about our favorite reads. When he eventually rejoined us, I tried to switch the topic back to something he was more likely to take part in, but he subtly pushed us back to books and continued to not say much.

His arm stayed across the back of my chair, his fingers playing with strands of my hair. It felt like a normal Friday night with friends and the only thing missing for me was Honor. She took her sister to the Brooklyn event on Wednesday so she didn't take up my invite to come here for ours.

Jack and I walked hand in hand back to the B & B with Elf, climbed into bed, and fell asleep. To anyone it would have looked like the perfect evening but something felt off the whole time. He kept bringing up how much I've achieved while I've been here. How he regrets giving me such a hard time at the start.

"You awake?" his sleep-drenched voice grumbles behind me.

"Yeah."

"I've decided to take the day off, so we can do whatever you want today."

I roll over to face him. I haven't told him how beautiful he is enough. "You'll get behind though."

He shrugs, wipes the sleep from his eyes, and yawns. "I'll catch up."

"Is it a waste if we have a calm day? I sort of just want to sit and look at you. Maybe eat. Then stare at you some more. I could probably do that from the store though. Just put me in a corner with a croissant."

I'm rambling. I can hear the nervousness in my voice and it sounds alien. "Permission to suggest something other than staring?"

Heat rushes to my cheeks. "Permission granted."

"There's an indoor farmer's market an hour away. I don't get time to go because I'm always at work on a Saturday, but I'd like to take you. There are tons of food options and other cool businesses. I think you'll like it."

"I'd love that. You want to shower with me?" I ask hopefully.

"If I ever answer no to that question just know it's a cry for help." Jack kisses my forehead and swings his legs over the side of the bed. He stretches his arms toward the ceiling; the muscles on his back ripple beneath the incoming sunlight.

Far too long later, I'm finally dragging a hairbrush through my mostly dry but still tangled hair. Having a man wash your hair is all fun and games until suddenly he's holding on to it while you're on your knees. "Baby, we need to leave if you want to eat something before it starts selling out," Jack says from his spot on my bed.

Why do men take just as long to get ready, but if they're done even a tiny bit before you, they sit somewhere in your eyeline and look like they've been waiting since the beginning of time?

"Take it up with yourself, mister."

"What can I do to speed this process up? What're you going to wear today?" he asks.

"My jeans that are over the chair in the living room and my black sweater that's hanging in the closet. I put fresh underwear on and my socks are in the laundry basket on the dining table."

Jack moves quickly to the closet, pulling the two shutter doors open. "Uh, Clara?"

I look at him over my shoulder. "Yeah?"

"Are you a serial killer?" He holds up a neon-pink sticky note. "And should I be concerned that there's a question mark under my name?"

"Do serial killers give their victims head in the shower instead of killing them?" I ask, finally working out the last knot in my hair. I braid it over my shoulder and stand from the floor to meet him at the closet.

He pulls out the black sweater he went in there for and there's another sticky note stuck to it. "True crime isn't really my thing so I'm not sure."

"It's my plan," I explain. "To help the town, not kill the town."

He sits on the bed in front of the closet, my sweater and the sticky notes still in his hands. "You really did have a plan this whole time. I thought it was a figure of speech or something."

I push my clothes out of the way so he can see the whole mess, peeling from the wall. "You made me realize when I first got here that for people to trust me they needed to like me first. So I decided to gain the town's trust by being proactive, helpful, and visible."

"You were visible all right. I felt like I saw you everywhere. You were like a ghost haunting me," he says.

"My plan got a little messy after that. I should've bought string. My main focus was raising the town's profile, getting more visitors, and earning everyone more money. But then I thought that the people involved in the Holly project needed something specific for them. I realized that everything all linked into my main focus—which is why I think I should've bought string, but you live and learn. Except for you, actually. Which is why your name's on my closet wall with a question mark."

"I was a phase of your plan?" he asks.

"In the achieving-my-goals sense, not in the dying-my-hair-black-and-listening-to-emo-music kind of way." I see him smile out of the corner of my eye.

"Walk me through it. It's interesting to see the town through your eyes."

Putting these sticky notes up feels like a lifetime ago. "Okay, but before I start, so many of these things had multiple people contributing. Please don't think I achieved them all on my own."

Jack kisses the top of my shoulder. "I know."

"I put Mel and Winnie in touch with my mom to do an event for her; it's a boost of income, which meets my earning-money goal.

"My mom loves them and she's giving their name to all her socialite friends. Obviously, the Small Business Saturday stamp book coincided with the most profitable Fraser Falls SBS ever, which also fits into the earn-money goal. Could just be a coincidence . . ."

"It wasn't a coincidence. You nailed it," he says.

"I stepped up to help Dove with the toy drive and emailed every single rich person I know. I don't know what the final donation number is and there's a truck of toys still to arrive that I ordered, but I think the donations are up significantly from past years."

"I heard that too," he says. "Raising our profile by telling people about it."

This is why I need string. "Yeah, I guess it is. I connected Miss Celia with my friend in publishing. Obviously the event last night brought dozens of people here and they not only spent money at the Green Light, but they went to other stores and we saw loads of them at Tommy's."

"You found Wilhelmina's nutcracker." There's a tinge of something playful in his tone.

"*We* found Wilhelmina's nutcracker. I gave Arthur a lesson on how to utilize the email mailing list opt-ins to push other things like the nativity and the ballet. I also showed him how to stop sending everything twice, but that was more for me."

"When the hell did you do that?" he asks. "I didn't even know teaching him was possible."

I wave my hand flippantly. "You were fixing someone's toilet or something. I wrote it all down for him, too, so you shouldn't get any calls about it. But that should help bring repeat visitors back to town, where they'll hopefully spend money."

"You've been busy," he says. "What else?"

"Well, Flo was the person I truly wanted to win over. I've been the most helpful, most visible, and most proactive with her. I've bought something from her every single day I've been here. Said yes to every little thing she's wanted."

"Dangerous territory. That's how it starts, now look at me." I do look at him. He's listening to my plan attentively and hasn't once interrupted to call me a scheming weirdo. I'm going to miss him so much it makes my bones ache. "Sorry for interrupting, baby. Carry on."

"I hoped I'd impress her with the stamp book, and I know she was happy, but I knew I could do more. That's why I got the news here for the Santa run. That's the best way I know how to raise a profile. Then the bad reviews happened and I helped get them removed, although I maintain that she needs to thank Sahara, not me. And finally the article."

"I think anything you do in town directly helps Flo, Clara. But you've done a lot for her and I know she appreciates you for it."

I look at the newer row of sticky notes beneath my original ones. "The more time I spent here the more things I picked up on. I'm sure even the hairdresser's and ice cream parlor need something so I put them on there somewhere. I've just run out of time. It's hard when you have to use your brain instead of your AmEx."

"You're missing one," he says quietly.

I lean against his shoulder, slowly breathe in his clean smell. "You're still a question mark, Jack."

"You don't think you've helped me while you've been here?" Above everything, he sounds confused. He grips my chin gently and angles my face toward his. "Clara, you've helped me in ways I'm not even sure I'll realize until you're not here anymore. But even at work things have been easier with you supporting me."

"When you say 'until you're not here anymore' it makes me feel like I'm never going to see you again. Makes me feel like I'm grieving before I'm even gone." The words hurt as I say them because the past forty-eight hours have felt different. Like we're both slowly crawling toward the end.

"It doesn't feel good saying it."

Jack kisses my temple and it takes every single shred of my inner strength to not burst into tears. This is not how this was supposed to go. I was supposed to skip my way back to New York and happily accept my promotion. Something I don't even know if I want anymore. "You know, you could charge like four times the price for your stuff if you moved your store to Brooklyn. You can keep the beard, we can pitch you as the tortured-artist type. Elf would love having so many questionable things to sniff."

"You could live here. Rent an office space and commute a couple of times a month. Or even better, quit and work for people who value you. Everyone would be happy to see you stay. Me especially."

I feel angry when I think about how easily Davenport hurt people in this community. They've strayed so far from our company values that it's borderline unrecognizable. The reason it hurt so much when Jack called me their first victim is because I can see the truth in his logic. He's right, I do need to stand up for myself. I have let them take advantage of me, of my ideas and my skills.

The fact he can tell knowing barely anything about my professional and family life is worrying. I think back to Max's urgent want to meet with me and it reminds me how paranoid I've become.

"We're going to miss the farmer's market," I say, reaching for my sweater. "We shouldn't waste your day off sitting here, you staring at me."

"You want to hide your murder closet?" he asks. "Or are you going to leave Maggie with questions and probably very serious concerns?"

"Close it. There's not much more I can do now anyway."

Chapter 38
CLARA

Dodging your father's calls should be considered an endurance sport.

It makes me just as sweaty and tired as any sport would, the only difference is there's no real reward at the end, because eventually I'll be forced to pick up the phone.

Just not today.

Today is the toy drive and I'm too excited to let a lecture about whatever's on his mind ruin my day. Or worse, he found out about Flo's videos before I've told him myself.

That's a problem for later. Today I refuse to let the ticking clock ruin my day.

Dove is in charge of the toy drive recordkeeping, her mom's old role. The truck driver called an hour ago to let me know he'd be arriving at the town hall around now.

Collecting donations has been more of a hobby than a task to complete, and I know that there are people who now *hate* to see my name in their inbox. I don't care. I'm perfectly happy to be a shameless pest to people who have the money to give.

I spot Dove upon entering the storage room, her face obscured by a wooden clipboard. She looks over it, squinting and widening her eyes. "I printed my list too small and it's making my eyes hurt but I don't want to waste paper," she explains.

"Flip it over and print it on the back," I say, putting her vegan croissant and oat milk latte on the table. I can tell that it immediately puts me on her nice list.

She looks at me like I just cured a rare disease. "This is why you get paid the big bucks in the big city."

"*Moderately-sized bucks* would be more appropriate."

"You'll get the big bucks when you get your promotion," she says confidently.

"I think they already gave it to my brother," I say, trying not to sound too disappointed. "He wanted to go for lunch to talk before the charity gala, but I told him I'm not leaving until I have to. We're not lunch-to-talk kind of siblings, so it's weird. Like, we do go to lunch, but we make small talk and bitch about petty things. We're not serious-lunch-meeting kind of siblings."

"If my brother asked me to go for lunch with him, I'd think he'd been kidnapped or something and it was his cry for help. But that sucks, I'm sorry. Maybe it's your sign to quit and work for a less morally bankrupt company?"

When Dove and Sailor visited me last week, aside from serious toy drive chat, we bonded over brothers and family business. Dove told me about how her brother basically left her to work the farm herself when their parents died, and even now he's reluctant to ever come back to Fraser Falls.

I told her about the promotion I've been working toward for two years, and how I was struggling to see my goals here and my goals at work as part of the same situation. Especially when it's always felt like Max has a bigger foot in the door.

Max isn't in any way a bad person, just like Dove's brother isn't, it just feels like they're playing life on easy level when we're playing it on medium. Maybe hard for Dove as a former teen mom with no parents around to support her.

It felt good to talk to someone who can understand loving your sibling so deeply and yet seeing them as this person whose motivations you don't truly understand. It was nice to hear Dove say she struggles to talk to her brother about even the simplest of things sometimes, because I'm the exact same with Max. My life would be so much easier if I felt I could just ask him things outright, but I don't. Competing with each other has been our thing our whole lives; being vulnerable by asking him questions feels like showing my hand.

He's always been the smarter sibling, but I'm the one who's put everything into Davenport.

"Sadly, places don't advertise whether they're morally rich on Indeed."

She smiles brightly. "That wasn't a no! I'll take it."

We fill the time looking up the quickest way to wrap masses of presents. When the truck pulls up outside and the door slides open, we're greeted with dozens of boxes.

"This is going to take forever," Dove says, watching the driver begin to offload them onto the sidewalk.

"I'll call Jack and see if he can come over and help. He might be able to leave work for twenty minutes."

Jack sounds bored as hell when he answers and is far too happy to be asked to skip work for a little while. He promises to call Tommy, too, and he's the first to arrive.

"You have a shopping problem, Clara," Tommy says, taking a box from our driver and carrying it into the building.

"It's a donation!" I shout after him. "I don't even know what's in the boxes!"

"You're not convincing," Jack says, jogging up behind me. His lips press into my temple briefly, hand patting my butt as he passes toward the back of the truck. "I'll grab that one, buddy."

Dove and I grab a smaller box, mostly pretending to help until the truck is almost empty. One of her jobs is to record every single thing that gets donated so they can be appropriately distributed, so we start opening the large cardboard boxes and putting the toys on the long table to categorize.

Tommy drops a box in the corner and Jack puts one on top of it. "Done!" Tommy announces proudly. "I gotta get back to the tavern. Have fun with your clipboard."

"Thank you!" we shout after him as he jogs off.

"Clara?" I turn at the sound of my name. Jack's standing in front of a box he just opened. I walk over to look in, slightly scared the warehouse sent something totally random.

There are lines etched into his forehead. "What's up?"

He gestures to a brightly colored robot in the box. "These are Davenport toys."

"I know. It's a donation delivery I've been waiting for all week. I told you about it."

I mentally go over every conversation in my head frantically. I told him I'd ordered a delivery of toys. I'm *sure* I did. My heart rate picks up as he looks over his shoulder at Dove, then closes the box. "I need to get back to the store," he says sharply.

"What's happening?" I ask quietly, anxiety spiking. I squeeze his forearm, desperate for some kind of answer. "Talk to me."

The kiss to my temple is brief and cold. "We can talk about it tonight. I really need to go."

All I can do is watch him leave. Dove walks to my side, watching him step through the door. "What's his problem?"

It feels like I'm back to square one. "Me."

Dove huffs. "Men. Ignore him."

. . .

I MISCOUNT THE STUFFED TOYS so badly that Dove kicks me out of her cataloging session.

Heading over to Jack's makes me feel like I'm volunteering to step onto a sinking ship. That stomach-wobbling unsettledness when you know you're walking into something bad, but you don't know what.

This place is making me soft because I've walked into fire before and escaped unscathed. I've never worried about what a man might say to me or how I might feel afterward.

But this isn't any man.

He's already upstairs when I head into the store instead of walking the long way around. Nancy gives me the nod to use his workshop as a shortcut to the stairs, and I take it as a positive that my access hasn't been rescinded.

I knock and wait for him to open the door, unsure what kind of mood I'll find on the other side of it. Elf rushes to my feet, whipping Jack's legs with his tail as he sticks his face between my knees. "Hey," I say carefully.

"Hey. You want a drink?"

I follow him into the kitchen, lean against the counter. "Sure. I'd really like to know how I've upset you."

He leans against the counter on the opposite side of the kitchen, mirroring me. It feels like there's a mile between us. "You haven't upset me," he says.

"But you're upset. You're hardly looking at me. Just come out and say it, Jack. I'm a big girl, I can take it."

"Davenport toys, Clara." He drags his hand over his hair, his head shaking gently. "You filled our town hall with fucking Davenport toys. The company that screwed us over. The toy drive is Fraser Falls' chance to give back to the community, and we're giving them *Davenport* toys."

He says my last name like it's a dirty word he hates to have on his lips. I stare back, not saying anything. Stuck between understanding, hurt, and anger.

"I didn't think it mattered—it's for charity. I told you I had a huge shipment of toys coming and you didn't say anything."

He rubs his fingers against his temple. The exact spot where I kiss him when I wake up. "Because I thought you'd bought them."

"Are you kidding me? You told me you didn't want me to throw money at things! I've raised *thousands* of dollars for Dove's toy fund using literally every person and business contact I have. Would you seriously have sick kids or kids who have nothing go without gifts *just* because of who their manufacturer is?"

"You're simplifying things, Clara. It isn't like I'm annoyed you bought Nike when I prefer Adidas. You know how I feel about the company. What can I say to my neighbors when this shows up as some kind of good-news story online?"

"It won't. Nobody knows, I placed the order myself. I didn't need authorization, it isn't on anybody's radar except Dove's, who I talked to about it before I even did anything." I laugh humorlessly, pinch the bridge of my nose between my fingers. "She gave me a lecture about microplastics in the ocean, then helped me choose what to order."

"Is this your way of telling me that I'm the only one upset about this?"

"It's my way of telling you that there isn't some great conspiracy. We . . . I was trying to do the best thing for the kids. Maybe I should've just bought them and let you be mad at me about that instead."

"Clara," he says, trying to interrupt, but I don't let him.

"I worked on some of those donations. Some of them in the design and innovation departments, some just marketing campaigns, some market research. Some of them I hauled from the stockroom over and over during holiday rush when I was just in high school and trying to survive working in retail. I'm proud of those toys. They make people happy."

"This isn't about you, this is about the message I'm trying to spread. I still don't want people to shop with them. I still think you're too good to work there."

"I'm sorry that we had this misunderstanding," I say. "I honestly am. I totally admit I didn't think enough about how you would feel. I was only thinking about helping sick and underprivileged kids."

He pins me with a glare, folds his arms across his chest. "You're making me sound petty."

I look down to avoid him and shrug, playing with the sleeve of my cardigan. "If it walks like a duck . . ."

I hear his heavy steps on the floor; his socks come into view. The snowman ones I bought for him at the market. He nudges my chin up with his finger until I'm looking at him. "I'm not angry at you, I'm angry at them for the fact we're even arguing over this."

I think maybe in any other scenario that would feel like relief, but it doesn't. We don't have a shared common enemy. I'm not praying for Davenport's downfall like he is. He doesn't seem to realize that it would be my downfall as well.

"There isn't a *them*, Jack. My name doesn't just disappear into thin air when I slip into your bed," I say, my voice tired. My everything tired. "You've created this divide between me and the company in your head, and I get it. I *really* do. What happened was unforgivable and I fully understand you holding that against the company forever. We said 'casual' and 'for now' and I'm leaving soon—"

"Because the videos are down."

At least I now know I haven't been paranoid and there has been a strange energy between us. "Because this isn't my real home, Jack. I can't stay here forever."

His eyes soften. "You know I don't want you to go."

"And maybe I'm on my own but I sort of didn't imagine we'd just never speak to each other ever again. Even if we're not going to be something, I at least thought we could be friends."

"You're not on your own."

"Then you need to find a way to deal with it, because I want to progress at my family company. I want to add to our legacy and I want to make it a company I'm actually proud to be part of again. Max probably got this promotion, which sucks for me, but there will be future promotions and—"

His hand slowly drops from my face. "What promotion?"

"The promotion to head of innovation. I've been working toward it for years but my brother wants to meet to talk in person, so I think he's going to tell me he's taking it."

"So you had an agenda the whole time you were here? It was never about proving anything? It was about a promotion." His voice is hard and cold. He's already taken two steps back. "You're fucking unbelievable, Clara."

"Don't make this something it isn't, Jack. Don't make me the villain again."

"You're doing a damn good job of that yourself."

I don't want things to escalate, but anger is burning me from the inside out. "You won't let me talk about my job or my family and you have the audacity to be outraged that you don't know something about my job and my family? It was never a secret that I was here for my job, Jack."

"No, I always knew who you were here to represent but I didn't realize what was in it for you. This whole time I've been telling you you're too good to work for them, and you've been using your good deeds as a bargaining chip to climb the ladder. Kind of paints it in a different light, don't you think?"

There's a thud that only I can feel when my heart drops. "I'm not standing here and letting you talk to me like this. You're always telling me to stand up for myself so I'm going to take your advice. What

I do with my career is *my* decision and wanting more for myself doesn't undo how hard I've worked to help Fraser Falls." He doesn't say anything. "I guess there's no point in me hanging around."

"I guess not." He leans back against the counter, and we're back to where we started. Opposite sides of everything.

"I've really loved being in this town, in your world, for the short time I've had." I hover in the kitchen because I don't know what else to do. I want to hug him goodbye, I mostly want to burst into tears, but I do neither. "Thank you."

Jack looks like he's going to tell me to stay. A flicker of regret across his face that I might've imagined. He doesn't.

I wait until I'm back at Maggie's with packed suitcases before I start crying.

Chapter 39

JACK

I'VE NEVER CALLED MYSELF A paranoid or self-conscious person, but people are definitely avoiding me today.

Neighbors who would normally stop and make polite conversation as I pass them on Elf's walk, Flo when I'm in the line for coffee at Bliss, Arthur when I walk past anything that looks slightly crooked.

Today I'd be able to hear the crickets if it weren't winter and they were around.

Total radio silence.

At first I like it; my whole schedule moves faster without the constant distractions. I'm grateful, given I'm already trying to distract myself from reliving last night in my head. But by late afternoon, I'm starting to feel unsettled. Nobody interrupted me in the workshop with a request.

The weirdest part was nobody stopped to pet Elf, and he's holding me personally responsible in the form of ignoring me too. When I tell him it's time to go to the town meeting he doesn't move an inch.

"I'll leave you here," I say out loud, like he's a child I'm trying to make behave in the grocery store. "I'm going without you. Watch..."

I open the front door but he still doesn't move. I feel like I'm losing it wondering if my dog is annoyed at me that Clara isn't here anymore. He's smart, but I'm pretty sure he isn't *listen to an argument and hold a grudge* smart. "Last chance, Elfy..."

Even town feels different today. The gray skies make the snow-covered ground feel dull; the tree lights are dim. The brightness has been turned down, me included.

The town hall is already full when I arrive, with people standing around talking, but nobody looks at me when I walk in. I hover near the back, ready to take a seat somewhere I'll have an easy exit. Meetings are usually quick in December, but I go anyway because if I'm not here to speak for myself, I'll end up with a to-do list longer than me.

I'm about to sit down when I hear, *"You!"* yelled from across the room. I look for the source of the noise, only to find Dove heading straight for me. "You pigheaded, stubborn man! I could kill you, Jack Kelly."

Her finger stabs me right in the chest and Luke pulls her back by her waist. "What the hell is wrong with you?"

Dove's face twists into something incredulous. "What's wrong with me? What's wrong with you!"

Flo appears beside her, brushing off Luke and putting her arm across Dove's shoulder. He mouths "Sorry" at me from behind Dove and disappears into the meeting crowd. I can't blame him, I'd do the same. Flo sighs. "Dove Pierce, stop shouting in public."

"But he—"

"I know what he did," Flo says. "But you need to lower your voice." Flo's volume and sharpness immediately rise when she adds, "And I'd like to know what on God's green earth you thought you were doing when you sent that wonderful woman back home in tears."

I guess I don't need to worry about being paranoid anymore.

Dove takes a deep breath, her chest growing and shrinking as she centers herself.

"A truck arrived here this afternoon and took back the boxes of toys Clara donated." The toy drive going ahead without Davenport toys is what I asked for, so I can't work out why I feel so shitty. "I don't know why you look so conflicted when it's what you wanted."

I've known Dove Pierce her whole life, and she's never talked to me like this. I think the only time I ever saw her this angry was at Luke when she found out she was pregnant.

"We'll replace the toys," I say confidently. I'll find a way. I'll email everyone the way Clara has. I'll put in the work.

Flo squeezes Dove's shoulder and if I weren't in the firing line I'd be confused about them uniting to shout me down. "Clara has already replaced them, Jack. We expect them to arrive over the weekend. She apologized for using her own money to buy them, she said she hoped we wouldn't think she was throwing money at us. She just couldn't see a way to resolve the hurt she'd caused while also not letting down the children."

"And now I have to f—freaking catalog them again," Dove says, huffing. "When there wasn't anything wrong in the first place! It's not like we gave them money! We got them for free!"

There's a tight squeezing in my chest, turning and folding in on itself. "She was here for a promotion."

"We know," they say in unison. "It was never a secret, Jack."

"I told her to quit her job," Maggie says, filling the spot beside Flo. "Her dad sounds like a terrible man. I didn't trust he'd give her the promotion even if she did turn things around here."

Dove nods. "I told her to quit, too, she's too nice to work there. I told her to start her own family legacy. She can make it whatever she wants it to be. It doesn't need to be attached to them."

"Well, I told her she should be sipping margaritas in Saint-Tropez and not worry about work because it would only age her prematurely," Flo adds. "Her father favors her brother anyway. Why get wrinkles and be second best?"

They continue to share their thoughts and opinions. Meanwhile I feel like the rug has been pulled out from beneath my feet. I want to ask how the fuck they all know but I don't, I know the answer because Clara yelled it at me last night.

I told her not to talk to me about her job or her family.

"The point still stands. She came here with ulterior motives. It was more than her just wanting to do right by us. She was out for herself, and I let her fool me."

Flo nods but I know she's not agreeing with me. I'm about to get it. "Did she beg you to convince me to delete the videos? Did she bring it up and pressure you? Want you to put out a public announcement saying you've forgiven Davenport?"

"No."

"No, she didn't," Flo says flatly. "Because Clara Davenport isn't and has never been the villain you've made her. And now she's gone, likely never to return, probably believing that nothing she does is ever good enough for you."

"That's not true," I argue. "I told her how much she deserves better."

"You really don't get it, do you?" Dove says, rolling her eyes. "I give up. You don't deserve her anyway."

"What did I miss?" Tommy appears behind me and I've never been more relieved to have backup.

Dove laughs. "Your best friend is a fucking asshole, how's that for an update?"

She pushes past him, before Flo can yell at her for cursing, and disappears into one of the side rooms. I turn ninety degrees so I can see both him and Maggie and Flo.

"Great," Tommy mutters, "so glad I hauled my ass over here for important town business."

I side-eye him. "You're not the one being yelled at."

"What did you do? Where's Clara?" he says, looking around for the familiar head of red hair. He takes one look at Flo and Maggie, then looks at me knowingly. "You're such a fuckup sometimes, jeez. Ow! I'm sorry for cursing, Ms. Flo, but he needs to hear it. I knew you'd do this, Jack. Why have you always got to be punishing yourself? Just be happy for once for God's sake—ow!"

When being pinched by Flo isn't stopping him from telling me how it is, I guess I can take Tommy's thoughts at face value. "I'm not punishing myself."

"You are," Tommy says softly. "It isn't a new thing, you've been doing it since we were teenagers. It feels like you've been extra hard on yourself ever since Davenport announced their copycat doll. Like you didn't even take a minute to be sad for yourself and your creation, you went headfirst into being angry for everyone, when we were sad for you and everything you've achieved."

Flo nods. "Couldn't have said it better myself, Thomas. If it wasn't them, it was going to be someone else. People try to steal magic all the time in commerce, but they can't steal what only you can make."

I don't know what to say to the people whom I love so much who are really fucking angry at me right now. Thankfully, Arthur takes the stage and bangs the gavel he bought for himself from eBay.

I take a seat at the back of the room so I can run if I end up being a topic on the agenda. It's one thing to listen to Dove and Flo lay into me, but I don't think I can deal with the whole town.

"It's a quick meeting today, folks. We're going to start off with requests and submissions, move on to upcoming events and updates, and finish with good-news stories. First up is . . ." Arthur checks his list; his rectangular glasses almost fall off the end of his nose. "Donald."

Excitement shoots through me as I reach for my phone when Donald stands up sporting his favorite Area 51 T-shirt. It's short-lived, replaced with an emptiness when I realize I was going to text Clara. She spent her whole time here wanting to meet him. He was so elusive that she started to believe she'd imagined him that first time she saw him with a net.

Arthur tells Donald that he won't be putting in a request to remove the cell towers and Donald storms off.

"Tommy, you're up next, unless you have the same request."

Tommy gets onstage with his laptop and I sit up a little taller in my chair. What the hell is he doing there? "I'm all good with the cell towers, thanks," he says, awkwardly connecting his laptop to the ancient projector system we have.

A presentation appears on the screen behind him. "I know you all probably know what I want to talk about, but I'm asking you to look at my request with fresh eyes. I have a presentation I'd like to share, then I can answer any questions at the end."

The first slide is a picture of a sketch I did to demonstrate how an extension to his patio would look. I don't think I ever gave him a copy. He clicks to the next page, which outlines the benefits of profitability, public perception, and return visitors. His slides are detailed and thorough and when he clicks the next slide to possible cons, he has proposed actions to make sure none of them impact the town.

"There's something more I'd like to add on—a retractable roof and walls." He brings up pictures of other bars with outside patios; one has clear glass walls and roof, and what look like heaters. "Fraser Falls is so beautiful people should be able to enjoy looking at it even when it's too cold. Being able to close off the patio will allow me to offer service to more customers through the winter."

He finishes up with some numbers and graphs and a slide that thanks everyone for listening.

I can't believe Tommy has been planning this and didn't tell me. If I weren't already sold on the idea, I would be now. Arthur looks like he is still processing and is possibly a tiny bit skeptical judging from the crease that has now appeared in his brow. "Can we talk after the meeting, Tommy? I have some questions but this all looks very promising."

Tommy hasn't looked this happy in forever. He unhooks his laptop and jumps down from the stage. "Sure. Thanks, everyone."

Arthur checks his list. "Luke?"

Luke stands, looking as shocked as me at the performance his brother just put on. "Not a lot from me. I'm getting a new website for the Christmas tree farm. People will be able to select a visiting time so I can see trends and plan staff cover better. It'll help with traffic flow and I'm happy to share the information with other businesses. Gonna introduce some email marketing and maybe try some targeted ads. Watch this space."

He sits back down and Arthur moves through his list. Winnie tells everyone how busy they are and that their mailable flowers are doing great. Dove is next.

"Dove & Friends received a large anonymous donation and I'll be using it toward improvements on the farm to make the animals more comfortable, and take on some more rescues if I can. The toy drive is the best it's ever been," she says, but she doesn't sound happy about it. "We've raised more than several previous years combined and we've received a record number of toy donations. If anybody is free to help me wrap them, it would be greatly appreciated."

"Thank you, Dove. We're nearly done, everyone. Jack, I have you next."

What? "Must be a mistake, Arthur. I haven't put my name down."

He brings his clipboard right beneath his nose. "Says it's to discuss changes to the doll process."

Flo and Dove both turn to look at me. "Definitely nothing to contribute," I insist.

Dove huffs and turns back to face the front. Flo gives me a tight smile and turns around slowly. "We'll move on then!" Arthur says cheerfully.

I zone out while Arthur talks about upcoming events around town. My name is mentioned but I don't even look up; something to do with the Santa letters, I think. Everything that's happening over the next few weeks will raise our profile, bring visitors, and get them to spend their money. Just like Clara wanted.

I genuinely feel sick as Arthur starts on the good-news-story section. Every single thing he mentions I can place on Clara's closet wall. Even the things she hasn't taken credit for. There's no way Luke proactively organized himself a new website, and Tommy couldn't have done a whole-ass presentation with a picture from my place without me knowing.

Is this what it's going to be like? Feeling her touch on everything and everyone? People staring at me whenever she's brought up in conversation? I've always said she's a ghost haunting me and I think I'm about to find out how true that is.

I'm the guy who drove her away, so I guess it's only what I deserve.

I don't leave the meeting even though I want to; I stay until the end, even linger so I won't have to walk back to Main with Flo. Tommy comes bouncing down the aisle, almost sending his laptop soaring across the room. He claps me on the back. "They said yes! They fucking said yes!" he whispers as loud as his hushed tone will allow. He looks back at Arthur over his shoulder to make sure he didn't hear him.

"Congrats, man. You did yourself proud up there."

"We should celebrate!" he says, and I couldn't be farther from his energy level if I tried. But he's my best friend and frankly, a change of scenery sounds good. "Where should we go?"

"Somewhere not in Fraser Falls."

Chapter 40

CLARA

I HAVE AN EMPTY HOLE in my chest that feels a lot like grief.

Like something's been taken from me without a proper goodbye and I'm full of regrets and things I wish I'd done differently. There are things I wish I'd said, things I wish I'd seen through, conversations I wish I'd revisited.

But it's over now. I'm back in my empty apartment, in my busy city, for my important job. Well, I'm not doing my important job today, because I called out sick for the first time in my professional career. I might not be sick in the traditional sense, but I feel sick every time I think about someone at work asking me about my time away.

What's the office-friendly way to say I was in love with Fraser Falls? Its quaint charm and its cast of lovable neighbors. The feeling of togetherness even among the most reluctant residents. The way excitement spreads. How there's a restaurant called Mr. Worldwide and I called it Mr. 305 four different times but nobody got the joke, they all just smiled politely.

But it's over now, like I said.

My cell phone lights up again but I ignore it. I told everyone that

I won't be checking my emails or be available for work questions and four people have texted and called me so far to see if I'm on the brink of death.

Max called twice, then texted to say Mom let him know that I'm home and ask if I wanted to grab lunch. I texted him back to say I'm sick and tossed my cell phone to the other end of the couch where it couldn't annoy me anymore. That lasted two minutes before I had it back at my side, just in case a call came through that I might want to answer.

God, being a depressed bitch doesn't suit me. I don't know what to do with myself other than mope and eat. Daytime TV has gone downhill and I've learned Mr. Eighties Perm likes to play Phil Collins during the afternoon too.

I could go for a walk but trying to get anywhere in the city in December is like trying to walk through Jell-O. It might be the only time of year where tourists outnumber the rats. It's funny how I've gone from wishing for more visitors in Fraser Falls to wishing people would stay home so I can pick up a Sweetgreen in peace.

Food is the thing on my mind when my doorbell rings and I have to question if I've ordered takeout and forgotten about it. The woman on my doorstep is holding a bag of food but it definitely isn't something I requested.

"Wow, you look like total shit," Honor says, eyeing me up and down.

I rest my head against my door. The coolness soothes the subtle ache I've had in my head since I woke up. "Remind me why we're friends again?"

She holds up the brown paper bag. "Because I brought you tomato soup and the ingredients to make you a grilled cheese."

I stand out of her way and let her in. "Yeah, that's a good enough reason for me. I've missed you."

She traps me in a tight hug. "I can't believe you're not just someone who lives inside my phone screen."

The noise of someone else in my space is an immediate comfort. I can't believe how quickly I've gone from being content living alone, to listening to every creak and groan my apartment makes. It feels too cold and empty and right now I wish I hadn't bought it.

"You going to give me a rundown on why you look so miserable to be home?" she says, pulling the container of soup out of the bag. She grabs a grill pan from the wall and sets it on the stove. "I'd like the long version. I have nowhere to be and you look like you need to talk about it."

I sit at the breakfast bar and rest my chin on the backs of my hands. Honor multitasks cooking and listening, eyes widening when I reveal that I've been messing around with Jack. I move past it quickly, recapping all the things she's already heard about, like my plan to win everyone over.

My grilled cheese is done by the time I reach the argument. I pick at the corner of the bread when I tell her what he said, what I said, how much I cried afterward. The too-quick visits to people that felt more like a handover than a goodbye. The shame I felt all the way home.

"He's a dick, you know that, right?" she says when I'm finally done. "He's pissed off on behalf of people who aren't even pissed. What's with that?"

I shrug. "He thinks it's his duty to protect everyone. Take over some legacy from his grandfather who was like the ultimate protective, helpful neighbor. His dad was a flake and Jack acted out as a teenager and now he just carries this *weight*, like a guilt, and *nobody* stops him."

"Striving to be their grandfather to undo the behavior of a shitty father. Where have I heard that one before?" Honor looks at me like she's waiting for me to realize. I know what she's saying, but I don't think it's the same at all. "Come on, Clara. You don't think you two were drawn to each other because you're the same person in different fonts?"

I shake my head. "I really don't. I don't jump to false conclusions like he does, for starters."

"Oh, really? Tell me more about how you think Max has been given your promotion."

The crust of my bread is now just a pile of crumbs on my plate. "Not the same thing. He puts everything on hold to do things for other people, often to his own detriment."

Honor's perfectly preened eyebrows quirk. "Bitch, you just moved to the middle of fucking nowhere to try to save a town you're not even from. How's that for putting everything on hold? You're not going to win this argument, I know you too well, and I'm telling you. You and that man are cut from the same cloth. You just handle things differently."

"Yeah, he handles things like a jerk."

I feel foolish to be this broken up over something that was supposed to be casual, no-strings fun. I'm not supposed to care about anything other than the fact I achieved what I went there to do. I helped the town and I helped the company by having the videos taken down.

I've never felt so utterly disappointed by achieving my objective.

Honor pins me with a look. One I know, from years of friendship, means she's about to tell me something I don't want to hear. "You knew how he felt about your job when you started fucking him. Do I think him not wanting to hear anything is childish as hell? Yes, I do. Do I think his reaction to the toys was fair? Maybe a tiny little bit."

Honor casually confirming my fear that I *was* in the wrong is the cherry on top of a terrible day. "You're kidding."

"I don't like saying it."

My skin prickles as an uncomfortable anxious feeling settles in the pit of my stomach. "What was I supposed to do? I wasn't supposed to buy them off. I was supposed to let kids go without?"

"You could've donated anonymously, babe. They'd have known it was you but what were they going to do? Anonymous is anonymous. It's okay to be proud of the toys your family company sells, but I think if you'd really thought about it, you'd have seen that reaction coming."

"And my last annual review said I'm good at solving problems before they occur. Where?"

"Listen, I think the way he talked to you about your promotion was not okay. It's his own fault he didn't know, and you'd have told him if he'd asked, right?" I nod. It was never a secret. "But I get him being concerned about the message sending out thousands of dollars' worth of Davenport toys gives after they literally stole his product. You know I don't lie to you, even when it's what you don't want to hear."

I want to say *But everyone else was fine with it* over and over but I've always felt like the betrayal from Davenport bruised Jack more than it bruised everyone else. It was his design, he does the majority of the work, and it was him who was approached about the small business program.

"All this over two dolls," I say, echoing what Honor said to me right at the beginning.

"I don't know why they don't just get rid of the Evie doll. It's so cheap looking compared to the one from Fraser Falls—is her name Holly? Paloma has that many damn toys. Obviously, her Clara doll will always be her favorite."

I smile for the first time today. "Because she has good taste. I wish they would but they won't. If it makes them money it stays. No matter who it hurts."

I don't know when I started saying *them* instead of *us*. I feel so mentally disconnected from everything Davenport brand. I clear my throat. "I don't think I'm appreciated at work."

Honor covers her mouth with her hand while she chews her

grilled cheese. "I've been telling you that for years. You're not appreciated. I don't think it's normal to be made to jump through so many hoops in different departments to work in the one department you're passionate about. Why do you need to know how to handle a crisis to make kids' toys?"

"Probably for the same reason my dad made me study business instead of design." I push my plates away, my appetite suddenly non-existent. "I don't know what to do."

Honor wipes her hands on a napkin and dabs her mouth. "You need to work out what makes you happy, then cling to it like your life depends on it. Maybe you need to go back to Fraser Falls and get real closure."

"Yeah, that's one thing I can say for certain I *won't* be doing. Jack might've acquired a pitchfork in the time I've been gone. Hey, should I buy a big plot of land in the middle of nowhere and we can just live on it with Paloma? You can be one of those online nurses who webchats with people about their rashes and stuff. I'll start a business of some kind doing something that doesn't make me feel like I'm losing my mind."

Honor looks disgusted. "In my fantasy life, I don't have a job. The fact that you work in your delusions should be a concern for you. I'll be your sugar baby."

It's funny, because what I don't say is that even in my daydreams I still work at Davenport in some capacity. It used to involve a great view on a high floor but now it looks more like a Davenport Toy Emporium franchise in a cozy town.

My heartbeat falters when my phone lights up beside me. It's Max again. "My brother keeps calling me to meet up."

"Answer it," Honor says.

"I'm not sure I can deal with any more disappointment today."

Honor rolls her eyes. "Just pick up the phone and stop being dramatic."

Tough love sounds great until you're the one on the receiving end. "Hi," I say, putting my cell phone to my ear.

"Have you always been this difficult to reach or are you avoiding my calls?" he says, sounding out of breath.

"What're you doing?"

"I'm at the gym. Don't change the subject. Why are you dodging me?" he asks. Wow, if only I could handle being as direct with him as he is with me. "I know you are."

"I'm sick." Honor rolls her eyes again. Getting attacked from all angles, jeez.

"Bullshit, Clara. Meet me for breakfast tomorrow before you go to the office. I'll send you the location."

Can't believe I'm being bullied into being an adult by my younger brother. My life really is going to shit. "Fine. See you tomorrow."

Max ends the call and I put my phone back on the counter. Honor is leaning against her hand looking smug. "Now, was that really so bad?"

"Yes," I mumble like a spoiled child.

Honor smiles and pushes my food back toward me. "Shush now and eat your food. You need your energy to spend a huge amount of one-on-one time with your family this week."

Chapter 41

JACK

THE PLAN TO CELEBRATE OUT of town went as far as getting to Luke's.

Luke's house is everything I want one day. Huge plot of land out back, big windows, tall ceilings, and a porch out front. He can keep the tree farm and being Dove's neighbor, but I love the rest of it. I'd love to give Elf a big yard to play in, but my place is tiny and already too quiet. I don't think I could live in a big house alone.

Which means I'm not mad about hanging out here and to be honest, I don't think I'd have fun anywhere we went anyway. Patio or not, I don't feel like I have anything to fucking celebrate.

Tommy sits at the dining table opposite Sailor, who's doing her math homework, and opens his laptop to start working out his renovation plan. He still needs to get real planning permission, but believe it or not, it's harder to get things past Arthur. He takes his role as town council president—a role made up just for him—very seriously. More seriously than his actual job, which is being Sailor's math teacher.

"Mom's mad at you," Sailor says when I pull out the chair to sit next to her.

I sigh and rub my eyes with my thumb and forefinger. "Your mom's gonna have to get in line, kid."

"She called you a selfish asshole," Sailor says joyfully as she pencils a fraction onto her paper.

"Hey," Tommy snaps from across the table. "Don't let your dad hear you cursing or he'll be upset."

"He curses all the time. Yesterday this rude guy tried to argue with him and afterward Daddy called him a di—"

I plant my hand over her mouth. I remember her being born. I changed her diaper more times than I can count. She once spit up milk all down my shirt five minutes before a date. I don't need to know she's old enough to know what curse words are.

Tommy is trying not to laugh behind his hand. Two lines appear between his eyebrows as he tries to look serious. "That's bad manners, Sailor. You should tell Pastor Akinola next time you see him. Maybe he can teach your dad about what words he should and shouldn't be using."

I release Sailor's mouth and she looks at me in disgust. "You want help with your homework, kiddo?" I ask her, changing the subject.

She has an entirely serious face. "Do you know how to count?"

Tommy's trying not to laugh again. "Most of the time."

Sailor doesn't look convinced in the slightest. "This might be too hard for you. It's a really, really, really long time since you were in school."

My day just keeps getting better and better. "Okay, well, I'm here if you need help."

Luke appears in the doorway and claps his brother on the back. "Congrats. You guys want a beer?"

Tommy lights up again. "Yeah, I'll take one. And thanks, I can't believe a PowerPoint is all it took. I'd have done that months ago if I'd known."

"I'll take one, too." Luke rummages in the refrigerator and I can't fight the question that's been nagging at me since the meeting. *Suspicion* is a better word than *question*, because I'm confident I already know. "Hey, Tom, where'd you get that picture? The first one with the sketch."

The uncomfortable look on Tommy's face tells me what I already know. "Clara made the presentation. I added some of the figures and moved things around a bit, but she did like ninety percent of it. Sorry, man."

Luke hands us each a cold bottle and a bottle opener and sits at the head of the table between me and his brother with a soda. "You don't gotta apologize. I just thought I knew everything she was doing in town. Realizing there's a lot I didn't know."

"She showed up at the tavern last week and said she'd been working on it casually in her free time. Asked for some help with the figures. She was real nice about it. She's the one who said to ask for retractable so I could say it'll be used in winter."

I sip my beer, wishing it were something stronger. "Yeah, she's smart."

I'm starting to think coming here wasn't the best idea. I should've gone home and thought about everything that's been said tonight. I've never seen Flo so disappointed with me. Not when she caught me getting high for the first time or when the cops brought me home or even when I crashed into the gazebo.

Dove and Flo being on the same team should've been enough to make me go home.

The problem is home is empty and quiet and full of things that make me think about Clara's watering eyes in my kitchen. My bedding smells like her perfume, my pillows like her shampoo. There's a sticky note on the molasses in my refrigerator that says *rehome me :(* that I can't bring myself to throw in the trash. My toy sketches that are usually stuffed in the coffee table drawer have pencil annotations with all the things she loves and what she suggests adapting.

Elf is undoubtedly pissed at me. Everyone is pissed at me.

Luke is asking Tommy about costs and start dates, lumber orders he'll have to sort out. It's a conversation I should be part of but I can't drag myself out of my own head. I stay quiet and drink my beer, not wanting to kill Tommy's excitement with my own issues.

"You okay, man?" Luke asks when Tommy goes to the bathroom. "I know you got it pretty bad at the meeting."

I don't need to tell him what's happened. He and Dove might not be together but they're still best friends. He knows everything she knows and there are no exceptions. At least he tried to pull her away.

"Will be. Your new website sounds cool." Luke's current website is one page and has his location, opening times, and email address. He's always been a simple guy who wants an easy life. "I didn't know you were looking to switch things up."

"Yeah, got talking to someone who knows about SEO and email marketing and stuff. I've been lazy because we've always done okay but I realized, because they told me, that me bringing people to the farm brings them to town. Helps other people's businesses . . . so I'm going to try harder. Might be a waste of time."

"Doubt it. Sounds like a really good plan. That person you met sounds smart."

He nods slowly, tapping his fingers against the table. "You want another beer?"

I hold the glass bottle up to the light; there's a mouthful left. "Nah, I'm gonna head home. Elf's been on his own for a few hours and he needs to be walked."

Luke doesn't push me to stay. Neither does Tommy when he comes back. Nobody stops me on my dog walk and I try to forget the way Elf pulls toward the B & B. By the time I'm falling into bed, the only thing I can think is I need to change my goddamn sheets.

. . .

It's amazing what you can achieve when you're trying to distract yourself and nobody wants to talk to you.

My inbox has never been emptier. Workshop never been cleaner. Dog never been more walked. The only thing I haven't done today is figure out how to make time move faster, because now that I'm alone in front of the TV, I have nothing but the opportunity to think.

I turn *Love Actually* off pretty much as soon as I turn it on; I don't need to hear about people in love at Christmas. *Miracle on 34th Street* gets the same treatment; I don't need to spend ninety minutes in New York. Any variation of Charles Dickens feels like I'm tempting fate and I don't have the energy to be shown my past, present, and future right now.

I'm about to switch off several more movies when my phone starts ringing. For the first time ever, I'm relieved that someone is calling me on a Tuesday evening. I dig my phone out of my pocket, noting Miss Celia's name on my screen. "Hello?"

"Jack, I'm sorry to bother you. Could you come to the bookstore? I—" She pauses; I hear her shuffling on the other side of the line. "I didn't have my glasses on and I knocked my tea onto my computer keyboard. It's making a sizzling noise and I don't want to lose all my invoices."

I turn the TV off with my free hand and trap my cell phone between my ear and shoulder while I stand up and rebutton my pants. "Okay, don't touch it. I'll be right over."

"Thanks, Jack."

After a couple of weird days, it feels good to be needed for something again. Nature is healing and all that shit Mel and Winnie say. I ignore the fact they usually say it when something bad happens to someone they don't like. I guess I'll find out if that's applicable here if Miss Celia's computer electrocutes me.

I make a mental note to empty the Santa mailbox when I pass it on my way back home. Responding to the kids' letters is the perfect way to distract myself when I inevitably need distracting.

The door to the bookstore is locked, lights only shining in the back of the store. I knock on it a few times before I spot Miss Celia emerging from the light. She looks apologetic when she opens the door. I stomp the snow from my boots on the mat and unzip my coat.

"Thanks for coming so quickly. It's in the back, come through." The six-foot-tall Matilda Brown banner from the book event Clara organized nearly falls on me as I pass it. "Sorry about that, I need to move it."

"My fault."

I squint against the light as we step into the area at the back of the store. My eyes adjust as several heads face me. Tommy looks the most guilty, followed by Mel and Winnie, then Luke and Maggie. Wilhelmina and Flo seem determined and Dove is still pissed.

"Jack . . . ," Miss Celia says slowly, like she's pacifying a horse ready to bolt.

"I didn't realize book club was happening tonight," I say, scanning the room. They're sitting in a semicircle with one chair facing it. You've *got* to be kidding me. "I haven't read it."

"Sit down, Jack," Flo says in her most authoritarian voice. She must realize because she quickly adds on a softer, "Please."

"I'm too old for this," I say, taking the seat facing everyone when Miss Celia sits in the semicircle's last seat. This one was clearly always going to be mine. "We're all too old for this."

"Don't act like such a baby then," Dove says, crossing her arms, then her legs.

"Dove," Luke says harshly. "Don't start."

"Come on," I say, rolling my arms as if to speed them up. "Let's get this intervention over with."

"Mind your manners, Jack Kelly," Flo says. "This isn't an intervention. This is to help you because you're clearly not going to help yourself."

I'm pretty sure that's what an intervention is but I don't voice that. I might be pissed right now but talking back to Flo with an audience is not something I'm going to do.

I'd like to survive this meeting.

"We all love you, Jack," Maggie says gently. "Most of us have known you all your life. We all want you to be happy and we know you're not happy."

"I'll be fine," I say like a reflex. "I'm always fine."

"Being fine and being happy aren't the same thing," Winnie says, Mel nods beside her in agreement.

There isn't enough oxygen in this room. My chest feels tight and my skin feels hot. I should've stuck to *Love Actually* and put my phone on airplane mode.

"We realized we owe you an apology," Wilhelmina says. "That's what this is. Not an intervention."

Miss Celia nods. "I went to a lot of interventions in the seventies and they didn't look like this."

"An apology? What does anyone have to apologize for?" I ask. It's a genuine question.

"Clara Davenport came here like a whirlwind and swept us all up. I'm sure you don't need to be reminded about everything she's done for us."

"I have a list though if you do," Dove says, interrupting Flo. "It's long as hell."

Flo sighs and carries on. "And honestly, we loved having her here. Not because she's beautiful and charismatic, not because of her determination to put things right, but because of how happy you've been."

"I'm confused." Really fucking confused.

"There's nobody who does more for this town than you, man," Tommy says, finally piping up. "Clara's getting credit for putting in a few weeks' effort and you've been doing it for fifteen years."

"We're sorry that you feel like you have to protect and take care of us. Even if it means messing with your own happiness," Luke says.

"I don't." Everyone looks at me like I'm telling them the sky is yellow. "You guys are blowing this out of proportion."

"You're your grandfather, Jack," Flo says, smiling like she's recalling a fond memory. "Always taking care of everyone else. Never asking for help. A skepticism that would be infuriating if you weren't both so handsome while scowling."

Flo is a dramatic person, she always has been, but it's hard not to want to listen to her talk about my granddad.

"It skipped a generation with your father, but you're Harry through and through," Miss Celia adds. "And we should've said to him what we're saying to you now: we're not your responsibility, we're your neighbors, and we want to support you the way you have supported us."

There's a baseball-size lump in my throat when I try to swallow. "I feel like you didn't need to lure me here under false pretenses to say this to me," I say, rubbing at my beard. "I'd have accepted an email."

"Oh, sweetie. We're not done," Wilhelmina says.

I sigh and lean back in my chair. "Of course you're not."

"I put your name on the list to speak at the town meeting," Dove says, picking at her nail varnish. "At first, I wanted to help, then I wanted you to suffer, and now, Flo tells me I want to help again. Clara told me how much goes into running Holly. All the emails and the packaging and everything. We need to help more. You should've told us—" She pauses when Flo nudges her. "We should've asked you if you needed help."

"We can talk about how we'll divide responsibilities up better when you're back," Wilhelmina says.

My eyebrow quirks. "Back from where?"

They all look at me with the same pitying expression.

"No."

"Yes," at least three of them say.

"She won't want to talk to me." Clara's watery eyes flash in my mind. "I messed up bad."

"You messed up, but we messed up by not thinking about how accepting a Davenport delivery might look," Maggie says. "Lesson learned, we can all move past it."

"I don't know how to fix it. She might not forgive me," I admit, dragging a hand down my face.

Miss Celia moves to my side and wraps an arm around my shoulder. "She might not, but you won't know if you don't try. And either way, she deserves to hear that you're sorry."

Flo leans forward with her phone. "And we have something important you need to show her."

My adrenaline starts pumping as my mind runs through the possibilities. "I don't even know her address!"

"You know where she works. Go there and win her back!" Flo claps her hands together, the excitement delighting her. "And get rid of that beard, for goodness' sake."

I guess I'm heading to New York with a clean shave.

Chapter 42

CLARA

Max's taste in restaurants has changed significantly since he became a real grown-up.

I didn't even bother looking up the location he sent me and assumed I'd be going to a Spider-Man–themed diner or something for breakfast. Instead, he's sitting in the corner table of a cute French-style café wedged in the middle of a residential block. My heart stumbles over itself when I think of who would love, but probably equally hate, it here.

Max is drinking a cappuccino when I sit down opposite him. "Morning," I say as brightly as I can muster, hanging my purse on my chair back. It wobbles when I shuffle forward and I quickly realize the legs are uneven. Another sting.

"Feeling better?" Max asks.

No, everything reminds me of them. "Tons better, thanks."

Max's eyes narrow. "You're being weird. Why are you being weird?"

"I've said four words! How can I be being weird in four words?" I argue. If Max brought me here just to get on my nerves, then I'm leaving. I don't have the time or the patience today.

"You just seem, I don't know, off or something. Your energy

is weird." My eyes narrow. What woman has taught my brother about energy? "It's whatever. I'm glad you're here. What do you want to eat?"

I pick the most festive-looking thing on the menu. A Gruyère and ham croissant with cranberry and a gingerbread latte. Max orders the same and a plate of French toast to share. "So, are you going to reveal why you're so determined to see me this week?"

Max looks calm and collected, which is why it catches me so off guard when he says, "I think you should quit your job."

I stare at him unblinking for what feels like forever. "I'm leaving."

Max moves when I move. "Don't. I have a reason, I promise."

I reluctantly sit back down; he slowly lowers back into his seat as well. "This could've been a text."

"No, it couldn't. Stop being so flighty and listen to me. I want us to go into business together."

A confused laugh bubbles out of me. "You're kidding, right?" His expression doesn't change. "Max, you can't be serious."

The server places my gingerbread latte down in front of me, giving me a moment of reprieve to collect my thoughts. Max looks serious. There's nothing about his demeanor that indicates he's fooling around. I just can't wrap my head around it.

"Why not?"

I feel like I'm being pranked. "Because our family already owns one of the leading toy companies in the market? Because I've dedicated my entire working life to learning as much as I can about every branch, every *twig*, that makes it happen?"

Max takes a sip from his cappuccino and cradles it between his hands. "And now that you know everything that happens there, do you think it's a good company? Do you think Dad is doing a good job of running things? Putting the right people in senior positions? Signing off on the right projects?"

"I can't make changes from the outside, Max. Can't fix what's broken without getting my hands dirty. Davenport isn't perfect, but it's our legacy. It's Grandpa's legacy. I can't just abandon it."

"What if we start our own legacy? We're not kids competing against each other anymore, Clara. I want to be your equal in something we build together. Something we can truly be proud of."

I'm stuck in the spot between hope and annoyance. "You've never worked for Davenport. I don't know how you think you know so much. It isn't perfect, sure. Yeah, there are tons of things I'd change, but that takes time."

"I've never worked there because I've watched them not value you for almost fifteen years. Do you know how crushing it is to watch Dad just not be interested? Be dismissive and condescending whenever you talk about work? It fucking sucks, Clara. And it's not even the worst part. Watching you tolerate it is. I'm asking you to choose not to tolerate it anymore."

If one more person tells me that I'm basically hated and used at my job I'm going to start screaming. People say it like they're doing me a favor by telling me. Like somehow, suggesting that I'm wasting my time will lift the wool from my eyes and I'll be thankful.

"You're not asking me to try a new restaurant or pick up a new hobby. You're asking me to give up what I've been working for since I was a child, Max. You want me to tip my entire life upside down. Dad would probably cut us off, you realize that, right? Sue us into oblivion so we can never use the name Davenport. Squash us before we even get started. He's vindictive and—"

"And yet you still work for him," Max says coolly.

I fold my arms across my chest as the food is laid out on the table in front of us. I don't even want it anymore. I thank the server and focus back on Max when they walk away. "For someone so well educated you sure do look at things through rose-tinted glasses."

He takes a bite of his croissant and shrugs. "Paid all that money for them to teach me that people start businesses that go on to be successes every single day. I've been thinking about this for two years. I know what your job means to you. I wouldn't ask you to take the leap if I didn't think it'd pay off."

"I need to ask you a question," I say firmly, brushing the pastry crumbs from my fingers. "You need to answer me honestly or I won't even consider what you're asking."

"Go for it," Max says.

"Did Dad offer you a job at Davenport replacing the head of innovation?" It's a question that's been on my mind for so long that it felt impossible to get the words out. Turns out, it was really easy. What isn't easy is seeing the look of pity on Max's face.

"He did. I turned it down."

My skin prickles and my lungs feel heavy. "When?"

"Last week. He forgot his wallet at home and Mom asked me to deliver it."

"He didn't even wait for me to come back from Fraser Falls. He didn't even wait to see if I could fix the problem he created." It's an interesting clash of devastation and relief.

I wasn't being paranoid. I was *right*.

"I'm sorry, Clara."

I pinch the bridge of my nose, trying to relieve some of the tension in my head. "I need time to think about everything you've said. You've dropped it on me at a really bad time."

I think Max is relieved I'm not immediately shooting him down. "Sure. We can talk about something else. We can talk about *J*—"

"Do not say *Jurassic Park*."

THE CAR TO THE OFFICE takes longer than normal when tourists decide to hold a photo shoot on a crosswalk in two different locations.

It feels strange that it's over a third of the way through December and I haven't seen the Rockefeller tree yet. It's cold and wet today; the gray clouds cast a gloomy hue across the skyline. I pass countless holiday displays, candy cane entrances, and elaborate light designs on the buildings. What would normally feel magical to me just doesn't right now.

Part of me wishes I opted to work from home today. I'm not excited to be in the office and I have Max's proposal spinning around in my head like a carousel. I have an email from my dad to come up to his floor to give him a debrief when I get to the office, so I head straight there.

I remember when Davenport moved into this building, and I couldn't believe that we needed so many floors. My dad's floor with its vast view felt like heaven at the time. His assistant tells me he's on a call and offers me a water while I wait. I take a seat by the window and concentrate on the river cruises. The reality is, there's no disparaging comment my dad can give me that will hurt more than knowing he offered the job to Max.

That all my work, all my commitment, all my determination, amounts to nothing next to my brother simply existing. It's not that I don't think my brother wouldn't be a fantastic asset—he's smart and creative and hardworking—but there are dozens of other jobs he could have.

"He's ready for you now," a polite voice says from behind a computer screen.

Dad looks up from his computer when I walk in, then goes back to looking at his screen. He clicks his mouse a couple of times, then leans back in his chair, hands interlinked across his stomach. "Welcome back."

I pull out the heavy leather chair and take a seat. "Thanks."

"You haven't been returning my calls," he says sharply.

"I've been sick." It's a lie I've told everyone so there's no point changing things up now. "Today is my first day back in the office."

"Well? What updates do you have for me?" He eyes me impatiently.

"The Fraser Falls videos have been removed. While we still can't consider the town a friend, the work I've done over the past few weeks has given them other things to focus on. I carried out a strategic plan to raise their profile to increase visitors and spending. It worked and now they have a focus that doesn't involve Davenport."

"That's all it took to convince them to take down the videos?" he asks.

That's all it took? Leaving home and convincing a whole town of people to trust me, while listening to their problems and turning it into an actionable plan that actually helped them? I nod. "That's all it took."

"Do you have anything else to report?" he asks, looking bored of me already.

I'm so tired of it. I *know* he would never treat another employee like this. "Nothing to report. I have a request though. I think the Evie doll should be discontinued immediately. It's a lazy imitation and it isn't right for the Davenport brand. Taking it off the shelves would close the book on the Fraser Falls situation."

"I find it ironic that you feel entitled to tell me what's right for the brand I built, Clara." There's no warmth to his tone. "If I wanted your opinion on the product, I'd ask for it."

"If I'm going to be head of innovation, then at some point my opinion is going to have to start mattering to you," I snap. "That's my reward, right? The thing you promised *me*."

There's a silence that settles in the room that's making my arm hairs stand up. Dad has always had a way of conveying how he's feeling with a look. I was on the receiving end of it frequently as a teenager. "I have a meeting in five minutes, and I think you're forgetting who you're speaking to. I'll see you tomorrow at the charity event. I hope you'll have a better attitude, Clara."

I uncross my legs and brush off my skirt as I stand. "I should let you know that I've been headhunted. Out of courtesy, I'm telling you I'm considering their offer."

There's a twisted sense of satisfaction that comes with catching my dad out. It happens so infrequently that it gives me the most incredible high.

I don't wait for him to respond. I don't bother with fake polite goodbyes or thanks. I keep my head held high and go straight for the door feeling like I'm finally beating him for once.

Beating him, but still too chicken to let the door slam behind me.

Chapter 43

CLARA

I'VE BEEN TO MORE CORPORATE events in my life than I think is normal for a thirty-year-old.

When I was younger, before the business was on the rise, Dad thought charity galas were the ultimate sign of sophistication and success. Having so much money he could freely give it away and be praised for it was always the goal for him. The charitable side was more of a by-product than anything else.

My mom would take me to fittings where I'd be stabbed and pulled until my dress fit like a glove, my hair would be blow-dried to within an inch of its life, and we would smile on someone else's red carpet and pretend to belong there.

Max was always allowed to stay home with Grandpa and watch *The Lord of the Rings* or *Star Wars*, but I was made to go to all the ones labeled as family events, whether that label meant anything or not. Usually, it meant I'd make awkward conversation with kids my age who would also rather have been home eating popcorn and staying up late for fun reasons.

When Davenport partnered with a children's charity and threw its first gala, Dad thought he'd finally made it, and so the annual

Davenport December tradition was born. Except this year, we're celebrating twenty years of the product that put us on the map. The one little Clara designed and received no credit for. The one that paid for that first gala.

I wouldn't say I feel bitter, but I do feel a deep sense of misalignment with what's happening today. I think I've been feeling that deep sense of misalignment with Davenport for a while.

The noise of my childhood home is a welcome change from the silence of my own home. The emptiness and distance from everyone that I once found freeing now feels suffocating. Even if the noise of my childhood home in question is my mother barking orders at her stylist, it's still better than the quiet.

"Clara, why do you look so miserable today?" Mom asks as she passes where I'm sitting in a Hollywood-director-style chair in the middle of the living room. My hair-and-makeup guy is running late, but I don't want to admit that to her or it'll make her panic.

I've always used the living room to get ready for these types of things, ever since I was younger. Now it would feel weird to get ready somewhere else, even if I'm not the best company currently. "I'm sick," I lie.

She moves closer until she's standing at my knees and presses the back of her hand to my forehead. The diamond sitting on her ring finger scratches just above my eyebrow. "Do you want me to heat you up some chicken soup?"

"No, thank you. I'll be okay."

"Did you try your dress on?" she asks, looking for it in the room. I nod. "It's perfect, thank you."

I thought I'd found the perfect dress the day I obliterated that kid's snowman. I sent my mom a picture and received a text back that just said "No" and the cowboy emoji, which I assumed was an accident. Twenty-four hours later, she sent me a video of (someone I hope was) a sales associate wearing a stunning red evening gown.

"I'm going to make you a hot tea to help you feel better." She kisses my temple and disappears into the hallway, and I'm left sitting alone again.

I could be doing something useful or interesting, but instead I'm staring at her perfectly decorated Christmas tree. The one that looks identical to the tree I found in my own living room when I got home on Sunday night.

I looked at it from every angle before deciding I hate it. I hate every color-coordinated bauble. I hate the delicate decorations with all the parts still attached. It feels sterile and out of place.

The tea does make me feel better but I'm not sure if it's the product or the act of being taken care of. I zone out while my face is poked at and my hair is forced into identical waves. I know as soon as people show up here it'll be difficult to have this time in my own head, and I have a lot to think about.

When Dad appears with his golf clubs, it's almost time to go. He does this every year, with zero care for how much it stresses my mom out. We could be physically in the car ready to leave and he'd be *just* getting into the shower. He argues that it doesn't matter when he gets home, he will always be ready to go before her, but he's only right half of the time.

Two minutes later, Honor and Max appear. "Look who I found lurking outside," Max says, throwing himself into the seat beside me.

"I wasn't *lurking*," Honor argues. "I was timing my entrance so I didn't have to make small talk with your dad."

"Very wise," I say, looking my best friend up and down. She's glowing in a way I didn't notice when I saw her two days ago. The black dress fits her like a glove. I don't think I've seen it before. "You look breathtakingly gorgeous and I've missed you."

She gives me a bright smile. "Right back atcha. And I missed you too."

"Didn't you guys hang out on Monday?" Max says, looking between us.

"You wouldn't get it because you're only friends with people on the internet," I say flippantly, reaching into my purse for my phone.

"Gaming with my friends online doesn't make them people on the internet. They're not bots, Clar. They're definitely people."

I hum in acknowledgment that I heard him but check my messages instead of getting into a debate with him. It's a quick task because I have none, and the only people who do contact me are currently in this house.

Great.

Max leans over. "Can we talk privately?"

This is honestly the last thing I need today. "Anything you want to say to me you can say in front of Honor. You're just saving me from having to try to remember what you said to tell her later."

Honor nods along with me. Max looks like he doesn't understand but accepts it anyway. "This is unprofessional, just so you know."

I'm not being lectured by someone who's spent more time in classrooms than offices. "You should vet your potential business partners better then."

"So you *are* still a potential business partner?" he says, and the hope in his voice hits me square in the chest. Somewhere that's taken quite a beating this week.

I want to rub the tension out of my head with my fingers, but my mom won't let me leave the house if I ruin my makeup. Maybe that's the solution to my problems. "I'm still thinking about it. I told Dad I've been headhunted. I didn't say it was by *you*," I say, answering his question before he even asks it. "I want to know what his countermove is before I make a decision."

Max unbuttons his suit jacket and rests his arm on the back of the couch. "And if he doesn't have a countermove, what then?"

"I'm going to ask him to credit me for creating the Clara doll. The twentieth anniversary is the perfect time to bring it up. If he does it, I'll know that he values what I've contributed to the business."

"And if he doesn't?" Max asks.

The reality isn't something I want to picture. I sip from my champagne flute. "Then I'll find out how I really feel about my future at Davenport."

Honor's eyes are focused on the doorway. "I think your dad is coming down the stairs, guys."

We swap conversations immediately and focus on theories about who will get too drunk tonight, who will make a pass at someone in front of their wife, who will donate the most money and whether it will be out of the kindness of their heart or as a flex. It kills time until Dad eventually appears and points to his suit. "See? Why ruin a perfectly good round of golf to rush back when your mother isn't even ready to go."

Max doesn't say anything. He *hates* when Dad treats Mom like she's some ditzy housewife who can't be taken seriously. When in reality, if you added it all up, she's spent months of her life supervising the planning of events.

Back when we only had the illusion of status, she'd plan everything herself. I remember when I was younger hearing her blaming the event coordinator for a mistake with some flowers, knowing that Mom had organized everything.

All Dad has ever had to do is show up, do a speech, and sign off on the bill.

Dad sits on the couch beside Honor and she smiles at him in the polite but awkward way she has done since we met. Honor became the unofficial third Davenport child at these events when we were teenagers. I would tell people she was my sister just to watch them be confused. I had to stop when someone started a rumor that my dad had a love child and Mom was furious with me.

"Have you written your speech yet, Dad?" I ask, half expecting the answer to be no.

He pats his chest, indicating his inside pocket. "Of course. This one was easy after looking at the doll for twenty years."

I swirl my champagne, watching the golden bubbles dance in the glass. "Have you mentioned that she was my idea in your speech? When you no doubt talk about her impact on the company."

Dad looks taken aback, an expression I'm not used to seeing from him. My father is cold and calculating; he's never shocked because he's always a step ahead. Except this week apparently, where I'm doing a number on his ability to hide emotion. "I haven't. I didn't see how it was relevant."

I stop swirling and drink. "It isn't, I guess. It would just be nice to receive some acknowledgment for my work. She's our star product after all, and she literally has my name."

"The work of a ten-year-old is not the same as the work of the people who have done every prototype, modification, and upgrade in the past two decades, Clara."

"But she was *my* idea. I sh—"

I don't get to finish my sentence because he holds his hand up to silence me. "If it is so important to you to get your fifteen minutes, then fine. I will tell everyone that you did a drawing that looked a bit like a doll that we now sell. Happy?"

He's gaslighting me, and the fact that he's doing it in front of Max and Honor is the truly astounding part. "A drawing that looked a bit like a doll that we now sell"? Sure, ten-year-old me was no salaried Davenport product developer, but under the guidance of my grandpa I worked hard on my idea. We did market research and different designs and variations, and while we didn't do prototypes or anything, I knew exactly what I wanted her to be like, feel like, down to the shade of her eyelashes.

And I handed it all over to my dad.

"I'm obviously ecstatic," I reply sarcastically, finishing my drink.

Mom walks in before things can escalate, finally ready to leave. Honor grabs my hand as we head toward the door, squeezing it tight. "Just survive tonight," she whispers.

"This sucks," Max says as he stops beside me. One hand is in his pocket, the other clutching a tumbler of whiskey like his life depends on it.

"Yep."

"I'll never understand how opulence is supposed to be good for charity," he says, scanning the room. "Everyone should just send a check and stay home."

"But how would Dad get to talk about how great and generous he is in front of all his rich frenemies if he didn't force them all into a room to listen?"

Max shrugs. "He could send a newsletter. Start a YouTube channel, I don't know. Not this."

"At least he's admitting he's brought everyone here to talk about his successes this year. It's got to be better than him pretending it's only about raising money for children."

It's so far away from Fraser Falls' toy drive that it's laughable. These are fake people with fake intentions, and I feel like I've put on glasses that help me see everything clearly now.

My stomach turns as I watch Dad embrace Daryl. I want to voice my disgust out loud, but I don't want to give Max an opportunity to pitch me a new job. I'm already nervous as hell waiting to see what Dad says.

Max finishes his drink and puts the empty glass on a passing tray. "His speech is in two minutes. Want to take bets on if he'll thank Mom for overseeing everything?"

I scoff. "I like my money, thanks. We both know he won't."

Dad climbs the stairs to the stage and taps the microphone, getting everyone's attention. He pulls out white cards from the inside of his suit jacket and neatens them on the podium. "Welcome, everyone. Thank you for joining us for our eighteenth year of raising money for incredible causes, and more importantly, the twentieth anniversary of our star product, the Clara doll."

Max leans in, his shoulder brushing against mine. "Did he just say a doll is more important than charity?"

"Without a hint of irony," I confirm, placing my empty champagne flute down and picking up another one.

"Every company has that one product that shines brighter than the rest, and for us, the Clara doll has allowed us to push Davenport Innovation Creative to heights I didn't think were possible twenty years ago.

"As most of you know, our story started with my father and his dream to open a toy store. I spent more time in that place than in school." He pauses to let everyone laugh at his scripted joke. "And I learned a lot from my dad. He always wanted to fill his store with his own toys—our home was covered in sketches and ideas—but didn't think that was achievable for a working-class man from Brooklyn. Well, Dad, it was possible, and I know if you were here with us, you'd be speechless at what we've achieved."

Max leans in again. "Why is he acting like Grandpa wasn't on the board before he died?"

I shrug, paying close attention to every single word Dad says.

"I'd like to thank you all for being here tonight to celebrate this monumental occasion. I'd like to thank the hardworking Davenport employees and our esteemed business partners who make products like Clara possible, and finally"—my heart slams into my rib cage—"I'd like to thank our customers, for fifty years of loyalty. I hope everyone enjoys their evening and drinks enough champagne to be extra generous this year."

The round of applause becomes a high-pitched frequency making my brain hurt as I watch my dad smile and wave as he walks off the stage.

He didn't credit me.

It's something so unsurprising yet so gut wrenching—to watch him do absolutely anything except acknowledge that I contributed something to the business. I only realize I'm storming toward him when Max grips my arm, stopping me.

"Clara, don't. I know how you feel and I know that you're hurting but this isn't the place. It'll feel good at first and then you'll regret it."

I spin on my heel to face him, freeing my arm. "How can you even say that when you get everything you want from him? And always have? How can you tell me you know how I feel when he's done nothing but create a pathway for you to stand beside him?"

Max's eyes widen. "A pathway? Clara, I don't *want* to stand beside him. I don't want anything to do with him or his greed and bad decisions. I hate what he's done to Grandpa's company. This is why we need to start again."

My brain fumbles over the words and the feelings, everything mixing together and leaving me spinning. "I'm yelling at you because I can't yell at him. This isn't your fault. I'm sorry."

"I know you are and that's okay. I'd be yelling at you if the roles were reversed." Max sighs. "You know you deserve better. As your brother, I want you to want more for yourself."

I've been thinking about this exact situation since yesterday morning and I still feel blindsided. Every time I think I've made a decision, fear talks me into something else. I said I'd know how I felt about my future at Davenport if he didn't credit me, and now I do.

I nod slowly. "Okay."

"Okay?" he says, gripping my arms.

"Okay." I nod, faster this time. "Let's do it. Let's try. I don't want to feel this, this, this *disappointment* anymore. I can't feel like this for the rest of my life."

Max pulls me into a bear hug, crushing me slightly, but it's reassuring that he's so excited. I let myself breathe properly, focusing on the future and not how my dad is going to react to the news. "Clar?"

I lean back; his hold around me loosens. "Yeah?"

"There's a guy over there that looks like he wants to kill me for touching you."

"What?" I follow Max's glare over to the door, where there is a guy looking just as Max described, standing next to Honor, and missing a beard.

Chapter 44

JACK

"It's Max, her brother, bozo. You can turn off the angry-bear act."

I don't admit to Honor that it isn't an act. It's the first time I've met her and she already thinks I'm a piece of shit. Adding jealous to that doesn't help my cause. She already doesn't like me because I upset Clara, but the fact I called every hospital in Brooklyn asking for her until I found the right one hasn't helped.

"Thanks for the heads-up." Now that they're apart, it's more obvious. "And for your help getting me in."

"I don't like you. You should know that straightaway. I'm not a pretend type of woman so I'm not going to be nice for the sake of your feelings," she says, not a hint of humor in her tone.

"Got it..."

"So just know, I could absolutely murder you and make it look like natural causes. I'm really great at my job. Do not fucking hurt her." Honor is a whole foot shorter than me and I'm still terrified of her. "Or I will hurt you."

"I promise you I won't."

Clara is still looking over in shock when I finally move away from Honor, luckily unscathed. It's only been seventy-two hours since I last saw her and it feels like a lifetime. I'm now thinking I should've called first, but I didn't want her ignoring me to persuade me not to come here.

I watch Clara take a deep breath. She hands her champagne flute to her brother, pulls the front of her dress away from her shoes, then turns a one eighty and speeds away from me.

I deserve that.

"Clara," I call after her, but she doesn't slow down. I pass her brother easily; he doesn't stand in my way or try to talk to me. She comes to a hallway, looks left and right before choosing to go right, which she quickly learns leads to an empty room with no exit other than the way she came in. I close the door behind us, shutting out the music of the event. "I just want to talk to you."

"Have you heard of making phone calls? It's generally considered the normal way to communicate with someone instead of showing up uninvited to a work event," she snaps.

Even when she's angry at me, I just want to be close to her. "I didn't think you'd answer."

"Locking me in a room is not the normal alternative to getting your calls screened." She folds her arms over her chest; her red hair is in waves today, scattered across her shoulders.

I take a few steps toward her, closing the gap and putting space between me and the door. "You can leave if you want to. I won't stop you from walking out, but I hope you'll hear what I have to say."

My heart smashes against my chest, body frozen waiting for her to move, but she doesn't. "I'm listening."

"I was wrong, Clara, and I'm so, so sorry." I take a step toward her, but she takes a step back. "I made you feel like you need to be a different person around me, and it was immature and selfish. I should've either accepted you for who you are or stayed away from you. It isn't fair that I wanted you but only the bits that didn't feel influenced by your family and job.

"The truth is, I want all of you. I need all of you. You take everything in life and make it better, make it brighter. I took that for granted but I need you to know that it won't happen again."

She looks down at her feet. "That's really easy for you to say but as soon as something happens that you don't like, I'm public enemy number one again. I deserve better."

I drag my hand over my jaw, shuffle forward, and this time she doesn't move. In fact she also takes a step forward. It's like we're playing an elaborate game of human chess, except it feels like we're both losing.

"I've been trying to fill the role of town protector my entire adult life. I'm sure a therapist can work out why better than I can. Flo, obviously, has her theories, which she's voiced loudly and publicly without warning."

"I think I could add a few theories too," she mumbles.

"I was embarrassed when everything happened with Davenport. I felt like I let everyone down and it took me back to being a teen. It was easier when we had this thing to blame, this common enemy in Davenport. Then you showed up.

"And you flipped everything I thought I knew on its head. You make everything feel achievable and exciting. It felt good to have this person who I started to believe actually cared about us. Me, and the people in my town who I love."

Her bottom lip wobbles. "I *do* care."

"I know, baby," I say softly. "I just forgot that when the toys showed up and I learned about your promotion. Flo had deleted the videos and I could sense something was off, and I felt like I was getting fooled again and I panicked. It's no excuse and—"

"I shouldn't have ordered the toys," she says flatly. "I'm sorry. You were right and I should've considered the message it was sending long before you told me. I was overly excited to be able to tick another thing off my plan. I should've thought of how it would make you feel."

"I should've let you talk about all the parts of you, instead of acting like your dad was going to show up like Beetlejuice if you said his name three times. It was petty and I'm done with it."

She wipes under her eyes with her thumbs and scoffs. "I can't promise you that won't happen."

I take another careful step toward her. "I'm never going to let you down again, I promise. I'm not saying I'm going to be perfect, I'm still going to keep molasses in the refrigerator and argue that *Die Hard* is a Christmas movie. But the insecure guy from three days ago is gone. He was put through an intervention that supposedly wasn't an intervention by his neighbors who are really sad that you're not around anymore."

She sighs, lets her shoulders drop. Beneath how beautiful she looks she seems drained. "I'm just scared you're never going to fully trust me, Jack."

"I understand that. I know that you think that because of how I've acted but I know that I can convince you otherwise." I fidget in my tux. It's a rental and doesn't quite fit me right. "And I'm going to have more free time. We're going to divide up the Holly responsibilities more evenly to reduce the pressure."

For the first time since I got here, she smiles. "I'm glad you're getting help."

"Thanks to you. Dove basically forced me to talk about it because you talked to her. I should've done it a long time ago." There's a stretch of silence where she doesn't say anything. My pulse starts to pick up in panic that we've come to a natural halt and this is where it ends. "I don't want this to be it for us, Clara. I'm not ready for this to be it."

I don't know if it's the moody lighting of the room or the topic of conversation, but I don't feel good. Clara looks wary and tired. "What happened to casual no strings?"

She finally lets me close those last few steps of space between us. I reach for her face slowly; she lets me hold it in my hands. Her eyes soften, hands reach for the front of my shirt. "I plan on falling madly in love with you, Clara Davenport. And I'd really like it if you were around to see it."

She moves onto her tiptoes. "I think that I'd like to be around to see it too."

My hands sink into her hair at the nape of her neck as I kiss her hard. Every nerve in my body seems to calm at her touch, then heighten. "It's been torture not being able to touch you," I say, breaking us apart to memorize her face.

She kisses me deeply, her hands cupping my cheeks. "I can't believe you shaved your beard."

The relief from her is palpable. "It was ugly."

She nods enthusiastically. "It was *so* ugly and you're so handsome." Clara moves me backward until my calves hit a leather couch lining the wall of the room; I sink into it and pull her onto my knee. "We can't have make-up sex in here because I'm going to quit my job and if we get caught everyone will think I've been fired."

I blink slowly. "Sorry, back up. You're doing what?"

"I'm going into business with my brother," she says, testing the words out like they're new to her too.

"Doing what?"

She laughs lightly. "Uh, I don't really know yet. We haven't ironed out the details but it'll be something toy related. It's all I know really. I know it's impulsive but I have a lot of savings and"—she pauses—"and I've decided I deserve better. I want to feel appreciated. Max and I push each other to be better, I'm sure we'll land on something that feels right."

I have so many questions. "But what about your promotion?"

"Dad doesn't value my input now, he isn't going to value it in a better role."

I chew the inside of my cheek, thinking how to ask my next question. "This isn't because of me, is it? Because I made you feel so bad?"

Clara rolls her eyes and audibly groans. "What? Why are men so self-centered? *No*, I'm not imploding my career for you, Jack. I'm imploding my career because my dad doesn't pay me enough attention. The way it was intended."

I wrap my arms around her and pull her closer to my chest. I kiss the top of her head and breathe in her shampoo. "You can joke about daddy issues all you want, but I'm so fucking proud of you. You're going to be amazing. Look what you achieved in Fraser Falls in such a short time. Imagine what you can do at your own company."

We sit together quietly, listening to the crackle of the fire in the corner of the room. It feels like another world beyond the door, one that I don't feel part of, but I'll try to for Clara. Eventually she breaks the silence. "I've missed you."

"I've missed you, too. I've been so miserable they tricked me into going to the Green Light to talk some sense into me. Oh shit, that reminds me. I have town updates."

That gets her attention and she sits up straight, eager eyed.

"Arthur approved Tommy's patio."

Her jaw drops. "You're joking!"

"I'd never joke about something so serious and important. Tommy did a presentation at the town meeting." Even in the moody lighting, I see her blush. "Knocked it out of the park."

"I'm so happy for him," she says gently.

"It's because you put together such a good case," I say, running my finger up and down the silk fabric of her dress covering her thigh. "Congratulations on another success to tick off in your serial killer closet."

"I didn't do that much. I just gave him some direction. I'm happy for him. Really happy."

"Donald's request to remove the cell towers has once again been denied," I say.

Clara looks like she's going to burst into tears. "Donald was at a town meeting?"

"He was only there long enough to have his request denied, then he made a dramatic exit in his Area 51 shirt."

"I can't believe I missed him," she says, voice just above a whisper.

"You also missed something else pretty significant." I dig in my jacket pocket for my cell and bring up the link Flo showed me yesterday. "Flo asked me to show you this and tell you that this is your achievement."

Clara's expression settles into something confused as she reaches for my phone. Her eyes scan the screen, the bright light illuminating her face so I can watch her every reaction.

"'The Best Town You Didn't Know About Until Now,'" she reads out. "Oh my God, he came."

"Keep reading."

Her fingers frantically move the screen. *"Dear reader, today I bring to you a secret that I have no intention of keeping. You can keep your Hallmark movies, because every holiday season, I'm heading to Fraser Falls.* Jack, this is incredible. He's got thousands and thousands of followers."

"Baby, keep reading."

"I need to be honest with you: this hidden gem of a town wasn't going to be on my winter itinerary. I actually canceled a trip there and boy am I kicking myself that I nearly missed out on this delightfully charming community. Thankfully, a kind local, whom we'll call C, emailed me urging me to reconsider. C, if you're reading this, thanks, girl." Clara's eyes are watering, but she keeps going. *"Reader, get comfortable, because I'm about to tell you all about the most magical place you've never heard of. If you've always wanted to travel to Europe but don't have the air miles, this one's definitely for you."*

"The B & B is booking up faster than Maggie can answer the phone," I say, pushing her hair behind her ears. "You did this, Clara.

And there's a lot of people who'd like to say thank you to your face. Will you make your one-time trip to Fraser Falls a hell of a lot more than that?"

She bites her lip, punishes me with a long pause. "I have conditions."

"I'd expect nothing less. Hit me."

Clara holds up one finger. "When you visit me, you're required to bring Elf," she says seriously.

I laugh. "Obviously. He would be here right now but someone's been feeding him reindeer-shaped dog treats and his tux wouldn't fit."

She puts up a second. "No more off-limits topics."

"Done."

A third finger pops up. "You get me a ticket to the nativity play. And you never grow your stubble out."

I scratch at my neck awkwardly. "Is it romantic or weird if I tell you I bought you one two weeks ago? Beards are out."

"It's definitely romantic." A fourth finger. "You tell me who the naked neighbor is."

I suck an intake of breath through my teeth awkwardly. "Can't agree to that one. Classified town secrets."

She looks shocked. "I know it's Arthur. I can feel it in my bones."

I kiss her slowly, savoring that we're ending today having this ridiculous-ass conversation. "I guess you'll have to move to Fraser Falls and find out."

Epilogue

JACK
One Year Later

THE FIRST SNOW OF THE year comes just before midnight.

A hot summer that stretched into fall is probably the reason for our constantly changing winters. It's almost definitely *not* the government like Donald tried to claim. Dove was so irritated by him that at the last town meeting she made everyone sit through a twenty-minute YouTube video about global warming changing weather patterns.

Flo, of course, was uninterested in Donald and Dove's varying ideologies because she was furious that we wouldn't let her buy snow machines last year. *This* was the kind of disaster she was hoping to mitigate, she claimed.

We're counting the absence of snow as a disaster these days.

"Our visitors expect it," she emphasized when it was unseasonably warm on Halloween. "We're the home of the magical winter wonderland experience!"

It's a quote from an article about Fraser Falls last year. Flo loved it so much she added it to the welcome sign as you drive into town. Recognition and praise have prompted her to dream up bigger and better goals, and I suspect weather manipulation might be one of them.

I'm behind the bar in the Hungry Fox, wiping down a counter that's already clean and trying not to look like I'm watching the door. Tommy's in an unnervingly good mood (mainly because he has been able to successfully twirl bottles tonight without dropping any of them), so much so that he actually invited me to come and stand behind the bar with him.

He said it was so I could have a clearer view of the door as I wait for Clara, but I suspect it was so he could yell drink orders at me while he lived out his dream of finally being Tom Cruise in *Cocktail* after Clara bought him a mixology course for his birthday.

"Clara said she'd be here, right?" he asks as he fills a mason jar with prosecco and hangs a candy cane on the rim before handing it to a woman across the bar.

"She wouldn't miss it for the—sorry, was that a mason jar full of sparkling wine you just poured?"

"Listen, man," Tommy says, rolling up the sleeves of his Fraser Falls Bears sweatshirt. "It's New Year's Eve. The lady asked for the biggest prosecco I could legally pour. It's good customer service."

I open my mouth to respond just as the door creaks open and I see her, cheeks red from the cold, hair wild from the wind, suede boots soaked, and wrapped up in a coat far too fancy for here. She works the buttons and pulls it from her shoulders, and that's when I spot she's wearing the sweater Wilhelmina crafted her for Christmas. Cream with a knitted version of Elf in the center. She's perfect. The sweater is especially perfect, and surprisingly accurate actually.

Clara makes her way to the bar, peeling off her gloves and stuffing them into the pocket of the coat draped over her arms. "Will it ever be my turn to play bartender?" she says, pouting.

Tommy pours her a mason jar of prosecco and pushes me out from behind the bar. "Your assistance is no longer needed, Jack. You were actually more of a hindrance than a help, if I'm being honest.

I won't be letting anyone else have a turn. Sorry, Clara. Blame your boyfriend for being bad at pouring beer."

"I understand. I feel like that when he stacks my dishwasher wrong." She smiles like she didn't just insult me and leans across to kiss me. "Do you guys know it's snowing? Looks like the White House finally read Donald's letters and flicked the switch to turn us back on."

I *love* how Clara says *us*. "Wonder what we did to get in their bad books," Tommy says, leaning against the bar.

"It was probably Donald's podcast episode criticizing their lawn," I suggest, but there's a long list of options.

The *Landscape of Lies* podcast launched in the summer and is doing great in the exceptionally niche *conspiracy theorists who like gardening* space. Turns out all that soundproofing he's done over the years gave him the perfect spot for a studio.

The thumbnail is him holding his net in one hand and a shovel in the other. I heard from Miss Celia that he's close to scoring his first sponsored episode.

Clara takes a sip from her mason jar, then pushes it back toward Tommy, shaking her head with disgust. "Is that laced with *peppermint*?"

Tommy sighs and moves the jar under the counter. "I bought too much and it expires in February. I thought it was a fun festive twist."

She looks genuinely offended. "Make mojitos then, weirdo. Don't ruin a perfectly good sparkling wine."

He shakes his head slowly. "I feel like you're just naming a drink with mint in it. I guess I'll try it, but it feels wrong after my class. I only use fresh, organic mint now. Peppermint isn't even the same thing."

She still looks unimpressed. "And wine doesn't feel wrong? Bizarre. Just try it. It has to be better than what you just gave me."

Clara leads me through the back door of the bar and out onto

Tommy's freshly installed, fully approved patio extension. The outdoor space is full of people, local and otherwise. A group staying at the B & B are by the indoor-friendly firepit; Sailor is asleep across Luke and Dove in the corner; Flo and Maggie have cocooned themselves in a blanket nest over by a heater. Mel and Winnie are laughing with some guys from the fire station.

"Five minutes!" Tommy yells from the doorway, clinking a spoon against what I strongly suspect is a jug of peppermint-laced mojito. "Anyone who doesn't vacate the bar in time for the countdown is at risk of being captured in Donald's net."

"I could sit out here all night watching the world go by," Flo says dreamily. It takes a lot for me not to remind her that she was the main person vetoing the plans for this patio for years.

As we file out onto the street, Sailor has woken up from her nap with fresh enthusiasm and is waving sparklers like she's directing traffic with her equally enthusiastic dad. Winnie and Mel are frantically trying to keep them from accidentally setting fire to each other's wool scarves, although a firefighter is probably a good date to have if that happens.

The group from the firepit prematurely pops a bottle of champagne, making Clara jump beside me. With her hand safe in mine, we venture away from the tavern onto the sidewalk with a better view of Arthur and Tommy looking intimidated by tonight's entertainment.

Her eyes are closed; she lifts her face to the sky, letting snowflakes land on her face. "Everything's perfect."

The countdown begins. Ten. Nine. Eight.

Tommy's yelling at Arthur to move away from the fireworks like he's trying to wake the dead. Donald jumps the gun and starts singing "Auld Lang Syne." A rogue firework zips sideways, hurtling toward the newly repaired church roof. We collectively hold our breath. Pastor Akinola does everything but fall to his knees and scream.

Seven. Six. Five.

The firework doesn't make impact, exploding just above the roof, showering the parking lot in vibrant pinks, purples, and blues.

Clara looks up at me. "I've never liked New Year's Eve much. Too much pressure to transform into someone shiny and new."

Four. Three.

I take her face in my hands. "Good thing you already shine just fine."

Two. One.

A chorus of *Happy New Year* rings out in front of the tavern, followed by cheers, laughter, a correctly timed rendition of "Auld Lang Syne."

Clara stands on her tiptoes and wraps her arms around my neck, pulling me in to her. She kisses me and all the noise and chaos of the street around us melts away. If this moment is the only thing I achieve this year, then I'll consider it a year well spent.

I TOLD TOMMY THAT HE didn't need to extend his opening hours to 2 a.m. for special occasions.

As I listen to him telling Pastor Akinola and Miss Celia, who are both completely sober, that they can't sing *another* karaoke duet, I think I made the right choice.

"I personally would've liked to hear their interpretation of Sonny and Cher," Clara says, lifting her hair as I pull her coat onto her shoulders.

She takes my hand for the second time tonight and leads me outside. I follow like I always do, because I'd follow that woman anywhere. The snow heading toward Main has been crushed into a dirty slush by all the people eager to get away from the karaoke and continue their celebrations at home. Clara pulls that way, but I don't move and tug her back to me.

"We're taking a detour," I explain, guiding her left.

"You're delaying me seeing my child," she says, the mojitos she's been guzzling making her giggly. She called them disgusting, but it didn't stop her.

"Elf is loving life being babysat by Joe. He'll be okay for an extra five minutes." Despite Elf having survived countless New Year's and Fourth of Julys without incident, Clara convinced herself he would be scared of fireworks if we weren't there.

It resulted in me paying Joe a hundred bucks to hang out at my place and play PlayStation all night. Peak rates, the hustling little jerk said. Made me drive him to Mr. Worldwide to get Thai takeout before I left to help out Tommy too.

"Okay, but if he's pissed when we get home late I'm going to tell him it's your fault," she singsongs.

"And he'll believe you because you're wearing his face on your chest. It isn't far, promise."

Tipsy Clara is less inquisitive than sober Clara because she hasn't asked where we're going yet. We walk past the antique store and she launches into how much her mom loved the mirror she bought her for Christmas—which her mom picked out for herself when she visited at the start of December, but Clara appreciates the praise.

When I take a left before we reach the intersection where the Christmas tree farm is, Clara starts staring up at me with suspicion. "I don't think I knew this lane existed."

"You didn't notice it during the Santa run? Or, y'know, the countless times we've driven past it?"

She shrugs. "Nope."

We pass the first house, then the second, and the third until we reach a big corner plot at the end of the cul-de-sac. I stop at the white picket fence and put my arm across her shoulders. She just looks confused. I guess if I wanted her to be sharp I should've done this pre-drinks.

"Are we breaking and entering?" she asks, looking around and straight past the Sold sign. "I know you like to bend me around like I'm a pretzel, but I'm not actually that flexible. There's no way I'm Catwoman-ing through that big-ass window."

I take her wrist gently and twist her palm up, dropping a set of keys into it. "I'd like to see you as Catwoman, but this time you can just use the front door."

"You bought a house," she says, more talking to herself. Her eyes widen and she grips my arms before jumping up and down. "You bought a house!" Clara throws herself at me, the keys jingling somewhere behind my head.

"I bought a house," I say, fighting to keep the painfully large grin from my face. "And you have an office."

"I have an office," she repeats. "You bought a house, and the house has an office."

"Okay, let's go inside, I think the cold is doing something to your brain," I say, nudging her through the gate. This time I take her hand and lead her up the porch steps to the door.

She fumbles with the keys until she finds the right one and turns the lock. Seeing her walk through this door is all I've thought about while dealing with the Realtor and bank stresses.

This year has tested how much change Clara can deal with. The realization that she was leaving Davenport, building a plan with Max, figuring out where they wanted to set up their business, figuring out where she wants to live. It's been hard to have to stand back and let her fix it herself as someone who just wants to make her problems go away.

Thankfully the one thing that was easy to agree on, and the one thing I could take control of handling, was that I needed a bigger place. Somewhere for us both to live when a newly launched business isn't taking up her every minute and thought. And for when she's ready to leave Uber Eats and reliable cell service behind.

It's more than that too. It's somewhere for me to come to and have separation from my own business at the end of the day. Somewhere for Elf to have the backyard I've always wanted for him. Somewhere that feels quiet and homely and *ours*. Somewhere to raise those kids we want one day.

As soon as she said she was putting her place in the city on the market, I knew it was the right time.

Clara takes it in, eyes bouncing from fireplace to light fixtures to windows. "It needs some work," I say.

She spins to face me, her face frozen into something unreadable at first. "I love it, Jack. This is the best surprise you could've ever given me."

I hold out my arms to her, embracing her when she steps into them and kissing her forehead. "I love you, Clara. Happy New Year."

She squeezes me tight and the keys drop to the floor. "I love you too."

"Look after those keys," I say, reaching down to grab them and laughing when she immediately stuffs them in her pocket. "That's your set."

"I can't believe I have my own key to your place and can finally stop stealing Tommy's." I side-eye her. She's never needed a key because I rarely lock the door, and I always know when she's coming. "I think you finally might trust me."

"Of course, I do," I say gently, knowing she's teasing. "Wait, since when has Tommy had a key to my place?"

She drags her fingers across her lips as if to zip them. "Classified town secrets."

Acknowledgments

THE FIRST THANK-YOU IN THIS book needs to go to my publishing team at Atria and Piatkus, who said "Okay, cool, we can make that work" when I turned around in February and said I wanted to write a book about a doll scandal in a nonspecific small town somewhere north of New York with a cast of eccentric characters.

The time frames have been tough and I recognize how hard everyone has worked to make this book happen. Thank you for all your efforts, sacrifices, and love for Fraser Falls.

Of course, thank you to my agent, Kimberly Brower, who didn't hang up when I said I'd spent the weekend watching Christmas films and felt inspired to try something new so could she please make that happen. Your unwavering support and guidance are so valued and I'm unbelievably lucky to have you.

To my assistant, Lauren, for all your hard work on this book and your wide conspiracy knowledge. Donald wouldn't be the same without you.

My husband, who didn't complain while I worked on this book as we traveled to eight countries. Thank you for always making sure I'm looked after while I work.

Becs and Torie, thank you for cheering me on and always being there to listen.

And thank you to my readers, old and new, for giving me a chance to try something new. I appreciate you more than you'll ever know. I hope you enjoyed your trip to Fraser Falls.

About the Author

HANNAH GRACE is an English author, writing adult contemporary romance between characters who all carry a tiny piece of her. When she's not describing everyone's eyes ten thousand times a chapter, accidentally giving multiple characters the same name, or googling American English spellings, you can find her oversharing online or, occasionally, reading a book from her enormous TBR. Hannah is the #1 *New York Times* bestselling author of *Icebreaker*, *Wildfire*, and *Daydream*, and a proud parent to two dogs.

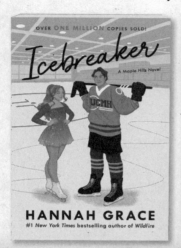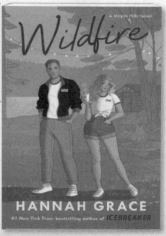